THE AGE OF LIGHT

WHITNEY SCHARER

PICADOR

First published 2019 by Little, Brown and Company
Hachette Book Group
1290 Avenue of the Americas, New York NY 10104

First published in the UK 2019 by Picador

This paperback edition first published 2020 by Picador
an imprint of Pan Macmillan
The Smithson, 6 Briset Street, London EC1M 5NR
Associated companies throughout the world
www.panmacmillan.com

ISBN 978-1-5098-8915-0

Copyright © Whitney Scharer 2019

The right of Whitney Scharer to be identified as the
author of this work has been asserted by her in accordance
with the Copyright, Designs and Patents Act 1988.

Excerpts from *Disavowals or Cancelled Confessions* by Claude Cahun reprinted here
courtesy of the MIT Press.

All rights reserved. No part of this publication may be reproduced,
stored in a retrieval system, or transmitted, in any form, or by any means
(electronic, mechanical, photocopying, recording or otherwise)
without the prior written permission of the publisher.

Pan Macmillan does not have any control over, or any responsibility for,
any author or third-party websites referred to in or on this book.

1 3 5 7 9 8 6 4 2

A CIP catalogue record for this book is available from the British Library.

Printed and bound by CPI Group (UK) Ltd, Croydon, CR0 4YY

This book is sold subject to the condition that it shall not, by way of
trade or otherwise, be lent, hired out, or otherwise circulated without
the publisher's prior consent in any form of binding or cover other than
that in which it is published and without a similar condition including
this condition being imposed on the subsequent purchaser.

Visit **www.picador.com** to read more about all our books
and to buy them. You will also find features, author interviews and
news of any author events, and you can sign up for e-newsletters
so that you're always first to hear about our new releases.

For my mother, with love and gratitude

Surely all art is the result of one's having been in danger, of having gone through an experience all the way to the end, where no one can go any further.

—*Rainer Maria Rilke*

PART ONE

PROLOGUE

FARLEY FARM, SUSSEX, ENGLAND
1966

Hot July. The downs have greened up from the past week's rain and rise into the sky like mossy breasts. From the windows in Lee Miller's kitchen she sees hills in all directions. One straight gravel road. Stone walls made long before she got here that divide up the landscape and keep the sheep where they belong, calmly chewing. Her husband, Roland, with his walking stick, wends his way along the bridle path. He has two of their houseguests with him, and stops to point out a mole's burrow that could break an ankle, or a cowpat that might be a little too much country for some visitors.

Lee's herb garden is just outside the kitchen and about as far as she ever chooses to walk. Roland stopped asking her to join him on his constitutionals years ago, after she told him that until he puts a sidewalk on the downs and lines it with café bars, she's not going to be wasting her time tromping through the hillsides. Now she thinks he welcomes the time apart from her, as she does from him. Each time she watches him leave, the hand that's clenched around her throat loosens a little.

Of all the rooms at Farley Farm, the kitchen is where Lee is most content. Not happy, but content. No one goes in here without her, and if they did, they could never find what they were looking for. Spice jars teeter in uneven towers, pots in various states of filth cover the counter and fill the sink, containers of vinegar and oil stand open on the shelves. But Lee knows where everything is at every moment, just like she used to know in her studio, the clutter confounding to everyone except her. When Dave Scherman, her photography partner during the war, used to come into her room at the Hotel Scribe, he'd always have some cocky comment ready—"Ah, making an installation piece out of used petrol cans, are we, Lee?"—and she thinks of him when she's in her kitchen and wonders what he'd say to her now. Dave is one of the few of her war days friends who hasn't made the trek out here to see her. She's glad of it. The last time she saw him, back when they were all still living in London, Lee overheard Dave say to Paul Éluard that Lee had gotten fat and lost her looks and that not being pretty was making her angry. Which isn't true, of course. There is so much more that's making her angry than the stranger who greets her in the mirror each morning, burst blood vessels blooming across her puffy face.

Lee trained at the Cordon Bleu a few years ago, and now she makes multicourse dinners almost every weekend and writes about them for *Vogue*. She is the magazine's domestic correspondent. Before that she was its war correspondent, and before that she was its fashion correspondent, and before that she was its cover model. In 1927, an Art Deco sketch of her head, cloche pulled low like a helmet, ushered in an era of new modernism in women's fashion. A remarkable career, everyone always says. Lee never talks about those days.

Vogue is on Lee's mind because Audrey Withers, her editor, is coming to dinner tonight. Audrey is most likely coming to fire her and making the journey to Farley to do it in person. Lee would have fired herself long ago, after the twentieth missed deadline or the tenth familiar pitch about entertaining in a country

4

home. She's loyal, though, Audrey, and the only fashion editor who ever tries to tell women about something more important than the latest trends in evening wear. Audrey will be buffered by some other guests: their friend Bettina, and Seamus, the Institute of Contemporary Arts' curator and Roland's right-hand man. Lee thinks that Audrey will not be able to fire her in front of Roland's friends. Maybe she can feel her out, turn things around, find her way back in.

Tonight's menu is a variation on one Lee has served before. Ten courses. Asparagus croûtes with hollandaise, scallop brochettes with sauce béarnaise, tots of vichyssoise, Penroses, mini toad-in-the-hole, Muddles Green Green Chicken, Gorgonzola with walnuts, beer-braised pheasant, a ginger ice, and bombe Alaska served flambé-style with the lights turned low. If Lee can't work for Audrey, she will kill her with butter and cream and rum-soaked meringue.

When Lee was reporting back from Leipzig and Normandy during the war, Audrey was often the only person she would contact. Lee sent her those first photos of Buchenwald, and Audrey ran them with the story Lee had pounded out on her little Hermes Baby, fueled by Benzedrine and brandy and rage. Audrey ran her words exactly as Lee had written them, with the headline "Believe It" and the photos full bleed, huge on the page in all their gruesome glory. Didn't care that somewhere in Sheffield a housewife turned from one shiny page advertising the latest Schiaparelli gloves to a bruised and beaten SS guard on the next, his nose broken and his pig's face covered in thick black blood.

It is noon and Lee starts on the Penroses, a dish she invented of thick closed mushrooms stuffed with piped pâté de foie gras and topped with paprika to look like the roses that grow at the edge of the herb garden. They are easy to do incorrectly, and the entire process takes hours. Roland often gets angry at her because she'll say dinner at eight and it will be nine, ten, eleven o'clock and all the guests will be tired and drunk by the time she brings out the first course. Lee shrugs him off. Once she made a grilled bluefish in homage to a Miró painting and even Roland agreed that it was worth the wait.

Tonight, though, Lee will be on time. She will emerge from the kitchen calm and regal, and dish after dish will reach the table like performers in a well-executed dance. There is magic to a multi-course meal, and on the best of days it reminds Lee of what it used to feel like to be in the darkroom, moving at exactly the right pace, no wasted effort.

Lee finishes the Penroses and leaves them on top of the ice-box. Next she makes the hollandaise, more than they'll need, whisking the yolks with the lemon juice in a copper pot, the whisk *ting-ting-tinging* against the metal. Outside, Roland and the early guests crest a hill, following one behind the other like ducks in a little line, and then dip down into a valley and disappear from view.

What will Lee say to Audrey? She has ideas for articles, none of them good. She has apologies. These feel better, more genuine. It's been a rough few years, moving out here, only getting to London a few times a month, cut off from everything. But she knows her writing is still good. Her photos are still good. Or they would be if she could do them, if she could shrug off the stultifying sadness that she pulls around with her like a heavy cape. She will tell Audrey that she feels ready now. She will tell her that she moved the junk out of one of the bedrooms and set up her typewriter in there, the desk pushed up under a small square window with a view of the drive rolling out and away from the farm. Lee even snapped a photo, the first she's taken in months, framing the window inside the viewfinder, a view within a view, and tacked it up next to her desk. Audrey will like to know that Lee has made a picture. That she's sat there, running her fingers over the type-writer's dented sides, watching the chickens peck their way across the drive. When Audrey asks, Lee will offer her sharp incisive sketches of country living. She will give her anything she wants of this life of hers, on time, with photos if she can manage it.

By four o'clock Lee has prepped almost everything and set up her *mise-en-place,* the small bowls filled with chopped marjoram, sea salt, anchovies, cayenne, and all the other spices she'll need to make the meal. She adds an ice cube to her tumbler and goes into the dining room. There is a long pockmarked trestle table, big enough to hold twenty-four people. The fireplace at the end of the room calls to mind Henry VIII, roast suckling pigs, flagons of wine. Above it hangs Picasso's portrait of Lee, which has always been the image of herself she likes the best, the way he cap-tured her gap-toothed smile. Around it are some of their favorite pieces from Roland's personal collection, crowded up against one another, Ernst next to Miró next to Turnbull. Over the years, they've mixed in some unknown Surrealist pieces as well: a taxi-dermied bird lying upside down on one of the frames, a railroad tie with a giant mouth painted on it, a doodle of a woman with wild tangled hair housed in one of the most ostentatious frames they could find. Lee sits down at the table. Her feet are starting to swell. She jiggles her tumbler a little, and the ice cubes dance in the whiskey.

Roland gets back from his walk at the same time that a low-slung Morris pulls up the drive, the loud engine growl alerting them to its arrival. He stands in the doorway to the kitchen—he often stands framed there on the threshold, never seeming to want to enter her domain.

"Good walk today," he says, rubbing his nose with his thin

sculptor's fingers. "We saw a bull snake on the path. Must have been five, six feet long."

Lee nods, not looking at him directly, moving a long-handled spoon in the pot in which she boils potatoes.

"Smells good in here," he says, sniffing. "Garlicky."

"That'll be the chicken."

He sniffs again. "What time is Audrey arriving?"

"I think that's her now," Lee says calmly, as if she hasn't been on edge ever since she heard the tires crunching on the stone.

"Do you want to greet her or shall I?"

"You'd better." Lee gestures to the mess. "I'm in the middle of a dozen things here."

Roland takes a long look at her before he walks away.

The water is really boiling now, the steam rising up around Lee's face as she leans over it. The rule with potatoes: start with water cold from the tap and cover them with more liquid than you think you need. Make sure they have room to wiggle. If they touch, they'll get starchy. Lee boils them whole and cuts them while they're still steaming. Most people don't think enough about potatoes.

From the front of the house comes Roland's voice booming, "Audrey! Don't you know friends use the back door in Sussex?," and then Audrey's high, refined voice in response. Quickly, Lee refills her glass from the bottle she has tucked away behind the Weck jars. She hears their feet on the gravel again, going back out to the car, and then the screech and snap of the screen door, loud as a gunshot when they return. The noise sends an electric jolt up her spine and suddenly Lee is covered with a spreading panic, blackness like a hood. There is a scorched smell in the air and she worries something is burning, but she can't make herself move over to the oven to check. Her vision goes dark at the edges as it always does when this happens, and even with her eyes open she is back there, Saint-Malo this time, her shirt soaked with sweat, crouched in the vault, the muscles of her thighs seizing up as she waits for the echo of the bombs to fade away.

She cannot stop the thoughts from coming. They lodge like bits of shrapnel in her brain and she never knows when something will bring one to the surface. This time, when Lee returns to the present, she finds herself huddled in the corner of the kitchen clutching her knees to her chest. She gets to her feet unsteadily and feels relieved that no one has seen her this way.

The glass is the thing. She picks it up, puts it against her forehead so she can feel how cold it is, takes one shaky swallow and then another. The timer dings. Lee startles again, tries to compose herself, digs a potato out of the pot, and tests it with her teeth, so hot she pulls back sharply and it falls with a soggy thump to the tile floor. Another swallow from her glass, the panic growing, the room around her bending and twisting like the reflection of her face in the pot's copper surface, and she wants to abandon the meal and go upstairs to her office, where she can look out at the sheep again, everything neat and orderly, the same as it was hundreds of years before they moved here.

She is almost out of the room, moving toward the back stairs, when she hears Audrey's voice.

"Lee!" Audrey walks through the kitchen door with her arms outstretched, a smile on her face. "This is where the magic happens. I've seen your pictures but it's so much more fun to see it in reality."

Audrey looks the same: tiny, immaculate, a fresh silk scarf tied in a bow around her neck. She has dyed blond hair that she still wears in pin curls, perfectly acceptable teeth that make her look a bit like a badger, and a habit of wearing corsages to work. She wears one now. Corsages aside, Audrey is the least vain person Lee has ever met, and that's quite an achievement for someone who's worked in fashion for over thirty years. Lee sets down her drink, rubs her hands on the towel she has folded into her apron's waistband, and holds out her arms. They squeeze each other tightly and Lee feels as if someone is blowing up a balloon inside her chest, pushing away the panic and making room in her. She has forgotten how much she loves Audrey.

They pull away from each other and Lee watches Audrey taking in the kitchen. She looks at the mess, she looks at Lee's glass on the counter, she looks—quickly, trying not to let Lee see the look—at Lee's housecoat, her snarled hair, the lumps of her heavy body. Lee sees herself through Audrey's eyes and it's not attractive, but Audrey has enough tact to move her gaze across the room.

"Are those the famous Penrose mushrooms?" she asks, pointing to the icebox. "November nineteen sixty-one. We got so many letters about them."

"In the flesh," Lee says. She's set down her tumbler, out of sight behind a bowl of lettuces, but keeps glancing at it. The panic is back, thick and suffocating, and she closes her eyes to force it away.

"Audrey," she says finally, gesturing to a chair, "please sit. Make yourself comfortable. Can I get you something to drink?"

"Oh, I'm sure you're much too busy to entertain me while you cook! Roland offered to give me a tour, but I wanted to say hello as soon as I got here." She comes back over to where Lee is standing and gives her another quick squeeze, her eyes kind.

Lee feels relief and doesn't try to stop Audrey as she leaves the room. With shaking hands she picks up her glass again and finishes her drink in one huge swallow that makes her eyes water. When the tears spill over, she lets them fall.

★ ★ ★

Nine o'clock and Lee is not done cooking. The guests are in the parlor. She hears the sound of their voices rising and falling, laughter, the clink of wineglasses. Roland has come back to the kitchen several times, saying in a low hiss that "they are waiting, they are hungry, do you have an estimate on when it might be ready?" Lee tells him no. They can wait, even Audrey, and it will be worth it.

Part of the trouble is that she's kept right on drinking, the extra bottle behind the Weck jars empty now and replaced with one she ferreted away in the back of the pantry. She's drunk so much that for once she can feel it: her nose gone numb and her fingers slick as sticks of butter. It is just so easy to keep topping up her glass, and there's no way to know how many times she's done it. Drinking makes her forget that Audrey is her lifeline to all she used to care about in the world: photography, writing, her old beautiful self. When Lee can fight off the urge to just curl up in bed and fall asleep forever, she wants to be the person she used to be, alive and hungry. But every time she hears Audrey's voice from the other room, that posh London accent, she keeps picking up her glass for one more swallow.

At nine thirty the asparagus is on a bed of lettuce with hollandaise drizzled across the platter. Lee picks it up and pushes through the swinging door to the dining room. From the adjacent parlor, the group quiets when they see her. Someone—Seamus, maybe, from the ICA—says, "Brilliant! I'm starving," and they all come into the dining room. Roland shows them where to sit— this is one of his talents, putting the right people next to one another at a dinner party—and then he comes over to her and takes the platter and sets it on the sideboard. Janie is there, the house girl, whose life Lee makes miserable by rarely letting her in the kitchen, and the girl serves the asparagus and then everyone looks at Lee where she's still standing by the door.

"Join us, darling," Roland says, indicating her place at the end of the table nearer the kitchen.

"More to do," she says, backing toward the door and wondering idly if she's slurring before deciding she doesn't really care.

"Sit, Lee," Audrey says. "You've been on your feet all day!"

Audrey's right. Lee's feet are aching. She takes off her apron and finds her seat and someone, not Roland, fills her wineglass, and the conversation begins again in fits and starts as people lift the shining asparagus stalks to their mouths and start exclaiming about how good they taste.

They eat and drink and it is not too daunting. Audrey is involved in a long exchange with Bettina about a spring fashion show she just saw. The new look was geometric cutouts, cropped jackets, sheath suits. After a while, Bettina turns to Lee and says, "You've always had such a good eye. What do you think of the new Yves Saint Laurent?"

Lee laughs. "Betts, I gave up on all that when I realized how comfortable my army uniform was—you know that. Now it's just trousers and housecoats for me."

Roland looks at her. He, like Audrey, knew her when she was modeling, when she could spot a dress from across the room and tell you the designer and the material and the season. That, too, is behind her, and good riddance. If women knew how comfortable army pants were, they'd all be wearing them. During Lee's last visit to *Vogue,* she cornered a few young models in the lift and told them how liberating it was to wear men's pants and not to stuff one's feet into the equivalent of Chinese finger traps. One of them recognized her.

"You're Lee Miller, aren't you?" the girl asked. She towered over Lee—it seemed every year the models got taller—and something about the question annoyed her. In it was Audrey's prompting: "Be kind to Lee. She's not the same since—Those things she saw—She was in Germany when they opened up the camps. Horrible, really. We never should have sent her." So when this girl recognized Lee, the devil in her came out.

"Lee Miller?" Lee said, leaning in so close she could see the girl's pores, the fuzz of plaque clinging to her straight white teeth. "I heard she died." The girl looked shocked and then the lift doors opened and Lee got out, the untied laces of her boots slapping along with her as she continued down the hall.

And here Lee is at dinner in boots too, the shirt she has on, formerly covered by her apron, tucked haphazardly into her trousers, with Audrey and Bettina and Roland staring awkwardly, the fashion conversation at a standstill.

To break the silence Lee gets the vichyssoise, which she serves in earthenware tots she and Roland picked up in Bath years ago. Janie helps serve, and Lee shows her what to do so that she can bring out the next few courses, which are prepped and ready when they want them. Each trip to the kitchen is an excuse for more whiskey, though, so Lee doesn't want Janie to do too much.

Finally, after the scallops and the chicken and the pheasant—all of it as perfect as Lee has imagined it would be, if not as timely—the conversation turns to Roland's work and gossip about the ICA and the latest exhibition troubles. Seamus's voice rises above them all, pontificating. Why do fat men always love the sound of their own voices? Lee and Audrey are the only people at the table not connected to the museum, so soon they stop listening and Audrey turns sideways in her chair and says, "Lee?"

Lee is ready—she has been ready—and says, "I have so many ideas, Audrey. Truly. I'm writing again. No more boondoggling."

Audrey sits back. Looks surprised. "That's wonderful!"

"I was thinking about that fish dinner I made—you remember,

I told you about it? The bluefish? Why not write a piece about art and cooking? Or I could do a piece about foraging. People bring me things, things you probably wouldn't know you could eat—fiddlehead ferns and different types of mushrooms—a whole piece on that, with photos to match."

Lee really is slurring now, she can feel it, the words coming from her mouth like puzzle pieces spilling out of a box. Audrey lifts her glass, her wedding band gleaming in the candlelight. In her eyes Lee sees the emotions she expected to see there, pity and embarrassment, her glance sliding away as if she doesn't really want to be seeing her.

"Lee," Audrey says, "there's something I want to ask you."

Lee moves to stand up. "I should—I need to serve the next course."

Audrey puts her hand on Lee's wrist. "It can wait. Roland and I had a nice long chat when he gave me a tour this afternoon, about something that's been on my mind for months. I want you to write a piece—well, Roland and I want you to write a piece—about your years with Man Ray. A feature. Thirty-five-hundred words. Some of his photos from that time. We think it would do you good to have a big project to focus on. It can go in the February issue. You could interview him if you want, or you could just write it from your perspective, your memories. Our readers will love it. The woman's touch. They've come to love you over the years through all the cooking pieces."

Lee looks at Roland, who studiously avoids meeting her eye. His shoulders are hitched up to his earlobes and he has that same penitent beagle look on his face that he gets when Lee is yelling at him.

They've come to love you through all the cooking pieces. All the fluff Lee's submitted to Audrey over the past few years, the portrait they commissioned of her in her herb garden, dressed in a goddamn gingham apron. And they do love her! They send her letters. *Dear Mrs. Penrose, I'm a homemaker in Shropfordshire and I tried your trifle last night. What a success! All my guests are still exclaiming over it.*

Today when Lee was in the kitchen measuring out fenugreek, Roland and Audrey must have been discussing her, cooking up a plan to get her to reengage, come back to herself, do something worth doing.

"I don't want to," Lee says finally, her tone petulant even to her own ears.

"Why not?" Audrey looks sympathetic.

Lee reaches for her glass and Audrey's expression hardens. Without letting her answer, Audrey says, "It will be good for you, Lee. A story with some meat to it. A story only you can tell."

"I don't want to, Audrey."

"Lee . . . I don't know how to say it . . . but it's this, or we'll have to renegotiate your contract."

She knew the words were coming but it doesn't hurt any less to hear them.

"I'm writing again, truly, Audrey."

"Then write this. This is what we need. We can't have . . . We're moving away from the domestic section, actually."

Just then Janie comes over to Lee and whispers in her ear, "Should I serve the dessert, ma'am?"

"No, no—I'll manage it, Janie," Lee says.

As the door to the kitchen swings shut behind her, Lee grabs the first clean glass she sees, one of her mother's teacups with a delicate rose spray pattern, and goes immediately to the Weck jars. The teacup rattles in its saucer as she fills it, so she sets down the saucer and holds the cup in both hands, gulping the whiskey so the fumes rise up and burn her nose.

An article about her time with Man Ray. With photos to

match. Lee could tell the story again the way she's always told it: "I met Man Ray in a bar on his way to Biarritz. I asked him if I could be his student and he told me he didn't take students. So I told him I was going with him, and before the train pulled into Biarritz we were in love." Tell it this way and it's romantic, a fairy tale, and if you tell something enough times it becomes true, just the way a photograph can trick you into thinking it's a memory. And why couldn't it be true? Lee was beautiful enough then to get what she wanted exactly when she wanted it, and there *are* photos of her in Biarritz with Man, her head tipped back to catch the sun, skin creamy as the inside of a seashell. Lee could assemble an entire history from the photos that would tell any version of the story she wants. But back then, that first summer in Paris, she didn't yet know the power of pictures, how a frame creates reality, how a photograph becomes memory becomes truth.

Or Lee could tell the real story: the one where she loved a man and he loved her, but in the end they took everything from each other—who can say who was more destroyed? It's this story that she's locked up tight inside herself, this story that she was thinking about when she hid all her old prints and negatives in the attic, this story that makes the delicate teacup tremble in her hands.

Lee takes a final swallow and sets the empty cup atop the pile in the sink. She calls to Janie, and together they carry the bombe Alaska to the table and set it in the middle of the group, and with a theatrical flourish, Lee pours the pitcher of rum over it and takes one of the long taper matches and sets it on fire, and the flames are instantaneous, hot and blue, rising up almost to the chandelier. Everyone gasps and claps loudly, and Lee forgets for a minute how sad Audrey has made her, just stands there and enjoys watching the alcohol burn.

After the cake is cut and everyone is served, Lee sits back down next to Audrey.

"When would you need it by?" Lee asks her, and watches as Audrey's face moves from surprise to pleasure.

"I'd want to see a first draft by October."

Lee nods. "I'll do it," she tells her. "But not his photos. Mine."

Audrey rolls the stem of her wineglass between her fingers. "I can't promise that. This is a story about Man Ray."

But it's not, Lee thinks. And that's been the problem all along.

CHAPTER ONE

PARIS
1929

The night Lee meets Man Ray begins in a half-empty bistro a few blocks from Lee's hotel, where she sits alone, eating steak and scalloped potatoes and drinking half pitchers of dusky red wine. She is twenty-two, and beautiful. The steak tastes even better than she thought it would, swimming in a rich brown roux that pools on the plate and seeps into the layers of sliced potatoes and thick melted slabs of Gruyère.

Lee has passed the bistro many times since she arrived in Paris three months earlier, but—her finances being what they are—this is the first time she has ventured inside. Dining alone is nothing new: Lee has spent almost all her time alone since she got here, a hard adjustment after her busy life in New York City, where she modeled for *Vogue* and hit up the jazz clubs almost nightly, always with a different man on her arm. Back then, Lee took it for granted that everyone she met would be entranced by her: her father, Condé Nast, Edward Steichen, all the powerful men she had charmed over the years. Those men. She may have captivated them, but they took things from her—raked her over with their eyes, barked commands at her from under camera hoods, reduced her to pieces of a girl: a neck to hold pearls, a slim waist to show off a belt, a hand to bring to her lips and blow them kisses. Their gaze made her into someone she didn't want to be. Lee might miss the parties, but she does not miss modeling, and in fact she would rather go hungry than go back to her former line of work.

Here in Paris, where she has come to start over, to make art instead of being made into it, no one pays much attention to Lee's beauty. When she walks through Montparnasse, her new neighborhood, no one catches her eye, no one turns around to watch her pass. Instead, Lee seems to be just another pretty detail in a city where almost everything is artfully arranged. A city built on the concept of form over function, where rows of jewel-toned petits fours gleam in a patisserie's window, too flawless to eat. Where a milliner displays exquisitely elaborate hats, with no clear indication of how one would wear them. Even the Parisian women at the sidewalk cafés are like sculptures, effortlessly elegant, leaning back in their chairs as if their raison d'être is decoration. She tells herself she is glad not to be noticed, to blend in with her surroundings, but still, after three months in this city, Lee secretly thinks she has not seen anyone more beautiful than she is.

When Lee has finished the steak and sopped up the last of the gravy with her bread, she stretches and sits back in her chair. It is early. The restaurant is quiet, the only other diners elderly Parisians, their voices too low for eavesdropping. Empty wine pitchers are lined up neatly next to Lee's plate, and on the far end of the table is her camera, which she has taken to carrying everywhere despite its heaviness and bulk. Just before she boarded the steamer to Le Havre, her father pushed the camera into her hands, an old Graflex he no longer used, and even though Lee told him she didn't want it, he insisted. She still barely knows how to operate it—her training is in figure drawing, and when she moved to Paris she planned to become a painter, envisioned herself dabbing meditatively at a canvas *en plein air,* not mucking about with chemicals in a suffocating darkroom. Still, Lee has learned a bit about taking pictures from him and at *Vogue,* and there's something comforting about the camera: both a connection to her past and something a real artist might carry around.

The waiter stops by and takes her empty plate, then asks if she'd like another pitcher of wine. Lee hesitates, picturing the dwindling francs in her little handbag, then says yes. Even though her savings are getting low, she wants a reason to stay a little longer, to be surrounded by people even if she is not with them, to not go back to her hotel room, where the windows are painted shut and the trapped air always smells oppressively of pot roast. Lately she's been spending more and more time there, drawing in her sketchbook, writing letters, or taking long afternoon naps that leave her unreplenished—anything to pass the time and make her forget how lonely she feels. Lee has never been very good at being by herself: left to her own devices, she can easily sink into sadness and inactivity. As the weeks have passed, her loneliness has gained heft and power: it has contours now, almost a physical shape, and she imagines it sitting in the corner of her room, waiting for her, a sucking, spongy thing.

After he has picked up her plate, the waiter lingers. He is young, with a hint of mustache above his lip so faint it could have been penciled there, and Lee can tell he is intrigued by her.

"Are you a photographer?" he finally asks, the word almost the same in French as in English, *photographe,* but he mumbles, and Lee's grasp of the language is still so rusty it takes her a moment to parse his question. When she doesn't respond, he tips his head at the camera.

"Oh, no, not really," Lee says. He looks disappointed, and she almost wishes she said yes. Since she's been here, Lee has taken a few pictures, but they have been shots any tourist would attempt: baguettes in a bicycle basket, lovers pausing to kiss on the Pont des Arts. Her initial tries did not go well. The first time, when she got the prints back from the little camera shop around the corner, they were entirely black; Lee had somehow exposed the plates to light before they were developed. The second set—made with more care, the plates inserted into the camera gingerly, a light sweat dotting her upper lip—came back as murky gray masses, so blurry they could have been clouds or cobblestones, but certainly not close-ups of the sculptures in the park she had been shooting. Her third set of prints, though, was actually in focus, and looking at those small black-and-white images, conjured not only from her mind but from a unique combination of light and time, Lee filled with an excitement she never felt when painting. She had released the shutter, and where nothing had existed, suddenly there was art.

Lee wants the waiter to ask her more questions—wants, so badly, to have an actual conversation, to make a friend—but just then the bell over the door chimes as a group of older men come in and the waiter goes over to show them to a table.

Lee sips her drink as slowly as she can to make it last. As the room gets more crowded, it occurs to her that the bistro is stodgy. All the patrons are years older than her. The men have thick gray mustaches like suit brushes above their lips; the women, while chic, have high buttoned collars and sensible shoes. But then a trio comes in: two men and a woman. At first Lee thinks they are actors because their outfits are so strange. The men wear gauchos and sashes tied at their waists, with white shirts and no jackets. They look almost like parodies of artists but they sit perfectly at ease and the waiter hardly glances at them when they order. The woman, too, is dressed strangely, in the Scheherazade style that was popular a few years back. Her hair is closely bobbed and gleams like polished walnut against her small head, and her lips are painted such a dark red they are almost the same shade as her hair.

Lee tries to listen to them without their noticing. They speak English with a hard northern bite to it, and though normally she wants nothing more than to put Poughkeepsie behind her, on this night the familiar tones of her hometown have the pleasure of sinking into a warm bath. They are talking about a man named Diaghilev, who is the head of the ballet and has diabetes and lives alone in a nearby hotel. The woman seems afraid of him, but Lee can't discern why; she clearly isn't a dancer—even seated it is obvious she is stocky, and her ankles look like *saucisson* stuffed into her T-strap shoes.

"If you're going to listen, you should join us," one of the men says, staring at the ceiling.

Lee sips her wine.

"Hey, Lorelei," he says, swiveling in his chair and snapping his fingers at Lee. "If you're going to listen to us, you better join us."

When she realizes he is addressing her, Lee is so surprised she is almost tempted to decline their invitation, but this is the thing she has longed for—a way to be a part of a world just beyond her reach. For a moment she is scared to let it happen. But her waiter has overheard them, and comes over to carry her drink for her, so the choice is made and she moves over to their table.

Once she is settled, the man who invited her leans toward her. "I'm Jimmy," he says, "and this is Antonio, and this is my sister, Poppy."

He holds on to the word *sister* for a beat too long. Lee knows she is to understand that Poppy isn't his sister, but she has no idea why he would say she is.

Poppy turns her shiny head and looks at Lee. "We were talking about Diaghilev, but I'm bored of that. I want to talk about a scandal. Do you know any scandals?" Poppy purses her lips and a line appears near her mouth like a delicate question mark.

Lee glances around, suddenly hot from all the wine and food. What does she have to say that would interest them? Her mind goes blank as paper, and the only things she can think of are the physical objects around them: the ceiling light swaying on its chain, the scuffed wood floor, the candle on the table with its small waterfall of wax.

"You're a scandal," Jimmy says to Poppy, reaching over and putting his hand on her knee. She ignores him, holding Lee's gaze, the challenge of her question continuing until at last she looks away and it is over. She turns back to Jimmy and he begins talking again, and just like that the tension eases and Lee is folded into their group.

"We were at the Ballets Russes," Jimmy offers.

"We had to leave," Poppy says. Lee wonders if they were kicked out because of how they were dressed.

Jimmy balances on the back two legs of his chair. "Poppy here has a very refined sensibility. She can't bear to see anyone suffer. The director has a reputation—a temper, let's say—"

Poppy cuts him off. "The dancer looked puffy. She'd been crying, I could tell. And Goncharova's set was all wrong."

"I liked it. I better have, all the time I spent helping her paint it." These are the first words Antonio has spoken. He doesn't take his cigarette out of his mouth.

Lee turns to him. "Oh, you paint!"

"No." Antonio takes a huge drag and then crushes his cigarette in the ashtray and lights another in a unified and graceful motion.

"Antonio does automatic drawings," Jimmy says, and Lee nods as though she knows what he means. Antonio just sits there, so Jimmy continues. "Incredible work. He really gets to the dream state. Time like gears unhinged. Screwy stuff."

24

"The opposite of you," Poppy says, looking at Lee again, and for a moment Lee is shocked, until she realizes that Poppy is pointing to her camera, which she has set on the table and is surprised to find is doing what she hoped it would do: signal her new identity. Lee reaches out and runs her fingers across its case, still cold to the touch in the warm room.

"I've been doing illustration work for *Vogue*," Lee says, eager to offer up something that might seem intriguing. "They hired me when I moved here to sketch copies of the fashions at the Louvre."

It is true, or was: for weeks Lee sat on her little folding stool in the Louvre's east wing, copying the Renaissance objects they had on display. A lace cuff with a rose point pattern, a belt with a giant silver buckle. She sent her sketches to the magazine, care of Condé Nast, but when she did he told her that they couldn't use them after all. *We have a man in Rome now taking pictures,* he wrote. *Much faster, and such a good way to see all the details.* Lee hasn't been back to the museum since, and she hasn't found a new job either.

"Fashion at the Louvre," Jimmy drawls. "How bourgeois."

Lee flushes, but before she can say anything, Antonio says, "Good light. I work there now and then."

Lee thinks of the slanting shadows cast down from a bank of the museum's windows, the silhouettes the statues threw onto the ground. "Yes," she says, and when she catches Antonio's eye he gives her a smile, warm and genuine. Jimmy twirls a finger in the air to call for more drinks, and Poppy shifts in her seat so that she's facing Lee and starts to tell her a long, convoluted story about her childhood in Ohio, and just like that, Lee feels she has lifted a chisel to the wall of Paris and tapped the first crack into its surface.

Later. More wine. Poppy's hand snakes along Jimmy's thigh, the white tips of her manicure pale moons against his trousers. A warm flush that started in Lee's stomach rises up to her neck, as if she is a carafe someone is slowly filling with hot tea. By the time the warm feeling reaches her chin, she is leaning back in her chair, her legs spread in an unladylike posture, laughing so hard at the things Jimmy is saying she forgets to hide her crooked front teeth with her hand. So when Poppy yawns, looks around at the restaurant, now half empty again, and says, "Let's go somewhere—anywhere," Lee is ready, doesn't even care where they take her.

"Drosso's," Jimmy says with authority, standing and throwing a sheaf of bills on the table—how many Lee doesn't know, but it seems to her a vast sum, more than enough to cover the cost of her meal—and then they are outside, and it is raining, so they pile into the back of a taxicab, pressed so close together that Lee can feel the stubble on Poppy's exposed thigh as it pushes against her own. Antonio is wedged against her other side, staring out the window.

"Careful of your glass," Jimmy says to Poppy, who has brought her wine into the cab and takes small sips each time they stop.

Poppy turns to Lee as if they are in the middle of a conversation, which maybe they are—Lee cannot recall. "A few weeks ago Caresse and Harry had us drive out to Ermenonville. They own a mill there, and we met in the field behind it. I got into Harry's car and Caresse got into Jimmy's car. Lavender leather seats, custom work. At first it was the wildest thing. One switch and you're leading a gorgeous new life. Harry gave me his gardenia—"

Jimmy reaches over and grabs Poppy's face roughly, pushing her cheeks together so that her mouth distorts into an unattractive pucker. He lets go after a moment and she takes a sip of her drink as if nothing has happened. She is quiet for the rest of the ride. Antonio pays no attention to them, and when Lee glances at him he is cleaning his fingernails with a penknife. Usually this would disgust her. He has huge hands, long tapered fingers. Artist hands,

Lee thinks. The knife blade reflects the light of the streetlamps as they drive, and Lee watches him for a while, then looks out at the city, watery and indistinct through her own reflection in the cab's fogged windows.

Drosso's turns out to be an apartment on the third floor of an unremarkable building in Montmartre. The exterior gives no hint of the opulent world they find inside, rooms opening one into the next like brilliantly lit jewels, furnished with silk settees and Persian rugs and piles of embroidered satin cushions. Drosso himself greets them, arms outstretched, dressed in the strangest and most fantastic coat Lee has ever seen, a long burgundy jacket with attached silk butterfly wings that flutter behind him as he approaches. He kisses everyone on both cheeks, awkwardly long kisses.

"Magnifique," he whispers, and holds Lee at arm's length and makes her twirl for him, ducking her under his wing and letting it brush over her like a curtain. When she has finished twirling, Drosso smiles and puts one arm around her and the other arm around Poppy and shows them to a dressing room, steps outside, and closes the door. A dozen brightly colored silk robes hang from hooks on the wall. Poppy begins disrobing immediately, piling her clothes haphazardly in the corner. At first Lee tries to watch her without looking as though she is watching her, but it doesn't matter: Poppy is uninhibited, shimmying her way out of her garter belt and stockings the same way she must when she is alone.

When she sees Lee watching her, she says, "Everyone changes at Drosso's," as if that explains things. After debating it for a few more moments, Lee follows her lead. She fusses over the buttons of her dress, folds the garment extra neatly before setting it on the floor, and after she sees Poppy remove her brassiere she does the same, feeling as though she is back in the dressing room at a

27

modeling studio. Once Lee is undressed, she chooses a sky-blue kimono and ties the belt tight at her waist, the silk cool and almost wet against her skin. She cannot bear to leave her camera—what if it gets stolen?—so she picks it up and tries to ignore how absurd she feels carrying it while wearing the robe.

As they emerge from the dressing room, Lee hears muted voices and low music coming from down the hall. Drosso is waiting. He leads them to the back of the apartment, to a library with gilded bookshelves, and then walks over to the shelves and pulls a lever. The bookshelf swivels open to reveal another huge room, this one painted deep eggplant, with several dozen people inside, most dressed in robes, reclining on sofas and the floor. In the center of the room is a low brass table with a hookah and a few opium pipes on it. A dark-skinned man sits cross-legged next to it, dressed in a brocade military jacket and a small close-fitting hat. He leaps to his feet as they come into the room and bows deeply. In a corner, a couple lies entwined, sharing sips from the valve of a hookah tube that snakes toward them from the table. The man's hand rests in the woman's hair, unmoving, and her eyes are closed. As Lee watches, the woman's head starts to droop forward, and his hand clenches shut in her hair and holds her steady. The woman opens her eyes and smiles sleepily at him.

It is as if they have stepped out of Paris and into a Bedouin camp, the room a tent whose curtained walls muffle sound and throw great distorted shadows when people move around the space. A Moroccan screen in a corner half hides a kissing couple. One man lies facedown near the center of the room, so completely still Lee wonders if anyone is worried that he might be dead.

Lee does not know what to make of this place, these people, the thick smoke that hangs low in the room and curls around her ankles like a silent gray cat. Everything is disorienting: the smell, cinnamon and something harsher, a scent like unwashed bodies that makes her surreptitiously sniff her own damp armpits to make sure it isn't her; the crouching man near the hookah, who has been staring at her since she came in and holds up one of the hoses each time she makes eye contact with him; the musician playing in the corner, a sort of low, droning cello that gives everything a nihilistic quality.

No one is paying attention to her, but Lee cannot stop thinking about herself: the way she's cinched her kimono, the cumbersome camera case still clutched in her hand as if she is some kind of gawking tourist on Indian holiday.

She is drunk, but not drunk enough to consider smoking opium. That was her mother's pastime—morphine, actually, the little blue vials lined up on the window ledge in her dressing room and glowing like sapphires in the sun. Lee looks around the room and sees her mother in all the drowsing women. "Go 'way, Li-Li. I'm tired." There were times when her mother locked herself in her bedroom and ignored Lee for days at a time, emerging puffy and haughty, her eyes smeared with the remains of her makeup.

Lee has been high just once: she and her best friend, Tanja, tried laudanum together, and sometimes when she is sick she can still taste it at the back of her throat, cloves and bitter herbs and alcohol, the numbness of her tongue and the floating giddiness that came after it. She hated it, had panicked, as if her life were a balloon and she had just let go of the string.

Now she is trapped. Thinking of Tanja has made her miss her friend, and she wishes there were someone here who knows her. The bookshelf is closed behind her. Poppy has reunited with Jimmy, and Lee sees them embracing in a far corner. Drosso kneels next to a young man and helps him steady a needle into his arm. Only Antonio remains nearby, so Lee turns to him and he catches her eye and gestures to a bar cart she hasn't noticed yet.

She nods, grateful, and lets him fix her a glass. The truth is that she probably shouldn't have more—she lost track of how much wine she had at the restaurant—but along with her nervousness she is filled with a reckless feeling.

Antonio brings her brandy, a man's drink, and the bitter liquid cuts through the fug and instantly makes her feel better.

"You ever been here?" he asks her, his voice low. He was so silent at the restaurant it is a surprise to hear him ask a question.

Lee shakes her head. "I've only lived in Paris for a few months."

"It's not all just this." Antonio gestures around them. "Drosso is an art collector. He's very wealthy."

"What does he collect?"

"Everything, I guess, though he loves modern work. He funds *Littérature*. That's why we're all here so often, suckling at the teat of our potential patron." He nods his head toward a few men arranged around a hookah.

"All who?" Lee takes another swallow of the brandy, which is opening up her chest in a strange way, pulling like a hot knife through her breastbone.

"Éluard, Tzara, Duchamp. All the Surrealists. Here to channel the unconscious." Antonio makes quotation marks in the air and smirks conspiratorially.

She knows these names, has heard them mentioned at New York parties, read them in literary magazines. Hearing Antonio say them is like feeling a key slide into a lock. "Do you know them?"

"Sure I do."

The drone of the cello stops and Lee looks at Antonio, looks him straight in the face and realizes how attractive he is. His mouth is full, his lips dry, almost papery. His eyes are a beautiful soft gray, ringed with black lashes.

"Can you introduce me to them?" she asks, leaning toward him and wavering unsteadily on her feet. "I know them—I mean, I want to know them. I want to meet them."

Lee is having trouble making sense, her words as wobbly as her legs, so she reaches out a hand and puts it on Antonio's arm, hard and warm beneath his robe. She hears everything now that the music has stopped: the burble of the hookah, the click and hiss of smokers' lighters over their pipes, the *tink-tink* of ice in her brandy glass. She takes another sip and then another.

"Now's probably not the time," Antonio says, his voice kind, and even though she tries to pull him in the other direction, across the room to where he said Duchamp is sitting, he gently leads her to an empty couch against a far wall and tries to take the brandy glass out of her hand. She won't let him. She needs the cold crystal, the warming bite of the liquor.

"Can you get me another?" Lee asks him, and he looks at her for a while and then shrugs and does as she's requested, trading her a fresh glass for her empty, and she lifts the new one to her mouth and takes a giant swallow.

"I'll be right back," Antonio says, or at least Lee thinks she hears him say it. In any case, he leaves her there, and the couch is deep and overstuffed and upholstered in a slippery fabric that's just begging for her to slide down on it, so she finishes the new brandy and makes herself more comfortable.

Just before Lee thinks of nothing she thinks of this: *That brandy is* not *just brandy.* The voice inside her head is indignant, and then she passes out.

It could be minutes, it could be hours. Lee wakes up, still on the couch, her cheek pressed into a heavily embroidered pillow. She rubs at her eyes, opens them. Drosso stands over her, his butterfly wings hanging at his sides and his big shiny face inches from her own.

"I'm fine, I'm fine," Lee mutters, batting her hand at him as if she is brushing away a fly. She lifts her head and looks around the room for Poppy or Antonio but doesn't see them anywhere.

"I must tell you a passionate secret," Drosso says in French. Lee is too confused to understand him, so he repeats himself a few times until finally another man comes over and says in English, "He says he has to confess something to you."

This man is smaller than Drosso, with thick curly hair springing away from his temples.

Drosso speaks to the man in rapid-fire French. He holds a champagne coupe in his hand and points at Lee, talking so quickly that even if she were fully cogent she wouldn't be able to follow him. The smaller man laughs and looks at her.

"He says . . ." The man pauses, seeming to debate whether or not to say what comes next. "He says that he's never seen such beautiful breasts. He says your breast is like a more perfect version of the glass he holds in his hand. He wants to draw it and then have it made so that he can drink champagne from it. He wants to drink champagne from your breast while touching your breast."

Through the whole statement, Drosso nods in furious agreement. Lee sits up. Looks down. Her belt is loose. Her kimono gapes brazenly from sternum to hip bone so that even in her fog she knows that Drosso must have been able to get a good look at her. She clutches the kimono's fabric to her chest, crunching the blue silk in her fist as tightly as she can, and then stands up and pulls the absurd robe even tighter around herself.

The small man is smiling at her, and though his expression is friendly and almost apologetic, Lee wants nothing more than to be far away from him.

"Please tell your friend," she says to him, twanging her American accent as imperiously as she can, "that he will never touch my breasts, not if I was falling from a burning building and my breast was the only thing he could hold on to, to save me from dying."

He bursts into laughter as Lee walks away from him. She goes toward the bookshelf but realizes she has no idea how to open it. With one hand still clutching her robe, she feels across the shelves with her other hand, desperately searching for a lever or knob or something that will let her out. But she is trapped.

"Wait," the man says. "Wait."

Lee looks around, feeling frantic. "How do I get out of here?" she asks a woman who lies nearby, eyes closed. The woman doesn't respond.

The man has followed her. He reaches for a small gold handle on the bookshelf, and it slides open easily. As she moves toward the opening, he gently circles her wrist with his hand.

"He's bent," he says, gesturing at Drosso. "He'd never try anything with you, or with any woman. Do you understand what I'm saying? It's all just silly. Theatrics."

Lee shakes her head no.

"Who are you?" he asks.

She shakes her head again. She doesn't want to tell him her name, doesn't want him to know another thing about her.

"It's all right," he says. "You're fine. I'm sorry he scared you."

"I'm not *scared*. I just want to leave."

"I understand. If you ever need anything, you can look me up. I'm Man Ray."

The pomposity of his statement—not "My name is Man Ray," but "I'm Man Ray," as if there isn't a chance in the world she wouldn't know of him—astounds her. True, she *does* know of him: his photography appeared in *Vogue* right next to her modeling spreads. He is as well-known as Edward Steichen or Cecil Beaton in the fashion world—she heard his name mentioned at many parties before she left New York.

Man Ray reaches into his coat pocket—it is only now that she realizes he is not wearing a robe—and hands her a small card with his address printed on it. All Lee wants is to leave, to be alone someplace where she can pretend none of this ever happened, so she says thank you and takes the card and turns away, walking out as quickly as she can without looking as though she's running.

It isn't until she has made her way back to the dressing room, found her clothes and put them on with fumbling fingers, taken a cab all the way back to Montparnasse, and is in her own cold bed, the coverlet pulled up to her chin and tucked hospital-tight around her body, that the black humor of the situation hits her. All these months spent hoping to meet other artists, and she meets Man Ray at an opium den, where she is too embarrassed to do anything but run away. Alone, she cringes at the memory, until she has another thought, much more disturbing: her camera, left behind on the couch in her hurry.

CHAPTER TWO

It is not until her camera is gone that Lee begins to understand how much she has grown to love it. For it is truly gone: the next day, she walked the six kilometers back to the apartment in Montmartre, found the door with its elegant bellpull, clenched her hands until her fingernails bit into her palms, and girded herself for Drosso's moon face, his wet lips. But it was a servant who greeted her, silently took her up and back through the maze of elaborate rooms. Lee knew the secret of the bookshelf and opened it herself, but behind the shelf the hidden room was empty. The whole place was empty, smelling jarringly of lye.

Without her camera, Lee returns to painting. She lugs her folding easel and stool out into the street, sets up along the Seine, bisects her canvas with a decisive horizon line as she was taught to do at art school. Hours pass. Lee wishes she felt inspired, but instead she is just achingly lonely. She watches two young women browse a nearby bouquiniste, their gloved hands trailing across the rows of book spines. They talk and laugh together, and for a moment Lee wants to join them, to abandon the pretense that she is trying to become an artist, and just while away her hours. But something in her is disgusted by their purposelessness, by the excess of the expat culture, all the rich Americans she sees, content to enjoy the favorable exchange rate and live like the hedonists they are.

As Lee wanders the city, she finds herself composing photographs in her mind instead of paintings. One afternoon she goes to the camera shop near her hotel to ogle the window display. The model she wants, a brand-new Rolleiflex Original, sits on a velvet cushion and costs 2,400 francs. Though she barely has money to pay her rent, Lee goes into the shop, ignoring the way the shopkeeper's eyebrows raise slightly in surprise when she asks to see the Rollei. In her hands it is lighter and more compact than her lost Graflex. She thinks of the pictures she took before and vows— if she can ever afford to buy another camera—to try harder, take more pictures, learn how to make something that is actually art.

When she has touched the Rollei's every knob and dial and finally handed it back over, the shopkeeper gestures to an ad for a Kodak Brownie on the wall behind him. In the ad the Kodak girl wears a flapper-style striped dress and stands at the top of a small hill, arms outstretched, her Brownie dangling from one finger. "Perhaps you would prefer something smaller, something a little simpler?" he asks her. "These are what all the girls are getting lately."

Lee shakes her head. Not this girl, she thinks, and bids him good day.

Instead of taking pictures, Lee reads the instruction manual she took from her camera case and stuffed in the back of her one desk drawer. She will use this time productively, and when she has saved up enough, she'll deserve the professional camera she wants to buy. Printed on one page of the manual are grainy pictures— sailboats, an excavator, a winding country road—followed by columns of numbers under the headings "Bright Sun," "Cloudy," "Hazy," and "Dull." Within these columns are more choices, based on time of day, and then there's a small sentence at the bottom of the page: "Exposures with stops larger or smaller than F8 should be respectively decreased or increased one-half with each succeeding smaller or larger stop used. Third group—May—Bright—9 a.m.–3 p.m. = 160—F8." Sitting on her bed, staring at the diagrams with no camera to reference, Lee finds it all so technical that it makes her want to scream, makes her feel like the living embodiment of the "Dull" column, too stupid to grasp even these basics of the art form.

Was this what her father was doing when he took her picture? Lee remembers him fiddling with the knobs on the camera's face, how he'd pace off the steps between her and the camera mount, which she realizes now he must have been doing so he'd get the focus right. But she remembers more the way he'd run his finger along her cheek to move her face toward the light, his pleased expression when he knew he had gotten the shot he wanted.

One session in particular stands out. Lee must have been nine or ten. The day would have fallen into the "Bright Sun" column in the manual, the contrast too high for shooting outdoors. Her father set up his camera in the parlor, drew the gauzy curtain liners across the windows, and endured her, with diminishing patience, as she ran through the room, asking him again and again, "Are you ready yet? Are you ready yet?," whipping the pocket door open and closed each time she came full circle.

When he was finally set up, he called to her and shut both doors, entirely cutting off the room from the rest of the house. With the wide doors shut, it was a small, close space, with such high ceilings the perspective seemed skewed, as if the furniture were clustered together at the bottom of a dumbwaiter shaft. Everything was dark, opulent, a wide band of mahogany wainscoting on the walls and heavy, low-lying mahogany furniture to match. Against the dark wood, her father's white hair gleamed, his body looked as thin and tough as a piece of jerky.

"Stand by the drapes," he said, and there are a few pictures of her in the first pose, clad in a knee-length organdy dress with a drooping bow at the waist and a sailor's collar. She wore black stockings, and all her running around had left them smeared with dust. Her expression in these first shots was insouciant; she stared at the camera with heavy-lidded eyes.

Now, running her finger along the grid of numbers, Lee understands how laborious the process was, why it was after only one or two exposures that he came over to where she stood and studied her with a puzzled, searching expression.

"Li-Li," he said, "the dress is too bright against the draperies. Let's try it without, shall we?" He helped her undo the fussy covered buttons that marched down the back of her bodice, unknot the sash cinched at her waist. His hands were warm and rough. As he helped her, his calluses caught on the band at the top of her delicate stockings; his fingernails left light scratches on her dry pale skin.

"That's going to be much better," he said, and he was right. Lee remembers the picture so clearly it's as if she just saw it. In it, her naked body is white and almost glowing, and she looks like a deer emerging from a dark forest, her eyes wide and startled like a deer's, full of all her love for her loving father.

CHAPTER THREE

As she does every few nights, Lee goes to Bricktop to hear the music. It is September now, two months since she was at Drosso's. The bar is small and dark, choked with smoke and packed with people. The jazz band sits on a small stage in the corner, the sweat making sparks of light on their dark faces. The music is loud, metallic; the high notes shake her eardrums.

Lee is down to just enough for three more weeks' rent if she is frugal. She thinks of the expensive clothing she brought with her from New York, already out-of-date, and wishes she were the sort of person who saved. A few days ago, Lee sent a telegram home and asked for a loan. She has wanted to be independent, but she knows her father will help her; he always has, even though he has also always insisted on being in charge of her finances. But the response she received this afternoon was a shock. *Kotex ad a scandal,* his telegram said. *Humiliated.* There was no mention of sending the money she requested.

On her way to Bricktop this evening, she stopped at the international newsstand and thumbed through the latest magazines until she found it: her picture in the August issue of *McCall's,* clad in a white satin dress, the words "Wear the pad even under the sheerest, most clinging frocks" written in looping script beneath the picture.

Lee remembers the photograph, one Steichen took of her, but had no idea it had been sold to Kotex. She can imagine her father's fury. He abhors social impropriety, loathes even more any discussion of the workings of women's bodies. Lee is mortified: by the picture, but also because she disappointed him. When she felt this way as a child he was the one she would run to, but now she is far away and he is the one she has offended.

Now, at the club, Lee taps her fingers on the table in time to the music's beat. What is she going to do? She cannot imagine going back to New York, but she doesn't know how she can stay here in Paris if she doesn't have a job or a purpose, and she feels paralyzed with indecision. It is all she can do not to start crying.

And then she sees them. Poppy and Jimmy. They come in a rush, trailed by another couple. All four wear matching black suits, bow ties. Lee is so lonely she is happy to come across anyone she knows, can brush aside the circumstances of their other evening together. She gets up and walks over to them.

"Poppy!" Lee says. "Can I join you?"

Poppy looks back with a face as expressionless as a Kabuki mask. "Pardon? You must have me confused with someone else."

"We met at a restaurant near here. We shared a taxi, we went to Drosso's together." Lee shouts to be heard over the trombone.

"So strange," the woman murmurs, and turns back to Jimmy and snakes her arm through his, and together they push their way up to the bar and leave Lee staring after them.

Poppy and Jimmy stand together at the bar with the careless quality of people who don't question their place in the world. They seem so casual, so relaxed, and Lee remembers that in New York she was like them, a girl who took what she wanted from life when she wanted it. This new version of herself—sad, alone, embarrassed—is not who she really is. The old Lee would have laughed off any whiff of scandal, made the Kotex ad into good gossip, found a man or three to pay for her drinks if she was short on funds, and not given Poppy and Jimmy another moment's thought.

Lee walks up to the bar and leans against its rounded corner. A finger snap is all it takes to get the barman's attention. As she waits for him to make his way over and take her order, she catches sight of her reflection in the murky mirror behind the bar. The humid room has flushed her cheeks. "Smile," Lee whispers, imitating a man's stern tone, and watches herself in the mirror as she does so. Her face is as beautiful as ever, her smile just how she wants it. Right now, she thinks, she'll get a gin martini, cold and clear as a glass of diamonds, and after she's finished the drink she'll go out into the crowded center of the dance floor and find someone to spin her around. And then tomorrow she'll take the card Man Ray gave her that she's been carrying around in her pocket and pay a visit to his studio. Ask him if she can be his student. Get him to teach her everything he knows.

It is just after two o'clock the next day when she arrives. She raps on the door and considers all the things she could say. Man Ray probably won't even remember her from that night at Drosso's, but if he does, she can laugh it off, or pretend to be someone else entirely, as Poppy did.

Time stretches out long enough that she begins to regret being there. Finally the door opens, and Man Ray stands in front of her, drying his hands on a dingy rag, his hair springing out from his head just like the first time she saw him.

"You're not supposed to be here until two thirty," he says.

Lee takes a step back. "I—I'm not supposed to be here at all."

He shades his eyes with his hand. "You're not my two thirty?"

"No, no...I'm...We met before—" The minute it's out of her mouth she regrets it but pushes on. "We met at Drosso's."

He steps out onto the doorstep and takes a better look at her, then laughs. "You! 'I wouldn't let you touch my breast if I was falling out of the sky.'"

"That's me," Lee says, smiling despite herself.

Man motions for her to come inside with him and shuts the door behind them. The foyer is filled with paintings and photographs in mismatched frames tacked haphazardly all over the walls, and a wide wooden staircase hugs the edge of the room and leads to a landing. Without another word he heads up the stairs, and she follows him. They enter a small parlor and Man walks over to a cart that holds an electric kettle and begins to make two cups of tea. Lee sits in an armchair studded with unnecessary buttons and watches him. He's as small as she remembers him, but this time he's dressed stylishly in wide-cuffed wool pants and a matching vest, and his body has a coiled, wiry energy to it. As he pours the water over the tea bags with one hand and arranges spoons and sugar cubes on saucers with the other, Lee likes how efficient he seems, some part of him in constant motion. He brings over the tea and sits on the settee across from her, and she likes, too, his dark brown eyes, the intelligence and humor she sees in them as he looks her over.

"I didn't expect to see you again," he says, his voice light. "You seemed rather angry."

"Well"—Lee leans forward and picks up her teacup with nervous fingers—"I lost my camera that night. I know you're a photographer. I thought maybe, when you left, you might have seen it?" She glances around the room as if she expects her camera to be sitting on a shelf nearby.

"You had it with you at Drosso's?"

"Yes. But I lost it."

"Not the best place to take something valuable. Lots of unsavory people go there. Addicts." He picks up his cup and slurps from it noisily. When he sets it down he scrunches his eyebrows together, as if concerned for her safety.

Lee switches tactics. "I'm a photographer—well, not really. I'm a model. I was a model in New York before I moved here, and I know Condé Nast and Edward Steichen. I know you know them."

"Has Steichen done you?" She can feel Man's gaze resting on her throat, her hair, her mouth.

"Of course. For *Vogue* and other places." Lee feels the familiar ground of modeling beneath her, sits up straighter and turns her good profile toward him.

"I'm better. After this two thirty I don't have any more appointments. I'll take your picture, you can use it here, get started. I know some people at Laurent's—they're always looking for new girls."

Lee sets down her cup. "I don't want you to take my picture. I want to *take* pictures. I want to be your student."

"I don't take students. I don't know what Condé told you. But you're luminous, truly. I can see why *Vogue* wanted you. I'll do you for free. You can put it in your portfolio."

Behind him a grandfather clock tolls once and is followed by the pound of the door knocker. Man rises. Lee knows this is her only chance to make this work. He thinks she's beautiful, that much is clear, and it would be so easy to flirt with him and keep his interest. But she doesn't want him to think of her that way.

"I've been thinking of how I'd take your picture," Lee says, just before he reaches the door. He turns to look back at her. "I'd lay you down on a table and put the camera at your feet. I'd make you look like a landscape." She blurts out the words quickly. As she says it she can see it: the ridges and folds of the fabric on his body like mountain ranges, the features of his face flattened to abstraction.

Man pauses at the door and considers her. "It wouldn't work. There's no way to get the focus right on a shot like that."

Of course not. Conviction and confidence, in an instant, replaced by the wide void of all she does not know. Lee stands up and clasps her hands together like a schoolgirl. "That's why I want to be your student. You can teach me these things. Condé mentioned I might come to you—"

Man waves his hand. "He's sent lots of people my way. I made the mistake early on of being helpful, and now everyone feels like they can come learn from me. I don't have time to support every person who wants to be the next Man Ray. I'm busy. Portraits to shoot—portraits to shoot for Condé's magazine, actually. He should know better."

"How would you shoot me?" Lee pulls down her shoulders and lifts up her chin and looks at him directly.

Man gives her a quick appraising glance. "Probably a close-up of your face, with your hand at your throat. Black background." His tone is clipped, a bit dismissive. Again the sound of the door knocker echoes through the room.

"That's boring," she says, to keep his attention.

Man chuckles and crosses his arms over his chest. "Oh? Then I'd put you near a window, half in light and half in shadow, and shoot you nude with your eyes closed, like you looked at Drosso's."

"You just want to see my breasts again."

He stares at her, surprised, then starts to laugh. "You're not shy, are you?" He takes a step toward the door and then holds up a finger. "Wait there. Don't go anywhere."

She can hear him run down the stairs and open the front door, then voices murmuring, footsteps. Man leads a woman past the parlor and Lee catches a glimpse of her, a column of gold-shot brocade topped with a towering pompadour, as they

44

disappear into what must be Man's studio. Lee sits for a while, waiting, watching the smooth sweep of the second hand on the grandfather clock, taking in the oils on the wall, the crowded bookshelves, the objects clustered on the mantel. A line of birds' eggs, arranged by size. A similar arrangement of enamel vases, the smallest no larger than a kidney bean. She walks over to the shelves and reads the titles on the book spines. She picks up a porcelain cow figurine and weighs it in her palm. She wants it, all of it. And then she walks out into the hallway where she can see into the studio, where Man is heaving a reflector light into place.

When he notices her standing there, he says, "Can you come help me with these lights, please?"

The studio smells of burning dust and bromine and it is like every other studio she has ever been in: white walls, light filtering in from wide windows, the camera on its platform with the huge black hood. But this time, she walks over to one of the reflectors, grabs a leg while Man grabs the other, and pulls and wiggles it into place. This time, she picks up a glass plate and hands it to him, watching attentively as he loads it into the camera. The woman in her beautiful dress chats with both of them. She is here to get a portrait done for her husband for their twentieth wedding anniversary. When the camera is set up the woman clenches her face into a small, tense smile. Man keeps up a friendly patter with her, clearly trying to put her at ease, and Lee sees immediately how good he is at connecting with his subject. But Lee knows a few things too, and right before Man goes under the camera hood, she tells the woman, "Relax your eye muscles when you smile," and after a moment's hesitation the woman does so, her face suddenly more natural. When Man emerges from the hood, he looks at Lee and gives her a nod of approval. She nods back, feeling the way she has hoped to feel since she left New York, as though she has managed to set something good in motion.

CHAPTER FOUR

"Bobby!" Man shouts when the man arrives. He is corpulent; his body fills up the doorway and blocks the light. Once inside, he smiles at Man, a gummy smile in a big bald head, like an oversize baby's. They laugh and shake hands and Bobby pounds Man on the back.

"It's been too long," Man says. "I couldn't believe it when I saw your note. Big Bobby Steiner, in Paris. Never thought I'd see it."

"When General Electric sets up the hoop, you jump through it. I'm head of the European division now."

"I heard. Terrific news. And you were smart to come to me. I'll take a photo of you that'll make you look like you deserve it."

"You better." Bobby laughs again and glances around. When he notices Lee, he stops short and raises his hands in a gesture of mock surrender. "Hello, looker!" he says. He walks over to her and offers his face for a kiss, one cheek, American-style. "This your new girl, Manny? You got yourself a new girl? I liked that last one you brought to New York."

Lee expects Man to clear things up, but he just laughs and mutters something to Bobby she doesn't hear and doesn't want to. She feels her face grow hot, not with embarrassment but with annoyance. Bobby stands looking at her for a few more moments,

46

letting his eyes drift up and down her body, and then the two men walk into Man's office and shut the door.

Lee is certainly not Man's girl, but she's not his student either. After the woman from the anniversary shoot left that first afternoon, Man asked Lee to stay behind, and explained that he had more work than he could handle and could use her help. Lee is not sure what she did to make him change his mind, but whatever it was, she doesn't question it. He has had other assistants, he told her. The last one left a few months earlier. The job isn't glamorous: keeping track of Man's finances, which he described as a holy disaster; scheduling sessions; setting up the studio equipment; and occasionally helping him print. To his description of all these tasks, Lee nodded her head, bobbing it up and down so insistently she was worried it might come unhinged from her neck. If she was expecting a huge salary, he continued, he couldn't provide it, but Lee could use the darkroom when he didn't need it and she could come and go as she pleased. She agreed before he even told her a number. When he did it was shockingly low. But she doesn't care. It is a beginning, a launching point into what she wants. The idea of working for a famous photographer is so appealing she probably would do it for free.

And now, after a month, she has settled into the rhythm of her new job. Mornings, she arrives at nine or ten o'clock—early by Parisian standards—and lets herself into the studio with the small brass key that Man has given her. She goes to the office and situates herself at his desk. It is her job to balance the ledger, a giant book that usually has to be unearthed from under all Man's detritus: birds' eggs, receipts from the tailor, toy soldiers, and, one day, a giant glass jar with a preserved octopus floating in it. He is like a crow bringing shiny treasures back to his nest, and Lee finds she likes the clutter his habits create.

Lee has a head for numbers, but still she does the work in pencil, carefully erasing any mistakes and redoing the figures in her round, even hand. The previous assistant was not as meticulous as she is trying to be, so when Lee has spare time she goes back in the ledger to earlier weeks and tries to untangle the web of errors her predecessor has left behind.

Here is what the numbers tell her: photography pays well. Man's other creative endeavors, painting and sculpture, do not. He has a lot of money, especially by artists' standards, but is terrible at managing it. He does not save. Instead, when a big job comes in he treats it like a windfall, an excuse to celebrate or buy something extravagant. There are more entries in the expense column than in the income column, and most of them are for ephemera: oysters at Le Select, two nights at a hotel in Saint-Malo—even, twelve months earlier, a Voisin, which he uses to drive out to the country or when he summers in Biarritz and otherwise has to pay an exorbitant fee to garage nearby.

Lee goes back to the records from 1928, where there were many entries with a single initial attached to them: "K rent," "Milliner for K," "Dinner with K," and sometimes simply a number with the initial next to it, no further explanation. One day she adds up all the K entries and is astounded at how much money Man has spent on this person. It must be the girl Bobby referred to, but who is she? So far Lee cannot ask. The many entries for K's milliner make Lee picture her as pale, concerned about her skin. Perhaps she is older—at least as old as Man. Lee is not yet sure how old Man is but he is certainly much, much older than she is. But where did K go? Dozens and dozens of entries, and then since January, nothing. A fight? Another man? Lee walks her fingers down the column of numbers and imagines their breakup, Man's secret torment. K has not been replaced—there are no initials after January. The only woman to be added to the ledger is Lee herself, and since she is now in charge of check writing, she gets the perverse pleasure of paying herself each week for her own hard work.

Man usually doesn't come in until eleven, so each morning Lee has a few hours by herself. She loves this time spent putting his house in order, loves having a list of things to tell him each day when he arrives. He usually shows up in one of three moods: distracted, his fingers covered in charcoal or smeared with oils from a morning spent painting; harried, when he knows an important client is coming in the afternoon and is anticipating a day spent doing work he does not enjoy; or gloomy, when there has been a lull in the stream of sittings or he has had to pay a bill he's forgotten about. Lee navigates all the moods with the same blend of professionalism and detachment, and Man matches her professionalism with his own, treating her with a courtesy she never knew when she was modeling.

In the afternoons, she assists him in the studio or in the darkroom, and these are by far her favorite hours of the day. Man insists he is a terrible teacher and that she'll learn nothing from him, but on the contrary, Lee finds him informative and patient. He's warm, surprisingly open with all the tricks he's learned. He tells her that photography is more like science than like art, that they are chemists doing experiments in a lab, and it does seem that way to her, as much about the technical work in the darkroom as it is about the original artistic vision.

Man doesn't print every day, or even every week, but when he does, Lee sets up the darkroom for him, donning rubber gloves and a rubber apron to mix the developer, stop, and fix baths. She places wooden tongs in the trays, uses a turkey baster to blow air off the enlarger, makes sure the safelight is working. She takes older prints off the clothesline and brings them into the studio, placing them carefully in one of the large flat file drawers with onionskin layers between them. As bad as Man appears to be at managing money, he is equally good at printing, and there are hardly ever any prints that have to be thrown away. Rarely, a first effort is too dark, or the contrast too low, but these prints he saves and uses in other projects, cut into ribbons and glued to a wood backing, or simply turned over so the reverse sides can be repurposed for sketching.

Sometimes the pictures are so beautiful Lee pauses in her work just to stare at them. Like the portrait of the dancer Helen Tamiris, whom Man shot dressed in a loose kimono, lying on the ground with her hair teased into a giant black cloud around her milk-white face. It is good, good work, and it is an honor just to be holding it, to know that she will one day develop prints in the same darkroom where it was made.

Lee has not yet broached the topic of her own photography with Man, even though Man mentioned it when he hired her. Above all she wants to keep things professional. But in her travels through the ledger book—and, though she doesn't want to admit she's this sort of person, in her early morning snooping through his desk drawers—she knows that Berenice Abbott, one of the former assistants, developed her own prints in Man's studio, with Man's blessing, and is now making a name for herself back in New York. Lee figures that there is time, that she is learning by observation, just as a scientist would do. Plus, there is not much to develop. Lee has three rolls of undeveloped film in her stocking drawer, but the last thing she wants is to use Man's supplies on pictures that any tourist might have taken.

Now, Lee stands in the studio and listens to the rise and fall of Man's and Bobby's voices in the office, their bursts of laughter. Her work is in the office too, so Lee doesn't know where to go or what to do. The situation and the visiting man remind her of the dinner parties her parents used to throw, the way she was shunted into a corner until it was time for her to help mix drinks. When she was young she looked precious, Lee supposes, all dolled up in Chantilly lace, with starched white bows stuck on her head like giant moths. But as she got older, it became discomfiting, the way the men leered at her when she brought them their cocktails, damp cigars clenched in their tight smiles.

Lee is still standing in the studio when the door from the office opens. The two men are in midconversation. "Sam's working for Lisowski now—did you hear? He made a pile off that property in Flushing," Bobby says.

"Yes, he wrote to me about it. Said the job doesn't give him much time for his writing."

"Minnie's glad he has some paychecks to send home, I'm sure."

Man scrunches his eyebrows together. "My mother is glad when any of us gets a real job and stops dithering around with art."

Bobby chuckles. "That's true. She told me to ask you when you were going to give all this up and move back home."

"She never gives up. Making you her messenger." Man laughs, but there is anger in it. He picks up a stool, walks to the center of the room, and gestures for Bobby to sit. Once Bobby's bulk is settled, his heavy legs spread in front of him, one ankle crossed over the other in his charcoal-gray spats, he makes a self-conscious face, squinting his eyes in a look of what he must think is confidence or concentration.

"You don't need much," Man is saying. "You look good like that, just a simple, powerful shot."

"Are you sure? This is for GE. We're not on Forty-Third Street anymore, Manny."

"Thank God for that." They both laugh again. Man turns to the camera, and Lee, standing near the door to the darkroom, clears her throat.

"Can I do anything?"

Both men look over. Bobby says, "I could go for one of those little stick sandwiches with the butter and ham."

"Ah yes, some food would be good. Do you mind, Miss Miller?" Man says, and even though she does mind, she tells him that she doesn't.

It is hot outside and the café is a few blocks away. Lee buys three *jambon-beurre* and eats hers on the street, like a gypsy. When she gets back to the studio, they have already finished the session. The door to the parlor is closed and the sweet stench of pipe tobacco seeps from the threshold. Lee plops the sandwiches on a tray and raps hard on the parlor door. More laughter and talking before Man opens it. She hands him the tray with a blank look on her face that she hopes subtly expresses her annoyance.

Man takes the sandwiches and turns away, then pauses and turns back to her. On his face is an expression she hasn't yet seen there, a sudden awareness mixed with gratitude. "Miss Miller," he says, "what did I do before you?"

"Got your own sandwiches, I imagine," Lee says, and feels his eyes on her as she walks away.

LONDON

1940

During the Blitz, bunked down with Roland in Hampstead, Lee wakes more than once to find her bed brown with menstrual blood. Something about the surprise of waking to the scream of the air-raid sirens sets her body off, starts her cramping. In the morning when the blackout lifts she rinses out the sheets in the sink, but stains remain, light copper blotches.

What Lee can never tell anyone is that she feels almost giddy when she hears the whistle of the bombs dropping, when she feels the room shake, when plaster dust coats her face and makes her sneeze. Can never tell them how much she looks forward to the mornings after, picking her way through the city with her camera, the bombed-out tableaux arranged before her like the work of some Surrealist set designer. A church destroyed, but a typewriter balanced on the rubble before it, perfectly unharmed. A statue completely decimated except for one beseeching arm. The wicked side of her loves the lawless nature of the blasts.

One night she and Roland wake to a different noise, a giant rustling, as if the house is a parcel being papered over. Lee pulls back the curtain and with a whoosh through the open window comes a ghostly silver fabric, almost consuming her, so much of it that she has to beat it away from her face in order to breathe. A barrage balloon, Roland tells her, laughing, and they go outside and work together to pull all the fabric back out of the house. The next day, she spends hours photographing it, the balloon's carcass draped over trees or twined around her body. None of the shots are right, but then a week later she is walking through Hampstead Heath and sees another downed balloon, pinned to the ground but still half filled with air, like a giant egg, two geese standing proudly before it. The photo she takes of it is a marvel, the war's first gift to her, and Lee feels buoyed aloft herself, filled with the promise of all that the coming days might offer her.

CHAPTER FIVE

It doesn't take Lee long to learn that Man thrives on change and gets itchy when days settle into a pattern. He does things Lee would never think of doing, like calling her up if his painting is going well and telling her to reschedule an afternoon's session, even if the client booked weeks ago. When she asks him what to tell them, he says "Gangrene!" or "Bus accident!" or "Surprise trip to Pamplona!," so Lee ignores him, and always says a family member has suddenly taken ill. Man's family, clients must think, is vast and constitutionally unsound.

One day, Man comes in and looks at the calendar: the afternoon is blissfully free. "Lovely day," he says.

He's right. As Lee walked to work that morning she'd felt sad she had to go inside, had stood on the stoop and filled her lungs to bursting with crisp air before she turned the key in the lock.

Man continues, "If I don't get that new cabinet, I think the whole operation is going to fall apart."

"Excuse me?"

"The flat file we need for extra storage." Man picks up his coat and puts it on. "The Vernaison will have one. Want to join me?"

So less than an hour later, Lee finds herself at the city's biggest flea market, where it seems there is nothing that's not for sale. Piles of empty gilded frames, giant Chippendale dressers, bundles of old letters, yellowed petticoats, war medals, brandy snifters, boxes of broken clocks, rusted skeleton keys, rows of prams filled with tattered silk pillows. Lee stops wonderingly at a hut where empty cans of denture powder balance on top of a motorbike. Man is a few yards away before he looks back to find her behind him. She smiles and hurries to catch up.

The November sun is brilliant in the cloudless sky and Man is the most lighthearted Lee has ever seen him. In two hours they haven't even made it to the furniture huts, where the cabinet Man purports to need might be, but he tells her those are off in the more expensive area of the Biron, and they'll go there later.

The dirt lanes they walk through are crowded with hundreds of vendors, their wares displayed on thick Oriental rugs in front of their stalls, which are filled with crowded stacks of what mostly looks like junk. Lee was puzzled when Man brought several large cloth shopping bags with him; now, as he pauses at a hut selling porcelain doll heads and begins to haggle with the rag-and-bone man over the price, she understands. Man has already filled two of his bags and—four doll heads successfully haggled for—is well on his way to filling a third.

A few huts farther down, they both stop to look at a display of glove makers' molds, the white hands stuck upright in a wire rack like a forest of small white trees.

"If I had my camera, I would take a picture of that," Lee says.

"Good eye." Man makes a square with his hands and holds it up to his face like a viewfinder. "What sort do you use?"

"I don't—" She pauses. "I meant, if I still had my camera. I never found it." She feels the loss again, as sharp as it was initially.

Farther back in the hut are mannequin parts, a jumble of elbows in a large wooden crate. Man picks one up and inspects it. "I forgot you told me that. What a shame. You'll have to get another."

Lee holds her tongue. Does he not realize how little he pays her? They wander farther down the lane. At the next stall, rows of stereoscopic pictures are arranged in boxes, organized by subject. Man thumbs through them. "These feel so dated." He holds up a picture of Trafalgar Square filled with carriages, the image doubled on the paper. Lee walks over to him and flips through another box.

"My father took stereoscope pictures," she says.

"Really? There's a technique to it. Was he a photographer?"

"Yes—we moved to a farm when I was little, and he built a lab there. I helped him with it."

Man glances at her. "No wonder you know what you're doing."

"Not really. I didn't do much." It's not true, so she's not sure why she says it. Man's sudden attention is making her uneasy, out here in the throngs of people.

Lee flips through some more pictures and stops at one of a mother in stiff Victorian dress, her young son perched on her knee. Both mother and child stare at the camera with the blank expressions the long exposure time required. At their farm, Lee's father's stereoscope collection was kept in his library, contained in several dozen dove-gray boxes lining the lower shelves of his bookcases. When he was working, Lee would go by herself into the room and kneel behind his desk, taking from its case the viewer she was not allowed to play with and inserting the stereo cards one by one into its frame. When she held up the device to her eyes, the small black-and-white images would hang for a moment in their separate fields of vision before converging into three-dimensionality, the scenes suddenly sharpened and made tactile. Sometimes when Lee looked at a scene of particular beauty—the Pantheon, or the palm fronds framing the Great Pyramids—she would, without even realizing what she was doing, put her free hand out in front of her as if to touch the images she saw, exactly as a blind man might feel for the edges of the objects around him.

Her father had literally hundreds of these cards; they were a sort of obsession for him, one of the largest collections of a man who collected everything.

Man has moved on, but Lee puts down the card and moves farther into the hut, where she starts flipping through another box, first some street scenes of Paris and Copenhagen, and then, behind those, photos of nude women, lounging on half-made beds, hanging coyly from brass poles, brushing their hair in front of vanity mirrors. These, too, are familiar. Her father had this collection as well, and alone in his office Lee would linger over them, memorizing what these women had done to capture her father's attention. Dark lips, dark hair, white skin. Fleshy rolls of fat where Lee was still slim. Shoes with pointed toes, hats with sequined veils or knee-high fishnet stockings. Until she found that box, she thought her father didn't look at pictures of any other girls but her.

After checking to see how far ahead of her Man has gotten, Lee picks up a photo of a woman dressed in nothing but three tassels, one on each nipple and one at the cleft of her legs; she's swiveling her hips to make them twirl. She holds up the photo and asks the rag-and-bone man how much, pays, tucks it in her handbag, and then hurries to catch up with Man before she loses him in the crowd.

At another hut there are rows of uniforms, blue as the sky, with metal helmets stacked upside down like bowls next to them. Lee fingers the wool collars, the steel buttons. Man disappears and returns wearing a helmet and brandishing an épée, which he whirls in the air and jabs at her.

"En garde!" he shouts. Lee laughs out loud. Man looks so silly in the helmet, and his lack of inhibition is surprising and wonderful. She grabs her own épée and feints toward him, then pretends she's been stabbed and staggers back against the uniforms. Man's eyes are bright. He sets down the sword and picks up a rounded piece of metal mesh, lofting it above his head and admiring it. "Ah, now *this*," he says, "this is coming home with us."

The object is curved like the spine of a nautilus, two feet in diameter, its purpose a complete mystery. Lee already knows he likes things like this, meshes and grids of wire or metal that take the light and break it into patterns. Man holds it in both hands, looking thrilled.

"What is it?"

"I have no idea—a cast of some sort?"

From the back of the stall the owner tells them it is a saber guard, for fencing. Man buys it and stuffs it in another bag. "I love coming here," he tells Lee as they move on, an acquisitive glint in his eyes. "You never know what you're going to find. One time I got a whole skeleton—a real one, from a hospital. It was just hanging there at the back of one of the stalls."

Soon they've made it to the Biron, where the road dust is brushed up with small bristle brooms and the shoppers' clothes are more obviously expensive. It doesn't take Man long to find the cabinet he needs—it seems everything is here, from console tables to butcher blocks to fainting couches—and he arranges quickly for it to be delivered the next day.

They pass a mother pushing a carriage and leading a small child by the hand. The child is whining loudly, his face sticky with what looks like syrup. Man and Lee both give a little shudder when they look at him, then catch each other's eyes and smile. "Not so maternal, are you?" Man says.

"Not really." The truth is Lee can't imagine having children. Nothing seems further from what she wants to do with her life.

"Art and children aren't a good mix, in my experience," Man says.

Lee wonders if he's cautioning her—does he see her as an artist? She doubts it. "You don't want them either?"

Man pauses at another furniture hut, opens a secretary desk, and looks inside. "Never. It's part of why my wife and I separated." He moves ahead to the next hut and Lee falls behind him a few paces. She had no idea he had been married. She wonders if his wife is the K from the ledger book, and walks more quickly to catch up with him.

"Was this here—in Paris?"

"No, no. Years ago, back in the States. A different lifetime."

"Where?" Lee hasn't given much thought to his past before, and feels a sudden hunger to understand him.

"That was in New Jersey. It was easier than living in New York. Cheaper. We had a good time—" Man pauses, coughs. "It wasn't really the question of children that made us separate."

Lee is not sure if she should prompt him to keep talking or not, but then he continues.

"We were so young. I was—well, I didn't even know what I wanted. I was supposed to be a tailor like my father, but I wanted to be an artist. My family supported me, to a point, but they never really understood me. My mother thought it was just a passing phase. A hobby. So I moved out of Brooklyn and rented a place in Ridgefield with a friend of mine. Have you ever been there?"

"I don't think so."

"Well, why would you? It's very small, very quiet. For a while my friend Halpert and I were really making something out there. We got a printing press and started a magazine, and I was painting every day. And then I met Adon, and she was interested in what we were doing—she wrote poetry, beautiful stuff, I had never met anyone like her—and we got married. But then when I needed to get even further away, to move to Paris, Adon—she wasn't interested. She was getting quite known in the literary circles. I haven't spoken to her in years."

Adon. So not K. And years earlier. "I'm sorry," Lee says.

Man shrugs and runs his hand through his hair. They have stopped walking and are standing at the edge of the market, where the crush of people is less intense.

"Well, no need to be sorry," Man says. "I'm not even sure why I'm telling you all of this." He shifts his bags so they're higher on his shoulder, and after a few moments says, "What made you want to take pictures?"

Lee tucks her hair behind her ears. She thinks of the stereoscope picture she just bought, thinks of all the photos her father took of her over the years, and says, "Oh, my father, I suppose... and I was sick of modeling. Of *being* photographed. I wanted to go around the other side and see how it was done."

Man nods, as if this makes sense to him, and then says, "Lately I think all the time about giving it up."

"You do?"

"It's not art. Not really. All I've ever really wanted to do is paint. Studio portraits—clients..." His voice trails off.

Lee thinks of the work of his she's seen so far, the recent portrait of Dalí he just shot, Dalí's face lit from beneath so that his eyebrows cast devilish spiked shadows on his forehead. She wants to tell Man how it made her feel, how it provoked her, made her simultaneously worry about all she does not know and eager for all she has to learn. It surprises her to hear him say he could give it up. If she had his talent she'd never stop taking pictures. "Your photography is so good, though," she says, and then immediately feels the inadequacy of her words.

"Of course. But try getting critics interested. They have no respect for photography as *art*. And part of me agrees with them. Photography's primary purpose isn't art, it's replication."

Lee looks at him curiously. "I think that portrait you took of Barbette—the double exposure—I think that's art."

Man huffs air through his nose. "Maybe. But I do get tired of all the studio work, traveling to the dress houses, and all the rest. It's such drudgery. If I had my way, I'd go back to painting full-time."

"Well, why don't you?"

He holds up one of his bulky shopping bags and smiles wryly. "Because painting does not pay for trips to the Vernaison."

A few blocks later, Lee and Man descend into the Métro, a waft of stale air blowing leaves up the stairs and around them. Man waves her off when she goes to buy a ticket and pays for her. As they board the train, Man shifts his heavy bags to his other shoulder and takes her elbow. An older man and woman bundled up in coats sit on the train's far side, watching them as they enter. To them, Lee and Man must seem like a married couple, he carrying her packages and leading her solicitously by the arm. There must be nothing odd about it to them, clearly old and married themselves. Man must have acted similarly with his wife, all those years ago. The thought of how she and Man look together is a strange one, and makes Lee strangely happy.

CHAPTER SIX

A few times a month Man pays student models a small stipend so he can work on pictures he is not being paid to take, and when he does he is always in a good mood. Today he's using a new girl, Amélie, small and dark-haired like all the models Man hires. Lee hears him whistling as he sets up the studio.

Amélie arrives fifteen minutes late, sniffling. Her nose is red and her eyes watery.

"Are you sick?" Lee asks. As she looks at the girl, Lee is convinced she feels a scratch in her own throat and vows to make a tonic when she gets home.

"No, I'm fine," Amélie declares, but after a few minutes in the studio it's clear she's not. She droops over the couch like a wilted flower, poses for pictures with her mouth hanging open since she doesn't seem to be able to breathe through her nose.

Man doesn't seem to notice that she's sick, or care. He's humming, cracking jokes, putting Amélie in strange poses and muttering "Brilliant!" under his breath. Lee has come to find his appreciation of his own work endearing.

"Now," he says, "I thought we could try out this object. Put you in front of the window and play with the shadows a bit?" He pulls out the saber guard he bought at the Vernaison and shows it to Amélie, who stares at him blankly until he brings it over to her and says, "Your arm, here." The metal mesh is delicate as lacework but sharp along the edges. Amélie places her arm through it and winces as she balances it on the table.

Man steps back. He tilts his head as he always does, looking for the through line the image will need. He kneels and grasps Amélie's hand, tugging it so that her palm is a bit more open.

"Like this," he says, tugging again on her arm and moving it at an awkward angle. Satisfied, he disappears under the camera hood. Amélie breathes shallowly and Lee finds herself slowing her own breath to match. Man is out of view for quite a while, calling out now and then for Lee to move the reflectors or adjust the curtains behind them.

Finally he emerges from under the hood. "All done," he says to Amélie, and then he leaves the room to let her get dressed in peace. She takes her arm out of the saber guard, her face a moue of discomfort.

"So sharp," she whines to Lee, rubbing a red mark on the pale white underside of her arm.

"Well, models must do what is asked of them." Lee doesn't try to hide her annoyance.

Amélie disappears behind the curtain after throwing a mean look at Lee. When she emerges a few moments later, Lee has left the room and stationed herself behind the desk in the office, where she busies herself with some papers.

"Bonsoir," Lee calls to Amélie as she walks by, artificially cheerful now that the young woman is leaving. After she is gone, Lee goes and looks for Man. He is in the parlor just pouring a cup of tea. He gestures to it—does she want one?—but she shakes her head.

"You shouldn't use those students anymore," she says, settling herself on the horsehair couch.

"Ah, she was fine. Needed some meat on her bones, but I was doing a lot of cropped shots and she has nice skin."

"She wasn't interested in it."

"They don't have to be interested. They just have to stand there and listen to what I tell them."

He sits down opposite Lee and takes a loud sip. She watches him, still annoyed and not completely sure why. The girl bothered her. Not just her germs, which Lee pictures as little fleas dancing on the couch, on the saber guard, all over the studio. It was more how unimpressed she acted during the shoot. Does Amélie even know who Man *is*?

"I saw it come through, when I used to model," she says.

"Saw what?"

"When the model didn't know why she was there. I've done it myself—" She stops.

"You?" Man seems to almost chuckle as he takes another sip of tea. "I bet you look ravishing in every picture anyone has ever taken of you."

Lee flushes and doesn't meet his eye. Since the day he hired her, Man hasn't commented on her appearance. It is what she thought she wanted—a working relationship free from all that—but over the weeks she has often caught herself wondering what he thinks of her. Just the other day she wore one of her nicest dresses to work to see if he would compliment her. He didn't, which was fine, but now his words send a tingle through her she isn't expecting to feel.

"It *is* easy for me," Lee says, "but not for the reasons you would think. I always felt like..." She pauses, suddenly feeling she is about to reveal too much.

"Tell me."

She goes over to the kettle. Standing with her back to Man, she says, "I would use this trick—I learned it, I think, when I was little, when I modeled for my father. I can make my expression practically anything—" Here Lee turns around and gives him a confident stare, her eyes narrowed. "But while I'm doing it I can send my mind anywhere. With my father sometimes I would pretend I was a queen, the Queen of England, and that posing was required of me for my royal subjects. Or later, when I was at *Vogue,* I could put on a gown and pretend that I was at a gala or whatever it was they wanted the photograph to look like. I guess maybe it's a bit like acting. I had a name for it, when I was little."

"What was it?"

"I called it my wild mind." She coughs, to cover up her embarrassment.

"Wild mind. I love it."

"Yes, well. Amélie doesn't have it. She was probably thinking about a mustard poultice the whole time she was here. That's what her face was saying."

Man sets down his teacup. "Would you pose for me?"

He sounds eager, and it thrills her. She wants to say yes. Part of her always wants to say yes, to please whatever man is asking something of her. And she knows Man's pictures of her would be beautiful, probably better than anyone else's have ever been, and that is tempting too, to help him make his art. But posing for him even once will change things between them. She will have given him something of herself, even if he doesn't see it that way, and he will always think of how his camera made her look when he sees her.

"I'm sorry, I can't—I have a lot of work left to do this afternoon." The words hang in the air.

"All right." Man's tone tells her he's not going to push the issue. He refills his teacup from the pot and plops two sugar cubes in it, then says, "I've seen some photos of you. I bought an old copy of American *Vogue* last week so I could see them."

An image of him stopping at the international newsstand on his way to work rises in her mind. Thumbing through dusty piles of magazines in the back of the shop, pausing at her picture. Seeking her out, assessing her—or, knowing him, critiquing the compositions. Pushing down his hat more firmly on his head as he leaves the shop, the magazine with her picture in it rolled up in a stiff tube and stuck into his overcoat pocket.

"Which issue?"

"Oh, you were wearing black satin and fur, I think. And there was a spread on pearls—you wore a choker. Nicely composed, actually. In any case, you've got clear talent. If you change your mind, I'd love to shoot you."

He slurps the last of his tea and sets down the cup loudly, then slaps his hands on his thighs and says, "Well, back to work," and disappears into his office. Lee sits there a while longer, touching her neck where those pearls had been, trying to remember what she had been thinking when the photos were taken.

CHAPTER SEVEN

Lee's new Rolleiflex has a beautiful face, two perfectly round lenses for eyes, and a focusing hood that looks like a chic little hat. Lee wears the camera around her neck on a short strap and can't believe how light it is—not even two pounds with the film loaded. When she puts her eye to the viewfinder she could swear the glass makes things look clearer than her eyes alone can do, and she finds she prefers the world boxed up, contained inside the camera's frame.

Lee still can't believe it's hers, bought with the Christmas bonus check Man gave her. Man left the envelope propped up on the fireplace mantel in the office with her name written in huge looping letters across the front. She gasped when she opened it: an almost ridiculously lavish gift, and bizarrely close to the price of the camera she'd had her eye on for months. But when she thanked him— grateful, awkward, the check pinched between her fingers as if she expected him to ask for it back—he waved as if it were nothing.

"One windfall deserves another," he said, referring to a new and unexpected commission he had gotten from his patrons, Arthur and Rose Wheeler.

"It's too generous," she protested.

Now, with her new camera in hand, Lee finds herself wondering if the gift will make her beholden to Man, if there is some subtext to it she's not understanding. And it is not just the bonus check that is making Lee wonder. Ever since Man asked her to pose for him, something has been crackling between them, a static where there used to be calm air. But what Lee cannot figure out is which of them is generating it. Just a few days ago, Man came up behind her at his desk, leaned over her shoulder to read the contract she was typing up for him, his cheek so close to hers she could feel his skin even though he wasn't touching her. Imperceptibly, she moved her face toward his, just to see what he would do, and when he did not pull back at all she was disconcerted. But it was probably nothing. He is always leaning toward her or needing to show her something, and up until now she has never thought anything of it.

The frustrating thing is that she doesn't *want* anything to change between them. This was her first thought when she opened the envelope with the check inside. *I hope this doesn't change things between us.* But he was so nonchalant when she thanked him that she decided any change she was feeling had to be in her head. And then, as if to confirm that her worries were unfounded, when she came in to work with the new camera a few days later, Man took one look at it and just said, "Good girl." His eyes crinkled up from his wide smile, and he took the camera from her and ran his fingers over it with the same covetousness she feels every time she touches it, mumbling to himself about its features like a fanatic reciting baseball statistics, the static between them gone silent. Lee pointed out a few features he hadn't noticed, and after a while Man handed back the camera and said, "Anytime you want to use the darkroom."

Lee thanked him and told him she'd let him know.

The Rollei is her friend when she is walking, a better pair of eyes she wears around her neck. On a frigid Sunday a few weeks after Christmas, Lee grabs it and starts wandering, angling up

Boulevard Saint-Michel and taking a left into the Luxembourg Gardens, where the wide gravel footpaths divide the lawn into orderly chunks. A dusting of snow has fallen and covers everything in white. At the lake in the park's center she stops and watches the mallards swim in the part of the water not yet scrimmed with ice. The day is so still they hardly ripple the surface. One dabbles at the edge, and Lee walks over into the soft mud and watches him bob up and down, up and down. She snaps a picture of his tail, sticking out of the water like a tiny iceberg. She cuts across the park and over to Église Saint-Sulpice, where the columns cast stripes of shade onto the building's facade. She takes a picture. From there it's to Café de Flore, where she sits at a table near the window and watches the people go by, bundled into thick coats and scarves. She is glad to have a cup of coffee, warm between her hands, glad to have the money to pay for it, glad for her job and her camera and the feeling that she is learning something from her time spent with Man. Nearby, a thin woman sits alone at a table, facing away from Lee. Her hair is in tight pin curls and she wears a white blouse. Every few moments, she reaches up to massage her neck. Her fingernails are filed into sharp points and painted in a reverse French manicure: black tips and white nail beds. Her hair is a rich auburn. She rubs her neck again; Lee snaps a picture.

The day is perfect, cold and clear. By the time Lee has walked to Les Halles she has filled two canisters of film, and she can envision each of the images spooled on the rolls: crisp, original, all her own. Lee has never been able to carry a tune, but as she walks home she sings aloud and doesn't care who hears her.

LONDON

1943

It is 1943 and British *Vogue* has a new editor, Audrey Withers, Oxford-educated, who has knuckled her way to her position from the finance department, more political than pretty, more savvy than chic. With her at the helm, *Vogue* wakes up, smells the cordite, stops treating the war as if it's not happening. Instead of making Lee chronicle the season's latest silhouette—cinched waists, sweeping skirts, sweetheart necklines—Audrey assigns her spreads on short hairstyles for factory workers, on staying fit in wartime, on the different cuts of women's uniforms. Lee ties her models' hair back in nets and poses them facing away from the camera, legs spread, feet planted in flat-soled shoes. She photographs beautiful women climbing into air-raid shelters, puts them in fire masks so no one will be able to see their pretty faces.

Lee visits the Women's Home Defence Corps, the Voluntary Service, the Women's Royal Naval Service. She takes photos of women carrying rifles longer than their own legs, slung casually over their shoulders like handbags. Takes photos as women pack parachutes, ducking their bodies under yards of hanging nylon, folding and twisting the strings and fabric into bundles. A single tangle could mean a loved one dead. Cord caught, bones shattered. Unthinkable, how it would fill the air with blood and cinder.

At night, Lee drags Roland to the Whitby, where all the press photographers spend their off hours. This is how they meet Dave Scherman, who shoots for *Life* magazine and charms them both with his lopsided smile and impish humor. Soon enough Dave moves in with them at Hampstead. He's broke and already half in love with Lee, and for a while she's with both of them, Dave and Roland, and all of it—the two men, the new assignments—is almost enough to make her happy.

But then one night Dave knocks on her door as she is getting ready for bed. Shows her his war accreditation papers and tells her they're sending him to cover the action in Italy. Lee tries to smile, to say congratulations, but his words bring back the dark black shadow she has never been able to name. She's furious when she feels her eyes fill up with tears.

"I wish they didn't want to send you," she says.

"Can't stay in London. There's nothing going here. What am I going to do, teach soldiers how to finger paint at camo school like Roland? I'd go mad. Wouldn't you?" And then he says, "You should get accredited too. Get Condé Nast to sponsor you. You're a Yank. Just as legitimate as the rest of us."

Lee laughs, a harsh sound in the quiet room. "Me. A soldier. No, I'll be stuck here, knitting socks or holding scrap drives for the war effort."

And then the tears really do spill over. Lee pretends to be coughing so she can wipe at her eyes, but Dave has seen them and moves to hold her. He thinks she's crying over him, and since it doesn't matter, she lets him.

A few days later, Lee is still thinking about what Dave said. Why couldn't she? She even floats the idea by Audrey, to see if *Vogue* would publish her pictures. Audrey is noncommittal, but says that if Lee could write some articles to accompany the photos, maybe they could do it.

Lee makes the call, fills out the forms. Four weeks later she gets her papers: she'll be a war correspondent just like Dave, traveling with the 83rd Division. A few days after that she is fitted for her uniform: olive-drab pants with a button fly, olive shirt, wool jacket thick as a horse blanket and just as flattering. The second she puts on the uniform she loves it, how shapeless it makes her, how little of her skin she can see beneath all the layers.

Before they leave London, Lee makes Dave get out his camera. She buttons her jacket to the collar, stands near a window so her U.S. lapel pins catch the light. Doesn't smile, doesn't try to look alluring. For the first time in her life, she doesn't need to.

CHAPTER EIGHT

It's been several weeks since Amélie was at the studio, coughing all over everything, but Lee has gotten the girl's cold, she is sure of it. Sandy throat, a viscous pressure behind her eyes. But Lee is out anyway, out with Man, surreptitiously wiping at her watery eyes and willing herself not to sneeze.

Man offhandedly invited her to the literary salon as if it were a common occurrence for them to spend their evenings together. And even though she is feeling sick, she couldn't refuse. The idea of being out on Man's arm is more appealing than she wants to admit, even to herself, and the reality of it is even better: Man pleasingly attentive, guiding her with a hand at the small of her back as they enter the bookstore, helping her shrug out of her coat before hanging it with his on the crowded rack.

The room is jammed with people and hazy with smoke, the bookshelves pushed to the sides of the room to make space for folding chairs, though no one sits, clustered instead in groups of two or three around the perimeter of the small space. Everyone looks stylish, but few of the men look as good as Man does, in his double-breasted jacket and new trilby hat. Lee has always loved a man who knows how to dress. In fact, she can't help but think they are the smartest pair in the room—even with her cold, Lee has put herself together. She wears her new panne velvet dress, peacock blue, tight through the hips and flaring out in graduated pleats that twirl around her legs as she walks. She worried before she arrived that it was too dressy, but now that she is here she doesn't mind standing out. If there is one way to make herself feel better, it is by getting dressed up.

Man scans the room, and while he is looking away from her, Lee blots quickly at her eyes with her handkerchief. Everyone is a stranger to her—though not to Man—and Lee wonders what they make of her being out with him. If they think of her at all. She is not sure if it is her cold or the cough syrup she picked up at the druggist's, with its incomprehensible list of French ingredients, but she feels a little more vulnerable than usual, as if her emotions have lodged just under the surface of her skin. Lee moves a few inches closer to Man and wonders what would happen if she threaded her arm through his. Would he like it? He has invited her out, after all. But he is not looking at her, so she, too, glances around at all the people filling the small space.

"Is that André?" Lee asks, inclining her head toward a man on the opposite side of the room, with thick brown hair swept back off his forehead in an elegant wave. He stands talking to a shorter man and a very tall and striking woman, with a bouquet of blond curls at the nape of her neck. As they walked to the bookstore, Man gave Lee an overview of who would be there, a jumble of men's names she is trying very hard to remember now. André is André Breton, and Lee stares at him and thinks of the few things Man has told her about him: political, collects masks, self-absorbed.

"Yes, that's André," Man says, "and with him is Tristan. He's the one I make the journal with. And the girl is Tatiana Ia— Iakovenka? Illokovenka?" Man shrugs. "I can never get those Russian names right. She goes by Tata. She's around a lot, mostly with Mayakovsky. You haven't met André? Let me introduce you."

Lee follows Man and tries to think of something witty to say. Tristan opens up his circle and shakes Man's hand. "We were worried you weren't coming," he says.

"Don't be daft," Man says, and then turns slightly toward Lee. "André, Tristan—my latest assistant, Lee Miller."

Tristan and André nod politely, and Tristan reaches out and picks up Lee's gloved hand, kissing it and then stepping forward to kiss her on both cheeks. Tata merely stares at her, her bright red lips pursed into a pretty pout.

"Charmed," Lee says to both men, smiling, but in truth she is disappointed. Man's *latest* assistant. One in a long string of assistants, no doubt, and probably all of them female. Lee thinks that perhaps she should flirt with these men, so that their interest in her will make Man notice her, but before she can act on this idea, a tickle begins in the back of her throat. She wills it away, swallowing and swallowing, but the feeling gets stronger, and after a few more swallows she can't stop herself: she steps away from the group and bends double, coughing violently into her handkerchief. Man looks concerned, asks if he can get her a glass of water, but she waves him off, unable to speak. Finally she manages one word—"Lav," in a strangled voice—and Tata points her elegant finger in the right direction.

Lee locks the door to the lavatory and coughs in glorious solitude. When she has finally pulled herself back together—doing what she can to her face, the eyeliner that has smudged into dissolute halos around her eyes, her blotchy pink skin—she opens the door and sees a line of people stretching down the narrow hallway, obviously annoyed at how long they've been kept waiting. Lee stands sideways to edge her way past and wants to apologize to each of them in turn. At the doorway back to the bookstore's main room, a man stands slouching against the wall, blocking her way. He wears a white jacket, buttoned to the neck like a chef, and has a sign pinned to his chest on which is written messily *Ask me about my reasons*.

"Pardon," Lee says to him.

The man doesn't move.

"Pardon me," Lee says again, and when the man still doesn't move, she squares her shoulders and says, "All right. What are your reasons?"

He has a long beaked nose and dark purple bags under his eyes, and his hair is trimmed close to the scalp but tufted here and there as if it has been hacked off with scissors. He looks at her intently. "A childhood dream. A mask. A lie," he says, his voice deep and raspy, and Lee, confused, takes a step away from him.

"Yes, well," Lee says.

"Art. The dance of the invisible." His mouth moves in a strange sideways oval when he speaks, his lips so pale they almost blend into his white face and disappear.

Lee wonders if he's insane. She fakes a cough as an excuse to get away from him, and pushes past to the main room, where Man spots her almost immediately and makes his way over to her. "Are you all right?" he asks. "You were gone quite a while. The reading is about to start."

"I'm fine." Lee is glad to see his familiar face. "Except I just met the strangest man in the hallway—he has on this suit that says 'Ask me about my reasons,' and I made the mistake of actually asking him. I think he might be crazy."

Man goes up on his tiptoes to look back at where Lee came from. He laughs. "You don't mean Claude?"

Lee follows his gaze and sees the man, clearly visible, making his way around the perimeter of the room toward the small stage. "Yes—that's him. I guess it's easy to spot the only person who has things written on his clothing."

Man chuckles. "Claude's a *woman*."

"No."

"Yes." His expression becomes almost gleeful. "I didn't know either, not at first. That's how she wants it. She's constantly performing. André keeps trying to bring her in, but she won't officially join. She's quite talented. Writes, takes pictures. I admire her self-portraits quite a bit, actually."

Before Lee has a chance to respond, André gets up on the makeshift stage at the far end of the room, and the crowd shifts, finding seats and settling in. A few poets perform one after the next. Lee tries to pay attention, but even when she isn't sick she has trouble focusing on poetry: her mind can lock in for a few lines, but then wanders, and minutes can pass before she realizes she's been thinking about what she ate for breakfast, or a conversation she had with a cabdriver, or a pair of shoes she saw in a shop window a few days ago. She looks over at Man surreptitiously. He is leaning forward, his elbows on his knees, the pockets of his jacket sagging with the weight of all the things he stuffs into them. His hands are folded together and he rests his chin on them, and there is something about the attentiveness of his posture that Lee admires, that makes her snap her own attention back to the readers. A murky sea, Odysseus, sirens' songs like bells ringing out across the water. The poem is quite beautiful, now that she is hearing it. Odysseus twines the sirens' hair around his neck, the hair is music, but then it's choking him, the sea pulls him down, and the poem ends.

The next person to take the stage is Claude. She—Lee can still hardly believe this person is a woman—jumps up and then stands silently for a few moments, staring out at the crowd. When she begins, her deep, raspy voice fills the room.

"What—can—I—do?" she shouts, commanding everyone's full attention. The audience is silent.

"In a narrow mirror, display the part for the whole?
Mistake the aura and the splatterings?
Refusing to throw myself against the walls, throw myself against
   the windows?"

Her eyes squint to slits, her mouth a black hole in her white face.

"While I wait to see all this clearly, I want to hunt myself down,
   to thrash myself out.
I want to stitch, sting, kill, with only the most pointed extremity.
The rest of the body, whatever comes after, what a waste of time!
To travel only at the prow of myself."

Claude pauses, lights a cigarette. No one moves, and Lee feels
her own breath held tight in her chest, her cold forgotten, her
eyes seeming to water only to give the scene more clarity. Claude
blows a smoke ring that hangs in the air before she sucks it back
into her mouth, and then she turns around and takes off her
jacket, beneath which, pinned to the back of her shirt, is a photograph of her own face, one eye heavily shadowed, her mouth
on that side done up with lipstick in a Cupid's bow, and on the
other side her skin bare and white. Both man and woman, neither
man nor woman. Claude stands still so that everyone can see it,
then reaches around with one arm, pulls the photo off, and rips
it neatly in two, letting it drop to the floor before she walks from
the stage to the crowd's applause.

Later, walking home, Lee is able to breathe deeply through both
nostrils for the first time in days, and to smell things—a fire,
or roasting chestnuts, she thinks, but then remembers that chestnuts are in New York, and this city must have different winter
smells she can't even identify yet. Her annoyance at how Man

introduced her to his friends has faded, and she feels relaxed and happy.

Man walks next to her, matching his pace to hers.

"I thought that was absolutely wonderful," Lee says, and then, softly, "Thank you for inviting me."

"My pleasure. I loved Tristan's new work. The frog poem."

Lee doesn't remember Tristan's poem. "I thought Claude was the best. 'To travel at the prow of myself.' Wasn't that good?"

"Yes. It's exactly what André was getting at in the manifesto," Man says, and launches into a long monologue about Surrealism that Lee has heard before. *The prow of myself,* she thinks. Lee doesn't know—or really care—if she has fully understood what Claude was getting at, but she wants to be how the words made her feel: alone but not lonely, needing no one, living her life with intention.

"I think what I liked about Claude," Lee starts again, when Man has stopped talking, "is that she just didn't seem to care if anyone liked her."

"I don't think *liking* her is the point."

"I just mean—" Lee is frustrated at how inarticulate she feels. "I guess . . . I don't know. She's just so *ugly.*"

Man laughs, and Lee continues. "That's not what I mean. Stop laughing at me."

"Why should I?" Man says, but kindly, and as they cross a street, she notices that they have matched their steps exactly. They walk a few blocks in silence, close to home now, and the streets and shops, shuttered and dark this late at night, begin to look familiar.

"Oh dear," Lee says, then sneezes several times in a row, pulling her damp handkerchief out of her purse and dabbing her face with it.

"Poor cricket," Man says, and pulls out his own handkerchief and offers it to her. "I've kept you out too long. Let's get you home. You're close to here, aren't you?"

"Two streets over."

Lee clutches Man's handkerchief in her hand. When they get to the door of her hotel, Man says, "You're going to be all right?"

"I'll be fine."

He nods, looking unconvinced. "My mother always recommends a hot toddy and a flannel around the neck. I never bother about the flannel, but the toddy helps. Here they make them with Lillet."

"That sounds nice."

"I could get you one." Man peers down the empty street, at a shuttered bistro a few doors down.

Lee forces a smile. "I'll be fine. I just need to go straight to bed."

"Of course." They stand together on the same step, the sudden silence awkward until Lee breaks it with another cough. She turns from him and fumbles with her key at the door. Once she's pushed it open, she gives him a wave because she can't think of what to say.

"Stay in bed tomorrow, if you still feel sick," he says. "Don't worry about work."

Lee locks the door behind her and leans against it, and inexplicably her eyes fill with hot tears. Sniffing, stumbling, she makes her way through the dark hallway and up to her room, where she sheds her clothes quickly and crawls under the covers, the pillow cool against her warm cheek and soon wet as the tears keep trickling from her eyes.

She wakes to voices below her, with no idea how much time has passed. In the hallway she hears the hotel proprietress, Madame Masson, arguing with someone in a loud whisper. Lee rolls over and tries to go back to sleep, but before she can, there is a sharp knock on her bedroom door. She pulls a blanket around her shoulders and opens the door to find Madame standing in the hallway.

"Ah, you are awake," Madame says. "A man at the door brought this for you." She holds a teacup in her outstretched hand.

Lee, confused, sleepy, takes the cup from her. "Is he still here?"

"I sent him away. It is far too late for visitors." She sniffs dramatically to express her disapproval.

Lee carries the teacup over to the window and stares down at the dark, empty street.

Back in bed she cradles the teacup in both hands. Lillet and whiskey, sweet and bitter both. As she sips it she is shocked to feel her eyes fill with tears for the second time this evening. Lee pictures Man carrying the cup down the street, the liquid spilling into the saucer. The tenderness of the gesture. Even though the toddy has gone cold, the warmth of the liquor goes all the way through her.

In the morning Lee is not better. Though it's freezing in her room her sheets are damp with sweat. When the weak January sun has risen high enough in the sky to pierce the curtains with light, Lee knots her wrinkled dressing gown at her waist and hobbles down to the kitchen, feeling deeply, profoundly sorry for herself. She puts the kettle on to boil, and rinses out the teacup Man brought her so that she can use it again.

The kitchen is cold, and someone else's dishes fill the sink. Lee can't stand the squalor, so she takes her cup and goes back to her room, and as she starts up the stairs Madame Masson calls to her from her office to tell her she has mail.

Mail! A letter from her dearest friend, Tanja, and another envelope, smaller and slimmer, on which Lee is surprised to see her father's handwriting. She hasn't heard from him since the telegram about the Kotex ad. But here is his handwriting on the creamy envelope, his script as tall and angular as he is. Lee carries the letters upstairs and climbs back into bed.

She is curious about what her father has to say, but starts with Tanja's letter, several pages thick and written in wobbly handwriting, as if it has been dashed off on a train. Tanja has been traveling through Europe for almost as long as Lee has been in Paris, accompanied by a chaperone named Mrs. Basingthwaite. Her letters read like excerpts from an Anita Loos novel, full of non sequiturs and gossip.

Last week I took this perfectly harrowing car ride through southern Spain with a man I met in Seville. We went to Ronda (I can't remember, have you been there? It's beautiful—that bridge!) but the man drove like we were racing on a backcountry road and not practically clinging by our fingernails to the side of a mountain. And he had this pair of what I thought were opera glasses that he kept on his lap the entire time, which I thought strange, because what was he going to do? Bird-watch on the motorway? But then he unscrewed one of the lenses and took a giant swig! That was when I thought Mrs. Basingthwaite might not be so ding-a-ling after all and I should interview my companions a little more thoroughly before I went on transcontinental driving trips with them.

Lee laughs and then starts coughing, and has to put down the letter for a bit while she searches for a handkerchief. She can almost imagine her friend sitting in bed with her, strands of her dark brown hair shoved messily behind her ears and a big smile on her face.

Lee has been more circumspect lately in her own letters. The last one she sent to Tanja, just a week or so ago, started out with a description of Lee's new life, but as she wrote, a story about the strange aristocratic woman who lives on her hotel floor morphed into a story about a photo shoot Man did of an actual aristocrat, and then became a description of Man's photos of Duchamp, and then a story about Man's work habits, and before long she had filled four pages and mentioned his name seventeen times. So she had ripped up the letter and started over, a more restrained missive in which she explained a new technique she had learned for studio work and mentioned Man only once, to say that he was an excellent teacher. At the end of Tanja's letter, she brings it up.

I'm glad for you. I'm glad this is working out. When you left New York I didn't think it was a good idea. You had such a wonderful life there, and I had this vision of you moving to Paris and being alone and penniless in an alley with an opium addiction. I'm sure that sounds a little extreme, but I was worried about you. But from all you've written, this sounds like the right choice. You're doing what you've always wanted to do, and I'm glad you've found a place where you can learn from someone as talented as Man Ray sounds.

Lee finishes her tea and then slices open her father's letter. A single page, front and back, beginning with pleasantries. The annual Poughkeepsie tree lighting was particularly well attended, and her brother Erik has been promoted to technical adviser at Carrier, where he is now in charge of an entire division. Lee flips the page over and continues reading.

Your brothers and I went to the cemetery last month, and they both commented on how hard it was to visit your mother without you there. I said a few extra words to let Ellen know you were thinking of her even though you are far away.

We think of you often and hope you are doing well. I tell everyone that soon we'll be seeing your photos in all the magazines as you said we would. When you have a publication, be sure to write to me and let me know, so that I don't miss it. Speaking of publications, a small journal put out by the Poughkeepsie Architectural Society just ran a few of my prints—some recent shots I took of the lovely new Deco building on Cannon Street. I'm hoping the work leads to further commissions and I enclose copies so that you can see my work.

Lee wipes her running nose with her handkerchief. She feels vaguely guilty about missing the visit to her mother's grave, but mainly because it must have made her father sad. Lee and her mother were never close, and by the time Lee started modeling, Ellen was actively jealous of her daughter's beauty and success.

But it is not the lines about Ellen that nag at Lee; it is the part of the letter where her father writes that he is now a published photographer. She reads through that section again, but doesn't look at the pictures, which are still tucked inside the envelope. Her father, published before she is. How like him to wait to write her until he has something to say about himself. And he doesn't ask her a single question, just assumes she hasn't had her work published, twists the knife by reminding her that everyone back home is waiting around for her to be successful. She is a disappointment to him, she thinks, and the flare of envious anger she felt when she read his words turns to frustration.

Lee thinks back over the past months, how she's delayed and delayed using Man's darkroom. What is she waiting for? Being his assistant has become a sort of habit, her own work something that lives on undeveloped rolls of film. How silly. *I will travel at the prow of myself,* Lee thinks, and gets back out of bed and goes into the hallway, where she dials the number to Man's studio and stands impatiently, waiting to be connected. Finally he answers.

"I wanted to thank you for stopping by with the drink last night," Lee says, her voice hoarse and scratchy.

"It's nothing. How are you feeling?"

"Not well, but I'm sure I'll be better soon," she says, and then, after clearing her throat, "I have a question for you. When I get back, if there is a light day where we don't have too many appointments, I have some film I'd like to develop, if it's no trouble." She hates how obsequious she sounds and wills herself to stop.

"I believe I already told you that you could use the darkroom whenever you'd like."

Is his tone interested or patronizing? Lee cannot tell, so she forges ahead. "Yes, I suppose you did. I just have a few rolls. I think I know what to do—I won't need your help."

"Have you done it before?"

"My father showed me how a few times—"

"But you haven't done it by yourself?"

"No, not by myself."

"Ah." Even through the phone his voice sounds smug. "Are these pictures important?"

Lee thinks back to what she shot, walking through the city the other day. "To me."

"I think I should develop them for you, and then you can print them."

"How am I going to learn if you do it for me?"

There is silence on the line, and then, "You're right," he says. "Let me help you the first time. Teach a man to fish and all that."

"Thank you." Lee swallows hard, which makes her cough, and she holds the phone away from her mouth. When she puts it back to her ear, she hears Man asking if she needs anything.

"No, no, I'm fine."

They hold the line for a few more seconds, the silence so thick she could reach out and touch it. "Thank you again for the toddy," she says finally.

"It was no trouble."

She thinks of how far he must have gone to get it, what he must have said to get a café to let him take its cup. "Well, it was delicious."

"Take care of yourself, Lee," Man says, and when she hangs up the phone she realizes he's never before called her by her first name.

CHAPTER NINE

The next day, Lee wakes up with a clear head, and it feels like a gift to have the energy for everyday tasks. Why doesn't she appreciate it more when she is healthy? She hums to herself as she gets ready to go to the studio, stepping lightly down the steps from her hotel's front door, her rolls of film tucked in her purse. As she walks along, she admires how her new suede step-ins look against the cobblestones.

What a beautiful day it is, Paris hers for the taking, the winter air crisp and invigorating. At the corner of Avenue du Maine and Rue des Plantes, she stops at her favorite street vendor and buys a croque monsieur, taking off her gloves before she removes its waxed paper wrapper. As she eats, she is filled with purpose and benevolence. Man is low on his favorite printing paper, and the shop is over a kilometer out of her way, but it will make him happy that she has taken care of this for him, so she heads toward the 15th, pleased with herself for thinking of it. She takes a short-cut through passage Dantzig and pauses to look at La Ruche, with its odd circular structure and oversize awnings that hang over the windows like half-closed eyelids. As always, there are a few people huddled near the gate. Beggars or drunks, most likely, but they could be artists who got home too late to be let into the ateliers inside. Lee crosses the alley and sets the rest of her sandwich next to a man sleeping under a rough brown blanket. That could be her, she thinks. If Man hadn't hired her, she might be living rent-free in the squalor of La Ruche with all the rest of the starving artists. She reaches into her purse to touch the film canisters and feels profoundly fortunate.

It is late afternoon by the time Man is ready to help Lee develop her film. She stands in the hallway waiting for him, as excited as she used to be on the first day of school. The developing room, near the end of the hall, was originally a broom closet. Inside it, Man has nailed a plank at counter height, and above that a small shelf with bottles and trays stacked neatly on it. Lee steps in, with Man behind her. The space is tight for one person, claustrophobic for two. Dim light comes from a small hurricane lamp sitting on the counter. Man closes the door and pulls a thick black curtain across it, fussing with it until it falls completely evenly. The room is so close that even when Lee leans against the wall she cannot help but brush against him. She rubs her tongue along her teeth, a nervous habit, and tries to give him room to maneuver in the small space.

Man is in professor mode. "Light is our tool," he is saying. "Film is just a surface for capturing and holding light, but until the film has been developed, extra light becomes the enemy." As he talks he arranges the supplies, lined up on the table where he has placed black tape to mark their spots.

"Always put everything in the same order. Otherwise you'll be fumbling around in here and you'll drop something. Place the tools in the order you'll use them: film, church key, scissors, metronome, developer, stop, fix, water bath." He touches her shoulder and moves behind her, an awkward dance in the small room. "Before you blow out the lamp, put your hands on the supplies and close your eyes so you can remember where they are."

Eyes shut, Lee moves her hands across the supplies. The room is silent except for the hiss of the lamp's wick.

"Ready?" Man asks, and when she says yes, he reaches around her and blows out the lamp. The flame turns to a sharp red point and dies out. The small room fills with the smell of smoke. Of course she knew it had to be pitch-black, but somehow it is darker than she thought it would be, the darkness thick and alive and warmer than when the room was lit. She feels Man behind her but cannot see him. His hand hovers over hers, heat radiating off his skin.

"I want you to get the feeling of it. This is where most photographers run into trouble. You can take the best pictures in the world but if you can't develop them properly you may as well not bother taking them in the first place."

Her hand is on the canister, his hand is just above hers, and she casually changes her grip so that the back of her hand brushes against his palm. As soon as she does, his comes down fully on hers, warm, his skin dry and a little rough, and then his hand is all she is thinking about, the closeness of it. It is that simple: first she is not thinking about him, and then she is. She has to shake her head to retrain her attention on what he is saying.

"Pick up the church key and pry the canister open," he says.

Lee follows his instructions. She has to try a few times before she lines up the key with the canister's lip, but soon she manages it, the top peeling back with a screech of metal on metal.

"Good," he says. "Now take the film out and try not to get fingerprints on it. Feel the skinny end? That's the starting point. You have to cut that piece off, and then hold the film by each end so you can dip it in the trays."

Lee fumbles in the dark for the scissors. Man moves a bit away from her, giving her room. "I think I did it," she says. She can hear his breath, smell the woodsy scent of his aftershave now that the smoke has dissipated, and by necessity he is practically hugging her as he helps her, checking her work. It is so intimate—she didn't realize how intimate it would be. She could so easily turn around and face him, and part of her is curious about what would happen if she did, what it would feel like to really touch him. But the dark is playing tricks on her. What she wants is her pictures, to get them right.

"Excellent," he says. "Now, start up the metronome, and then dip the film strip into the developer, back and forth, so that it all gets an even amount of time in the solution. A few minutes should do it—I usually count to two hundred and then move to the stop bath."

Again she follows his instructions, reaches out in the dark for the metronome and sets it ticking, then finds both ends of the film and tries to move it smoothly through the water. Once the film is wet, though, it gets slippery, and as she tries to change her grip the whole strip slithers out of her grasp and down to the ground.

"Oh, damn it!" She is mortified, and if it weren't dark he would see that her face is crimson.

"It's all right," he says, patiently. "Don't move your feet. The last thing you want to do is step on it."

"But now it's probably all covered with dust, and—"

He has squatted behind her and she can hear him fumbling along the floor, his head level with her thighs. Lee stands as still and quiet as she can, willing herself not to move, achingly conscious of where his head is.

"It's okay. It's not the worst thing."

Lee takes a shallow breath. "What's the worst thing?"

"When you're commissioned to take pictures of Pablo Picasso and you get what you think are the best shots of your career and then you manage to mix up the developer and stop bath so that not one—not a single picture—is usable. That is the worst thing."

As he's talking he has found the film. He stands back up and takes his free hand and rubs it down her forearm until he finds her hand, and the feeling makes her shiver. When he holds her hand for what seems to be a beat too long she stays perfectly still, waiting, before he gives the film back to her.

"What did you do?" she asks.

"Bought the Master a drink at his favorite bar and begged him to let me take pictures of him at his home the next day."

"Did he let you?"

"Yes, actually. I'll show you the prints sometime."

Lee holds the film and begins to dip it back in the tray. The metronome is like another heartbeat in the room with them. She lets out her breath in a rush.

"Almost there. Another minute, maybe, then move the film to the stop."

As she does it he rests his hands on hers again. It is less startling now. She lets him guide her, and the strip moves smoothly in their grasp. It is only a few short minutes, but it feels longer. When they get the film into the final water bath, the metronome has stopped and the room is silent. "Excellent work," Man says. In the dark, Lee smiles.

Without thinking too much about it, she flails her hand around until she finds his, and gives it a squeeze. "Thank you."

"It's nothing—you're here to learn, as well as work."

"I know...but still. Thank you."

"You're welcome," he says. His voice is quiet and she likes the way it sounds, raspy around the edges. She wants to say something more, but nothing comes to her, and eventually he says, "Ready for the light?"

"Ready," she says, but she's not ready at all. She wishes they could stay in that darkroom for hours. As Man turns, she could swear he brushes against her unnecessarily. He pulls back the curtain and opens the door, and she is startled by the sudden brightness. It calls to mind emerging from the cinema after a film, the confusion of finding the day just as she left it.

In the bright hallway light, she looks at Man. There are grooves on either side of his mouth she has never noticed before, and when he drops his head for a moment, she notices the neat way he has parted his hair. She pictures him standing in front of his bathroom mirror, going through his morning routine. There is something so private and vulnerable about the white line in his scalp, and she goes warm with a rush of emotion and moves her gaze to the floor.

"I have a few more rolls to develop," she says to the carpet.

"Yes. Do you want my help with that too?" His tone is all business, and he shakes his watch down his wrist and glances at its face.

She doesn't know what to think. He seemed so eager to help, and now he seems eager to get away from her.

"No, I can do it."

"Good. I have to—I'll be in the office if you need me." He turns and disappears down the hallway.

Lee goes back into the developing closet. Part of her wishes she asked Man to help her. She thinks of his body behind hers. There is something so electric about him, a coiled energy that animates him and makes people—herself included—want to be close to him. But he is not interested in her. If there is one thing she is good at, it's telling when a man is interested, and—with the exception of bringing her the hot toddy—Man has shown none of the signs she is used to.

Lee peels open the next roll of film and then dips the film in the developer in a rhythmic back and forth motion. When she has finished all of her rolls, she turns on the overhead light and holds up the strips to it. A few of the images at the beginnings and ends seem underdeveloped, but she counts at least five or six that have come out. There is her lake picture, the picture of the woman's hand, all the images reversed so the duck is a white blob on black water and the woman's nails are dark spots against the brilliant white of her hair. Lee doesn't yet know if they are good, but right now she only cares that they are hers.

She hangs up the film on the clothesline to dry and is surprised to see that it is already five o'clock. The day has gone by quickly. As she goes back through the studio and into Man's office, she decides she will ask him to get a drink with her, to celebrate this small accomplishment, the first photos she's developed herself. Why not? But the office is empty and so is the parlor. Lee's giddiness seeps out of her like a pinpricked balloon. She so wanted to share this feeling with someone. Perhaps Man has just gone outside for a cigarette.

To pass the time she investigates the books in the library cabinet. There are dozens of literary and art journals, a shelf with a matched set of classics that she feels certain Man has never read, a few novels. There is even an Italian edition of *Lady Chatterley's Lover,* which she has heard whispered about but is shocked to see Man owns. She is half tempted to thumb through it to find the dirty bits but then imagines how she would feel if he saw her.

Instead, she lies down on the couch and stares at the ceiling. There have been many men in Lee's life. More than she would admit in pleasant company, more than she has even admitted to her close friends. When she was fourteen, she met a boy named Harry at the bakery in downtown Poughkeepsie. She was buying rolls for Sunday dinner, he was standing behind her in line, he had soft brown eyes fringed with black lashes. Their interaction didn't mark the first time she knew she had power over men, but it was the first time she consciously made use of it, and she felt no embarrassment when she asked him if he wanted to meet her outside the grounds of her school the next day at lunchtime. With Harry she found that the flirting she'd read about in dime novels actually worked, so she bit her lip and fluttered her eyelashes and gently placed her hand on his forearm as they walked, and she told him that he seemed strong. They went to an abandoned hayloft in the woods behind her school and she liked the feeling of his lean body pressed against the length of hers. She touched him everywhere, curious, but also oddly detached, as if she were floating somewhere above their two bodies, observing herself, saying, *This is what a boy's stomach feels like, this is how his hand feels when it is running up and down my back*. They did nothing more than pet but the memories stuck with her all the same.

Lee waits almost an hour for Man to come back. Finally, feeling too keyed up to lie still any longer, she heads out on her own.

There is a bar a few blocks away called Le Bateau Ivre, and the building looks like its name: squat and fat and listing to one side like a man who can't hold his liquor. Man has mentioned it to her. It's one of his favorite places, but she tells herself she goes there with no hope of seeing him, that she is choosing it out of convenience more than anything. It has six outdoor tables unoccupied in the winter chill, and inside is empty of patrons too. It was decorated decades ago to look like a pleasure yacht, and Lee climbs the nickel-plated spiral staircase to the second floor, where the bartender, a rail-skinny woman in a gray dress and black apron, sits at the bar with a glass of wine.

Lee sits down a few seats away and takes off her hat. She lays her Rollei on the counter and runs her fingers over it, a comforting habit.

"A drink?" the woman asks.

"Pernod."

Rousing herself from her stool, the woman moves behind the bar and bends into the icebox and fills a small glass to the brim with cracked cubes before pouring the viscous liquid over it. The ice pops as it begins to melt.

Lee takes a long swallow, the mix of cold liquid and hot licorice a familiar and pleasant burn.

The glass was stored in the icebox and as Lee sits there she cuts patterns in the frost on its surface with her fingernail. Her elation over her pictures has dissipated. When she imagined coming to Paris, she envisioned an immediate ascent into the bohemian circles her father had always warned her about. She thought it would be more open than New York, more welcoming. But here she is, still alone.

The bartender has been staring at her rudely the entire time, and finally says, "You look familiar. Are you an actress?"

"No. I work nearby. I'm a photographer. I'm actually studying with someone. Man Ray. He comes here sometimes."

"Ah! Of course." The bartender's demeanor changes. "We all know him. Lillet with a slice of orange."

"I guess so."

"But he is photographing you, no?"

"No, I'm his assistant."

The woman laughs. "And what does Kiki think of that?" she says.

"Kiki?" Lee asks, but even as she says the name aloud she knows who it is: the K of the ledger.

The bartender laughs again, louder, and then shouts something to the kitchen behind her in French too rapid for Lee to understand. A shout comes back, and then a loud rendition of a chanson.

"Who is Kiki?" the bartender asks. "How can you know Man Ray and not know Kiki?"

Lee doesn't respond. The woman has made her feel embarrassed, as if here again, even in this one small slice of Paris she has fit herself into, she doesn't quite belong.

The man who has been in the kitchen comes out, and they begin singing the chanson together, adding some sort of bawdy dance. The bartender shakes her shoulders and shimmies back and forth, and the man sticks out his tongue and leers at her until they both fall against the bar, laughing loudly.

The man turns to Lee, holding up his arms and saying, "You can catch our next show at the Jockey on Saturday night. Hortense and Pierre of Montparnasse!," and then he returns to the kitchen, still chuckling.

The bartender says, "Don't mind us—we just saw Kiki perform a few nights ago."

"She's a dancer?" Lee remembers the tailor fees, the milliner.

"You really don't know her? She's a dancer, a muse, a singer. She's everything. Some say she's the most beautiful woman in Paris. She's been with Man Ray for years now. Treats him horribly from what we hear. But she can treat people however she wants—that's just how it is."

Lee nods, picks up her Pernod, and goes over to a table in the corner where she can look down at the street below. She has left midconversation but she doesn't care if she is being rude.

So this is the mysterious K. Some sort of beautiful chantey singer. And with Man, for years. Lee wonders if Kiki modeled for him, wonders if things would have gone differently if she, Lee, agreed to be his model the one time he asked her. He hasn't mentioned it again, and all of a sudden Lee wants him to notice her, to want her. His hands on hers, his body behind her in the dark. What if she turned around in the darkroom, put her lips near his? Would he have kissed her?

Lee orders another drink, and then another, sipping each so

slowly that a few hours pass before she is done. As she sits there, staring out at the street below, the bar fills up around her. Each time someone new comes up the stairs a part of her expects it to be Man. Instead, more and more strangers. Women with rolled stockings and Eton crops. Men in jackets with wide lapels and homburgs cocked just so. They come in pairs, in groups, they sit close to one another at tables so their shoulders touch, and they do not notice anything beyond their own circles.

Just then a man ascends the spiral stairs and walks straight for the bar. He has a thin mustache, a gray tweed suit. He sets his hat crown side down on the counter, and as he looks around the room he spins it with his fingers, like a top. His hair is slicked down so perfectly it reflects the line of lights from across the room. Lee thinks he is American from his tie, wide with orange and red checks. A Parisian man would never wear something that loud. She makes eye contact with him, not dropping her gaze until he does so first. He turns to the bar and speaks to the bartender, but as soon as he has ordered, his gaze is back on Lee, who tilts her head at the empty chair next to her and cocks her eyebrow up at him. He smiles, nods, walks over after getting his drink.

"These seats are much more comfortable than the bar," she says to him in English.

"They do appear so. Are you waiting for someone?" She was right—he is not Parisian. But his accent is British, not American, and up close he has that apologetic half smile she has always found so attractive in Englishmen.

"I'm waiting for you," she says, brass bold.

"I doubt that very much." He pulls out a chair, waits for her to speak again before he sits down.

"Oh, no, really I am. None of these Frenchmen will talk to me." Lee gives him a flirty pout.

"I think they might be intimidated by you."

"You think so?"

"I know so. You're the best-looking girl I've seen since . . . well, maybe ever."

Lee laughs. She feels her good mood, the mood she was in when she developed her photos, come back over her.

She leans toward him. "I used to be a model."

"I'm not surprised. What are you now?"

"I'm a girl who hasn't had a glass of champagne since I left New York."

He throws back his head and laughs so she can see the fillings in his molars. With one quick tip of his hand he finishes his drink and lifts his finger in the air to signal the bartender, who comes over and gives the two of them a sharp look.

"Jouët split," he says, but when Lee looks disappointed, he says, "Full bottle, please."

The bottle comes in a nice silver stand that sits next to their table, and the champagne bubbles are like kisses tickling Lee's throat on the way down. The man's name is George, he is from Dorset, and he is in Paris for three days on business. He is a financier, which means nothing to Lee, and she lets him prattle on about his work as she used to let men do night after night in New York City. He has green eyes and a tender-looking mouth, and if she charmed him when he was sober she charms him much more the drunker he gets. Soon the sun has set and they are both sitting with their arms on the table, their elbows touching.

"Can I tell you something?" she asks him, stifling a small burp from all the champagne.

"Anything."

"I haven't kissed anyone since I got to Paris."

"Isn't that a crime of some sort?"

"I think so. City of Love and all."

"Is that what they call it? I thought it was the City of Light."

"Maybe it is. But that doesn't change the fact that no one's kissing me."

George clumsily picks up their latest champagne bottle and fills both their glasses again, spilling just a little on her arm. He says quietly, "I come here every few months or so, and for me this has been more like the City of Sadness. I'm always walking about all by myself, mooning around and wishing I had someone to share it with."

"The City of Sadness—that's how I feel too." They stare at each other and he gives her a small smile and she feels a rush of power. She licks her lips, lightly, and takes a sip of champagne.

"I'm tired of mooning about," George says, and Lee leans toward him as she wishes she had done with Man, and finds his lips with hers, and they are so warm, and they are kissing in the bar, across the small table, their tongues hot and wet against each other, until they bump the table and the champagne flutes fall to the ground with a spectacular smash. They both gasp at the same time and look toward the bartender like two children caught stealing from the candy jar. George puts a wad of bills on the table and they leave as fast as they can, their arms around each other, and he holds her hand as she goes down the spiral staircase, as if they are executing some sort of quick and elegant dance.

George is staying at the Saint James Albany, and it has been so long since Lee has been on a bed this comfortable, with fat pillows three deep against the upholstered headboard and little round bolster cushions she sweeps to the floor with one fist. She lolls on the bed while he removes his tie, letting her legs fall open so he can see her garter belt and up her thighs to her underwear—her good ones, thank God, blue with lace rosettes along the edge. He stands above her and struggles with the buttons of his shirt, his suspenders, his belt. She can tell he is already hard. She doesn't help him undress, but she moves down the bed and puts her foot on his leg and wiggles it up until it is touching him as he unbuttons his fly and pushes his pants down. Once he is undressed he leans over her and says, between kisses as he helps her out of her dress, "You . . . are the most . . . perfect . . . woman . . . I have ever met."

Lee smiles and pulls him on top of her, and he continues to kiss her, soft kisses on her lips and trailing down her neck. She tips her head back and is distracted by the view out the window, where white clouds scud across the dark sky. His kisses are so gentle she can barely feel them. She puts one hand on top of his head and pushes it down and wills him to bite her nipple. He doesn't do it. She arches her back and presses her chest against his face, but he moves away, so she reaches down and grabs him by the hips and pulls him up until he is inside her. For a few moments the hot slick slide of him is the only thing she's thinking of. But then he falters, pausing above her with his eyes squeezed shut, and murmurs some sort of apology, and they wait like that, his body unmoving. She kisses him again and pulls his bottom lip into her mouth and bites down before she releases it. He lets out a small moan and begins again, slowly, too slowly, and she wraps her legs around him to be able to feel it deeper. And then he moves faster, but moving to the time of what he wants. Lee feels her mind detach, as it often does when she has sex, and she is floating somewhere above the bed and looking down at herself. She watches from above as he comes and falls over on the mattress next to her. She watches as she takes his hand and pushes it between her legs, watches as he touches her until she comes too. But she doesn't feel it. She watches these two strangers as they lie next to each other on the bed, and feels nothing. And all the time, while she is watching, what she is thinking about is Man.

CHAPTER TEN

Lee does not mean to spend the night with George, but the champagne sends her into a deep sleep and she wakes to find him rubbing her bare arm and smiling at her. In the daylight filtering in through the organdy draperies, he looks mawkish and needy. He suggests breakfast on the hotel terrace but her head is pounding and she doesn't want to be outside with him, so they call for a service cart and eat omelets with snipped tarragon in bed while they try to make conversation. The way she feels is familiar: caged, choked, but above all deeply, deeply bored. She knows George's mind is pinwheeling through thoughts of more lovemaking, followed by a day spent wandering Paris together, but before he has a chance to suggest anything specific or reach for her again across the mattress, she finishes her eggs and gets up, sliding so quickly back into her clothes that she barely gives him time to register that she is leaving. Her apologies are false but firm. Yes, she does have to go to work; no, she cannot be late; yes, she will try to meet him at Le Bateau Ivre again that night and won't be able to stop thinking of him until she sees him there. And then, like a prisoner emerging from a secret escape route, Lee walks out into the frigid city and lets out her breath in one big exhale.

The day is bright and her head feels full of last night's champagne bubbles, which seem to ping against her skull as furiously as the thoughts of Man's hands, the feeling of him behind her in the dark. She walks quickly back to her room, where she will lock herself in the shared lav and submerge herself in the hottest bath she can manage. She feels as if she hasn't had a good bath since she left New York—there is always another tenant pounding at the door and rushing her. Not that she blames them, since she herself does the same whenever she is late getting ready.

Lee splashes water on her face and stares at her reflection in the cracked mirror. Puffy bags beneath her eyes. The beginnings of an angry red pimple in the middle of her chin. She pinches her cheeks to give herself some color and sticks out her tongue at her reflection, then slides the latch on the door and fills up the tub to the brim.

She is unnerved at the thought of going back to the studio. She could call up Man and say she's not coming in today. But she thinks of her negatives, hanging on the drying line, and knows she can't not print them. She almost itches to get back to them and see if they are any good. She'll print the one of the duck first; that one, perhaps, has some potential.

When Lee gets to the studio an hour or so later, it is quiet, and for a moment she thinks maybe Man is not there. She goes up the staircase and into the office, which is empty too. But then she hears him in the darkroom, humming loudly, the way one does when one thinks he is alone.

What will she say to him? She tries things out in her head. *I can't stop thinking about you. I keep remembering your hands on mine. I looked for you last night at your favorite bar.* Every option seems absurd, trite. Her previous encounters haven't made her feel this way, and she has no idea how to go about telling someone like Man that she is interested in him. She's a little in awe of him, perhaps, or maybe it's just that she doesn't know how he would react

103

if she told him. For all she knows, he is still in love with Kiki, or with someone new.

But then Lee remembers Man hasn't seen her negatives yet. They can talk about this, a subject much less fraught than whatever she's feeling for him. Maybe he is looking at them right now. She wants so much to hear his opinion of them, lets her imagination spool out a different scene in which she walks into the darkroom and he is standing there with her work in his hands, a look of surprise on his face. "These are what we developed?" he will ask. "They're wonderful. I never knew you were so talented." And she will offer a few halfheartedly modest refutations, and then she will print the photographs, and soon enough some art collector will come to the studio and see them and offer to hang them in his gallery, and all of them will sell within the first month, and everyone she has ever known, including Man himself, will be jealous of her success.

She does their special triple tap on the darkroom door, and Man opens it, wearing rubber gloves with his shirtsleeves rolled up. She has been thinking about him so much for the past few hours that when she sees him, there is a vague sense of disappointment. The solid realness of him doesn't match up with what's been in her mind, though she doesn't know what she expected, if the disappointment lies in her inability to have remembered him accurately or in the reality of the person standing before her, his face unshaven and his eyes closer together than she remembered them being. But seeing him eases some pressure in her that has been growing since she left the studio yesterday. He is just a man. There are many men in the world.

"You're very late," he says, his eyebrows crunching together in a frown. Behind him she can see her negatives on the drying line exactly where she left them.

"I know, I'm sorry—"

"This *is* a job."

Lee knows she should feel bad—she has no real excuse for being late and should have called him, but she feels anger snap beneath the fug of her exhaustion. "I know. I'm sorry—I forgot to tell you I'd be late today."

He sighs. "I've been waiting all morning for you to help me with the prints from the session with Amélie."

"Have you started on them?"

"Yes," he says, his tone softening a bit. Lee goes over to the sink, and floating there is the picture of Amélie with the saber guard. The shot is cropped close, showing only her chin and shoulders, the mesh of the metal crosshatching her skin with geometric shadows. Man picks up the paper at the white border with his tongs, and the water runs off the photo's edge and plinks into the tray.

"It's a good start," he says. "The way the metal looks against the skin. The softness of the cheek and that sharp line of the metal. Startling, I think."

Lee is barely looking at the image now, has turned her gaze so that what she sees is Man looking at it, the small smile on his face and his hand holding the tongs over the fix bath.

"I like it," she says, which sounds trivial. Embarrassed, she turns away.

He holds up a second image, similar to the first. "What do you think of this one?"

Lee comes over and they look at it together. It's a more straightforward shot of Amélie with her head lying on top of the saber guard as if on a pillow. The composition is beautiful, but Lee knows Man wants something from her, a suggestion or small critique. The truth is she finds the image a bit boring, a bit expected, but she can't say that to him—she knows already how defensive he becomes when someone critiques his eye. What she needs to do is suggest a darkroom fix, not comment on the artistry. But she does not feel she has the language for that yet.

She points with a pair of tongs. "It looks too light on this side, where the light from the window is coming in."

"Yes," he says, pleased. "What would you do to fix it?"

"Print it darker?"

"Hmm...but then the right-hand side would be too dark. Why don't I show you dodging and burning?"

He rattles the darkroom door handle to make sure the door is fully closed. Then he lights the red lamp and turns off the white lamp, and everything is amber, as if lit by a campfire. He sets up the enlarger and Lee watches as he exposes the paper, using a small handmade tool, a stick with a round piece of cardboard taped to the end of it that casts a small shadow on the image. He takes the stick and moves it around quickly for twenty seconds or so, never letting it sit in the same place for very long.

"People always ask me, 'How do you get your prints so even?'" he says. "It's simple, really. Everyone thinks photography is like a magic trick, but there's no magic involved. There are only two colors to mix together: black and white. Add more of one, take some of the other away. You want both in your picture. True black and true white. If you have those, you can have as many shades of gray as you want and the image will still look good. Most of the time, if you develop a print and it doesn't have at least one part that is pure white, either the image is unusable or you've done a lousy job of printing. You want a white spark on someone's mouth where the lipstick reflects light back to the camera, or in the whites of their eyes, or in something they are wearing. Not too much white—most of the time, just a little bit to put everything else in contrast to it."

Man moves easily through the small space while he is talking, turning off the enlarger and then gently sliding the paper into the developing bath. The same image appears on the paper, first just the outlines, like a footprint in the sand, and then the rest of the image fills in. This time, the print is much more even, and Lee can tell just from looking at it that Man will be satisfied with it.

"Voilà!" He holds up the print for her inspection, waiting until she nods and smiles, indicating that she feels just as pleased as he does. "Now, you try," Man says. He turns to the enlarger and hands her the dodging stick.

It is like the developing closet again, and her nervousness comes back in a rush. He stands behind her, closer, she thinks, than he needs to. They slide the paper into the frame and Man reaches around her to light the lamp. She grips the dodging stick and waits for him to instruct her. The lamp lit, the image glows on the paper, Amélie's face black in the reversed image. Lee thinks of what he has just said, the need for a pop of pure white sparking on someone's lips. She fumbles the stick and inexpertly begins to move it around above the paper. She feels suddenly dizzy, swallows and tastes old champagne on the back of her tongue and wonders if Man can smell it on her, the drinks and the cigarettes and even the stranger, George, whose scent she is worried must be lingering on her even though she's bathed since she was with him. Man is so close behind her she can feel his breath against her cheek.

"Is this right?" she asks.

"You're doing fine." She glances back at him, but he has his eyes trained on the print and does not meet her gaze.

They work together in what seems to be a companionable silence for the next few hours. The room is only marginally larger than the closet where they developed the film. There is an enlarger with a mercury lamp, a large wooden sink for fixing and rinsing the images, and a developing basin that they have to share. The afternoon passes in a blur. Together they print dozens of images from the session, and if Lee were feeling more herself she would be thrilled at all that Man is teaching her. But instead she has to focus on keeping her mind on the task at hand, her way-ward thoughts a heavy book she must repeatedly slam shut. The room is small, but does that explain how close to her Man seems to stay? The images are wonderful, but surely he doesn't usually print so many from the same session? Everything seems to be sending her a message: the way he pulls off his rubber gloves and massages his hands, the way he doesn't move out of her way when she brushes past him but instead seems to consciously fill up space so that she has no choice but to come in contact with him. She wills herself to focus.

Finally, after hours of printing, he gestures to her negatives still hanging on the line.

"Are those the ones we developed last week?"

"Yes—there's probably not time to print them today, though."

"Why not? We've gotten a lot done. Go ahead."

Lee checks her watch and sees that it is not as late as she thought. She finishes what she is working on, then takes her strips of negatives and cuts them in thirds and arranges them on a sheet of paper. Man has started singing out loud as they work. "I'm longing to see you, dear / Since you've been gone / Longing to have you hold me / Hold me near." His voice gets louder and louder, and with his Brooklyn accent the sad lyrics seem absurd. Lee clears her throat.

"What?" he says, turning toward her. "Oh—was I singing out loud? It's a bad habit of mine."

"It's okay," she says, and he starts up again, this time doing it even louder, and adding in some exaggerated dance moves until she is laughing.

"Do you sing, Miss Miller?" he asks, with mock formality.

"Only when I'm completely sure no one is listening to me."

"Yes. We'll see about that. A few months of lessons with me and you'll be ready for the stage."

"You're going to teach me to sing? You do seem to be a true maestro." As she says it, she thinks of Kiki. Would they sing together? Certainly Man has watched her, hundreds of times, probably. "Is that one Kiki sings? You . . . know her, don't you?" Lee keeps her tone light and even.

He lifts his head from his work and glances over at her. "Kiki? Yes, I know her," he says, "though I don't think she's ever sung that song."

"I've never heard her . . . I went to Amélieeau Ivre last night and the bartender was talking about her." Lee is on a dangerous path but the words keep coming. "I like it there. Nice bar. They make a good Lillet."

A good Lillet? Yes, they are so adept at pouring one type of alcohol into a glass.

Man doesn't seem to notice. "I like that bar. The spiral staircase and the view from the second floor."

"But Kiki doesn't sing there, does she?"

"At Amélieeau Ivre? No, Kiki's usually at the Jockey."

"I haven't been there yet. I should go, to hear her."

"Mm," Man says, and starts singing again, but more quietly. Lee wonders if she shouldn't have brought up the other woman—perhaps now Man is thinking of her, remembering all the good times they had together. The hats he bought her to protect her delicate skin, the lavish restaurants he took her to.

Lee makes the contact sheet as Man has shown her, and then, hardly waiting for the fix to drip off the paper, she takes the wet sheet by the corner with her tongs and carries it into the studio, where she lays it down on some newsprint and looks at it with the loupe. Each image makes her throat close a little with excitement. She wants to see them enlarged, so she hurriedly chooses one and makes an X next to it with wax pencil, then goes back into the darkroom, where she places the negative in the enlarger. It is the picture of the woman at the café, shot from behind and close up on the woman's hair and neck.

Lee flicks on the mercury light, counts to forty slowly. Flicks it off. Carefully, she carries the paper over to the developing basin and slides it in, agitating the liquid as she has learned how to do. Within seconds her image spreads across the paper. First there are just the faint outlines of the woman's hair, then the outline of her shoulders, and then the bright parts of the image show up: the woman's hand, her nails, the contrast of the light shining on each of her curls. Sparks, Lee thinks, bright white sparks against her hair. Lee looks up for a moment to see if Man is watching. To her it is incredible: her own picture, appearing before her eyes. But he isn't paying attention. She returns her glance to the image just in time, before it gets overexposed. Once the image has set in the fix, she stares at it. She feels that it is good without knowing how to articulate why. It is just the nape of a woman's neck, her fingers scratching at her skin, but the image sends a shiver down Lee's spine.

Just then Man turns around and sets his own paper in the developer, and she watches as another image of Amélie appears before them. His work sits next to hers and when he doesn't immediately say something, she starts to panic that hers is banal, amateur. Finally, after what seems like forever, he peers at her photograph in the stop bath and says, "That's excellent work. Is she a friend of yours?"

"No, just a stranger."

"You set this up and took it without her noticing?"

"Yes—is that not allowed?"

Man laughs. "No, no, of course not. It's fine. I'm just impressed, that's all." He says it lightly, as if he doesn't realize how much it might mean to her.

"You really like it?"

"Well, I think we can tweak the exposure time a little bit"—he points with his tongs at some dark shadows in the woman's hair—"and burn in this corner a bit, but for a first print? It's very good."

If Lee was feeling strange before, now she feels even stranger. His words make her hot and achy at the same time, flushed with pride, and she looks at her print with new confidence and thinks that if she tries she might actually be able to make herself into a photographer. The confidence emboldens her, and her two desires—to work and to be with Man—come together in that moment. There doesn't need to be one or the other. The way he said "we"—"we can tweak the exposure." Perhaps someday her work will be on the same level as his. Perhaps they will work together to create it. A partnership of sorts. So she turns around to face him, and she is not sure what she is going to do until she does it.

"I had a different idea for the saber guard," she says. "If you still want, I could model for you, if you let me set it up."

Man raises his eyebrows. "Last time I asked you to pose for me you said no."

"I know. But if we do it together—I could frame the shots. I have an idea about it."

"Really? Well—yes. Let me just get things cleaned up in here."

As Lee is waiting for Man to come into the studio, she stands next to the camera and looks around, at the cloths draped over the couch, the half-drawn curtains, how bright and white and clean everything is. She whips the drapes off the table and the wall and replaces them with some black ones, draping the couch too. Then she goes into the office, picks up the saber guard, and turns it over and over. When she goes back into the studio, Man is waiting for her.

This is the first time Lee has done anything but follow his directions. Despite that, or maybe because of it, she feels she knows what he wants to see, has known it ever since she met him, but didn't realize it until she saw her own work in the developing tank, saw him appraising it as he did his own.

"You had Amélie near the window," Lee says, and takes the guard over to the couch, where she balances it on the arm, "but what if you had had her here?" Then she goes over to the camera and says "May I?" before lifting up the hood and going underneath it for the first time. The dark cloth smells of tobacco and cedar, a musty, masculine smell. Lee looks into the viewfinder and swivels the camera slightly so that all she can see is the couch and its black coverings. Through the viewfinder the room appears upside down, the couch hanging from the ceiling. It is disorienting, and Lee almost gasps when Man himself appears in the frame, walking across what looks like the ceiling and then sitting, absurdly, higher up than when he was standing.

"You need something to focus on," he says, and his voice comes to her through the cloth as if through water, murky and indistinct. She turns the focusing knob back and forth a bit, watching as Man blurs and sharpens, blurs and sharpens. Upside down, he is a stranger. She does not recognize his eyes, his mouth; if she saw him on the street she would not know him. It is disorienting. She comes out from under the camera hood and everything is right side up again, Man sitting on the couch, watching her as she walks toward him.

Lee goes over to the changing area in the corner of the room and stands hidden behind the screen. Slowly she undoes her blouse, first the buttons on the cuffs and then the placket, letting it drop to the floor when she is done. Then she undoes her trousers, unbuttoning three of the five buttons at the fly and pushing the trousers down so they hang on her hip bones and expose the full flat expanse of her stomach. And then she reaches behind her back with both hands, thinking of how the shadow of the pose must look silhouetted on the screen, her arms sticking out like a swan's wings. She unhooks the back of her brassiere before shrugging it off and letting it drop to the floor on top of her shirt. She keeps thinking about swans as she undresses, the ones she photographed in the park the other day, the muscle and bone of their wings and the power it must take them to beat the air into flight. She walks back and sits where Man has been on the couch and settles the metal guard over her face like a veil.

Up until this moment, Lee has felt calm, her actions at a distance from the emotions that prompted them, almost the way she used to feel when her father took her picture. But once she is sitting down, and able to see Man's face, the slight raise to his eyebrows the only hint of how he is feeling, she comes back to herself and goes cold all over, her nipples puckering into hard points.

Man clears his throat, and his voice, when he speaks, sounds high and thin. "Hold that pose." He moves over to the camera and goes under the hood.

The saber guard is heavier than it looks, and its sharp scent makes Lee's mouth go sour. What injury was it meant to protect from? She imagines the curved slice of a fencing sword, the bone-deep bruises from a blunted blade. Lee closes her eyes and holds her head just so.

"Oh, that's good!" Man shouts, his voice muffled by the cloth. "Hold it just like that."

Lee doesn't want to sit still, doesn't want to do exactly what he asks of her, so she moves instead into different poses, her arms stretched out along the back of the couch and then held tight between her knees, her head tilted so far to the side she feels a hard pull in her neck and the saber guard pressing into her clavicle. She keeps her eyes closed and tries not to breathe in the smell of metal.

"I think you were right," Man says as he reemerges from under the hood and comes over to her. "Having it over your face like that—it's good."

Lee stands up and takes off the guard and sets it down. Standing so close to him, she feels the difference in their heights. His eyes are just level with her jawbone.

"The shots are going to be very good," he says.

"I know," Lee says, taking a step closer to him. Her bare nipples graze his linen shirt, sending an ache shooting down to her groin.

Man takes a deep breath. "Lee, I—"

"I know," she says again, and moves a step closer.

And then their mouths press hard together, their teeth clicking. His arms come all the way around her and pin her own to her sides. They stand that way for what seems like hours, days, just kissing. Man takes her hand and leads her to the parlor. She kicks off her trousers while he does the same with his clothes, hurriedly, and then in the dimness of the falling twilight, Man lays her down on the couch and kneels next to her, running his hands over her bare skin. She arches her back to get closer to him, but it is not close enough, so she pulls him down on top of her and breathes him in. His skin on hers is warm as water, and she is wet with it, and for once her brain shuts off completely, leaving only feeling. The one thought she does manage is that there is no going back from this, and for that she couldn't be more grateful.

NORMANDY

JULY 1944

France is metal, the smell and feel and taste of it. Hot steel helmet on Lee's sweat-soaked hair. The scent her field camera leaves on her hands. The nib of her pen when she licks it, ink bluing her tongue. And the hospital. Bone saws. Disinterred bullets in a bowl. The stink of infection in the air, sweet like licked pennies.

Photos everywhere she looks, compositions formed of horrors. Lee shoots and shoots and swallows down the bile that rises in her throat—even that tasting of metal. Her assignment is to photograph the post-invasion duties of the American nurses, so Lee records plasma bags, penicillin, surgical procedures. She takes pictures of American women working side by side with German nurses, tamps the blast hole of her growing loathing for the Krauts down tight.

She sends the pictures back to Audrey accompanied by essays, knows the censor will scissor away most of what she writes. Even her letters to Roland get censored, blank spaces where her words once were. His notes back to her get censored too, and arrive weeks and weeks after he sends them, but the words they still contain are normal, soothing. They tether her to a world outside the war.

At the end of one day Lee hears a voice calling to her from a hospital bed. She turns to see a man bandaged up like some sort of mummy. "Ma'am," he says, his voice so weak it's almost a whistle. "Take my picture, so I can have a laugh about it when I go home."

His eyes and mouth and nose are black holes, obliterations. His hands are bound up as big as oven mitts. "Say cheese," he whispers, and Lee grips the dark metal box of her camera and tries to focus.

CHAPTER ELEVEN

Three months have passed. Man has moved her to a new apartment a few blocks from his in Montparnasse. Paid the first month's rent, bought her furniture, given her art to hang on the walls. Together they wander through Printemps like an old married couple. Man helps her pick out sheets, coffee cups, lavender sachets to tuck inside her linens. They paper her bedroom with a geometric print and lay an Art Deco rug on the floor, its thick pile soft beneath her feet. He gives her one of his own blankets and when he isn't with her she burrows into it for comfort. Lee has never cared too much where she lives but she finds that the apartment becomes an extension of what she feels toward Man. It is not a large space—when he spends the night she stacks their shoes by the door, liking how the heels of hers nestle inside his—but it is sized just right for her, and she feels a sense of calm when she is there that she has never felt anywhere else.

At night they lie on her bed, the mattress sagging in the middle so that they continually roll toward each other, their bodies warm and their skin sticking together in the unseasonable April heat. He kisses her toes, her wrists, the cleft of her buttocks. In the mornings she finds that his stubble has chafed her skin and left it stinging.

Always, always, he is photographing her. His camera is a third person in the bedroom, and she flirts for it and for him as he takes her picture. They print the images together, standing hip to hip in the developing room, her body blooming on the paper while they watch. This way they get to have the moments twice, the images calling up the feelings from the day before until sometimes they stop what they are doing and make love again, quickly, her hands gripping the edge of the sink, the pictures forgotten and gone black in the developing tray.

For days at a time Man takes no clients. They lock the studio door behind them. She does not answer the phone when it rings. Instead, they print pictures of Lee, or Man paints or sculpts— he is filled with an almost manic energy that he says comes from her, from being near her. He begs her to stay close when he is painting and often Lee does so, sitting curled in an armchair near his easel, breathing in the smell of camphor and turpentine and watching his expression while he works. Sometimes he paints abstracts; other times he uses her seated figure or one of their photographs as inspiration—the line of her neck becoming a guide for a tightrope walker, her breast becoming a grain silo becoming a mountain. Where he is meticulous in the darkroom, here he has an almost frenzied focus. He wants her close but sometimes forgets that she is there, until Lee grows frustrated and takes the brushes out of his hand to call him back to her, kissing him insistently until he is hers again.

Sometimes Lee looks at him as they are eating dinner, or just sitting next to each other, and wonders how she ever thought this might not happen. It feels inevitable. He looks like a different person than he did when she first met him. He has become dear to her. The fringe of his lashes, the whorl of his ear, all of him now more familiar than she is to herself. His smell—almost piney.

Even after she bathes she can smell him on her. She nestles her nose into her own shoulder and breathes him in.

At parties or cafés, she is aware of where he is in the room without looking; they catch each other's gaze and hold it longer than they should. Their connection feels so obvious, as if everyone around them can see, just from looking at them, what they have been doing in the bedroom. Their need for each other. All the other people in the room must hear her heart thumping, the naked *tum tum tum tum tum tum* of it.

When Lee is not with Man, she does her own work. She finds herself as eager as he is to create things. As the weeks pass she wants to walk more than she wants to shoot in the studio, so on the days when Man is taking clients, she puts her Rollei around her neck and takes long afternoon strolls through the city, cutting across the wide boulevards and crossing over the Seine, losing her way in the Marais, where the Jews look at her curiously, the tall girl with the camera and the bright blond hair. Maybe she should be fearful wandering the city alone, but the camera not only gives her purpose but feels like protection. She likes the serendipity of shooting street scenes, juxtaposing people and objects in weird positions, playing with perspective. Each time she prints one of her photos and Man likes it, she grows more confident, feels more like who she has always wanted to be.

When she returns from her walks she brings back paper bags full of fruit pastilles, or macarons so light they melt on her tongue, and feeds them to Man. He licks the sugar off her fingers. She comes back as the sun is fading in the west and the light lies like thick striped taffy across the bed, and before it gets too dark Man takes her picture: her neck and torso banded with shadows, her legs tangled in the sheets, the curve of her ribs as she lies on her side. And then he puts aside the camera and spreads out next to her and touches every bit of her, all the parts he's photographed and all the parts he hasn't. She closes her eyes and wills her mind to stay in it, the good feeling, and it is better than it has ever been for her. And when her mind drifts, it drifts only to their pictures.

It is spring now, the leaves just pushing their bright green way out of the trees, and one evening when Lee goes back to her apartment, she is stopped at the door by the sight of a woman sitting on the stoop, brown hair bobbed at her jawline, her eyes closed and her face tipped up to catch the warmth of the sun. A valise sits next to her, a small veiled hat on top.

"Tanja?" Lee asks, incredulous, and Tanja hops up and they are embracing, jumping up and down and making small squeals of happiness.

"Oh Li-Li," Tanja says, "I missed you!"

Lee takes Tanja upstairs and settles her in a chair in the corner of her room. Tanja starts recounting her latest travels, and Lee lets the stories wash over her, a sweet river of words. She has always liked how easy it is to be with Tanja, and it does not take long for Lee to revert to the old version of herself, cracking jokes and talking in shorthand with her friend.

"You should have seen it, Li-Li. We get to Milan later than we would have liked, it's already dark, and we take a cab to the hotel my friend Ruth had recommended—remember Ruth? Well, it's called the Casino Hotel and Ruth had told me it's right in the center of all the action. She was wrong: it *was* the action. I'll never forget Mrs. Basingthwaite's face, standing there in the lobby, surrounded by what I'm fairly certain were ladies of the night. She hustled me out of there so fast it made my head spin."

Lee laughs. "How long can you stay in Paris?"

Tanja grimaces. "Just the weekend. Mrs. B won't let me out of her sight longer than that. *Please* say there's somewhere desperately seedy you can take me."

Lee hesitates. She is supposed to go to a party with Man that she has been looking forward to for ages. It would be easy enough to include Tanja, but the idea of sharing Man with someone is unappealing. Yet, another piece of her wants to show him off— to show her life off—so eventually she says, "There's a party I was planning on going to tonight, at an apartment just a few blocks from here. Do you want to come?"

"Do birds sing?" Tanja says, and dances around the room, trilling, "A party! A party!"

Lee gets dressed and they walk together to Tanja's hotel. When Tanja used to come down to New York for visits, they joked that their sightseeing was merely a backdrop for their chitchat: they talked about the same things at the Met as they did at a cabaret. And now, Paris is no different. They stroll along and talk and talk. This time, though, Lee has her camera with her, and every once in a while she breaks free from Tanja's arm and takes a picture. She feels her mind operating on two levels and she loves it: she listens to her friend, but there is another track in her brain and it is focused on what she is seeing, on getting the last of the evening light, images composing and dissolving as she moves her gaze around. Some images she wants to keep, they tug at her, so she frames them, focuses, releases the shutter. She decides to take a picture of Tanja, her hands gesturing as she tells a story, and watches in amusement as Tanja realizes what Lee is doing and gets self-conscious.

"So will Man Ray be there tonight?" Tanja asks her. "Is it still going well with him?"

Lee opens her mouth to tell her friend about what has happened between her and Man and finds she doesn't know what to say. Both Man and the pictures—her pictures—feel so new. Lee doesn't want to answer questions; she wants to keep it all to herself, a little pearl locked in a shell.

After a long pause, Lee clears her throat and says, "I haven't told you yet, but Man and I—we're . . ." Her voice trails off.

Tanja's eyebrows go up. "Really?"

"Yes." Blushing, disconcerted, Lee turns away and takes a picture of one of the gargoyles on Notre Dame, silhouetted against the iron-gray sky. When she puts down her camera again Tanja is still giving her a look, but doesn't say another word about it.

At the hotel, Lee can't help but covet the outfits Tanja has collected as she's traveled across Europe, day dresses with fuller skirts than Lee is used to seeing, and little bolero jackets with shoulder pads sewn in. The two women are practically the same size, so while Tanja gets dressed Lee tries on her crepe de chine and pearls, and when her friend sees her she tells her she should borrow them. Lee stands in front of the mirror, admiring herself: the flush in her cheeks from the walk and the anticipation of seeing Man, the way her lips always look now, tender and swollen. Tanja comes up behind her and examines her with a critical eye, then turns the necklace backward so that the pearls hang down Lee's back like a cape, and as they go outside, Lee feels more Parisian than she has the entire time she's been here.

In a secluded corner of Le Dôme, where Lee has taken her for a drink before the party, Tanja leans down and takes a sip from the full rim of her martini. She looks at Lee while she does it, her kohl-blacked eyes narrowed. "He's *paying* for your apartment?" she says. "He's serious about you. Why haven't you told me?"

Lee focuses on a group of people over Tanja's right shoulder. One of the women looks familiar but Lee can't think where she would have met her. A friend of Man's? Did she come to the studio? Lee has met so many of Man's circle now that it's hard to keep them all straight.

"Li-Li." Tanja waves her hand in front of Lee to get her attention. "You should have told me. All those letters and you didn't tell me."

"I know." Lee tries to sound contrite. "I just felt—it was so new. It was all happening so fast." She doesn't want to make eye contact with Tanja, so she keeps looking around the room, and then realizes they are sitting right beneath the portrait of Man and his friends that has hung on the wall for a decade. Pointing to where Man stands glowering in the center of the group of a dozen men, she says, "That's him on the wall. With his Dada group. They used to meet here." Man has told her how different Le Dôme was then, pipes and politics instead of gossip and champagne cocktails. Lee points to the grainy picture. "That's Tristan Tzara on the right—you'll meet him tonight, I think. He and Man publish a journal together, *221*. Have you seen it? Man said—he told me it might be a good venue for my pictures someday." Lee cannot keep the pride out of her voice.

Tanja takes another sip of her drink. "I know he's going to be here any minute, but I..." Tanja fishes out the cocktail onion from her glass and pops it in her mouth, chewing it slowly and looking at Lee with an appraising expression before continuing. "You work for him, the only people you know are the people he knows, and he's paying for your apartment. Li-Li, just...what happens if it doesn't work out? You know how you are when you get tired of someone."

Lee looks down peevishly at her hands, folded in her lap, and is distracted by a smudge of ash on her glove, which she tries to rub out with her finger. The spot gets larger, a gray smear.

"Argyle is still pining for you," Tanja continues when Lee doesn't respond.

"How pointless of him." Argyle. One of Lee's lovers before she left New York, who flew her out over the sparkling ribbon of the Hudson in his two-seater plane before taking her home with him, his skin smelling of gasoline when they made love. The last in a string of men Lee treated badly. As soon as they told her they loved her she never spoke to them again. Tanja was there for all of them, knows all the details—which is probably, if Lee were to think about it more deeply, part of the reason she doesn't want to talk to her about Man. If Lee *doesn't* talk about him, he can't be flawed like the other men and Lee can be better too.

Finally Lee says, "It's not like that this time. And honestly, can't a girl grow up? Just because I've been stupid all my life doesn't mean I'm stupid now."

Tanja reaches across the table and gives Lee's arm a squeeze. "You've never been stupid a minute."

"Well, once or twice, maybe?"

"All right, possibly," Tanya says, and laughs before growing serious again. "You really like him, don't you? When you mention him—there's something different about it."

Lee nods. It *is* different. When she thinks back on her other lovers, all she remembers is her restlessness, her dissatisfaction. They were always wanting more and more of her and she had no interest in giving it. She would sit across from them at restaurants or lie next to them in bed and most of the time she'd be thinking about how she could get away. It was as if the closer they wanted to get, the less emotion she was able to express, until it felt as if her body was a wooden box she had nailed down tight. She tried to explain this to Tanja once, years ago, but her friend only looked at her curiously, unable to understand. So now it feels impossible to explain what is different about Man, how when Lee is with him she feels open, pliable; no way to explain that the more time she spends with him the more she craves him. "I really like him," is all she says. "I'm glad you get to meet him."

When they arrive at the party, Man is surprised and pleased that Lee has brought a friend. He links arms with both of them and leads them smoothly from conversation to conversation. After some small talk with two of Tristan's friends, Man takes them over to an older couple and makes introductions.

"Arthur, Rose," Man says. "So wonderful to see you."

Arthur and Rose Wheeler are Man's main patrons; they have funded his films and always seem to swoop in with a commission when work is going slowly. Man is very close to them. In past summers, he even traveled with them to Biarritz—Lee has seen some photos from the trip, has heard a story about a day spent shooting pictures of sheep when they blocked the main road and trapped them in the countryside for hours. In Man's photos the sheep crowd together, the whites of their scared eyes popping like bright marbles.

Rose turns to Lee, a radiant smile on her face. *"You,"* she says, "you must be Lee Miller. We've heard so much about you—and we've seen you too, in Man's beautiful pictures."

Man smiles and pulls Lee closer. "Yes, this is my love. I'm so glad you finally get to meet her. And this is her good friend, Tanja Ramm, visiting from New York."

They all continue talking, elegant cocktail patter, and Lee participates in it, but all she is thinking of is Man's expression as he looked at her, his brown eyes full of feeling. The words he used: "my love." Lee could swear that people are noticing, their glances filled with admiration and envy. Lee is so lucky to be the one with Man, so lucky that everyone knows it.

Tanja's earlier skepticism has dissipated, and within moments of meeting him, Man has charmed her. Lee is not surprised: Man is in a sociable mood, and he is always at his best in a crowd like this, where he knows most of the guests and doesn't have to posture. He is dressed simply but elegantly, in dark trousers and a white shirt, and he's wearing the electric cuff links he made, red lights that wink off and on in a random pattern. As he gesticulates in the center of a knot of people, Lee can see them flashing.

Lee can tell Tanja charms Man just as much as he charms her, but of course Tanja charms everyone. It's part of what Lee likes about being her friend: her ease in any social situation, her uncomplicated nature. They are opposites inside and out: Lee has always thought Tanja had an angel's soul, clean and unblemished, whereas when Lee pictures her own soul she sees it as thorny, a dark tangled nest. Unlike Man and Tanja, Lee often feels tense in crowded social settings, too aware of how she appears or how she is supposed to be acting.

Now Lee scans the room for Tristan. Ever since Man mentioned that he and Tristan might publish her photos in their journal, she has been itching to talk to him. As she looks around she sees someone else familiar: shaved head, corpse-pale skin, baggy suit. "Look—it's Claude," Lee says to Man. He glances over and gives a small nod. "I want to tell her how much I liked her poem," Lee says, excusing herself.

Claude stands alone in the corner, furiously smoking. Lee goes up to her and smiles. "This was months ago now, but I wanted to tell you I loved the poem you read at Monnier's."

Claude blows a smoke ring and closes one eye, seemingly so she can look at Lee through the circle's center. "It wasn't a poem."

"Oh. I thought—what was it?"

"My manifesto. My refutation of the self." Her English is thickly accented.

Lee wants to roll her eyes but restrains herself. In the past few months, as lines that Claude spoke continued to ping through

Lee's head, she forgot how odd she is. Now Lee glances around and tries to think how to elegantly get away.

"You are the one with Man Ray," Claude states.

"Yes." Here again Lee feels a flash of pride.

"The *muse*," Claude says, drawing out the word and waggling her fingers in the air derisively.

"I'm a photographer, actually."

"Are you?"

Lee tries to match Claude's derisiveness with her own. "You are too? I think I heard that."

Claude hands Lee her cigarette, the tobacco wet on the end that has been in her mouth, and begins to look through her jacket pockets. She pulls out a stack of small cards and hands one to Lee. On it is a photograph of Claude dressed as a weight lifter and an address on Boulevard Raspail. "I'm having a show," she says.

Lee doesn't recognize the address, but still she's impressed. Claude must be even better than she thought. "I don't know this address," Lee says. "It's a gallery?"

Claude curls the corner of her lip into a scornful smile. "*Gallery* is too much of a word for this. The owner calls it a gallery, but I would call it a hallway between two other buildings. But then again the owner is a—how you say? A son of a cunt. The whole thing has been miserable. First it was just my work; now it's my work and twenty other photographers. I've been thinking of backing out, but I like the idea of seeing my prints on the walls too much. Wouldn't you?"

Lee doesn't answer, but an image rises in her mind: her own work, framed and mounted. A crowd of people clustered in a room, moving silently from print to print. The pictures—her pictures—staying in their minds afterward, haunting them.

Claude scans the room. Lee follows her gaze and sees she is looking at Man, who is still holding court in the corner, his cuff

links blinking in the dimly lit space. Claude flicks her eyes pointedly between him and Lee, suggestively enough to express that
she can envision everything that is going on between them. "Big
man," Claude says, but her tone says she thinks the exact opposite
is true.

It occurs to Lee that she can walk away, so she does, stamping
out Claude's cigarette in a heaping ashtray and helping herself to
a glass of wine from a passing tray.

It is a relief to be near Man again, and Lee leans into the familiarity of his rumpled jacket, his solid arm that comes around her
waist and holds her tight. Tanja gives Lee the dazzling smile she
always has when she is drunk, all gums and teeth. The Wheelers
have left, and Man and Tanja are talking with an older woman
who has ten or twelve strings of pearls looped around her neck,
her drink held high above her head like a torch.

"And I *said* to Rémy," the woman shouts, "I said that what is
going to ruin art *isn't* the young people, the young people are *fine,*
no matter what anyone says about their heads being completely
empty. What's going to ruin art is *commerce.*" The last word is said
imperiously, with the hoisted drink waggled for emphasis, liquid
sloshing.

Tanja leans toward Lee and in a whispered imitation of the old
woman says, *"Commerce."*

But Lee is interested, and waits for the woman to continue.

"If you think that Americans are going to be sitting for portraits
now," the woman says, pointing a long maroon fingernail at Man,
"you are very mistaken."

Man clears his throat. "Is it that bad? We haven't felt the effects
here yet. In fact, I was just talking to Arthur Wheeler about this
very subject—"

The woman cuts him off. "I'm from Pittsburgh," she says, shaking her head. "I went to get money out for this trip, and can you

imagine, but they told me they didn't have it. My bank! Didn't have *my* money."

Man nods, frowning, and questions the woman again, his voice pitched lower so Lee can't hear him. Tanja turns toward Lee and says, "Who was the bizarre person you were talking to before?"

"Claude Cahun. She's a photographer. She's going to have her own show at a gallery near here." Lee hands Tanja the card. She looks at it for a brief moment and then hands it back. Tanja has never cared much about art.

"Lord, I hope she does something about her hair before then," Tanja says, and they both laugh.

"She's actually very talented," Lee says. "It's not everyone who gets to show their work in this city."

Tanja raises a shoulder in an elegant half shrug. "Soon enough it will be you."

"I hope so," Lee says, but only part of her believes it could really happen. She remembers a snippet from her father's last letter. "My father's photographs are being published," she says.

Tanja looks at her, surprised. "His photos of you?"

"Some sort of architectural shots he took."

"Ah."

Tanja has known Lee's father since their girlhood, and has never liked him, though she sat for art portraits with him just as Lee did. They even did portraits together, which Lee is still a bit embarrassed by, her father's staging making them look more like women in love than friends. Lee still has not responded to his letter; she has just stuffed it in the bottom of a drawer and tried not to think about it.

"I like Man," Tanja whispers now, changing the subject, her voice smelling of wine as she leans in close to Lee.

"You do?"

"Yes. He seems to really love you."

Lee reaches out and touches Tanja's forearm. "What did he say?"

"He spent almost our entire conversation—before that woman joined us—telling me how talented you are. Some picture you took of a broken umbrella? He went on and on about it."

Lee flushes with pride and takes a sip of her drink to cover it up. She didn't know that Man liked that photo, though she herself was quite happy with it. Man is still talking to the woman, so Lee asks Tanja if she needs another drink, and they set off together for the bar, where they stand for a while, nibbling on pickled eggs and downing their drinks so that they can grab fresh ones. When they get back to Man, Tristan Tzara has joined him, and the conversation seems much the same as it was when they left, though a larger crowd of people has gathered around them. Every time Lee sees Tristan, he is politicking, and she can tell by his deeply earnest expression that tonight will be more of the same. He is a man who should travel with his own soapbox.

"How do we justify making art when class is still such an issue, when people are struggling?" Tristan shouts.

"Art is always justified!" someone shouts, and a few people rap their knuckles on the tables in agreement.

Lee moves over to Man and kisses his cheek. Tristan nods at her, then continues talking, switching to French and speaking quickly and loudly: they must liberate people from bourgeois concerns; under the rod of the capitalist system people are exploited; exploitation is death. Lee tugs on Man's sleeve, wanting to ask him about the journal and whether or not they can ask Tristan to include some of her photographs, but before she can speak, Man says to her, "We're going to make the entire next issue of *221* about this. A new manifesto about the role art and photography play in freeing the mind from complacency."

More manifestos. Talk, talk, talk. Perhaps all their talking makes a difference, but so far Lee hasn't seen it. She likes the conversations she has with Man about art when they are alone much better than these public shouting sessions, when confrontation and conflict seem to be the point. At the studio, they talk about desire, how much it is like hunger, how love is as important to art as revolution. Lee has found this much more interesting, but even those ideas struck her as slightly false. Or perhaps it isn't that the ideas themselves are false, but that she doesn't quite believe that art always needs an underlying message. Her favorite pieces of Man's are the ones that don't require an explanation or larger context, the ones that simply make her *feel* when she looks at them.

Still, there is something energizing about what Tristan is saying, the passion that guides his thinking. Lee looks back at where Tanja stands behind her, obviously bored, and realizes that over these past few months some of what he and Man are saying has begun to affect her own work. That having a reason and purpose behind the photographs she creates is important, even if she doesn't quite know yet what that purpose is.

But tonight she is here with her friend, and as Lee looks at her she feels the lifetime of their affection for each other. She steps slightly out of the circle of people surrounding Tristan, throws her arm around her old friend's shoulder, and clinks her glass against Tanja's with a smile.

CHAPTER TWELVE

Lee lies with Man on the couch in the studio. She has smudges of paint on her stomach and thighs where his hands have been. He rests his head on her, tells her the past months are the most creative he has known. The photographs, the paintings, the sculptures—they are the best work he's ever done.

"It's you," he says. "All you."

"What about with Kiki?" she asks him. In the four months they've been together, Man hasn't mentioned her, so until now neither has Lee, but she has wondered about her again and again. Lee has never cared about any man's former lovers, but with Man she finds herself dwelling on his past more than she'd like to admit.

"It was different."

"Different how?" Lee sits up and starts buttoning her shirt.

"She was young—"

"I'm young."

He looks at her, starts again. "She was young. I was young. I met her at a café. There was a misunderstanding—you don't care about this."

"Yes, I do."

Lee drags the story out of him. He had just arrived in Paris.

He went to La Closerie des Lilas and saw a woman sitting in the corner with a friend. He knew, even fresh off the boat from Brooklyn as he was, that she didn't belong there. She wore no hat, had her hair unpinned and cheeks rouged to a consumptive brightness, and was speaking too loudly in a fast stream of words with a guttural rasp to them. Back home in New York, Man had been doing nude studies, and Kiki's loose hairstyle reminded him of the prostitutes who often posed for him, easy in their bodies and grateful for a job for which all they had to do was stand still. From the moment Man first saw her he wanted to protect her. He watched as a waiter approached Kiki and told her that she must leave the restaurant if she did not cover her hair. Kiki screamed that she would not leave. The waiter insisted, and she rose from her seat and stepped up onto and over the table. In two quick steps she was down and walking toward the door. As she was passing, Man reached out and grabbed her arm, offering her a place at his table so that the waiter would not bother her anymore. He spoke hardly any French and Kiki no English, but somehow they enchanted each other. He took her to dinner and then a show and then his studio and then his bed, and they were together for ten years before he left her.

"Why did you leave her?" Lee wants to know because she wants to confirm she is better than Kiki, wants to know all the ways in which the other woman failed.

"She was jealous."

"Jealous of what? What did you do?"

Man looks at her with an injured expression. "Nothing! She was volatile—such a performer. She spent every night singing songs about betrayal and pretty soon she saw it everywhere." He stands up and crosses over to the office. "Here, let me show you something." He returns with a small black address book. Inside are dozens of names, all written in Man's neat hand, but as Lee looks closer she sees that some of the names and telephone numbers have been altered, run over again and again in thick black pen until the letters look like misshapen animals.

"I came home one day and found it like this." He flips through the pages, chooses one, and hands her the book. "My cousin Flora, who lives in Philadelphia. My grandmother. Every woman's name that was in there."

"Had you been with someone else?"

"No, no, nothing like that."

Lee thumbs through the book. The markings are pressed into the pages so hard they are visible on the other side, and there are gouges where the pen's tip caught against the fibers. On one page, Kiki has written *merde merde merde* in the margins. Lee imagines Kiki in Man's bedroom, white-knuckled, furious. But as she keeps flipping through, something about the other woman's anger tugs at Lee, and she is surprised to find herself feeling empathy, or even kinship. "There must have been some reason she did this—"

"There's not. I was devoted to her." Man's tone is sharp. "When I was with her, I did everything I could to help her along. She wanted to paint, so I bought her canvases, let her use my oils. She wanted to act, so I took her with me to the States when I went home to visit my family and set up meetings for her in New York. She wanted to write—she had this idea that she'd write a memoir, so I read some of her early pages and helped her translate them into English. And I introduced her to a friend of mine, Broca, because he put out a newssheet about Montparnasse and I thought he might be interested in Kiki's stories. Well, he was more than interested. She started working with him all the time. *Writing.* And then she moved in with him."

Lee is confused. "So . . . she left you?"

Man takes the address book out of Lee's hands and sets it down on the side table, then walks across the room and stares out the window. "No, I left her. I made it very clear that her behavior was unacceptable. And it was. Broca turned out to be a drinker and a drug addict, always wandering through the street and muttering to himself. Kiki wasn't with him for long—I think she left him for her accompanist, actually. An accordion player."

It is clear from Man's tone that he is still angry about what happened. He has not answered Lee's question about why Kiki was so jealous of him, but she doesn't want to push him much further. She goes over to where he stands at the window, wraps her arms around him, and kisses his ear.

She waits a few moments, then says, "I want to meet her. I want to hear her sing."

"Well. She can be cruel. She knows we are together."

"Are you worried she's going to be mean to me?" Lee puts on a pout, bats her lashes.

Man rubs his finger along the side of her face and down her neck.

"You want to know? I'm worried that you two are going to become best friends and Kiki is going to tell you terrible stories about me that make you regret all of this. She could do that. She *has* done that."

"And all along I thought you were worried for *me*."

"Worried for *you*? I think you're quite capable of taking care of yourself."

When Lee walks through Montparnasse she keeps seeing broadsheets advertising Kiki's performances, and no matter what she does she can't get the woman out of her head. Later that week she asks Man if she can see his pictures of Kiki. She can't help herself. He never misses an opportunity to show off his work, so she's not surprised when he goes over to the flat files and starts pulling out folders.

At first what she feels is utter relief, tension she didn't know she had unknotting in her neck. This is the most beautiful woman in Paris? To Lee's American eye, Kiki looks bloated as over-yeasted bread, her makeup garish, her hairstyle outdated by two decades, her derriere wide and sagging as a half-filled flour sack.

But some of the compositions are uncomfortably familiar. Here are Man's bedroom curtains, the same as they are today. There Kiki tips back her head—Man has taken a close-up of her neck. It could be Lee's neck, the shot is so similar. Man doesn't seem to expect Lee to say anything and keeps up a quick patter about what he was thinking when he shot a certain image, or pauses to inspect one and explain how he would print it differently now.

He shows her at least a hundred pictures. When he is done she is still quiet. Man asks what she thinks. Lee hesitates and then says what she thinks she must: Kiki is very beautiful.

"Of course," Man says. "But what do you think of the work?"

CHAPTER THIRTEEN

"Biarritz," Man says.

Lee is balancing the ledger; Man is sitting at the table in the far corner of the room. He has appointments booked solid for the rest of the week.

"Biarritz?"

"Let's go," he says. "I can get the car out, we can drive there. You've never been, have you?"

She makes the phone calls for him. Apologies—Man Ray is very sorry, but there has been a death in the family. Can they rebook? Part of her knows Man should be worrying about money, about angering the clients who pay the bills, but it is simple for her to ignore that thought. If he isn't worried, she shouldn't be either.

It takes her an hour to tidy up, go home, and pack her valise, and when she comes downstairs from her apartment he is already idling at the curb in his Voisin, the big long car growling like an animal. Lee has never been in a car this nice. She ties a striped scarf over her hair and props her arm on the leather-covered door, feeling glamorous and louche. She rests her hand on Man's thigh for most of the ride.

It's a long drive on lousy roads, so they stop in Poitiers for the night, strolling like tourists through its cobblestoned streets, eating dinner at a small restaurant where they are served brown bread and *boeuf bourguignon,* the gravy rich with cognac and studded with carrots and potatoes and pearl onions. Lee eats so much the waistband of her dress is tight when they leave the restaurant. At night they make love in their small hotel room, lit only by the full moon that glows like a lamp through the curtainless windows, and in the morning they eat croissants in bed, their fingers slick with butter and smelling of sugar and yeast. When they go outside, shielding their eyes from the bright sunshine, so different from the light in Paris, Lee takes pictures, the towers on the Palais de Justice like men in jester's caps, and she feels happier than she has ever felt, free and clean and light inside. As they cross over a footbridge, she turns to Man. "Let me take your picture."

"No one takes my picture."

"That's absurd," she says, and holds her camera to her eye.

Shrugging, smiling, he agrees. She frames him with the wide stone railing running off to a point on the horizon, holding the camera slightly off axis so his body is parallel with a lamppost just behind him. He wears a white scarf, cream-colored linen pants. He is still smiling, just a little, and the wind catches his hair and his scarf and blows them straight out sideways. He looks old, a bit tired, and for some reason that makes her love him all the more.

Biarritz, when they finally arrive after two days of solid driving, is a postcard. The sun is setting as they pull into town, and Man puts the Voisin's top down and takes them along Esplanade du Port Vieux to Villa Belza, which rises narrowly from the road as if it has been gouged out of the sandstone cliffs. Man parks nearby and together they walk up the path to the villa's front door.

Man books a room while Lee waits, admiring the lobby's elegant furnishings and thick velvet drapes. He comes over to her with a giant key, and when she sees it in his hand she feels dizzy.

They cannot move fast enough. She walks in front of him up the stairs and brazenly he puts his hand between her legs as they climb, his fingers hot on her skin right up above the lace at the top of her stockings, so high he must be able to feel the wet heat between her legs. As soon as the hotel room door closes behind them they are on the bed together. The window has been left open and as Man makes love to her—hard, fast, the way she likes it—she smells sea and salt and thinks that from now on she might always think of salt when she thinks of him. When they are finished she lies back on a gigantic pillow and looks around for the first time. The hotel room walls are covered in red brocade. Red curtains are suspended from the ceiling and drape over the headboard. Even the vanity and sitting areas are upholstered in red fabric.

"What *is* this place?" she asks him.

"Isn't it amazing?" he says, laughing at her expression. "Just wait until you see the cabaret."

They nap and make love again and emerge from their room for dinner, where they stuff themselves with seafood dishes: *moules marinières,* amberjack in orange marinade, a crudo made of some fish Lee has never had before. They refill their wineglasses again and again. Lee feels as though she will never stop being hungry. Eating like this—ordering whatever she wants, scraping the last bits of frosting off her dessert plate—makes her feel like a child again, and for a moment she grows antsy. But then Man takes her into the cabaret, which is as lavish and ostentatious as he promised, and she relaxes. They sit at a mirrored table with their knees pressed together. On the stage, women in sequined brassieres and tall feathered headbands dance the Charleston. The music is loud and brassy and when the show ends and the music continues, most of the patrons get up to dance. Man pulls Lee up onto the floor. He is a wild and uninhibited dancer, not particularly graceful, but so full of joy she cannot help but get caught up in moving with him, following his steps and growing wilder and wilder herself. When they are sweating and winded, Man nicks a wine bottle and two glasses off their table and they go upstairs and climb into the giant red bed and talk until three o'clock in the morning. Art, inspiration, the difference between painting and photography. The conversation is its own dance, looping and circling back on itself until she is practically breathless.

"I had this idea," Man says, "a series of self-portraits I want to do. Maybe six or seven of them, all with subtle variations. A close-up of my face and on the desk in front of me a mask, a death mask. The change in the images would be in the other objects on the desk. I'm not sure what they are yet. Maybe in one a noose, in another a feather. Like how it feels to be an artist—"

Lee nods with excitement. "Yes! How one day you can't think of a single original picture and the next day there's almost too many of them—and how do you capture that, or how do you hold on to the feeling from the good days—"

"And not let the noose days be all you're thinking about."

"Yes," Lee says. She tips the last drops of wine into her mouth and sets down her glass. He trails his fingers across her arm and she moves her hand to his, lifting it up and pressing just her fingertips to his.

"Let's set it up when we get back to the studio," she says.

"Yes," he says, and kisses her.

In the morning they walk to the Rocher de la Vierge and then to the Grande Plage, where they take off their shoes to stroll along the hard-packed sand. It is mid-May, before the summer season, and the beach is not that crowded. There are rows of empty sun shelters, and when Lee expresses interest, Man rents one. They open its canvas doors and watch the rise and fall of the white-capped waves. Lee lies half in, half out of the sun, marooned under a gigantic sun hat she buys from a passing pushcart, sitting up only to sprinkle water on her legs so she can feel the sea breeze on her skin. The water leaves a filigree of salt when it dries. Man naps next to her in a sun chair. She watches him, his jaw slackened, skin loose around his neck, perfectly at peace. Lee decides to take a walk while he is sleeping. She grabs her camera and heads up to the sidewalk where the chic hotels line the waterfront. Everyone is beautiful. Men in straw caps and cuffed trousers walk hand in hand with women in gauzy palazzo pants. Lee takes a picture of the rows of sun shelters sprouting like button mushrooms from the sand, another of a couple carrying a gigantic parasol and arguing while they walk. At the edge of the beach a woman sells neck-laces made out of sea sponges, which charms Lee enough that she buys one to show to Man. It smells of brine and ocean rot, but she puts it around her neck anyway and heads back to him. He is still sleeping, so Lee sits down near him, her head tipped back to the sun. After a few minutes he opens his eyes and sees her and picks up her camera. She doesn't move, closes her eyes as he takes pictures of her, the sun warm on her face, melting into her bones like butter.

Before they leave they go into the shelter, close the doors. In-side the thick canvas enclosure the sound of the sea is muffled to a whisper. They lay their towels over the soft white sand and lie down, and Man kisses her, a long deep kiss as if he is drinking her. Lee is astounded at how much she desires him. She takes his hand and puts it at her waistband, and he unbuttons her pants and thumbs aside her underwear and touches her until she is spent and trembling, her skin damp and lightly textured with sand. After-ward she lies against him, her body completely relaxed. He holds her close, and she wants the moment to last forever, for nothing to break the way she feels.

Lee hears the phrase in her mind but wants Man to say it first.

She directs all her attention to him and wills him to say it, even nuzzling her head into his chest and clearing her throat a few times. *I love you*. They are both silent for a long time, listening to the soft sucking hiss of the surf.

Finally he says, "I wish you hadn't gone for a walk while I was sleeping." Lee sits up slightly so that she can look at him, but he has his eyes closed.

"Why on earth not?"

"We're in a strange town. I didn't know where you were. And you alone—it worries me. I don't like to think about other men seeing you."

"Other men *seeing* me?" He can't be serious. "So the entire time you were napping, I was just supposed to sit here waiting for you to wake up?"

Man opens his eyes and looks at her. "I guess when you put it that way, it sounds a bit ridiculous. I just...I need you, Lee." And then, more softly, he says, "Don't ever leave me." He pulls her down so that she is lying on his chest again, and strokes her hair.

The words are not what she wanted him to say. Still, there is something thrilling about them. The vulnerability. The power he is giving to her. She wants to reciprocate, to show him that she knows he's revealing something of himself, so she rests her head on his shoulder and says, "I won't."

If by staying with him she can always feel as happy as she has felt on this trip, then it will be an easy promise to keep. "Can we come back here every year?" she asks him.

"Nothing would make me happier."

Lee imagines it, a ritual they will create together, and thinks of how it will be in twenty years. His hair the silver that right now dusts his temples, the creases in his face more pronounced, his eyes deeper set. He'll have old man complaints, and Lee will be the type of woman who finds them endearing, who carries his tonics in her handbag. He will make her into that woman by loving her.

Man squeezes her closer and they lie in silence until Lee begins to overheat. It is stifling inside the shelter. She pulls away, sits up and adjusts her clothes, and ties open the doors again, staring out at the blurred line where the ocean meets the horizon, admiring the way the doorway frames the view.

SAINT-MALO

AUGUST 1944

The rumble and whine of the planes fill the air before Lee sees them nose-diving toward the citadel. In perfect unison, they straighten, and the engine growl is replaced by the hiss and scream of bombs. In an instant everything is chaos, the citadel exploding with fire. Lee gets a shot of a bomb dropping, and one of a soldier against the haze, his body a silhouette of flame. After the war she'll find out this was the Americans' first use of napalm—explaining not only why they censored her photos but also the way the fire seemed to stick like syrup to the soldiers' skin.

The attack doesn't last long. Ears ringing, Lee makes her way down the fort's steps and back toward headquarters, but the gunfire follows her, and when shots go off so close she can feel their reverberations, she ducks into an underground vault and cowers there, crouched down and clutching her camera against her chest. The vault stinks of war and decay; the walls are covered with what might be blood. When Lee takes a step forward, her heel lands on something fleshy, and she panics and heads back up to the street and begins to run. Her ears ring so loudly she can barely focus, so when someone shouts at her at first she doesn't realize she's being asked a question. She turns to find four GIs staring at her.

"Are you a ... dame?" one of them asks.

Lee is surprised he noticed. She knows what she looks like, so grimy she can flake the dirt off her skin with her fingernails. But these men are delighted to be near a bona fide female, and one from New York to boot. *Keep talking,* they beg her. *We miss the sound of our girls' voices.* More gunfire rings out and they take cover in what turns out to be a nearby wine cellar. Crates of wine bottles line the walls: sauternes, Languedoc, Riesling. When the gunfire stops, the soldiers take as much as they can carry, and back at the hotel later that night, during the blackout, Lee and the men drink it out of stolen crystal polished to a shine on dusty sheets.

"What's a girl from Poughkeepsie doing in a place like this?" one soldier slurs, pointing in Lee's direction so that liquid from the glass in his hand sloshes out on his pants. Razor burn and pimples cover his cheeks; his jacket has the single chevron of a private first class.

"Didn't think you should have all the fun," Lee responds. The other soldiers laugh. Lee keeps her eyes on the private. "You killed any Krauts yet?" she asks him.

"I was at Anzio."

"But did you kill any? Yourself."

The other men's conversation has moved on, so Lee scoots closer to him. He nods, not looking at her. "I shot one fella, a sniper. He killed my friend, sitting right next to me. So I shot him."

"What did it feel like?"

"Didn't feel like nothing." The boy's voice is thick with wine. "But I keep thinking about him. He had real blond hair, like white hair. I don't know why, but I keep thinking about how his momma must miss him."

The sick soup of hatred rises out of Lee's stomach. "His momma is a monster. They're all monsters. I wish I could've shot him."

The private gives her a curious look, and then from across the room another soldier tells Lee he wants to show her a picture of his girl back home, so she leaves the boy and goes over to him. In the photo, the girl wears a demure pearl necklace and has a trusting smile, and Lee hates her too, clean and coddled and safe at home in Indiana.

The bottle goes around and around, and they stay up all night, drinking and talking. As the morning sun makes a bright line on the seam of the blackout curtains, the other soldiers start to yawn. Some bed down in borrowed blankets or sleep sitting slumped against the wall. Lee pours herself another drink, stares for a while at her reflection, fish-eyed on the surface of the wineglass. Then she stands, and on unsteady feet she walks over to where the private with the razor burn has fallen asleep, his mouth open like a child's. Lee kicks gently at his leg with her boot until he wakes up, a confused smile on his face as if she's part of the dream he's having. "C'mere," Lee whispers, and he follows her down the hall to an empty hotel room. She pulls him inside and then pushes him so that he is sitting on the edge of the bed, where he looks up at her with surprise and expectation. He must be fifteen years her junior.

"Ma'am?" he says.

"Shh." Lee takes off his boots and then while she's undoing the laces of her own he shimmies out of his uniform and lies back naked on the bed, his skin so pale it's almost translucent. His chest is smooth and hairless. Lee wants to punch him. She crawls onto the mattress on her hands and knees and motions for him to move behind her, and when he is in the right position she reaches her hand around to help him slide inside her.

"Do it," she says, her voice in the quiet room like an angry stranger's. Adrenaline courses through her, and she conjures the image of the blond soldier this man has killed and lets the hate boil her blood. Lee doesn't know when she became this person, fueled by rage, but she loves how it feels not to hold back, to let her emotions judder out of her uncontrolled.

"Harder," she says.

The boy is happy to oblige, but it's over before it's hardly begun, and when he rolls away from her on the mattress and whispers that he's sorry, she can barely stand to look at him.

When Lee gets outside again a few hours later the sun is hot in the cloudless sky. With all that smoke from yesterday, it doesn't seem possible that it could be so bright. Around her the whole city is a crater, the buildings empty shells of rubble. Lee is empty too. She walks for miles to get back to her convoy. Nothing she passes seems to have been spared the bombs' destruction.

CHAPTER FOURTEEN

By now it is June again, and Lee realizes she's been in Paris for an entire year. The city is still fresh to her, but she has settled in, found her haunts, and begun to feel as if she belongs. On balmy days, she wanders through the Cimetière du Montparnasse, just a few blocks from her apartment, or spends an afternoon at the Bois de Vincennes, watching the rowboats and the swans float across the placid lake. She always brings her camera, and loves taking pictures of the carousel with its carved pigs, the fierce expressions on the children's faces as they wait to spear the iron rings. In the early evenings, she and Man take a sidewalk table at Le Select or La Coupole and nurse aperitifs, often so content they don't even feel the need to speak. One particular toy vendor Lee likes often stations himself in front of Le Select, and whenever he comes to their table Man buys her one of the toy dogs he is selling. Lee has a whole collection now that she keeps on top of her dresser.

She barely ever gets hit with the dark moods that were so frequent when she first arrived in Paris. When she thinks back to those early days in the city, the memories are tinged with loneliness: wandering the city with her arms crossed tight across her chest, sitting cross-legged on her bed with her sketchbook on her knees, catching the reflection of her wistful face in a store window. Moving here was harder than she thought it would be. But now, the memories feel as though they are from much more than a year ago, and the girl she was then is distant and unfamiliar.

Some evenings—more now that there are so many stories about money and its lack, so much more anxiety—Man has been going out with his circle. To Drosso's, where they try to ingratiate themselves to their host in the hope that Drosso will buy their work. To Tristan's opulent apartment, paid for with a family fortune that is never mentioned. Sometimes to Le Dôme, where Man mutters darkly about the prices and the atmosphere.

Lee tried to go to Tristan's with him once, but it was a disaster. She was the only woman in the room, and her presence set the men off-kilter. Even Man was different—brash and boastful. The talk revolved around sex: fellatio techniques, homoerotic desire, the depiction of penetration in Surrealist art. Everyone kept looking to Lee as if for her opinion, referring to her as Madame Man Ray, but she wasn't sure how she was supposed to act. At first, she went along with the conversation, laughing gamely. She has always been adept at double entendres and loves the visual ones Man creates in his work—his photo of an eggbeater that looks like genitalia, or the close-up he shot of the peach—but when she tried a bawdy joke with the group, Man cast a disapproving look at her that made her unsure what he wanted from her. She wondered if she was supposed to act shocked, if having a woman there as a foil to the conversation freed up the men to not act shocked themselves. By midnight, with everyone tittering like schoolgirls and sloppily drunk, Lee decided she was ready to go home.

So now on most of the nights when Man goes out with his crowd, she stays in, or goes back to the studio to get in a few more hours of work. That is part of the beauty of the darkroom for her. Completely sealed off from the rest of the world, time loses meaning there, measured only by the metronome as she guides her prints from developer to stop bath to fix. The transition from the amber-lit darkroom out into the city at night is an easy one, and often she goes home and straight to bed, diving deep into a dreamless sleep from which even Man, returning late, cannot rouse her. Other times she is antsy, filled with energy, and on those nights she pulls her hat down low and walks the blocks around her apartment until she wears herself out. The sun doesn't set now until almost ten o'clock, and after it does the sky retains its echo, bluing the clouds and obscuring the stars for hours. On the nights it rains, steam rises from the pavement and curls around Lee's ankles as she walks.

Man has put off writing his essay for *221,* but now the deadline is looming, and with every passing day, his anxiety grows. It turns out that as a writer Man is insufferable. In his office he sweeps aside papers and pounds on his big Remington in noisy bursts. Sometimes he poises his fingers over the keys for five or ten minutes, and then types furiously for a while, only to later rip the paper off the platen and toss it on the floor. Lee's work is relegated to a small side table, where her concentration is interrupted by his sighs and constant questions.

"How about this?" he says, and reads out loud. " 'The mode of the artist is one of perception. In perceiving, in replicating, reality, the artist comes to create automata of his experiences, that are simultaneously new modes of reality as seen through the eyes of the artist, and also ultimately inferior simulacra of lived experience.' "

"Hmm," says Lee, putting down her pencil. "What are you *actually* trying to say?"

He groans, stands up, and crushes the paper into a ball. "I'm trying to say that when I look at a picture of you, I want to feel exactly as good as I felt when I was taking the picture. Photography can capture reality, but how does it capture emotion? Isn't the emotion what makes reality real?"

"So why don't you say that?"

"I *am* saying that! Or at least I'm trying to."

"Sometimes a direct approach works better," Lee says, and goes back to her correspondence.

One night when Man is out with friends, Lee goes alone to the little gallery on Boulevard Raspail to see Claude's pictures. The show is called *Masks* and every photographer has interpreted the word differently. Claude has three photos in the show, and in each she is dressed in a different costume: the weight lifter outfit from the show's postcard, a swimmer with spit-curled hair, a matron in a Parliamentary wig and burlap dress. The work is good. Arresting, even. Lee walks up and down the narrow cramped hallway a few times—Claude was right: the gallery is less a room and more a passageway between two buildings—and takes it all in, her body aching with envy as she looks at all the pictures.

When Lee leaves she decides she is hungry, that she will plug the ache she feels with food. A small bistro down the street has a seat at its marble-topped bar; Lee orders a thick slab of pâté studded with pistachios that comes with a little pot of mustard, and washes it down with white wine. The meal is delicious but leaves her feeling bloated and tired. Instead of going home she goes back to the darkroom, where she prints from the same negative a dozen times, each attempt marred by something different: one is underexposed, the next has a hair on the surface, another a dark patch in the corner. Each time it comes out wrong, Lee growls with frustration and sets up the negative to print again.

It takes Man right up to and past the deadline to finish his essay. That night he stays at the studio until 3 a.m., and though Lee has gone home she imagines him in the office, drinking and running his hands through his hair until it stands up like a feather duster.

As he is quietly slipping off his clothes so as not to wake her, she murmurs sleepily, "Did you finish?"

"Yes. It's done. I called it 'The Light of Our Time.'"

"'The Age of Light,'" she says. "That would be better."

"That's good," he says admiringly. "You're good at this."

"I'm good at lots of things."

"You certainly are," Man says, and lies down next to her. Lee snuggles up against him until she has fit her body completely against his.

The idea comes to Lee one afternoon while she is walking. A woman, not Lee herself, kneeling behind a desk. On the desk's surface a bell jar, with the woman's head lined up so that it appears to be floating inside the glass. Lee likes the idea so much she makes sketches of it, and soon she has filled an entire notebook with ideas. Until she composes it through a camera's eye, though, she can't be sure it will work, so she tries it out in the studio without a model. It is then that she begins to understand the allure of an Amélie, an interchangeable person she can bring in to pose for her. For some reason, she doesn't want to tell Man about her project, wants it to belong just to her. So she puts up a note at the art school where he has advertised before and a few days later gets a response.

Lee makes the model come to the studio at seven in the morning, long before Man arrives. The light is good, the model compliant and pretty, though seemingly surprised to find another woman behind the camera. Lee feels herself grow decisive and directorial. It takes only an hour to get the shots she wants.

CHAPTER FIFTEEN

The dress is borrowed. Somehow Man has finagled it. Acid-green moiré, with an intricate bodice of pieced silk shaped like overlapping leaves. A smart row of buttons marching down the front to a trim waist, higher and tighter than the styles have been lately. The gown sweeps the ground and falls into a short train, and it fits Lee as if it was made for her. When she puts it on Man cannot stop staring, and now that they have arrived at the House of Patou she feels the eyes of everyone else on her as well, men and women both. Someone once said to her that dressing up is done mainly for other women, and as her eye is drawn around the room to where the women stand out like hummingbirds against the background of men, casting side-long glances at one another, Lee believes it to be true.

"Impressive, isn't it?" Man mutters to her. He takes her elbow and guides her through the lavish room. He has done a lot of work for Jean Patou over the years and has said before that he does it just for the parties. "You'd think they could pay me a little better. Let's drink our weight in champagne to make up for it."

It doesn't seem as if that will be a challenge. Dozens of waiters circle the room, their trays laden with champagne flutes, and at her first opportunity Lee takes one and moves off to an alcove, thinking how pretty she must look framed against the windows.

This is actually more her type of crowd than Man's. He is a bit awkward in his tuxedo, and she wants to tell him to stop pulling at his bow tie. If she were in New York she would know lots of people, but there is something nice about knowing no one. Across the room Lee notices two extremely handsome men, so similar they must be brothers. She tries to look at them without being obvious, but they are scanning the room as well and she realizes that they seem to be heading right toward her. They wear their suits as though they were born in them. She admires the way their narrow tuxedo pants break over their shiny shoes.

Lee searches her mind for a quip to respond with when they compliment her—it is clearer than ever that they are coming over expressly to talk to her—but before she has thought of something to say they are in front of her.

"Man! We have missed you!" one of them says, speaking English with a thick but very polished Russian accent.

They barely glance at Lee. Man tugs at his shirt collar. The other one—they are so alike they could almost be twins—says, "We are meeting at Dmitri's house next Thursday. You will be there?"

When he asks the question, the man reaches out and helps Man adjust his crooked bow tie. Then he runs his fingers up Man's cheek. The movement takes only a moment, and it would have been easy for Lee to miss it. But she doesn't. The gesture is careless, intimate, like accidentally using a lover's pet name in front of strangers, and something in it makes her wonder.

Man looks visibly uncomfortable, and tells them maybe he will come. For what seems to be the first time, the brothers glance over at her. They say a few more things to Man, none of which makes much sense to her, and then they excuse themselves.

"So nice of you to introduce me," Lee says after they go.

Man gives her a look. "Alexis and Deni Mdivani. I assumed you knew them—or knew of them."

"I don't."

He relates a convoluted story about a prank the brothers played at a recent party, where they changed into dungarees halfway through dinner and insisted they had to leave early to get to their jobs at the factory.

"They work at a factory?"

Man huffs air through his nose. "They're related to a czar or someone. They just did it to be funny."

"Sounds hilarious."

Lee's mood has soured and it is clear Man's has too. They both finish their champagne and reach for more.

"What were they inviting you to?" she finally asks.

Lee can tell he doesn't want to answer her, but she stares at him, silent, patient, until he is forced to respond. "Paul and Tristan— they both come from money; you know that—so they travel in the same circles as the Mdivanis. We get together once a month or so and discuss art."

"You discuss art."

"Yes," Man says, but as he says it he tugs again at his collar. The room is hot. He is sweating. She cannot understand what he could possibly be lying about, or why.

It is late by the time they get back to Lee's apartment, where she has insisted they stay because of how complicated it is to take off and store her dress. Man fumbles with the covered buttons. She raises her arms and he helps her shimmy out of it. As he pulls the stiff silk over her head, Lee realizes just how drunk she is, champagne sloppy, and before she goes to brush her teeth she sits on the floor for a few minutes, hiccuping at her reflection in the mirror and listening to Man stumble around in the other room. The sour mood still lingers, and for the first time that she can remember, when they get into bed they pull the covers up to their chins and keep a wide distance between their bodies, even though Lee has to brace herself so as not to roll toward the middle of the mattress.

Finally she says, "You made me sad tonight." Man moves to hold her, but she puts out her arm and pushes him away. "What happened? Why wouldn't you tell me…whatever it was you wouldn't tell me?"

A car pulls up outside. There's the sounds of people laughing, the car door slamming. Farther away there is a sharp insistent bleat of a siren.

"Have you ever…" Man's voice is pitched high and hesitant. "Do you like…"

She waits for him to finish.

"Sometimes I like…to be tied up."

The room is too dark for her to see his expression. Part of her wants to laugh, she feels so on edge. But she can hear in his voice how much he has been wanting to say this.

Lee is so drunk she can barely feel the outlines of her body. Man waits for her to answer. She can hear him breathing; she finds she wants to make him wait. From another floor there is the creak of someone pacing.

She waits until she knows he is about to say something, to apologize or explain, before she gets up. The floor is cold on her bare feet. She stumbles. On her chair is her striped scarf and she feels for another in her armoire.

Lee kneels next to him. "Will these work?"

Her bed has a low brass frame that squeaks when they make love. She holds his wrist between her thumb and index finger and feels their pulses racing.

With Man's wrist in her hand she thinks again of the two brothers, the way the one reached out and touched his cheek.

"Have you *been* with them, those brothers?" Lee cinches his wrist tight to the headboard.

"Yes," he says.

"How many times?"

"Not that many. Not once since I've been with you."

Lee is not surprised at Man's answer. She doesn't know why. It is as if she knew the minute the man touched him at the party. If it were women she would be furious, but there is something about the image of these men together that arouses her: one brother or both, Man tied, submissive. The power in it.

She cinches his other wrist.

"Did you like being with them?"

His voice is so low she can barely hear it. "Yes, but—"

Lee cuts him off. "I don't care what you did with them. Just don't do it now that you're with me."

Man still has the covers over him. Lee stands and pulls them off, leaving him exposed. His body and face are in shadow, the whites of his eyes bright spots in the moonlit room. Lee stands looking down at him, waiting for her breath to come more slowly. Then she kneels and takes the length of his penis, already erect, in her mouth, following the motion with her hand. She does it only a few times, then stops and stands up again so she can look down at him. Teasing him, making him wait. His eyes don't leave her. She puts her hand between her legs and touches herself, loves having him watch her while she does it.

"Lee, please . . ." Man says after a while, his voice small.

She waits to bend down to him again until she cannot make herself wait any longer.

Later, afterward, what surprises her most of all is how much she likes it. How good it feels to be in control.

PARIS

DECEMBER 1944

The bennies make Lee's teeth ache but they also help her get the writing done. Dave has nicked some more for her from the other soldiers and now she's got a cache of them that will see her through her article. She takes one as soon as she gets out of bed. Cracks open the inhaler and eases the paper strip from inside, rolls it into a pill, and downs it with hot water because no one has any coffee left. Then she sits at her makeshift desk, puts her fingers on the typewriter keys, strokes their curved edges. Soon her veins will start singing and the words will come, the words she sees behind her eyelids when she lies in bed at night, too agitated to sleep but too drunk to get up and start working. Outside her hotel window is her stash of jerry cans, some filled with framboise, others with gin, all within arm's reach and very tempting. She has to get the draft done first.

Her most recent photos sit on her desk. On top is the shot of surgeons gathered around an amputee, holding him like some sort of gruesome Pietà. When Lee took that picture she wasn't able to hide her revulsion, and she was glad the soldier was unconscious so he couldn't see her face. Looking at it again wakes her up even hotter than the bennies and she types a few lines as quickly as she can. But then she reads them over, black marks on the page that are nothing like what she sees in her mind. The words are not right. Nothing is right. Her photos are shit and the article is going to be shit and she's a disappointment to Audrey and everyone who has ever put their faith in her. Was she really naive enough to think she could become a writer? The anxiety starts in the pit of her stomach and rises into her throat like a trapped bird, fluttering and frantic. Lee slams the lid of her typewriter case shut and pounds on the wall for Davie. He is there in an instant and she knows he can tell just by looking at her that she's too wound up, but he doesn't say anything, just comes over to her and rubs her neck and shoulders until her heart stops racing.

When he has calmed her down, he picks up the stack of photos from her desk and flops on the bed.

"This one," he says, holding up a shot she took in Paris right after the surrender, a picture of a woman modeling a Bruyère coat in the Place Vendôme, framed through the shards of a shattered shop window. "Jesus, that's a good one. The way you foregrounded the bullet holes."

"You really think so?"

"I know so."

His praise brings the words back into focus. Lee turns around and pounds out a paragraph, only stopping once to worry that it doesn't sound right. When she is done, she pulls the paper off the platen and hands it to him. He reads it slowly, but this time Lee doesn't need him to tell her it is good. She already knows. While he's reading, she eases the window open and grabs a jerry can, fills up two glasses to their brims. It's not even noon, but lately she's turned everything into an opportunity for celebration.

CHAPTER SIXTEEN

One hot July night a month or so after the Patou party, when Man is out again, Lee stays late in the studio. She has been working on her bell jar images. There is a small series of them now, and she is very pleased with them. Their framing makes the model's head appear to float inside the jar, trapped like a specimen under the glass even though she was kneeling behind it. In a few shots the woman has a dreamy expression; in others she has her eyes closed and her head tilted to one side. In all of them, there is a sense of claustrophobia that feels both provocative and familiar. Lee has started to understand her work in this way: she is consciously evoking a feeling rather than just lucking into a successful image.

Lee decides that if she can get the series done tonight, she is going to show it to Man. It is her best work so far, and she has been waiting until she has all the images printed. Perhaps four of them could be mounted in a frame, or there could be a triptych of them in *221*. They work best in a grouping, as if they themselves are a collection of specimens. Maybe, if she ever has a show, the pictures can be pinned to the wall rather than framed, or they can be displayed *inside* bell jars. That might be the most provocative of all.

Lee moves through the darkroom easily now. It is almost a second home.

When Lee is done printing, she goes back into the developing room. There is one roll of film left from the bell jar sessions, and she is curious to see what it contains. She lines up her tools as she's been taught and turns off the light. It is still a shock to be plunged into darkness. She has her hands on the film and the church key. She peels open the canister and is getting ready to start dipping the film in the developer when she feels a skitter-scratching run across her shoe and dart up her leg. Lee lets out a shriek, drops the film, shakes her leg frantically, and, in her panic, reaches up and pulls the cord to turn on the ceiling light.

The first thing Lee notices in the sudden brightness is the tail of the mouse as it runs under the table. The next thing she notices is her film, curled in a heap on the table and almost certainly ruined. Quickly she turns off the light. What to do? The chances of the film being salvageable are minimal. But she loves the photos so much—they are the final roll of her bell jar session, the one she thought might be the best of all.

Out of indecision more than anything else, she goes through the motions of developing the film. When the images are finally in the fix, she sees that they aren't entirely black, as she would have imagined them to be; they are murky, low contrast, fuzzy compared with the others from the session. She feels a crushing sense of disappointment that she knows is related as much to Man and her growing need to impress him as it is to the loss of her work. Hanging from the clothesline to dry, the negatives are like a sad little ribbon of failure, and she goes home immediately, not even wanting to print the other work she has planned to complete. When Man returns, she pretends to be asleep.

The next morning when Lee comes into the studio, she takes

down the negatives to inspect them under the loupe. They're altered, certainly, but when she sees them magnified, she notices that they seem almost reversed, as if the light and dark crystals on the film have switched places. Intrigued, she chooses one and prints it. As the image appears in the developing tray, she draws in a sharp breath. She was correct—there has been some sort of reversal, and all around the image, where the light and dark areas of the composition meet, there is a fine black line, as if someone has traced it with a soft pencil. The image itself is extremely low contrast, which is unfortunate, but paired with the ghostly effect of the black outline, it is like nothing she has ever seen.

Rushing, Lee prints another few images from the series. In each the effect is subtly different—perhaps, she thinks, because of where that particular frame was positioned when the light came on—but they all have the black outline and the same ethereal quality. By the time Man arrives, she has printed several more and cannot wait to show him.

He comes over and kisses her, but she has no time for kisses.

"Look." Lee shows him the prints and explains what happened in the developing room. He takes one of them, still dripping wet, out into the light so he can see it better.

"Very curious," he says. His finger hovers just above the surface of the print and traces the outline along the bell jar. "So you mean to tell me that you turned on the light—the overhead light—in the developing room, and this is what you got? That really doesn't seem possible."

"I know. I thought I had completely ruined them, but for some reason I developed them anyway, and here we are."

"Lucky mistake," he murmurs, and Lee clenches her teeth in annoyance. He looks at all the other prints, holding up one image and saying, "You know, we could experiment with this. See what would happen if we exposed it to light for longer or shorter times. How long do you think the light was on?"

"Maybe ten seconds?"

"We could try five, twenty—and we could lay the film out on the table purposefully so that the exposure is uniform." He is moving from print to print as he talks.

"I was thinking that if we underexposed the film to begin with maybe it wouldn't be so murky."

"Ah, yes—we should try that!" His face fills with excitement. "All we need are some terrible pictures we can experiment with." She follows him as he leaves the darkroom. He grabs both of their cameras from the office and throws his coat back on, and then fills his camera bag with extra film.

Outside, Lee poses on bridges, makes funny faces, takes pictures of Man doing the same. Since the goal is to use up the film, they take pictures of pedestrians, shadows, signposts, trash cans, antique store windows. Soon it devolves into a game to see who can do the oddest pose in a shot with a stranger, so Lee goes and sits behind someone at a café, puts a napkin on her head like a babushka, and stares at the camera with a look of surprise. Man leans on the back of a car that someone has just parked; Lee takes a picture of him sticking out his tongue while the driver, not noticing him, opens the car door. For each roll, they experiment with under- and overexposing, making careful notes about which roll is treated which way. After less than an hour they've used all the film, and they head back to develop it.

In the studio, they are methodical. There are twelve rolls of film; they make a chart and hang it on the wall, marking out how long they will expose each roll to light and if it was underexposed to begin with. Only one roll of film can be in the developing bath at a time, so they work as a team: Man does the exposures and dips them in the developer; Lee agitates them in the stop and fix and hangs them up to dry. When they speak, they speak only about the work.

"This one is twelve seconds."

"I think we should mark them with tape once they dry so we don't get confused, and then we can match that to the chart."

When she and Man make eye contact, she can tell he feels it too: a sense that they are doing something momentous. To be able to manipulate the negative itself, its chemical properties, the very nature of it, rather than to alter it manually by scratching or cutting—it feels as if they are creating a new medium altogether. She hopes so much that it works, that it wasn't some weird fluke when she did it the first time.

Without acknowledgment, it seems that they have both decided to wait to look at the images until they develop all the film. Lee hangs them up and marks them with tape without even holding them up to the safelight. Finally, after several hours, all twelve strips hang together on the drying line, and Man rubs her back as they stand there looking at the film.

The three little words come unbidden out of the ache she feels in her stomach. "I love you," she says.

Man puts his arm around her shoulders and pulls her tight. "I love you too," he whispers.

It is the first time they've said the words to each other, and it should be huge, but it just feels of a piece with the work they are doing together. Lee hugs him back quickly and then moves away, grabbing one of the still-damp negative strips and taking it out into the main room. Immediately, it is obvious that they've re-created the effect that Lee produced accidentally. Lampposts glow white, outlined against white streets. Man's hair against the parked car is traced with a black edge. Lee's eyes are shockingly dark against her ghostly skin. She feels as if she is looking at pictures from another planet. Together, she and Man choose twelve images, one from each roll, and print them, moving around each other in the darkroom as smoothly as dancers.

When the prints are laid out side by side, it's clear that there's a pattern—that their experiments with underexposure have created subtle variations in the effect. They talk about the images for a long time, appraising them. Which effect works best with which image, what they would tweak if they did it again. They both scrawl copious notes, and after a while, Lee puts down her pencil and stretches, rubbing at her neck where tension sends threads of pain into her shoulders.

"Are you hungry?" Man asks her, moving her hands aside and placing his own on her neck to dig into her muscles.

She rolls her head back and closes her eyes. "Mm. Starving. But I don't really want to stop."

"It will be here later," he says, and they grab their coats and walk to Le Dôme, where Man orders a dozen oysters and champagne. Lee is almost too worked up to eat, but the first oyster hits the back of her throat like a gulp of the sea and suddenly she is famished. Brine and lemon, the delicate fizz of the champagne when she swallows, Man's hand on her leg, the hum and clatter of the restaurant around them, everything amplified, larger and better than it was before.

"Can you work after we drink this?" she asks, gesturing to the bottle.

"No—but let's be done for the day. It will be there tomorrow."

So they drink the bottle and order another. Around them the crowd ebbs and flows, new faces replacing old. They see people they know and ignore them. The longer they sit there, the less Lee hears the noises and clatter, as if a thin shell separates them from everyone else. They see no one and no one sees them.

When they get home, electrified, tingling from liquor, they hurry to bed. Man starts at her feet and begins kissing her, delicate kisses all along her body. When he gets to her mouth, he lingers, and then he stops and reaches for the nightstand and gets out one of the scarves they have been using. Lee lifts her arm to let him tie it. But he shakes his head no and folds the fabric on itself to make a blindfold, then moves to put it on her.

She pushes her hand against his chest to stop him. All of a sudden her heart is racing, she is sweating, she cannot breathe.

Man freezes. "What's wrong?"

Lee cannot speak. The blindfold has terrified her. She swings her legs over the side of the bed and sits with her arms crossed over her stomach. Man runs a gentle hand across her back. Her heartbeat thumps in her neck, and she tries to take a deep breath to calm herself down, but she can only manage little sips of air. Man gets up and brings her a glass of water. She drinks it down. He waits for her to speak.

Lee holds the empty glass in her lap, and closes her eyes. Fragments of memory come, unbidden and unwanted. Uncle—Lee never allows herself to think his name, but the outlines of the word catch in her mind like a burr. She was seven, staying at a family friend's house in New York City. Everyone else had gone out ice skating, but Lee had had a fever, and even though she was feeling better, he was called to mind her while they were gone. He gave her a giant stick of horehound candy and watched Lee while she ate it, the flavor not so dissimilar from the medicine she had been given before he arrived. He took her into the parlor and asked her if she wanted to play sardines. "But there are only two of us," she remembers saying. "That's all right. We'll hide together." He found a scarf, tied it tight over her eyes, spun her in a circle. She heard his footsteps receding as he went to find a place to hide. Lee remembers counting, remembers taking a first step, stroking blindly at the air in front of her; remembers how worried she was she'd break something in the pretty, cluttered parlor. After a count of twenty, Lee found him in the butler's pantry, and he caught her around the waist and settled her on his knee. The rest is a blur, flashes of sensation Lee does not want to let herself recall: the wet sound of his breath in her ear, a cloying bittersweet scent in the air, the pressure of his huge hot body between her thighs.

Lee never talks about the memory, and is usually adept at pushing it away. But tonight the images keep coming. She can tell Man wants her to say something, to explain what is going on. He wants to know how to comfort her, but she can't bring herself to speak. Finally her racing pulse slows, and Lee is able to pull more air into her lungs. She says, "I can't—I just don't want you to do that. To cover my eyes."

"My God, of course." He grabs her robe, puts it around her shoulders, then rubs her back through the soft fabric. He has a fine line of worry between his eyes and a look of concern on his face, but he doesn't push her to say anything else.

She takes a few breaths. "Could you make me a cup of tea?"

Man goes into the kitchen and she follows, needing to stay near him. When the kettle whistles she startles again. He hands her a mug and she wraps her hands around it, the heat a thing to focus on, a small comfort. For a long time they sit in silence, and Lee is grateful for it.

In the familiar gloom of the kitchen, Lee bends her head to the teacup and smells the flowery scent of bergamot. As soon as she does, she regrets it. Another flood of images. Lee in the bathroom with her mother. After the rape, once a month for several years her mother had to swab Lee down there with iodine and picric acid—that was what her mother called it, *down there,* her lips compressed in a tight line as she administered the gonorrhea inoculations. The acid in the bottle a urine yellow with a bitter scent so strong it made Lee's eyes water. Her mother on her hands and knees in the bathroom afterward, bleaching any part of the room Lee had touched. Her expression as she did so—a revulsion at the chore that Lee knew extended to a revulsion for her daughter. Thank God for her father—how when he held her afterward the cedar scent of his soap overpowered the bitter smell, how he stroked and stroked her hair until she calmed down.

The teacup has gone cold in her hands before Lee is ready to go back to bed. They do that quietly too, and she pulls Man near and lets him hold her until she falls asleep.

The next morning, Lee watches the sun cast changing shadows on the ceiling. Man sleeps next to her, his hands tucked up under his pillow. She eases herself out of bed, trying not to wake him, and when she is sitting up she notices the scarf lying on the floor, still folded over into the blindfold. Again her heart starts racing. She kicks the scarf under the bed, and then wills herself to think of something different. But no matter what she thinks of, she keeps coming back to last night, her sudden panic. In the bathroom she splashes cold water on her face and looks at herself in the mirror, her hair snarled from sleep, dark hateful smudges under her eyes. There is a low-level electric buzz in her head, and when Man gets up soon after, she waits for him to ask her about last night, about what happened. She is glad when he doesn't.

They spend the day at the studio working on prints from a fashion shoot Man was hired to do for *McCall's*. Their time spent experimenting yesterday has left them behind schedule, and Lee is glad of the urgency of the deadline, the banality of the assignment. Glad too for Man's gestures of affection, his hand placed lightly on her shoulder as he moves around her in the room. By the end of the day she realizes it's been several hours since she thought about what happened the night before, and though she's not sure if Man is trying to give her space or feels too awkward to talk about it, all she feels is relief at his continued silence.

★ ★ ★

A few days pass, and they neither make love nor discuss what transpired between them. Lee feels her shame about her panicked reaction receding, and she knows that if she lets herself, she'll be able to pretend it didn't happen. That soon, in another day or two, she'll be able to have sex with Man again as if nothing is different. It would be so easy to push the thoughts back down from where they came. To close herself off as she is so good at doing. She wonders if he will let her. But another piece of her knows that if she does not tell him—if she keeps him at the same distance she's always kept everyone—their relationship will never deepen past where it is now. They will never truly know each other. It is how she acted with every other lover she has had, only letting them in a certain amount, then pushing them away or leaving them entirely. She doesn't want that. So far she has been able to be different with Man, and she wills herself to keep it up, to create something better and more lasting than what she's had before.

Three nights later, they lie nose to nose in bed, the room lit only by the little stained-glass lamp Man bought for her nightstand, and Lee looks at him—the familiar contours of his face, his long eyelashes—and closes her eyes and knows that every piece of him exists in her memory as detailed as in reality. She clears her throat, but at first she cannot get the words out. The air grows charged between them. Man takes her hand and pulls it to his chest, pressing it there, warm against his skin.

Finally she whispers, "When I was little, a bad thing happened to me. I've never told anyone about it."

"Tell me." His voice is calm. He gives her time. Sweat prickles in her armpits. She can feel her heart erratically thumping. Finally she continues.

"I went to stay with friends of the family because my mother was very sick. They lived in New York City. The man, we called him Uncle—" She almost says his name but cannot. "I was left alone with him one day. My parents came to get me. I was seven." She relates the story as it always comes back to her, disjointed and fragmentary, and by the time she is done she is exhausted.

"My God, Lee. I'm so sorry." Man squeezes her hand gently.

Lee tries to get her breath. Man waits. "After, my parents took me to an analyst for many years and it was very helpful. The analyst helped me realize that what happened—it had nothing to do with me. I should put the memory in a little box and throw away the key. It worked, but sometimes...the memories come back."

"Of course they do."

"He also told me that what had happened was just my body, and had nothing to do with my...well, he called it my soul. He said when I got older, I would find someone who loved me, and it would be entirely different."

Lee's mouth feels numb, and she hears the words as if they are coming from someone else. The room is very dim and she is glad she cannot see Man's expression.

"This *is* entirely different," Man says.

"I know."

"I am so sorry that happened to you. So, so sorry." He moves his arm around her waist and she rolls over so that he is holding her. The feeling of his body is pure animal comfort. Lee feels herself relax a bit, feels her heartbeat slow.

"I love you so much," he tells her.

"I love you too."

"Has this been hard for you?" Man asks. "Us together? The things I've wanted you to do?"

"I don't think so," Lee says. She is confused. "But—the blindfold. It scared me."

"I'm so sorry. We don't have to do that. Of course we don't have to."

"I think part of what scared me is I want you to."

He wraps his legs and arms around her even tighter and she lets the warmth of his skin sink into her. Very gently, he runs his hand through her hair and kisses her cheek and neck. They lie like that for a long time, and finally she says, "I think I want you to do it."

"Are you sure?" He sounds as nervous as she is.

"Yes, I think so."

He gets up to grab the scarf, and then stops. "No," he says. "Maybe someday, if you really want me to, but not now."

Lee watches him. He pulls her against him again, and they stay that way for a while, and then Lee finds his lips with hers. She feels hollowed out and hungry, as if she has made room inside herself by telling him. He is gentle with her still, his kisses tentative, but suddenly she wants him closer to her, and she pushes her mouth harder against his and presses the full length of her body to him. When Man moves on top of her, she closes her eyes and puts her arm over them, imagining what the darkness of the blindfold would feel like. With her eyes gone black, all that is left is touch: Man's thumbs against her nipples, his thigh between her legs. Behind her eyelids beautiful bright flashes explode. And then as Man starts to move inside her, he is all she thinks about—she could not make her mind think of anything else if she tried. She is alone with him in the darkness she has made and when he calls her name she feels herself dissolving, into sparks, into film grains, and by the time they are done she does not know where she ends and he begins.

It becomes even more than it was before. He cannot get enough of her. In the mornings, he takes her picture as she stretches like a cat getting out of bed. At the studio, he puts her next to the window, he bends her down against the wall. Instead of using the studio camera, he puts a small one around his neck and gets close to her. He runs his hand through her short hair and pulls her head back, takes close-up, blurry pictures of her neck. In the images her skin doesn't even look like skin but like a river, the muscles turned to water rushing over stones. He runs his fingers over her breasts and takes pictures of the goose bumps he raises on her skin. He cannot get close enough, takes dozens of pictures of just her lips, just her ear, just her eye.

In the darkroom they perfect the technique that she discovered, figuring out the right amount of time required to re-create the haunting, double-exposed effect. And when they try it out on pictures of her, when she sees what they have made together—her torso glowing like a ghost, manipulated into someone she almost doesn't recognize—what Lee feels is heat and pride and love, all at the same time.

Solarization, they decide to call it. It feels like that to her, dazzling, as if they have untethered her body and brought it closer to the sun.

After a few weeks of experiments, they make one print they both agree is perfect. It's simple, just a shot of her face in profile. She is set against a gray background, and the solarization gives her face a nimbus of black. She looks like an etching, set out of time. She looks more beautiful than she has ever looked before. Man takes a pen and writes along the print's white border "Man Ray/Lee Miller 1930," then puts his signature below and hands her the pen. Lee scrawls her own signature with shaking hands. There is nothing better than seeing their names together on the page.

A few weeks later Lee finishes her bell jar series, a triptych the way she has imagined. The first image shows the model with her eyes open, staring out and past the viewer. In the second her eyes are closed and her head is tipped slightly to the side, appearing to rest against the glass. The third image is solarized and has a submerged, underwater quality to it. The pictures feel very personal. As if they are telling a story or revealing something she hasn't been able to say.

Shyly, Lee shows them to Man. In her heart she knows they are good but while he looks at them she is stricken with panic. She has no eye; she is a fraud. He spends a long time looking, and she tries to remember that this is what he always does.

Finally Lee can't take it anymore. "I'm not sure about the print quality—maybe the first one should be darker to balance out the last? Or maybe I should only use two images instead of three? The first and the last, maybe? Or the second and the last...?"

Finally Man says, "These are incredible. The three of them together—they're what we should print in *221*. I'll talk to Tristan."

That night, elated, Lee goes to Bricktop to hear the music. She goes alone and chooses a table in the back. Josephine Baker is singing. Her voice is gravelly, the song slow and sentimental. "Blue days, all of them gone / Nothin' but blue skies from now on."

Lee closes her eyes and rests her head on the wall. The song feels exactly right.

PART TWO

CHAPTER SEVENTEEN

PARIS
1930

At the end of August, on a suffocatingly hot day, Lee stands at the threshold of her apartment for the last time. She has already sent her boxes to Man's, has sold what little furniture did not come with her rooms. She looks around the space, emptied of her possessions, and hopes she is making the right decision.

There are a thousand reasons to move in with Man. Money has become a worry in the past few months—things are still relatively inexpensive in Paris, but more stories roll in about the crash from family and friends back home, and some of their acquaintances who have been living in France for years are heading back to the States. Man has fewer portrait bookings, and the magazines are cutting back as well, printing issues with smaller spreads. Man seems unconcerned, but he agrees it will be nice to pay less rent instead of skimping on other things. They are both terrible at skimping; Lee has gotten used to helping Man spend his money, and when he wants to spend it on her, she has a hard time saying no.

They haven't spent a night apart in months, and before they even talked about living together, more and more of Lee's possessions had migrated to his apartment. But now, gazing around her bare rooms, she feels a little worried. As Tanja so rightly pointed out when she visited, Lee and Man work together, they socialize together, and now she won't even have a space to call her own. Their worlds are completely joined. What will happen when she needs to be alone? What will happen when she is irritable or sad and has no choice but to be those things in front of Man? Lee pictures herself doing what she did when she first got to Paris—whiling away the hours at empty cafés—but now she will be going out to find some space for herself, and not because she's hungry for human interaction.

For Man, living together is a simple proposition. One of their beds sits empty every night—it is a waste. And he loves her. He loves being with her and hates when they are apart. What good does it do to keep two apartments?

They have been living together for several weeks when, over dinner, Lee asks him, "Did you live with Kiki?"

He takes a bite of salad, chews, and swallows before he responds. "Yes, for a few years. You should have seen it. This little place off Rue Didot. It was my studio too. I rigged up a curtain I could pull around the bed when people came for their portrait. It's a miracle anyone ever took me seriously."

"How long had you been together when she moved in?"

Man takes his napkin off his lap and dabs his mouth with it. "She moved in with me right away, but you have to understand: Kiki had no money. None. She just stayed with one man after the next, so after we got together, it made sense. I haven't thought of that place in a long time. You had to walk up four flights of stairs, and it was stifling—even hotter than tonight. No air. I could never go back to living like that."

"Kiki just traveled around from man to man?" Lee frowns with distaste.

"Lee, this was twenty-one, twenty-two. Paris was wilder back then."

Lee sighs. "I get so tired of stories about how wild Paris used to be."

"Well, they're true."

"And where did you live with Adon? What was it like?"

"Small. Cramped. Four rooms in a square, with a tiny garret where I used to work. We had a lovely view, though. When it was clear, you could see all the way beyond the Hackensack to Paterson. And Adon put flower boxes in the windows."

The flower boxes sound lovely, domestic in a way that Lee isn't and that she can't imagine Man wanting. They seem wholly out of character for him, and make real for Lee as nothing else has that Man had an entire life before her that she barely knows anything about. The closest the two of them have come to flower boxes is a rose he gave her once, which she left in a vase in the office until it died, the overblown petals dropping in a brown heap on the desk.

She must look worried because Man says, "Another lifetime," and reaches for her hand across the table.

At their newly shared apartment, Man is painting a picture of her mouth. He hangs the canvas above their bed and paints her lips red, the color of the lipstick Lee wears almost every day. It comes in a cold gold tube with an etched cap that pulls off with a pop, and the lipstick twirls up almost obscenely from the case, moisture beading on its surface in the humid summer weather. When Lee puts it on it has a matte finish that looks nice, but it's a nightmare to remove. Dozens of cotton balls in the waste bin, cold cream stained bloody, a stubborn red filigree veining the surface of her mouth.

Man mixes a red paint to match it, a blend of cadmium scarlet and Winsor rose. Pots and pots of it. His canvas is huge—eight feet wide—and on it, her mouth floats disembodied and elongated in a mackerel sky.

Man says she has the most beautiful lips he's ever seen. But then he says that about her eyes and her ears and her skin and even her snaggly front teeth. When she admits to him that she hates her teeth, he tells her he loves them, rubs his finger along their surface, licks them with his tongue. In a way it is the most intimate thing he has done with her.

Man works constantly on the painting. Lee now understands how single-minded he can be. His behavior reminds her of the first few weeks when they were together: he cancels appointments, skips meals, gazes past the world with bloodshot eyes. But for her it is not the same. Now that she has her own work, she finds she doesn't want to just watch him, gets jumpy if she sits next to him for too long. He insists that he needs her there. So even though she often doesn't want to, for hours Lee lies on the bed as he works above her, her head cocked toward him just so. By the end of the day the drop cloth and her skin are dusted with a fine spray of paint spatters.

Most of the time he paints in silence, but sometimes, if he's struggling to get something right or needs a break after focusing for a long time, he'll talk to her about what he is hoping to accomplish with the painting. He tells her that her lips are like their two bodies at rest, that the horizon behind them joins them as it does the earth and sky. Behind her mouth, at the edge of the painting, he paints the observatory they see every evening as they walk home down Boulevard Saint-Michel.

"I want the painting fixed in space," he tells her, "so that everyone will know it's you I'm painting."

When Man is silent, sometimes Lee thinks about nothing, or just lets her mind wander. Other times, if she lies there long enough, she starts to think about her life as one long string, all the things she's done interconnected and stretched out from the past into the future. She finally feels she is here at the prow of herself.

All she's learned. So much that she can see her modeling years as something important, as a way for her to understand the images she now wants to create. The pictures in *Vogue* or *McCall's* whose artistry used to be so impenetrable to her she now views with a critic's eye. The bones of the compositions feel more obvious to her, and she finds herself questioning the lighting choices or holding her hands to the page to crop an image differently.

"Man," she says one morning while he is painting, "what has Tristan said about my pictures? For *221*?"

He looks down at her and a sheepish expression spreads across his face. "You know . . . I'm so sorry. I haven't even seen him since you asked me last. I'll ask him soon—next week."

"All right," Lee says, but she is disappointed. She feels as though she heard Man talking about seeing Tristan just the other day, but maybe she is wrong.

Man paints for a while, and then he says, "Another thing I forgot—I can't believe I didn't mention this to you. The Philadelphia Camera Society liked my essay so much they invited me to submit photos for their next exhibition."

Lee knows that the Philadelphia Camera Society is respected worldwide for exhibiting some of the most interesting work of the moment. To many photographers, its annual exhibition is the holy grail, and Lee has long suspected that Man has been annoyed not to be asked to contribute before. "That's wonderful! What are you going to submit?"

"I'm not sure yet. I have some ideas, but I want to think about it a little longer. It has to be something really spectacular. Groundbreaking."

Lee knows what this opportunity might mean for him and tries to feel a selfless happiness for his success, but the thought of how he has forgotten to talk to Tristan about her work snags in her mind. "Wouldn't it be fun if we both had work published at the same time?" As soon as she says it she regrets the words, which even to her ears sound petty.

Man sets down his brush and looks at her. "Lee—I told you, I'll ask him. Things are fraught for him right now. I have to pick the right time."

"Of course. I'm sorry I brought it up again."

Lee closes her eyes and lets him paint her, imagines what the finished painting will look like hanging on a gallery wall.

CHAPTER EIGHTEEN

All the squares on the calendar are blank.

"Nothing? How many days in a row is this now?" Man's voice sounds tired.

"Not that many." It has been three weeks since their last paying client, but Lee knows better than to tell Man this. He has been so obsessed with his painting and his artist statement for the Philadelphia prize that he hasn't even noticed, and having finances pointed out to him will just make him huffy about how glad he is to have time to spend on his *real* art.

Man comes up behind her and stares over her shoulder at the empty white calendar page.

"I'll start on the perfume bottle spreads," Lee says.

"No, I've got a better idea. It's beautiful outside. No reason to work when there isn't any. I'll get the car out and we can drive to Chantilly, have a picnic." As soon as he says the words Man's entire demeanor changes, and within moments he has dug a picnic basket out of the closet, along with a pile of blankets and the traveling cocktail set.

While Man gets the car out of the garage, Lee fetches supplies, stocking the basket with bread and radishes and butter, cold pulled turkey and *saucisson sec,* their favorite little éclairs from the patisserie down the street. She nestles the food around an iced bottle of Sémillon and is on the front steps of the studio before Man gets back with the car, her coat buttoned to her neck, its rabbit fur collar soft against her cheeks. Man rounds the corner and she waves at him, but just then a young Western Union boy on a bicycle stops in front of the studio and runs up the steps to the door, an envelope clutched in his hand.

"For Man Ray?" Lee asks him.

The boy squints at the typed name. "No, for Monsieur Lee Miller."

"That's me."

The boy's eyebrows push together in confusion, but he holds out the telegram and receipt book so Lee can sign for it, and then rides away on his bicycle. Man is idling in front of the door, the growl of the car engine loud on the quiet street. Lee holds up her finger to Man and opens the telegram, already expecting the worst: someone dead or sick or maimed in some horrible accident. But instead,

```
LI-LI COMING TO PARIS OCT 1 ON THE SS
ALGONQUIN FOR BUSINESS AND YOU STOP
ERIK AND JOHN SEND THEIR LOVE STOP
YOUR LOVING FATHER
```

Man honks the horn a few times in a row and Lee shoves the telegram in her bag and runs down to him, strapping the picnic basket onto the back of the car and then settling herself in the passenger seat. She pulls her beret lower over her ears.

"Anything important?" Man asks her.

"No, not really. I'll tell you later."

"Okay, then off we go!" Man shouts, his voice full of the joy of abandoned responsibility. As he drives he keeps up a steady stream of chatter. Lee is quiet. She has her handbag on her lap, the telegram inside it. Impersonal typeface, the message stilted, nothing like her father, but still it is enough to bring him back to her. *Your loving father. For business and you.* He will be here in less than a month, in their apartment, poking around the home that she and Man have made together. She has imagined how her new life might appear to him, but now the thought of him actually being here makes her uncomfortable. What will she tell him? How will her world look through his eyes?

Man continues north out of the city, and soon the road opens up into farmland, alternating fields of pasture and plantings, punctuated here and there with stands of beech trees, their leaves not yet turned to fall colors.

"This is wonderful," Lee says, and rolls down her window a little so she can breathe the air, tinged with the smell of a distant controlled burn that smudges the sky with gray.

Lee is aware of how it could appear: she has moved from one man taking her photo to another. This new man is not her father, of course. Still, she cannot bear the idea of having her father see their apartment, where many of the pictures Man has taken of her hang.

In Chantilly, Lee and Man visit the château and spend a while in its gorgeous library. By early afternoon they are famished, so they drive farther onto the château grounds and park the car next to a stream with a view of a pretty little footbridge. The day is still, the water so placid it reflects the trees and clouds above it. Lee sets out the picnic blanket, cuts thick slabs of butter and presses them into rounds of bread, tops them with razor-thin radish slices, and shakes salt on top from paper pouches. Man eats with his eyes closed, blissfully, and they wash down the meal with the Sémillon, not cold anymore but still delicious.

"Sometimes I think about being a chef," Lee says, popping a slice of Morbier in her mouth and loving the way the ashy rind tastes against the radish and the wine.

Man opens his eyes and looks at her. "I've never seen you cook anything."

"I cook! Well, I would if I had any of the right things. Pans, a larder. I used to cook when I was growing up."

"What did you make?"

"All sorts of things. I never used a recipe. Soups and stews—I'd just throw things in a pot until it tasted good."

"And were you successful?"

"My father always thought so." Lee remembers serving him at his desk, the walk down the hallway with the tureen clutched between two pot holders. She'd set it at his elbow and hover nearby until he put down his newspaper or pencil and took a bite, waiting for the moment when he'd look back at her and smile. Oh, how she used to adore her father.

"Maybe I'll cook for you sometime," Lee says to Man.

"Maybe. I like taking you out, though."

"We'd save money," she says, and then, after a pause, "He's coming to visit—my father. That's what the telegram this morning said."

Man sits up and grabs the wine, refilling first her glass and then his own. "I didn't even know you were in contact with him."

"I'm not." The last time Lee heard from Theodore was when she received his letter about his photos being published, which she didn't answer. She mentions him now and then, but each time she does Man never seems interested. He has purposefully cut off contact with his own family, and doesn't ever seem to regret it. It's a philosophy he shares with many of the other members of his circle. Like them, he says he wants to be free of the tangled alliances of his past, because being free will help him focus on his art.

"Do you want to see him?"

Lee watches a bird poking around in the mud at the edge of the stream and ponders his question. "I'm honestly not sure. I've been angry at him for not contacting me, but I'm to blame for that too."

"You just have to decide if being in touch with him will make you happy. And if it will, you should see him."

Lee nods. After a while, she says, "When I was little, my father had this album—actually, lots of albums—and he kept records of everything I did. My first steps, my first visit from the doctor when I got a fever as a baby. All my school papers, and these silly little poems I wrote and gave to him. He was always so proud of me. And he took so many photos. Sometimes I think every memory I have of my childhood comes from looking at those pictures."

"Did he make the albums for your brothers too?"

"I think so, but I was clearly his favorite. And I needed him more than they did."

"Why's that?"

"Because . . . because of what happened."

"Of course. God, I'm sorry."

"You don't need to be sorry. It's just that I . . . I miss him. He was always there for me. He loved me."

Man shifts on the hard ground and then winces as he stretches out his legs in front of him. "Well. Of course he loved you. That's what parents do. But I only meant you don't *have* to see him when he visits if you don't want to. You're a grown woman. You're not beholden to him."

Lee nods again. Part of her agrees with Man: just because Theodore has finally sent her a telegram doesn't erase all the months that they haven't been in contact. And he's not even coming to see her, if she's reading the message correctly: the trip is business and she's just tacked on. But "loving father" keeps running through her mind; there was a whole childhood when those words were true.

Man stands up, stretches, and pats his belly. He walks down toward the bank of the stream, picks up a stone from the water's edge, and sends it bouncing a few times over the surface of the still water. Lee joins him, starts collecting stones and fills her pockets with them.

"Want me to teach you?" Man asks.

Lee pulls a stone from her coat. She palms it for a moment, remembering, then with a neat twist of her wrist launches it smoothly toward the stream, where it skips almost twice as far as Man's before sinking. "Ha!" she shouts, pleased.

Man whistles. Lee throws another stone and another, the technique coming back more fully each time she does it. She and her brothers spent whole afternoons down at the pond on their property, skipping stones, catching fish, Lee's pants rolled up over her calves, the ladylike white bows her mother insisted she wear in her braids drooping and mud-splattered. Man stops throwing his own stones to watch her, and she revels in his attention, a different kind of attention than when he takes her picture.

"You were a wild child, weren't you?" Man asks.

"I suppose I was." Lee knows he means *wild* like free, and she was that way, especially when she was very young. Back then there was no difference between her and her brothers. Whole days were spent outside, exploring; she remembers feeling as though she could hoard the whole world and eat it with a spoon. Before what happened with—she almost hears his name inside her head but stops herself as always. Her childhood is split that way, two neat halves, before and after. It was after when she went truly wild, but not in the way Man means. When her wildness became a thing she felt she had to hide from everyone.

Lee stops skipping stones and stands staring at the water. Maybe

Man knows what she is thinking. She's not sure. All she knows is he is quiet, and she appreciates it.

After a while he says, "Can you show me how you do it, that little flick of your wrist?"

She goes up behind him and puts her small hand on his larger one, their fingers joined around the cool round stone, and she demonstrates a couple of times before Man tries it on his own. His first attempt goes plunking into the water, but it is not long before he has it mastered, the elegant snap that Lee learned all those years ago. When they tire of the diversion, they walk over to the footbridge, where they stand together and look down at the water, its surface smooth as a mirror once the ripples of the stones have disappeared.

Later, as they drive home, Lee takes off her shoes, tucks up her feet on the seat, and lays her head on Man's shoulder. She feels content, warm, and drowsy. She thinks that it will not be so hard to have her father here. To show him her new life. She is about to say this to Man when he says, "Those albums your father made—did your mother help him?"

Even in Lee's contentment the mention of her mother fills her with sourness. "I doubt she ever looked back on pictures of me, even when I was little."

"You never talk about her."

"I never *want* to talk about her. I told you how we never got along, not even when I was really young. And then the older I got...I could never make her happy. I kept getting into trouble at school. Everything I did was a disappointment to her. And she was jealous of me." As always when she talks about her mother, Lee can't keep the bitterness out of her voice.

"Jealous of you?"

"It's true. When I was young she was jealous of all the photo shoots my father did with me, and when I was older she was jealous of my modeling career. She was a beauty when she was young, but I was always prettier than her, and she was scared of getting older and losing her looks."

They are getting closer to the city, and Lee looks out at the modest homes that dot the landscape. Man says, "I don't wonder that your mother took issue with the photo shoots."

He keeps his hands steady on the steering wheel. Lee lifts her head to look at him. "Yes. She hated that my father and I were so close."

Man opens his mouth as if to say something, then closes it. They drive in silence for a while. Then he says, "I would just think, after what had happened to you, that your father would have been a little more protective. It just seems odd, what you've told me about those pictures."

"No no no," Lee says, and sits up and untucks her legs from beneath her. "You see, he did those shoots with me to make me feel *better*. To help me regain my confidence."

"Ah."

Man doesn't say anything else, so Lee continues. "I'm sure it's why I was able to be successful as a model so quickly. And then modeling led me to Paris, and then to you." She leans over and kisses Man's arm and rests her head on him again.

They have turned onto a smaller road, and a horse-drawn wagon blocks their way. Man has to focus to keep the car from stalling. The air, now that they have lost the breeze, is thick and heavy, and Lee fans herself ineffectually. Finally they reach a place where the wagon can move into a ditch to let them past, and once it is well behind them, Man accelerates quickly, sending a spray of gravel out from under the tires. They crest a hill and then Paris is spread out before them, even from this distance seeming to teem with life after the calm of the country. At first the buildings are low-slung against the horizon, but as Man drives farther into the city, taller buildings crowd out the sky, the sloped lines of the mansard roofs more beautiful to Lee than a mountain vista. Cars choke the road, people press up against one another on the corners. As Man turns onto Boulevard Raspail, Lee realizes how comforting the city is, how much it feels like home. The smell of their neighborhood, granite and garbage—she lifts her head and breathes it in.

"I think I *will* see my father while he's here," she says.

Man squeezes her knee. "Whatever you want to do."

"I want him to see—I want to show him what I've done since I left New York. That I'm fine here on my own."

"Better than fine."

"Yes, so much better."

Lee watches the buildings vibrate past them and pictures her life through her father's eyes. How far she's come. How proud she will have made him.

CHAPTER NINETEEN

When Theodore gets to town, Lee goes to meet him at the train station, arriving almost an hour early. The October day is blustery and cold, and the wind cuts between her hat and collar, making her wish she brought a scarf.

Lee has spent the past few weeks envisaging exactly how Theodore's visit will go. The things she'll do and say to impress him. Now, as she waits for his train to pull in, she runs through the activities she has planned for them, the carefully curated examples of her artistic life in Paris. A visit to a bistro, where she will introduce him to dishes he's never tried. A tour of Montparnasse, complete with casual references to streets and buildings where artists and writers she knows he admires work and live. A visit to the studio, so that she can show him the darkroom equipment, maybe even some of her photos if he asks to see them.

The train whistles in right on time and Theodore is one of the first people to disembark. Lee sees him before he finds her in the crowd, and she is shocked at his appearance—it has been only a year, but he looks much older; the skin on his face seems to sag off the bone. Even bundled in his thick coat he looks skinnier than ever, diminished, perhaps, by his long journey. When he sees her, his stern face breaks into a smile. Lee has planned to kiss both his cheeks, a breezy bonjour, but he walks toward her with his arms outstretched and before Lee realizes quite what is happening they are embracing, she is pressed against his coat, enveloped in the smells of cinder and travel. "My Bitsie," he says. "I've missed you."

She has not heard or thought of his pet name for her in ages. The word cracks her resolve to appear independent, and she feels herself give over the weight of her body to their embrace. Though it is not what she intended, she responds, "I missed you too, Daddy," and hears her voice tremble when she says it.

Theodore gives his bags to a porter and sends them to his hotel, then he and Lee walk together to the bistro she has chosen. It's a cozy place, with red paisley tablecloths and wax-spattered candlesticks on every table, but Theodore insists on sitting outside, even though it is so cold they have to keep their coats on.

"Dr. Koopman says that everyone should get six to ten hours of fresh air a day," he says to Lee, ignoring the hovering waitress, who is waiting for them to change their minds and move inside. Theodore has always avidly followed the latest diet and exercise fads. For years he has walked six miles a day, not eaten certain foods together. No cheese with meat. No fruit with grains. Lee has almost forgotten, and scans the menu now, trying to imagine how his habits will translate into Parisian dining. Not well, it turns out: he spends five minutes interrogating the waitress in broken French until Lee has to step in and order for him. Roasted chicken and potatoes, a small salad. Once they have finally settled in he looks Lee over.

"You look good. Healthy. A little plumper, but not too much. I can see it in your face."

"So nice of you to say so, Daddy," she says, frowning.

"Well, if you want to slim down again, just follow—"

"The Koopman method. I know."

Lee switches to pleasantries, asking about his business travels, her brothers. He tells her that his company, DeLaval, is branching out, and he is here to meet about a potential new separator that a Frenchman has patented. Hoover's tariff bill is causing problems for the company, and in order to stay profitable, Theodore needs to expand its scope. He saws methodically at his chicken while he talks. Lee picks at her food and then sits back in her chair and inspects her manicure. The conversation is familiar, the kind of talk she used to overhear when she was young, when he would let her slip under the table and sit on the rug with her back pressed against his shins, waiting for the adults to finish dinner.

Lee wonders when he will bring the conversation around to her, ask a question about her life here, but it is not until they are done eating that he does.

"Tanja's parents dropped by for a visit a few months ago," Theodore says. "They say you're studying with Man Ray?"

Lee is surprised that he knows this, but it does explain how he got her studio address. "Not really studying. I work with him."

"His fashion work is very impressive." Theodore considers himself an expert on fashion. Ever since Lee started modeling, he has filled his albums with pictures of Lee and other models he admires.

"All his work is impressive."

Theodore peers at her over his glasses and Lee feels momentarily uncomfortable, then reminds herself that she is a twenty-three-year-old woman and that her relationship with Man is none of her father's business.

"I'd love to meet him while I'm here," Theodore says.

"He's—" Lee starts, and then pauses. "*We're* very busy at the studio. I'll see if he can make the time."

The next afternoon, in preparation for her father's visit, Lee tidies the studio, folding drop cloths, filing prints, stacking magazines, and straightening frames. She's not nervous, but she wants the space to look its best when Theodore gets there. When Man comes in and sees that she has organized his collection of birds' nests on the mantel, he huffs air through his nose.

"He's coming at two?" Man asks. "Is he—what have you told him? Does he think I'm your lover or your employer?"

"Employer."

"Ah. Then while he's here I'll refrain from talking about fucking you senseless."

He says it jokingly, but Lee can tell he is troubled. "Love," she says, going over to him and wrapping her arms around him from behind, "we can tell him if you want. I just—he has this way of asking a thousand questions, until you find yourself wishing you hadn't said anything in the first place."

"I'm worried you're embarrassed of me."

"What? Why on earth . . . ?"

Man pulls away from her embrace and turns to face her, gesturing at himself from head to toe. "How old is your father? Fifty? You realize I'm closer to his age than I am to yours?"

"I don't care how old you are. Besides, you're wise. Not old."

"Wise."

"Yes, wise. I love that you're older than me, that you've done more than me. And anyhow, my father is fifty-six."

"That *still* puts me closer to his age."

"You're nothing like my father," Lee says. "This is a perfect example of why I don't want to tell him we're together."

"Fine." Man pulls her close to him again. "We won't tell your father I'm your wise, ancient lover. I'll stay ten feet away from you at all times, and if he asks any questions, I'll just pontificate at him. Wisely." Again his tone is joking, but he leaves the room soon after and goes into the developing room and stays there while she is cleaning.

Lee's father is punctual as always. She brings him inside and notices how he has to stoop when he stands in the low-ceilinged foyer. He looks around appraisingly, pausing at the Braque and Léger on the walls, mixed in with Man's own work.

"Cubists," he says, sniffing and reaching into his pocket for his handkerchief and blowing his nose. "It's not what I'm interested in but it's very popular." He puts away the handkerchief. "I'm fairly certain I'm getting sick. I find the air in Paris to be quite fetid."

"What does Koopman have to say about it?"

Theodore doesn't pick up on her tone. "Oh, I've been eating more cruciferous vegetables since I've been here to counteract it. But it's hard to do it right—so many potatoes on these menus."

He is such a hypochondriac, a trait he's passed on to her. Even hearing him talk about getting sick makes her throat tickle.

Just then Man comes down the stairs. "Mr. Miller!" he shouts. "What a pleasure. My lovely assistant here has told me so much about you."

Lee feels a rush of gratitude for his hospitable manner.

"Mr. Ray, the pleasure is mine," Theodore says. He pumps Man's hand up and down a few times. They are dressed similarly, in high-waisted black pants and white shirts. After Man's earlier comments, Lee has to force herself not to make comparisons.

Man leads him upstairs, making small talk as he would with a client, and as they ascend, Lee lags behind them, purposefully slow, trailing her hand along the banister.

In the office, her father has already moved their conversation to photography, and Lee hears him peppering Man with technical questions, the sorts of things she would now be able to answer if he asked her.

"You know," she hears Man say, "I spent a lot of time fiddling with exposure times. When I was working on one of my series, these images I called rayographs—"

"Objects laid directly on the photographic paper. Yes, I read about it."

Lee doesn't even have to look at Man to know this pleases him. "You must be quite knowledgeable about the field. Not very many people in the States have heard of them."

"Oh yes. I always like to stay up on the latest technologies. Photography is a particular passion of mine."

Theodore wanders around the office, inspecting the photos hanging on the wall. Most are older work—Man is lazy about changing them—but a few of them are of Lee, and she feels a growing agitation as Theodore moves around the room. By the fireplace there is a portrait of her looking over her shoulder, her back bare, her expression loving. She desperately wants her father not to see it.

"Daddy," Lee says. "Let me show you the darkroom equipment."

Theodore turns and seems surprised to see her standing there. "Oh, of course, Bitsie," he says, and then, with an almost apologetic glance at Man, follows her into the other room.

Lee knows Theodore has never seen equipment as professional as Man's. He seems particularly interested in Man's photoflood prototype on the stand in the corner, with its rheostat controller, and he inspects it from all angles. He's also intrigued by the xenon unit, saying, "I should get one of those. Or a klieg light. Does Mr. Ray have one of those?"

"I don't think so."

"They're so bright it's like having the sun there when you shoot indoors. I read about it."

"Aren't they mainly for movies?"

"So far, but their advantages for studio work are obvious. Remember all the times I made you shoot outside when you didn't want to?"

Of course she remembers. A whole childhood of it. Indoors,

outdoors, hundreds of photos. Her fourteenth birthday, when he had a vision of Lee as a modern dryad, stolen from the pages of Ovid, her head crowned with branches as she stood next to the small creek just south of their house. She'd been so sad that whole year—nothing could shake her dark mood—and he told her the shoot would be fun, like acting. "It will cheer you up," she remembers him saying, but it didn't. He meant well, but that day she felt uncomfortable in front of the camera. She couldn't find the words to tell him. In the photos she is hunched and shivering, her arms crossed over her naked torso, her eyes round and dull as the river stones that cut into her feet while she was posing.

Lee doesn't want to spend any more time thinking about the past. "Let me show you something," she says, and takes her father over to the flat files and pulls out some of her recent pictures, including one from the bell jar series and an abstract shot she took recently of a sailboat in a child's regatta. She lays them out on the table and gives her father time to look them over. He picks up a few photos and inspects them more closely, holding them carefully by their edges. Lee stands expectantly on the other side of the table. They're good, she thinks. She waits for him to say it. Theodore picks up the sailboat print and stares at it for a long time. Lee bends down to another drawer and pulls out more of her work, street scenes and studio shots, her whole portfolio. Taken in total, the collection is impressive, but the longer they stand there, and the longer Theodore spends picking up a print, setting it down, picking up another, the more off-kilter Lee feels.

"Elizabeth," he finally says, "all of these are yours?"

Lee nods and starts to respond, but just then Man comes into the room, a scarf looped around his neck. He glances at the table and then at Lee. "I thought I'd step out for a quick coffee. Would you two like to join me?"

Embarrassed to have Man see her showing off her work, but relieved again that he is being friendly, Lee begins to hurriedly push the prints into stacks and shove them back into their folders. "I'd love one. Daddy?"

"Certainly. I wouldn't miss a chance to get more advice from Mr. Ray here."

As they walk outside, Lee pulls Theodore aside and whispers, "Just call him Man. Or Man Ray. No one calls him Mr. Ray."

They go to Café de Flore and sit crowded around a small outdoor table. Man orders a double espresso and a pastis, then turns to Lee. "Same for you?" It is what they always drink when they come here together.

"Alcohol during the day is terrible for digestion," Theodore says to both of them, then turns to the waiter and, in his broken French, says, "I'll have a hot water with lemon, and my daughter will have black tea."

"Actually," Lee says, "café crème, please."

The waiter nods and moves away, and into the silence that follows, Man says, "Pastis is a digestif. For digestion. It always calms my stomach—isn't that the point?"

Lee sighs. Man has given Theodore a perfect opening to explain his eating habits, and as he launches into a lecture, the mood at the table grows tense. Lee can tell Man is annoyed; he thinks all theories on diet are from charlatans, which he actually says out loud.

"Taking care of yourself is not hoo-ha," Theodore says with dignity.

Man coughs, then busies himself pouring water from the jug into his glass and stirring the clouded liquid with a long-handled spoon. "But only eating certain things together? It all ends up in the same place in your stomach the moment you swallow. It seems, if you will forgive me, absurd."

Lee has thought the same thing, many times, but still she wants to smooth things over. "I think people should do what feels right for them."

Man gives her a sharp look. "You *do*?"

"Yes," Lee says, then raises her eyebrows at Man before she turns to her father and, pointedly changing the subject, says, "How was the opera last night, Daddy?"

Theodore smiles. "Wonderful. Just wonderful. I've always wanted to see *Guillaume Tell*. And the Garnier is so much more ornate than the Collingwood. Have you been yet, Bitsie?"

"No, not yet."

"That surprises me. You used to love the opera." To Man he says, "You've never seen a little girl so focused. Her brothers got bored after twenty minutes, but Elizabeth was in love with all of it. She said she wanted to be Sarah Bernhardt when she grew up. Or a film star."

"Oh, remember when we saw her?" Lee must have been ten when Bernhardt's farewell tour came to Poughkeepsie. She still remembers everything about it: the immense arrangement of lilies in the lobby, filling the air with their syrupy scent; the people of Poughkeepsie crowding the tiers and theater boxes, almost unrecognizable in their finest clothes; the domed ceiling that rose above them with its beautiful Italianate frescoes. Lee sat rapt through the entire performance: the silent film they showed as a curtain-raiser, the *tableaux vivants,* and then finally the divine Sarah herself, resplendent in thickly draped maroon velvet, making her way around the stage with the help of an ivory cane before reenacting the death of Cleopatra by swooning onto a chaise longue the exact color of her dress.

Theodore chuckles. "Remember how afterward you had to act out the locomotive scene from the film they showed?"

"Did I? I don't remember that."

Theodore turns to Man. "Elizabeth's brother built a child-sized locomotive in the barn behind our house, including a wooden track that went down the hill into a field. Quite impressive. He's an aeronautical engineer now. After Elizabeth saw that silent, she insisted on riding on the engine, backward, holding her Brownie like the camera stuntman in the movie."

"That's right!" Lee says. "I had forgotten all about that old locomotive. I wanted you to pay me danger money, just like a real cameraman."

"And I did. I gave you three dollars after we developed your pictures."

Lee laughs with the pleasure of the memory. Man watches the two of them but doesn't say anything.

"One could say I was your first paying client." Theodore reaches out and pats Lee's leg, then leaves his hand resting on her thigh, a self-satisfied look on his face. Lee drains her coffee and grows silent. Man's gaze keeps moving from Theodore's face to where his hand is lying in Lee's lap.

When they've finished their drinks, Man gets up to pay, but Theodore waves him off. "Allow me," he says, and makes a big show of signaling the waiter. Man puts his billfold back in his pocket and doesn't say a word.

When they're outside the studio, Lee figures it is time for her father to go. It's four o'clock, and he will want to rest before dinner. But when she says this to him, he doesn't answer, turning instead to Man and saying, "Before I go, I would love to have my portrait taken with my daughter. Do we have time for that?"

Lee is mortified. It is so presumptuous. "Daddy..." she says.

But Man, who also has a startled expression on his face, says, "No, of course! I should have thought to suggest it."

"It's getting late," Lee says. "There's probably not enough light."

Man stands on the step below her before the studio door, and just for a second he puts his hand on the small of her back. "It's fine, Lee. We have enough time to get it in." Lee looks at her father to see if he's noticed Man's touch, but he is fiddling with his scarf, not paying attention.

Together they go into the studio. Man drags a high-backed chair into the center of the room and seats Lee's father in it, then runs some light tests. Lee stands off to the side with her arms crossed. Her father sits with his back ramrod straight, and she stares at his profile, his aquiline nose, his meticulously razored sideburns.

Lee moves to take her place beside him and tries to relax her face into a less tetchy expression. Man makes a couple of exposures of them like this, and then Theodore says, "Bitsie, this is a portrait, not a foot drill. Come, sit with me." He takes her hand and pulls her toward him, and she complies, and before she knows it she is sitting on his lap as she used to do when she was young, her head resting on his shoulder.

From under the dark cloth Man calls, "Ready?"

Her father's jacket is scratchy against her cheek and smells familiar: herbs and loam, the cedar from his soap. Lee stares directly at the camera, almost through it, and then she is floating outside herself and seeing the picture from Man's perspective: the bodies upside down in the viewfinder, Lee clinging to her father's neck. Docile, passive, exactly who she does not want to be. The pose feels so normal—she has sat on his lap a thousand times—but having Man as a witness is suddenly intolerable. Lee tries to pull free but her father's arm at her waist holds her steady, and instead she stiffens inside his grasp.

After a few more exposures, Man comes out from under the cloth and says, "I have to get another plate." His voice is stilted and professional, and he walks quickly over to the supply closet, his heels thudding hard on the wood floor.

Lee stands up. "How many did you get?"

"Five or six."

"I'm sure they're fine," Lee says, and then to her father, "Man works quickly. You won't be disappointed."

Even though they are done, Theodore wants to linger, but Lee can't get him out the door fast enough. Man is clearly happy to see him go. Lee escorts Theodore to his hotel, walking so quickly that she grows hot beneath her coat, and even her father, with his long stride, can barely keep up with her. He moves to kiss her cheek at the hotel's entrance, but she steps away from him and leaves him standing alone.

A block away she ducks into a bar and takes a seat at the counter, breathes deeply, and orders one brandy and then another, drinks them until her empty stomach burns. It is not until she has finished both drinks that she pays attention to her surroundings, lifts her head and looks around at the other people in the bar. Paris a city full of strangers still. Everyone is paired or in groups of three, their faces round and blank as moons. They talk and laugh around her, their actions exaggerated as if they're in a play.

Lee wishes she hadn't agreed to see her father while he was here. Having him see her new life has diminished it somehow. Diminished her. She remembers the rages she used to fly into when she was young: screaming, kicking at walls, pulling at her hair until it came out in clumps in her fists. All that rage, and in the end it led to nothing. To acquiescence. The submission her father required of her when she was a child—she felt it again when Man was taking their picture, when Theodore's hand was on her thigh. She thought that part of her life was behind her, but having him here in Paris has brought it back, like two sides of a stereoscope coalescing into one image. And how different is her relationship with Man? She complies with all he asks of her too.

★ ★ ★

When she gets back to the studio, she realizes she has forgotten her key, so she rings the bell and Man meets her at the door.

"I didn't know if you were coming back until later," he says.

"I just dropped him at the hotel, and stopped for a drink on the way home."

Man's face twitches with what seems to Lee like disgust. "I can smell it on you."

She climbs the stairs and goes into the parlor, Man following her. "Should we have another?" she asks. "I think we should have another."

She busies herself at the bar cart, pours two brandies into matching tumblers. When she hands one to Man, he says, "Thank you, *Bitsie*."

He gives the word a hard edge and Lee winces. "Don't. Just . . . don't."

"What *was* that? You, your father—it was like you were trying to make me jealous."

"What do you mean?"

"Letting him pay for the coffees . . . Making me take your picture . . ."

"I didn't *let him* do anything. He does what he wants. And besides, you should have offered to take our picture." Lee doesn't really think this; she was just as uncomfortable as Man with Theodore's request for a portrait, but she wants to lash out at him.

"Oh really?" Man says. "It's not taking the picture I minded. It's how superfluous I felt. Like you didn't need me." He says the last few words quietly, his voice self-pitying and needy, which makes her even angrier.

Lee sets down her tumbler on a side table and then takes Man's from him as well. She hooks her fingers in his shirt collar and pulls him toward her, kissing him on the mouth so hard it almost hurts.

"Stay there," Lee says. She goes into the hallway and gets his scarf, the one he was wearing that afternoon. Back in front of him, she runs the length of it through her hands.

"Lee—"

With one hand she pushes him onto the couch and then straddles him, putting her mouth back on his insistently. Though at first he resists her kiss, through their clothes she feels him grow hard. It pleases her, how irresistible she is to him. She picks up the scarf and ties it around his eyes, pulling it tight in a knot at the back of his head and then pushing him down so he is lying on the couch. It is the first time they've done this. The sight of him with the blindfold on excites her much more than she thought it would. She feels so aroused she is almost ashamed. Maybe it is anger—she wants to hurt Man, wants to cause him pain. Together they strip off his clothes and then she takes off her own. She squeezes both of his wrists so tight she can feel the bones slide. And then she reaches between her legs, pushes him inside her, and begins to move on top of him.

"Lee, this—I don't think—" His voice is almost fearful, but she releases his wrists and rests her hand on his mouth briefly so he cannot speak. She grinds against him, paying attention only to what her own body wants, speeding up the tempo, so fast she feels his balls slap against her. He groans and calls out her name as if it's hard for him to say it, grabs her waist and helps her slam herself down on top of him, again and again and again.

He tries to move her to a new position, to slow her down, but she won't let him. She keeps going, faster and faster, until she feels his whole body stiffen and he cries out her name again. Even then she won't stop, pounding against him, and when she comes she rakes her nails across his shoulders.

Afterward, she lies on top of him, skin on skin, and reaches around to help him push off the blindfold. Man pulls her closer to him. Now that they are done, she worries he is going to want to keep talking, so she closes her eyes and pretends to be falling asleep. He strokes her hair for a while. When she doesn't respond, he gently moves her over and slips out from under her. She hears him getting dressed and then feels him lay a blanket over her. She lies there for hours, until the light fades from the windows and the room goes dark, wishing there was somewhere she could go to be alone.

LEIPZIG

APRIL 20, 1945

It takes the 83rd forever to reach Leipzig after the Germans surrender the city. Lee is hobbled by her regiment. She knows Margaret Bourke-White has gotten to the city ahead of her, probably others have as well, while Lee sits in the mud in the GI jeep and urges it to go faster. In the end they are only half a day late. Old women in dirty brown dresses greet them in the streets with flowers; they wave and smile and hold up their children. Around the corner the fighting continues, and the sound of gunfire intermittently drowns out the women's cheering.

Lee hears stories of what the Nazis will do to avoid capture, but she doesn't know if she should believe them. Poison, gunshot, hanging. A factory director invites a hundred guests for dinner. When the 69th takes the city, he pushes a button, sets off an explosion that kills everyone at the table. Friends point guns at one another, counting to three and pulling the triggers. Someone tells her every Nazi in Leipzig's *Neues Rathaus* has committed suicide, and it makes her loathe them even more, the cowards.

When Lee gets there, the *Rathaus* is quiet, everything coated in thick white dust. She goes from office to office, alone. A bomb explodes somewhere outside and more plaster drifts down from the ceiling. On the second floor, she pauses at the threshold of an opulent room. A window hangs open. Oiled leather furniture is the only thing not completely covered in dust. A mother and daughter lie sideways on the couches. A man sits in the desk chair, his head resting on the blotter before him. Lee feels for a moment as if she has walked in and caught everyone napping, but on the desk an empty bottle of cyanide serves as the paperweight for the family's documents.

The daughter must be almost twenty. She wears a nurse's cap, a Red Cross armband on her black jacket. Her hands are folded over her stomach. Lee takes a wide shot and then gets in closer, so that the girl's face almost fills the frame. Blond hair cut like Lee's. Cheekbones sharp as bird wings. Her lips are parted, her jaw relaxed. Her teeth are extraordinarily pretty, and after Lee takes the picture, she reaches out and touches them, just so she can feel the bone.

CHAPTER TWENTY

The posters start appearing all over Montparnasse, pinned to signposts, stacked near café entrances, taped up in the Métro station. On them is the image of a woman in a gigantic feather boa and a low-cut dress, her mouth open, smiling ecstatically. LE RETOUR DE KIKI is printed beneath her image. Lee cannot escape them. Every time she walks by Le Jockey—which is often; it is only a few blocks from their apartment—she watches the raucous crowd spilling out of the doorway, seemingly having the time of their lives, and she wonders anew what all the fuss is about.

It is embarrassing the amount of time Lee spends thinking about Kiki. Man has insisted he isn't in love with her anymore, that the only person he loves is Lee, so why does Kiki still fill her imagination?

One day a cold October wind rips a poster off the side of a building and it wraps itself around Lee's shin, and she peels it off her leg and takes it home. When she walks in the door, she holds it up and says to Man, "I want to go. Tonight."

He groans. He is already in his dressing gown, sitting on the couch with a large book on his lap. "I thought we were staying in."

Lee scans the dates on the poster. "Okay, not tonight. Thursday?" With a sigh, he agrees. She puts the poster on the table in front of him, and he glances at the image.

"That photo is about ten years out-of-date," he says.

"Really?"

"Kiki looks older now. She's gotten too fat to dance."

Lee is pleased. "I don't care how fat she is. We're going. Besides, I thought you liked a little jiggle in the middle."

When Thursday arrives, Man keeps his word. He is quiet as they walk to Le Jockey. He wears a new pair of flannel trousers and his beret, which he keeps fussing with while they walk. Lee wears her smartest dress and imagines herself shimmying on a café table— Lee of Montparnasse.

"How long has it been since you've seen her?" Lee asks as he takes her arm and threads it through his.

"I saw her just last week, at Éluard's."

Lee thinks back to the previous week. "You didn't tell me that."

"I see Kiki now and then. She poses for a lot of people. I run into her. We're still friendly."

"I thought you said she was jealous."

Man looks over at her, an amused expression on his face. "She was. I was too. It was a part of it. Actually, it's how I knew we were in love."

"Because she was jealous?"

"Because we were both jealous. For a time at the beginning we had an open relationship, but that didn't work out for us. And even when we agreed not to be with other people, I still imagined her with other men whenever we weren't together."

Man says this lightly, but Lee does not love this side of him. She is reminded of how displeased he was when she left him on the beach at Biarritz and went for a walk on her own.

"Let's never be jealous." Lee's voice is firm.

"Sometimes jealousy is a good thing." There is some trash on the sidewalk, and Man pulls her closer as they sidestep it.

"I remember Kiki onstage one night. She was singing some old chanson—I could barely understand the words—and I looked around and every person in the room had stopped what they were doing to stare at her. When she dances she has this one move: she gets really low, her knees pushed together, and somehow she shakes her hips and makes her dress fly up a bit. It's hilarious, and sexy . . . You can't stop watching her. I knew that night that I was in love with her, and I remember thinking that I knew it because I saw how badly all the other men and women wanted to have her and that she was mine. I was jealous of them getting to watch her, but really they should have been jealous of me. And maybe they were."

Lee pulls away and stops on the sidewalk, facing him. She bends her knees and starts to twist her hips, and her dress climbs up her thighs until her garter clips are showing. "Like this?" Lee asks. "Is this what she used to do?"

"Hmm . . . sort of. But your version is more . . . Yankee." He reaches out and grabs her arms and pulls her toward him. They are standing in the middle of the sidewalk, which is filled with people out for their evening strolls. They become a logjam in the river of the crowd: people behind them have to stop and go around them, bumping up against one another and then adjusting their course.

"Do you think all these people are jealous of us right now?" she asks.

"I think anyone with eyes would be jealous of me with you."

"And what if I wanted to be with one of them? Like that man, over there." Lee points across the street to where a fat man is just getting out of a taxi.

"You and that man?"

"Sure. Why not?"

Man laughs, uncomfortably. "I don't want to think about that." His tone is final, but Lee doesn't want to let it go.

"We never talked about it, whether we could take other lovers. Not even at the beginning." Lee has not thought through what she is saying. All she knows is that they are going to see Kiki, and what she wants is for Man's attention to be on *her*, Lee.

"I don't want you with other men." They are still standing in the middle of the sidewalk. She wonders if they are about to cause a scene.

"And what about you?"

"I haven't wanted to be with anyone else since I met you. Not for one minute. I want to spend my life with you, Lee."

Man doesn't break eye contact, his expression serious. Lee knows his words should please her, but she finds herself thinking of what this means in a literal way, all the other men she will not get to go to bed with, strangers to her now and always, and then she pictures a different future, those men standing in her bedroom and shrugging off suspenders, their hard stomachs, her hands pulling at the top button of their pants and bringing them down to lie on top of her, the way their tongues would feel, soft and hot as her own. She pictures dozens of them—a hundred, even—all in a line stretching into her future, and then replaces the image with Man. Almost as a test, she leans forward and kisses him on the mouth. He kisses her back, and it feels as good as every time they are together—better, even—and the pedestrians on the sidewalk continue to slip past them like water, and Lee doesn't care even a little bit that these people are seeing them, not even when Man grabs the back of her thigh under her dress and tucks his fingers inside the top of her stocking. She finds that she wants the other people to see them, so she wraps her leg around him to pull him closer.

After a little while they separate.

"Should we go to the Jockey?" he says, and puts her arm through his again.

* * *

Inside Le Jockey every table is full and every person looks interesting. The room is spacious but divided up by large columns, each painted with a different scene of cowboys and Indians. In the corner is a small stage where a man with an accordion and a feral-looking monkey are performing a chanson Lee actually knows. A visible haze of cigarette smoke hangs in the air. Man turns to her and asks a question, but it is so loud she can't hear him.

"What did you say?" she shouts.

"Do you want a drink?" he shouts back, miming someone sipping from a glass.

"Yes. Get me a drink!" He merges with the crowd and she moves over to lean against a column painted with a picture of an Indian warrior rearing on his horse.

Soon Man is threading his way back to her with two gin martinis, perfect corkscrews of lemon peel suspended in the glasses. On the way, though, he gets stopped by a pair of men, and he talks to them for a minute and then gestures with a cocktail in Lee's direction. Just then the accordionist stops playing, and the noise level in the bar lowers slightly. Lee walks over and Man introduces her, two names she does not recognize. The men look her over wolfishly. Man finds two empty chairs and pulls them up to the table. As soon as they are sitting, Lee takes her martini and downs most of it in one big gulp. She wants to get another but Man and the two men are deep in conversation, hunched over the table and practically excluding her. Then she feels a tap on her back and turns around to find a seated man holding out a Tom Collins glass filled to the brim with bright fizzy liquid. He stares at her intensely and she takes the glass from him.

"I make films," the man says in accented English. He has thick brown hair curling back off his forehead, a long straight nose, dark brown eyes. He is sitting backward in his chair, and his lips are so close to her ear and his voice so deep that she can hear him perfectly.

"I take photographs," Lee says back, and takes a swallow of the drink.

"I am making a new film. I've been inspired by the paintings here and I need someone to play a statue. Have you been in films? You're very beautiful."

His directness is unnerving, and his gaze never wavers from her. Man is still having his own conversation with the two men at their table, but his glance keeps sliding toward her too, which makes Lee feel that no matter where she looks she will accidentally meet the eyes of someone. She takes another sip of the gin fizz. It is delicious, light and lemony—a shock since all she can smell is smoke.

The man doesn't blink, which is disconcerting. "I don't see why you need someone to play a statue," Lee says. "Can't you just get a statue?" She makes her tone teasing.

"The poet is looking for a muse. The statue comes to life. You have the look." He leans back and seems to compose himself. "I'm Jean Cocteau," he says, grabbing her hand and kissing it lightly. "Have you heard of me?"

"I haven't." The drink is already gone and Lee is finding this man too intense. She looks over at Man and when she catches his eye she makes a subtle *help* expression and flicks her eyes in Cocteau's direction. Man realizes what is happening, stands up, and comes around the table to her.

"Jean!" he says. Lee feels a rush of pleasure at having him come to her rescue.

"Hmm—mm—mm," Cocteau hums through closed lips. He doesn't even look up at Man.

"Jean," Man says again. "It's been a long time. I don't think I've seen you since our last session."

214

"Mm," Jean hums again, and it is clear that he is humming a little tune, as a child might do. Lee feels deeply uncomfortable and wonders if she can move to a different table.

Just then everyone starts applauding. They turn their chairs to face the stage.

Kiki appears through a side door and walks primly up to the stage, moving exaggeratedly in what is almost a waddle. She sets one foot on the stair and then pulls it away, laughing. The room is silent. She sets her foot back on the stair and sticks out her arms as if she is walking a tightrope, then slowly and carefully steps up. The stage is empty except for a café chair, which she turns away from the crowd and straddles. Her dress is short, and even from the back of the room Lee can see her knickers. Kiki laughs again and everyone laughs with her, including Lee, though she isn't sure why she is laughing. From a small bag sitting next to the chair Kiki takes a mirror and some makeup, and proceeds to do her face. It is fascinating to watch her. She picks a red lipstick and traces her lips, then presses them together to blot them. She takes a bright blue eyebrow pencil and draws two arches above her eyes, almost an inch above where she has shaved off her real eyebrows, then gazes out at the crowd with her mouth in a surprised O. Her eyelids she paints green, the apples of her cheeks get coated with vivid pink circles, and then she slowly and painstakingly puts all the makeup and the mirror back in the bag and sets it on the floor.

Throughout all this, which takes about five full minutes, Lee keeps glancing at Man, who rolls a cigarette and presses it to his lips, taking short full drags and keeping the cigarette only inches from his face as he exhales. Behind Lee, Jean directs his complete attention to the stage.

The piano starts, and Kiki leans forward into the curved wooden frame of the chair so that her breasts are pinned against it and her legs are spread even wider than they were before.

There is no longer any doubt in Lee's mind: Kiki is ferociously ugly. Her nose is wide and flat; her mouth, even with all the lipstick, is too small; her hair is pulled back so severely Lee can see the skin of her forehead stretching; and the view up her skirt reveals thighs rippled with fat. And yet when Kiki opens her mouth to sing, Lee begins to understand her appeal. Kiki's voice is high-pitched but gravelly, as if she has just woken up from a too-long nap, and the sound of it makes Lee think of the bedroom. It is almost as if Kiki's ugliness makes her more sensual. The song she is singing is as louche as her appearance. It is some sort of French limerick about a boy in school and a circle of desks and a mean old teacher with a whip. Kiki performs so well that Lee doesn't even need to follow all the words. When Kiki says the word *whip,* she shoots up one of her sky-high eyebrows, which curls on her forehead before snapping back into place. She sings a song called "La Connasse" and grabs at the rolls of fat on her belly before reaching down provocatively between her legs. She commands the room with these gestures, and when she lowers her singing voice to a whisper, the room goes silent to hear her.

After a dozen songs, Kiki announces that she will sing one more and then be done. Moans go through the crowd. She shakes her finger in the air, *non non non,* and tells everyone not to be sad. Then, coming to the lip of the stage, she looks pointedly in Man's direction and says in French, "This is a song for the great Man Ray, who is here with us tonight and gave me many years of happiness." And she smiles sweetly while everyone claps and turns to look at him, raising their glasses to the lover of Kiki, the lover of Montparnasse.

Lee thinks she adores Kiki for a minute then. She looks so sweet, standing in the bright light on the platform, and Lee is glad Kiki found happiness with Man. Perhaps Lee will be able to as well, real happiness that lasts for years and years. It pleases her to hear Kiki praise him, pleases her more to see all the people in the bar toast him while he sits there looking neither embarrassed nor self-congratulatory. He has a small smile on his face and relaxes in his seat as if this scene is nothing out of the ordinary. And perhaps it isn't; maybe this happened to him all the time when he was with Kiki.

Kiki begins to sing again. At first it seems fine—cats in the moonlight or something along those lines. As the song continues, though, Lee sees Man stiffen and cross his arms and look over at her worriedly. Lee smiles at him to show she is having a fine time. Man gets up and walks over to the bar, where he orders a drink and stands smoking and staring at the stage.

"One for you / Two for you / There is only me and you," Kiki sings, and, leaning forward, begins to undo the buttons on her blouse. There are many buttons, and some ribbons as well, but soon enough she has it open to her midriff. Looking directly at Man where he stands next to the bar, she reaches into her shirt and pulls out one of her breasts, letting it swing exposed like an udder as onlookers rap on their tables with their knuckles and cheer. She does the same with her other breast and then squeezes them with both hands, singing, "Not for you / Not for you / Not since you went away."

The reality of Kiki is much worse than Man's photos of her. She is so much more, well, *real,* and Lee realizes that this has been a mistake. She can't look at Man. She doesn't want to see his expression. Instead, she shifts around and looks at Jean, who is not paying attention to the stage anymore and is instead jotting something down in a small notebook. He glances at Lee and says, "Shameful," dismissing the half-nude Kiki with a shake of his head.

Lee laughs. It is nice to see a man undistracted by a pair of exposed breasts. She pulls her chair closer to him.

"Everyone seems quite taken with her," Lee says. People are whooping and cheering, leaning forward in their chairs and rapping their knuckles on their tables even louder than before.

"Pigs. Are you here with him?" Jean gestures toward Man.

"Yes."

Jean rolls his eyes. "I want you to come see my studio, where I am making my films."

"Now?"

Kiki is still singing and gyrating onstage, but Lee does her best not to look at her.

"No, during the day, when the light is good. Perhaps tomorrow?" Jean says. "Would he allow it?"

"Man?" Lee straightens in her chair. "Of course—I mean, I don't ask him what I can and cannot do."

Jean leans forward and whispers, "He doesn't like me."

"He was pleasant enough when he said hello to you."

"He thinks I am someone worth knowing. Which I am."

While they've been talking, Kiki's act has ended. Demurely, she does up her blouse and then concludes as she began, stepping slowly and exaggeratedly from the stage. Lee expects her to walk over to Man, and she steels herself for this, but instead Kiki starts wending her way through the crowd, coming closer and closer until she is standing right in front of Lee. Up close her makeup is lurid, meant for the stage and not for such close proximity.

"I know who you are," Kiki says in stilted English, and a small piece of spittle shoots out of her mouth and lands on Lee's cheek. Lee flinches, reaches up, and wipes it away. The people around them murmur and shift in their chairs.

"Who?" Lee says, and stands up. She is a good six inches taller than Kiki, so Kiki has to tip back her head to keep looking at her.

Man starts moving toward them, holding out his arm as if he is trying to hail a cab.

"Putain!" Kiki shouts, loud enough that dozens of people look over. Man is still halfway across the room. "You are Man's *putain.* *Tu es fille d'un gay et d'une pute. Je te pisse en zig-zags à la raie de cul!"* She reaches up and slaps Lee across the face and is just going for a second slap when Man grabs her hand and stops her. Lee can feel heat throbbing in her cheek.

The café is quiet. Man holds the writhing Kiki and pins her arms to her sides. Jean has stood so quickly he has knocked over his chair. He comes over to Lee, dipping a napkin in a water glass. He holds the napkin to her face. Kiki starts shouting again, her eyes narrowed, her mouth a red circle of fury. "Don't come here, don't ever come here, you bitch, you whore, you ugly little cunt."

Lee's body goes cold. She cannot believe how quickly Kiki has gone from her stage persona to uncontrolled anger. It is as if her rage is another kind of performance, and perhaps it is: Lee feels every eye in the café trained on their table. She has never been slapped before. She wants Man to do something, to comfort her, to do absolutely anything besides what he is doing, which is holding Kiki and whispering to her to calm down. To someone who didn't know what was going on it would look as though they are lovers wrapped in an embrace.

"You shouldn't stay here," Jean says. Without thinking much about it, Lee lets him push her through the café. Lee turns and exchanges a last look with Man, who drops his arms from around Kiki and starts to move toward her. But Lee just keeps going, letting Jean steer her toward the front door, which has a small bell over it that tinkles cheerily as they go out into the streets, still crowded with people, the night air cool on Lee's hot face. Together they walk up Boulevard du Montparnasse and turn left on Boulevard Saint-Michel, where they head into the Jardin Marco Polo.

It is late, and unlike the sidewalks, the gravel path they walk along in the park is practically deserted.

"How is your face?" Jean asks.

"It hurts."

"You should put meat on it. A steak."

"A steak?" Lee thinks maybe her translation of his French is incorrect.

"Yes. It will take the bruise away." He makes the shape of a slab of meat with his hands and then pretends to press it against his cheek.

She can feel the gravel through the bottoms of her shoes, crunching with every step. Above them, elms rustle in the breeze.

"Ah, here is what I wanted to show you," Jean says, and points to the large fountain at the edge of the formal gardens. The base of the fountain has bronze horses leaping out of the splashing water, their bodies turned to fish tails and their eyes rolling in fear. At the top, four women hold a globe aloft and stare up at the sky.

"See that woman there? That is the one who reminds me of you. She's why I think you should be in my film."

"You want me to play that statue in your film?"

"Not her, no. You'll be Calliope, the muse of art for the poet. But this is what you'll look like. A gorgeous, untouchable statue. But then you'll come to life—you'll see. It will be brilliant. All my films are."

His confidence should seem obnoxious, but Lee is only half focusing on him. She can't stop thinking about how Man went to Kiki instead of her. Her mind replays the scene over and over; she's trying to understand what he was thinking, but she can't make sense of it. He abandoned her—and after their conversation about jealousy, it makes her especially angry.

They stare at the fountain for a while, watching the water pulse up and seem to hang suspended for a bit before splashing down into the marble bowl below. Lee tries to stop thinking about Man, and wishes she had her camera—she would take a picture of the horse's eye with the arc of water surrounding it, and the long exposure time would make the water a smooth blur against the stone.

"I need to go home," Lee says, breaking the silence. "I feel exhausted."

"Where is home?" Jean asks. "With him—with Man Ray?"

"Yes."

"The two of you are in love?" Jean asks.

Lee nods but doesn't say anything at first. Of course she loves Man, but after the scene in the café, she doesn't want to discuss her feelings with a stranger. What do the words mean, anyway? She and Man have barely said them to each other: just the time when they were doing the solarization, and later in bed. She dislikes the formality of the phrase, the weight of the history of all the other couples who have said it before them. Or maybe she doesn't like how vulnerable the words make her feel: how they show her to be a person who feels deeply and demands reciprocation of that feeling.

The water rises up and slaps down, rises up and slaps down. Lee could watch it forever. She is not sure what to say to Jean. Finally she decides to be honest—he is so earnest, so intense, he brings it out in her.

"Sometimes I worry I don't even know how to be in love with someone."

Jean gives her an appraising stare. "There is very little *how* involved. It is like breathing. As simple as that."

"Yes," Lee says, but there is hesitation in her voice. There have been moments when it has felt that easy—lying in bed, her body twined with Man's, so close Lee felt they were one creature—but often, especially lately, she has found herself observing their relationship from a distance, narrating her love for him: *There is the man I love. Look at us, how we care for each other. What a lucky girl to be loved so deeply.* Lee knows this isn't normal, but sometimes it is the only way she can feel grounded in the moment. But she is not going to tell Jean this. Instead, she says, "Is that what your film is about? Is it a love story?"

"Ah, not so much love as a story about art. But these two are connected, no? The film will be an exploration of art and dreams, of the struggle between life and death. A grand experiment."

"I have always, always wanted to be in a film."

"And now you shall! I knew the moment I saw you that you would be perfect."

Lee is flattered, but then her thoughts go back to Man—where he is right now, what he would say if she told him she was going to do the film—and just as quickly, she thinks that he should be *happy* for her. He should want her to have this opportunity. And if he doesn't—well, maybe he's the one who doesn't fully understand what loving someone means.

"You know I have a job, as Man's assistant."

"And I imagine he is paying you in . . . knowledge?" Jean smiles wickedly. "We have plenty of that at my studio. Film is the future. And I will give you one hundred francs a day as well."

"How much time will it take?"

"One week, maybe two? Not every day each week. All the days are money."

Lee looks up at the statue and pictures herself covered in delicate gold leaf, breaking free and emerging radiant in a goddess's robes. "I want to do it. I just have to tell Man and make sure it's all right."

"Wonderful!" Jean bounces up and down on the balls of his feet, and his enthusiasm makes Lee laugh. They move away from the fountain and head up the path that leads farther into the gardens. They walk for a while, making small talk, until finally she stifles a yawn and tells him again that she needs to get home.

"Where is home?"

"Rue Campagne Première."

"I know where it is. It's near his studio. I've been there a few times for him to take my portrait."

"You didn't seem as though you liked him at the Jockey."

"People often don't like other people. It doesn't stop them from working together."

Jean starts to walk her home, but then she stops him. Lee imagines getting to the apartment and seeing it dark and empty, imagines Man still out somewhere with Kiki.

"Where is your apartment?" Lee asks.

"Just there, two streets over."

"Is there any way I could sleep there tonight...just sleep?" Lee feels she has to clarify.

Jean stares at her under the dim streetlight. "If you had a beard, and a cock, I would be interested in you. Otherwise, you do not need to worry."

She laughs out loud, tucks her arm through his, and lets him take her to his home. For one night, Lee thinks, let Man worry that he has lost her.

CHAPTER TWENTY-ONE

In the morning Lee wakes up in Jean's big white guest bed, in a high-ceilinged room with soft morning light streaming in through the tall windows. It is a beautiful room, white and spare. Lee thinks how good it would be for pictures. She lies there for a while, luxuriating in the cool hand of the lemon-scented sheets. At home, she thinks, Man is waking up too, perhaps just realizing she never came back. Or maybe he isn't even there—maybe he went to Kiki's. Lee can't decide which scenario seems more likely. If he is home, he is surely furious with her.

Jean has left her a note saying that he had to get to the studio but that she should make herself at home, so Lee takes a quick bath and inspects her cheek in the lavatory mirror. It doesn't appear bruised, but it feels tender and hot to the touch. Nothing can be done about her hair. There is not a single sign of a woman's presence in the entire bathroom, not even a comb. Lee picks at the tangles with her fingers before giving up completely.

When Lee gets home the apartment is empty. She goes from room to room but there is no sign of Man. The previous night's events come rushing back to her again. The song, Kiki's fury, Man soothing her as Lee left. She goes into the kitchen to make an espresso on the stovetop, lighting the burner and measuring out the coffee as she has learned to do. The grounds froth up and the kitchen fills with their acrid smell.

Their space. In the bright morning light, after being in Jean's apartment, Lee finds this place small and unkempt. The table where she sits to drink her espresso is cluttered with unsuccessful prints, empty glasses, a plate crusted with brown gravy. Lee is no housekeeper. Until this moment she has not noticed what a mess she has made—she *and* Man, for he is not exactly tidy—and all the piles of dishes and clutter remind her of the time they spent together, how easy it's been, over the past months, to ignore the simple chores of everyday life. Now she is disgusted by the mess they have created. She begins gathering things up, arranging them in tidier piles and filling the sink with dishes.

Lee has not spent much time alone in this apartment. It is unsettling. She misses Man, his charged presence. Without him here, the rooms have a dimness to them. She notices dust clotted in the corners, the repeats in the chinoiserie wallpaper that don't line up at the edges, the pattern of cherry blossom branches breaking where the paper has peeled away from the wall.

Where is he? She remembers one of the pictures Man showed her of Kiki, her back to the camera and face in profile, imagines the two of them together now, his fingers tracing Kiki's spine in a delicate curving pattern. Her breasts, pale and swinging, Man's square workman's hands kneading them like dough. Without meaning to she imagines Kiki flung facedown on Man's bed, her hands tied behind her and his body between her legs. The thought makes Lee jittery. She can actually feel the espresso coursing through her. As she moves around the space, three mugs corralled by the handles in one hand, a stack of plates balanced on her forearm, the light from a window hits a framed picture at just such an angle that she can see herself mirrored there—her dress wrinkled, her hair dried to a spoiled snarl—and the sight of her disheveled reflection depresses her, sadness coming in a wave so sudden and strong it almost knocks her over. Lee sets down the dishes and drops into a chair.

What has she done? What if Man is truly angry at her? Without him, what does she have? She has done nothing to create a life apart from him. She wants to crawl into bed, yield to the sadness, wait for Man to comfort her when he gets home. Whenever that will be.

Or she can leave. Lee has always been good at solving problems by leaving, ducking out of parties she no longer wants to be at without saying goodbye, moving across an ocean to get away from a job she no longer enjoys. If she leaves, maybe she can stave off the sadness that threatens to engulf her.

In the bedroom Lee fixes her hair. Pulls on a different dress, puts a dark slash of maroon lipstick on her lips and hangs drop earrings on her ears. She does it all quickly, no wasted motion, and as she leaves the apartment she lets the door shut with a crash. The heels of her oxfords clack against the pavement as she walks away.

The film studio is in chaos when Lee arrives. Jean is behind the camera in the middle of a scene, the main actor shirtless onstage and pounding his chest in apparent agony. Twenty or thirty people rush from place to place and none of them even glance at Lee as she stands at the threshold and takes it all in. Jean shouts *"Arrêtez!"* and the actor relaxes, cracking his knuckles and rolling his head around in a lazy circle. Jean approaches him and starts talking excitedly.

"You're the poet," Jean says, holding on to the actor's wrists and shaking them. "This is your blood. You must feel it. On the film I see none of this. I see *ptthtttht.*" He makes a noise like a balloon losing its air and then stares at the actor with a hopeful expression. "We try it again, no?"

"Sure," the man says. He rolls his head back and forth again, stretching so far that the tendons pop out in his neck. He has dark eyes and sandpapery stubble. He hitches up his trousers and lets them settle back down on his hips while Jean watches him, an intent look on his face.

"Here's what I want," Jean says. "You are living in complete solitude. In this moment I want you to be understanding that what you stole from your childhood you cannot get back from destiny. Do you understand?"

They go through the scene three more times. Lee thinks the actor is straining to be authentic, but perhaps she does not fully understand the difference between still photography and this newer medium. She wants to make the actor take a few breaths, to slow down; if Man were shooting, he would tell him to forget there is a camera there at all, to picture himself alone in a calm, green field. Jean does none of this. The more keyed up the actor gets the more tensely Jean responds, the muscles flexing in his arm as he winds the film with the crank.

Finally, after the third time through, Jean seems satisfied. "Good. Fifteen minutes and we begin again," he calls, and the actor and all the other people who are rushing around move away from the stage. The room quiets. Jean goes to a nearby table and lights a cigarette, inhaling and then letting the smoke out slowly, so that it curls up around his nose like a gray mustache.

Lee stays where she is, leaning against a post at the edge of the room.

"Jean," she says.

He looks around, notices her. A smile spreads across his face.

"Ah, my Calliope! Your keeper let you out of the cage."

Annoyance flares in her. "There's no cage."

Jean nods. "Good. Have you come to work, to start today? Or just to see what there is to see?"

Lee looks at the stage, the black floor scuffed and dirty. The simple walls, white plaster with a single fake window. In the center stand a small wooden table and two chairs. What will Man think when he finds out she is here?

Two hours later they've cobbled together what they need to make Lee's costume. It is meant to look like the hard shell of a woman's torso, wider than Lee's own, with the arms cut off at the elbows to resemble Greek statuary. This they drape with a white cloth like a toga so that she is covered entirely from the neck down. She cannot sit or move her arms, which are strapped to her sides with thick cord. The fabric is covered with a stiffening compound, painted on in several coats with a wide brush and left to harden. Lee itches and sweats inside it. Jean and three other men gather around to discuss her. They take a large sponge and coat her face in white stage makeup, layer after layer, and Jean runs back to look at her through the lens and then returns, muttering that it isn't good enough, it isn't statue-like enough, it isn't *right*. Soon they decide to try the compound on her face and hair, and instruct her to stay completely still as they apply it.

"It's *burning*," Lee tells them, her jaw immobilized so that she has to force the words out through her teeth.

"It will stop," Jean tells her. This is not at all what she has been picturing. Where is the gold leaf, the radiance?

By the time the compound is dry, the burning is gone, except for Lee's tender cheek, which becomes the part of her body that she focuses her attention on so as not to feel all the other parts that are aching. The main actor, Enrique, is called over. He and Jean and the stagehands stand around discussing her as if she is a prop, and she can feel irritation heating her up inside the costume so that she starts to sweat with aggravation as well as discomfort.

"It's the folds in the fabric. They aren't right," Enrique says. "They're not hanging the way marble hangs."

The men move around the room looking for something they can use, and an Italian stagehand comes over and starts describing something, gesturing as if he is stirring cake batter in a bowl. Then there is butter and sugar and an actual bowl, and the man stirs it up for them and they spread it with a knife along the folds of Lee's outfit. It smells good, like shortbread baking in the oven.

Another hour passes. Still the men aren't done with her. They try her out in various poses on the stage, make her walk so that the bottom half of her body appears to be gliding, but Jean isn't satisfied. Lee grows more and more uncomfortable and soon she desperately needs to use the lav, but there is nothing she can do until it's time to take off the costume.

"She's still a woman," Jean says, disappointed.

Of course she is. What is it that they want from her? Lee is used to pleasing men when they point cameras at her. She walks again across the stage, not lifting her feet from the floor, but it still isn't right. Her whole body aches. Tension coils in her neck and shoulders and the heat of her own trapped skin oppresses her. She has an almost irresistible urge to move her arms, to scratch, to crouch down, to crack open the stiffened fabric and get free.

Then Lee remembers a scene from one of Man's movies that she saw recently, made before he gave up on film entirely. In it he has Kiki lying down, staring up at the camera, and then, when she closes her eyes, painted eyes appear on her lids. She moves to the center of the stage and closes her eyes, knowing that this is what they need — her blindness — and then she moves tentatively across the floor, unseeing and ghostly.

Jean loves it, and when he comes to adjust her costume one final time she tells him through clenched teeth about Man's idea to paint the eyes on Kiki's closed lids. A slow, competitive smile spreads across his face. He gets out an eyebrow pencil and she can feel its pressure through her closed lids. Lee opens and closes her eyes once to show him the effect and leaves them closed for the rest of the day's filming.

With her eyes closed, the power shifts. Lee suddenly feels as if she has gained control. The men in the room cease to matter. She is separate from them. She walks when they tell her to walk, shifting her body to face things she cannot see, but they are nothing more than sounds to her. After a while she loses her ability to distinguish where the sounds are coming from, everything in the room distorted and murky as if they are all trapped in a giant fishbowl.

And then the tension eases and she floats out of her aching body, as she has done so many times when her picture was taken. But this time she doesn't use her wild mind; she stays in the moment. Eyes closed, she watches herself glide across the room, while also still seeing the play of light and shadow across her eyelids from the shifting of the stage lights and the dark spots of the other actors moving past her. And then Lee can't feel her body at all, but she can see it there, under the plaster, can see how powerful she will be when she brings the stone to life on-screen.

When the bright lamps are turned off for the day, Jean comes up to Lee and moves her to a chair, where he and a stagehand begin getting her out of the costume. They remove the armor and the cord that holds down her arms. When they are done, she stretches her arms over her head and almost gasps at the pure pleasure of full movement. And then Jean places his hands on the sides of her face and pushes gently until the makeup cracks and he can begin peeling the layers of compound and batter off her like an eggshell. He does this slowly, almost tenderly, and when he is done he gets a big cloth and wipes away as much of what remains as he can.

As they all leave for the day, she tells Jean she is going to stop by Man's studio, and he and Enrique offer to walk her there. The men are subdued, but as they walk, Lee feels more and more alive. The day has changed her. Everything about it—the crush and bustle of activity on the set, the frenetic energy—was so different from a photo shoot, so much more alive.

At first Lee walks a bit ahead of them, but then Enrique moves next to her. "Have you acted before?" he asks. "I've never seen you."

She shakes her head no.

"You did great. It's batty the things Jean makes people do."

Lee laughs, but already the agony of the costume feels like a distant dream, and what remains is a strange feeling she can barely articulate, as if her emotions have experienced the equivalent of a slap that has brought them, like blood, to the surface.

The air is still, and in it hangs the odor of decaying leaves on the wet earth, rubbish bin fires, the yeasty scent of bread and the sweet rot of old vegetables from the restaurants and bakeries they pass. Lee realizes she is ravenous: she cannot stop thinking about food, a thick veal stew, perhaps, and a jammy red wine to wash it down. She has cake batter in her hair and her dress is smeared with plaster dust and stage makeup, but she doesn't care. As she walks she swings her arms back and forth. Jean glances at her occasionally and smiles.

"We are lucky to have her, no?" he says to Enrique as they wait to cross the street, watching her as she twists her body to wring the last stiffness out of it.

Enrique nods and gives a terse smile. He is just as intense as he was during the filming, and he seems almost angry at Jean in a way that doesn't make sense to Lee.

They reach Man's studio, and the familiar sight of his door with its simple brass knocker sets her stomach fluttering—whether from anticipation or trepidation she isn't sure.

Jean says, "Lee?," and she realizes he has been talking to her. "We'll see you tomorrow?" he asks, and Lee nods yes.

The men leave and Lee stands on the stoop for a few moments. Man is inside, or he is not inside. She doesn't know which would be worse. She opens the door and lets a crack of light into the darkened hallway.

CHAPTER TWENTY-TWO

Inside, the air is still and quiet. Lee climbs the stairs to the second floor. First into the parlor, then the office. Man is not there. Her stomach grows nervous, a feeling stronger than her hunger. The studio is dark and shadowed, the camera lurking in the corner like a giant sleeping animal.

Lee considers running home to look for him, but as she walks back toward the darkroom she sees that the amber warning light is lit beside the door.

Triple tap. He doesn't respond. She goes to knock again and as she does Man pulls the door open. He stands holding a wet contact sheet and at first he doesn't really look at her. But then his gaze flicks to her face and he notices her appearance. Brushing past her to take the print over to the table, he says, "Instead of coming home you slept at a glue factory?"

It is true: she must look very strange. Lee raises her hands to her hair and feels the cake batter crusted there, looks down at her clothes, smeared with plaster dust.

"I was at—"

He cuts her off. "Why didn't you tell me where you were going? You could have been anywhere. With another man. How was I supposed to know?"

Her own anger snaps to match his. "Well, I didn't feel much like talking to you after you ran to Kiki when she *slapped me in front of everyone*."

"I had to get her under control. When she gets like that—you have no idea."

"You're right: I have no idea. And I don't want to. I can't believe you were with a person like her for *ten years*."

"By the time she was calm you were gone. Gone! I had no idea where you were."

Lee throws out her arms in a defiant gesture. As she does it she can smell herself, batter and plaster and the sweat under it from the hours of filming. "Well," she says, feeling wobbly, out of control, "I didn't realize I had to tell you where I was every minute of every day as if I were a child."

"A child. So then I'm your father? I wouldn't think you'd want to bring your father into this."

"What are you trying to say?"

Man pauses and seems to consider his words. "You're being ridiculous. You and I both see the difference between knowing your every move and having you never come home."

"For all I know you never came home either."

"That's because you weren't at home."

Lee makes a sound that is half growl and half sigh. "Jean took me to his house and I slept in his guest bedroom."

"Jean? You and *Jean* are on first-name terms already?"

Lee's stomach growls audibly and she crosses her arms over it. "He asked me if I wanted to be in a movie he's making. He took care of me."

"Lee, not every man can want you. Let the homosexuals alone." Man smiles at her as if he is being funny, and his smile fills her with rage.

"I'm going to be in his film," Lee says. "I won't be coming to work here. For a week, maybe a little more."

"You can't do that."

"It's a week! And he'll pay me."

"I mean you can't work for him. Cocteau—he's such an unctuous little sycophant. His politics are anathema to what I'm doing. Tristan can't stand him, André can't stand him—I'm not alone in this . . ."

Lee wants to push Man and see how far she can make him go. "But that's exactly the problem: *you* don't like him. It's *your* art. But I'm not *you*."

Man rubs a stiff spot in his neck. "You're not *not* me."

"What is that supposed to mean?" As always happens when she is angry, Lee feels her eyes well with tears. There is a chair near her and she slumps into it, rubs her forehead, and watches plaster flake off onto the floor.

Man lifts up his chin. In a small voice, he says, "Last night—when you didn't come home—I realized things have changed between us. Those things I said to you about jealousy, when we were talking about Kiki—that's how I felt when I was with her, but it's not how I feel with you. I need more from you. I'm no longer—I can't be happy, can't be with you unless I have some sort of commitment from you."

"You need more." Lee stares up at him.

"You want to know what I did last night? After you left, I put Kiki in a cab and sent her home. I didn't want to spend another minute with her—all I could think about was you. Do you know what you're doing to me? I'm not like this. I'm not this sort of person. And I went home and I sat in the kitchen and I waited for you and I waited and waited and you never showed up. And I imagined *terrible* things—" Here his voice breaks, and she can see him cross his arms tighter to keep from trembling. "I imagined you hurt, or with someone else, and I couldn't stand it. I truly could not stand the idea of you with someone else."

"I wasn't with someone else, I told you—"

He stops her. "It doesn't matter. I just can't *ever* have you be with someone else. I need you to agree to that...or..."

Lee stands up and crosses her arms, suddenly cold. "Or what? I don't really know what you mean." She turns away from him. "I need a drink."

She walks through the office and into the parlor and goes over to the bar cart and pours a glass of Scotch. Man follows her and she hands him the glass and pours herself another. She holds her glass tight and rubs her fingers over the etched design on its surface. When Man speaks again his voice is much steadier.

"Commit to me and you can work on this film," he says. "That's what I want. That's the way it has to be."

"But I don't even know what you mean: commit to you."

"Promise me I will be the only person for you."

"Forever?"

"Yes."

Lee doesn't know what to say. The Scotch isn't warming her up the way it usually does, so she takes a bigger sip. This is not at all how she thought this conversation would go. It is Lee who is supposed to be angry—Lee, the one who was left to fend for herself last night. She sees again Man's arms wrapped around Kiki, his mouth near her ear as he whispers things to soothe her.

"All those people saw you go to Kiki and not to me. How could you do that to me in front of them?"

Man pushes his fingers into his hair. "I just had to get her under control. I had no idea what she was going to do next. She could do anything, truly."

"You make her sound like some kind of wild animal. Who were you scared for: you or her or me?"

"I don't know. I wasn't thinking it through. And then by the time I looked up you were gone."

"I couldn't be there. I hate that woman." Lee's voice sounds childlike when she says it and she feels a few new tears streak down her cheeks. She wipes them away and then actually laughs. "I do. I hate her."

Man sets down his drink and moves closer to her. He clears his throat. "Lee...what I'm trying to say is this is not just love for me. The things I feel for you—it's something more, something stronger. It's making me—changing me back into someone I used to be, that I had forgotten how to be. Last night in our bed—it was so big and empty. I kept moving over to your side and hoping I'd feel you there. And this morning—I barely slept; I'm not all here today, I'm sure you can tell—I walked the long way to work so I could see the Seine and the whole time I was walking I imagined you next to me. I'm not explaining it very well. I wasn't imagining it. I *saw* you next to me. I couldn't not see you, everywhere I looked."

He reaches out and takes the glass out of her hand and sets it down on a side table, then takes her hands in his. They feel hot. She knows he is waiting for her to say something but she is not sure what it is. He's never spoken this way before. They've discussed marriage, but only their mutual dislike of it. They agreed it's not for them. But this—this is something different. Man's voice is ragged; he holds her hands uncomfortably tight, as if he can squeeze her into understanding what he is saying.

Before Lee can speak, he continues. "I want to give you everything. Me. Not some other man. And I *have* given you so much—I've made you so good. You're so talented now. And every time you show me your work and it's better than the work you've done before, I feel more justified in loving you, in these feelings I have that I can't even make sense of."

She stares at his fingers wrapped around hers, the short dark hairs between the knuckles. He is so serious, but the words don't mean much to her. Commit—to say yes, to agree. And if it will gain her a permanent place here at his side, in this studio, then isn't that what she wants? So she nods, and she says it. "All right, yes. You know I love you."

He squeezes her hands harder and she feels her bones pressing against one another. "I want you to love me forever."

"Forever," she says, nodding, and then because she doesn't want to say anything more, she pulls her hands free and wraps her arms around him and lets him hold her and rock her back and forth. They stay like that for a while. Finally she pulls away. Man squares his shoulders and looks as if he is trying to regain control of himself.

"I should get to work," she says, and starts walking toward the darkroom. She turns to see if he is going to follow her. Instead, he picks up one of the birds' nests on the mantel, cupping it in one hand.

"Lee," he says as she leaves the room. "Do the film."

"All right," she says again. Of course she's going to do the film; she's already decided. But what is the harm in letting him think he is a part of her decision?

Outside the darkroom Lee looks down at the contact sheet he has on the table. "What are you printing?" she calls to him.

"Pictures of you," he says. "What else?"

Lee picks up the loupe. The contact sheet has nine images on it with hardly any variation, as if Man just released the shutter again and again as fast as he could. In the images Lee lies in their bed, sleeping. She has one arm flung above her head, the other wrapped around her torso. She is under the sheets, but it's clear from the folds in the fabric that her legs are spread wide, and the angle at which Man shot the pictures makes the shadows in the sheets point like an arrow toward the center of her. Lee has no memory of him taking these—it could have been yesterday or months ago. Man has taken pictures of her while she is sleeping before; it's never bothered her. But now, as she looks at her sleeping self, tripled in every row, she doesn't like the pictures. Not because it makes her uncomfortable to think of Man watching her while she sleeps, the voyeuristic aspect of them. No, what she doesn't like is the implicit *trust* in them, what it reveals about their relationship. The vulnerability she sees in herself.

Lee wonders if this is what Man means by asking for a commitment. If what he wants from her is total surrender.

Later they go home together. Man seems satisfied by their conversation. He holds her hand while they walk to the apartment, gently moves her out of the way of a pothole in the road. When they get inside, he runs a bath for her, and when she has dried off and gotten into her dressing gown, she finds him in their small kitchen, where he has scrambled her an egg. It sits steaming on a plate on the counter, and Man spreads butter on a slice of toast and adds it to the plate. Lee is famished, eats the egg and then another. She feels warm from the food in her stomach and warm from the bath and from the robe she has knotted at her waist. She and Man barely speak, but there is comfort in their silence. If this is not love, then what is?

DACHAU

APRIL 30, 1945

If Lee uses a wide angle and takes in the landscape, getting the tidy lawns of the nearby village in the shot, she can show how close the trains were to civilians, how they knew, how they *must* have known—

If she frames the shot through the open train car door, foregrounds the dead man's skull, his cheekbones almost slicing through what's left of his skin—

If she takes a photo of one of the rabbits they raised in the camp, its clean white fur, its plump rolls of well-fed fat. Bred to be a muff for an overfed Frau to push her fists into. A prisoner feeding the rabbit grain out of his dirt-blackened hand—

If she takes a photograph of someone else seeing what she sees. Prisoners, their eyes haunted, starving, looking on as bodies are tossed in a pit. An SS guard, jaw broken, watching blood spurt from another guard's punched nose—

If she tries different angles, gets in close. The empty tin bowl, the number on a wrist, the man's foot half gone when he takes off his boot—

If she takes photos of the ones in charge. A German official, vomiting next to a stacked pile of dead. Another of a suicide, his tongue a black worm pushing out of his mouth—

Sometimes Lee puts her camera to her face just so she can close her eyes. Sometimes she takes the photos blind.

If they knew—they had to know—there is no way they didn't know—

If she—the smell. She will write of it to Audrey.

One by one members of the press corps leave. Lee stays. She must bear witness. The film canisters fill her pockets, grenades to send out for publication.

CHAPTER TWENTY-THREE

Jean has picked up cast and crew members all over Europe. They are a ragtag group, but as soon as Lee shows up on the second day, resolute and motivated, she becomes a part of it. Most of them don't even speak the same language, but when they are together it doesn't matter: they crack jokes and talk in long looping soliloquies about everything, and somehow enough of it makes sense to create a fellow feeling. A woman named Anush is a palm reader, and one night everyone on the set gets their fortune read, which makes them reveal things they otherwise would never mention. Another evening they drink brandy and empty a metal trash can and have a fire right there on the stage. After only a few days Lee thinks she could count these people as her friends.

Some afternoons, when filming has wrapped for the day, they raid the dressing rooms, pulling out costumes. They cinch themselves into Edwardian gowns, men and women both, the corsets so tight their breath comes short and fast, or they don chain mail tunics and battle with dull-bladed swords. They act out skits and fall over one another laughing. When Jean is happy with how the day's filming has gone, he acts as their ringleader, and the scenarios he invents for them to perform are crazy and wonderful.

Lee finds she loves acting. Freed from the constraints of the statue costume at the end of the day, she is loose and uninhibited. She'll place Nefertiti's crown on her head and feel her whole bearing change, growing languid and queenly, and her real identity will slip away. The other cast members are surprised she's never acted before. She basks in their praise and finds herself working hard to impress them. The film inspires her photography too; there are similarities between her own process and what's happening on set. She begins to understand photography as cinematic. When she takes a picture, she is laying claim to one moment out of a moving stream of a thousand potential moments, and the act of choosing it, of removing it from its context, is part of what makes it art.

Behind the cine camera, Jean is a master. Lee sees that now. His way of winding up the actors, angering them, even, is effective for getting what he wants. Enrique in particular. The two of them together engage in what she soon realizes is the same dynamic both on and off set: that they are lovers suffuses all their interactions. The relationship is a tempestuous one. They scream at each other in full view of the rest of the cast, and Lee even sees Enrique reach out to strike Jean at one point. Everyone studiously ignores them, and instead just comments on the range Enrique displays in the dailies. In the end, Lee thinks, their personal drama makes their art work, and she can't help thinking of herself with Man, the way she can't separate her feelings for him from the work they do together.

Even though she is glad to be on her own, Lee thinks of Man often while she's on the set. The lightness inside her while she's there, like a fountain bubbling over, fills her with guilt, and sometimes the thought of Man, alone at the studio, makes her wish she wasn't having such a good time. She's not sure she deserves to feel this way; being here without him should not make her this happy. But then in the next instant she finds herself laughing so hard she forgets to cover her teeth with her hand, and all Lee thinks is that she can't wait to share all this with him, to let him in on all the fun.

One afternoon, after a long shoot of a bizarre scene in which the poet's mouth separates from his body and reappears on his hand, Lee sits on a wobbly chair at the edge of the stage. They called her in for some of the crowd shots, and she loved being on film without all her makeup. Around her, other actors are talking and relaxing. Someone brings out a brandy bottle and passes it around. Another man rolls cigarettes on a barstool and hands them out, and soon the stage is hazy with smoke. It could be four in the afternoon or the middle of the night. Like the darkroom, the film set has a timeless quality, and Lee wants to linger. Her stomach is empty and the brandy settles in it like a hot-water bottle, all comfort and heat. After a while the bottle is empty and one by one everyone starts to get up to go home, gathering coats and hats and saying their goodbyes.

Soon Lee is one of the last people there. She picks up her coat and heads backstage for one last look around. The dark space smells of smoke and wet wool and some sort of herbal cleaner, and she breathes it in with pleasure. Only a few more days and they'll be done filming. Lee doesn't want to let it go.

Someone comes up behind her and puts his hand on her arm. She jumps, then sees that it's Jean. "You scared me!"

"I am sorry." He takes a deep breath. "You stay too—I've seen you. I never want to go home."

"Me neither." She turns to face him and he gives her an appraising look.

"I am headed to the ballet tonight—it is Lifar's first production. Would you like to come?"

Lee smooths her hair and looks down at her wrinkled dress. "I look a fright."

"You look a vision. Plus, we will sneak." Jean makes a gesture with his hands like a little animal creeping, and she laughs.

They walk out of the studio together as the sun is setting. Masses of purple clouds gather, and through them the sun sends sharp rays of light.

"Oh, look," Lee says, and they stop to stare until the sun shifts and the rays disappear. Then, companionably, Lee loops her arm through his.

"Enrique didn't want to go?" she asks.

Jean sniffs. "Enrique does not like to be seen with me."

"That can't be true!"

"Lately it feels that way."

"I'm sorry."

Jean shrugs. "And you? Man Ray is not taking you out tonight, wooing you?"

"Man doesn't need to woo me anymore," Lee says, and laughs.

Jean gives her a look. "Certainly you always need wooing. Someone should tell him that."

The facade of the Palais Garnier is one of the most beautiful in Paris, studded with statues of the Muses of poetry and harmony. Lee heads toward the front entrance, but Jean moves her around to the south side, where they enter through a small unmarked door.

"We really are sneaking?" she asks.

"Yes—like little mice. You should see backstage."

They walk down a narrow hallway and emerge into the costume room. From a delicate metal frame bolted to the ceiling, dozens of tutus hang suspended in the air. Against the dark wood of the room, the tutus are ethereal clouds scudding across a nighttime sky. Lee immediately reaches for her camera and takes a few pictures, but the light is fading from the small windows and she knows the shots won't turn out well.

"Can you bring me back here another time?" she says to Jean, but he is already leading her farther into the building. They ascend a short flight of stairs and emerge backstage. The room takes Lee's breath away. Dark wood and shrouded set pieces. A vast floor, stained black and scuffed from thousands of ballet shoes, the scent of dance tallow lingering in the air. Lee walks toward the stage and, as her eyes get used to the darkness, notices the sets that must be ready for use that evening: beautiful tapestries with pastoral landscapes, a cloth painted to look like a four-poster bed, a scene of a dining room table laid out for a sumptuous party. Like the tutus, each set panel is suspended from a series of cables, and Lee likes the way the ropes crosshatch the ceiling, lets her eye be drawn up to the top of the room, where the last of the sunset filters through a row of small windows. In the light the dust motes twirl and sparkle.

Lee watches for a while and then notices a person up in the rafters, standing on a wooden platform suspended between two ropes. He extends a leg off the platform and grabs a cable, then crosses over to another ledge, nimbly climbs down a ladder, and moves closer to the ground. She can see him better now. He is dressed all in black: tight black pants, black shirt, black scarf tied around his waist like a belt. When he moves again, pulling a different cable so that he can adjust one of the set pieces, she sees the power in his body, the lithe maleness of him. When she finally tears her eyes away to look at Jean, she realizes he has been watching too, and they exchange a smirk.

"Caruso!" Jean shouts at the man. "We see you!"

The man turns to them, and Lee picks up her camera and frames him in the viewfinder, his shadowy form silhouetted against the ropes. She focuses, releases the shutter, and puts her camera away. The man climbs down and jumps neatly to the ground, the thump of his feet sending up a puff of rosin powder.

Jean goes over and embraces him, which the man endures without reciprocating.

"Caruso!" Jean says again. "You are here—why are you here? I need you on my set!"

Caruso doesn't respond but gives Jean a brief smile. Then he glances over at Lee, and his face shows a flicker of recognition.

As their eyes meet, Lee recognizes him too. Soft dark hair, sharp cheekbones, shirt unbuttoned with a sprouting of straight chest hair visible. Full dry lips. His first name comes to her immediately. Antonio. From Drosso's.

Antonio reaches into a back pocket and pulls out a flattened pouch of tobacco, then sits on a chair and starts to roll a cigarette.

"Caruso, Caruso," Jean says. "I need you for my last scene. I need you to paint me a billiards room."

Antonio licks the edge of the cigarette paper and twists it closed. "You know how much Lifar's paying me? Good money."

He lights the cigarette and takes a huge drag, his lips going white with the force of his inhalation. He moves to hand the cigarette to Lee.

"I don't smoke," she tells him, but he ignores her and places the cigarette to her mouth. His boldness surprises her, and when his fingers touch her face she thinks at first he must have burned her with the ash, the feeling of his skin on hers sends such heat through her. The effect is absurd, outsize, makes the world seem sharper, as if she has rubbed her eyes and brought everything into better focus. As if she has just come awake. The part of her cheek where he touched her feels separate from the rest of her face, and separately awake. The smoke burns her throat as she exhales, and she is desperate not to cough. Antonio lights two more cigarettes, one for himself and one for Jean, and as he does so Lee tries to look anywhere but at him. But every time she looks, Antonio is staring right back at her, rolling the cigarette without even glancing at it. His eyes are gray, clear like chips of river ice, and he doesn't seem embarrassed to be looking at her so intently.

The three of them smoke for a while. Lee wants to reach out and touch Antonio again to see if the same feeling will happen. She can't even focus on the small talk they are making, so she moves away from them and walks over to look at one of the set pieces. The panel is dupioni silk, painted with sweeping brushstrokes to give the impression of a forest. Here and there intricately painted birds are just visible within the looser lines of the branches and leaves. A draft from somewhere makes the silk vibrate.

"I remember you," Antonio says, coming up behind her. The night at Drosso's rushes back.

"You're friends with Poppy and Jimmy," she says.

"Those two. Not really."

Lee is flooded with the memory of her behavior that night, all the drinks she had in an effort to feel comfortable, to belong.

"I saw Poppy once since then," Lee tells him. "She pretended she didn't know me. I still can't figure out why."

"You're probably better off. She's always putting on some new act."

"What do you mean?"

Antonio shrugs. "She and Jimmy—there's always some swindle. I didn't figure that out until later, but they're no good."

Lee wonders if they were the ones who stole her camera. It was the only thing she had of any value. When his cigarette is done, Antonio looks at his watch. "Almost time," he says, and just as he says it the first dancers and stagehands appear backstage. Lee makes to leave but Jean crooks his finger at her and leads her over to the curtain. It is massive, made out of heavy-pile velvet and edged with dense rows of braided fringe. Jean pulls it open and sticks his head through.

"Come—you have to do this," he says, so Lee goes over and they swap places. She sticks just her face through the fabric, letting it encircle her like a heavy veil, and she looks out over the still-empty opera house, the rows of seats receding into shadow and flanked by the beautiful gilded boxes. Everything is silent, and the room is filled with a sense of expectation. What would it be like to perform on that stage, blinded by the bright lights and unable to see the hundreds of people you know are there? To feel the orchestra reverberating under your feet? Lee drops the curtain and moves to take one step forward but realizes the backstage has gotten crowded. It is time to go.

As she leaves, Lee glances around for Antonio. He stands in the corner talking to another stagehand, but as she looks over at him, he catches her eye, and a devilish, unexpected grin spreads across his face, as if he and Lee are sharing a joke from across the room. Lee smiles back and a string pulls tight between them.

Lee and Jean are among the first to be seated, and they watch as the giant hall fills up around them. They talk of their film, and of ballet; Jean tells her all he knows about that night's production. Then the lights dim and the music begins. The dancers fill the stage, their legs and arms hard as marble but moving like ribbons when they dance. They are all so beautiful—Lee has never seen such powerful bodies, men and women both, and as she watches them she feels shivers go down her back. Almost as beautiful as the dancers are the sets, which rise and fall with an elegance that is itself almost dancing. Lee pictures Antonio up in the rafters, his body moving the scenes he has created, the rooms and landscapes he conjured now under his control.

Lee watches in what becomes almost a trance. One part of her mind watches the ballet; the other thinks about how it would feel to be touched by Antonio, like a dancer himself, all hard muscle and bone. The air in the opera house is full of perfume, but beneath it Lee smells Antonio's tobacco, lifts her fingers to her lips to smell it better. She likes the way his belt sits at his hips, how tall he is, the flex of his thighs when he jumped to the floor. Onstage, two dancers promenade, and then the man's arm circles the woman's waist and he lifts her up above him as easily as stretching. As she lands she drapes herself across his body. The thoughts leave Lee plucked and twanging like the ropes behind the stage when Antonio leapt down from them.

At the end of the performance, the entire audience stands, clapping furiously and shouting "Bravo! Brava!" again and again as the dancers return to the stage to bow. Lifar has done it; he is a success. Jean applauds for a while and then puts his arm around Lee. She claps until her hands are burning.

CHAPTER TWENTY-FOUR

When Lee wakes up the next morning, she reaches for Man across the bed, their two bodies warm beneath the blankets. They haven't made love since she started working on the film, and she misses him, kisses his shoulder and then his neck. Her body hums with longing. Man returns her kiss, and Lee presses against him, but she can tell his mind is elsewhere. Hers is too: the ballet still fills her thoughts. So she tells him about it. Lifar's first production. What she does not mention is Antonio, the way she can still feel his fingers on her face as he held the cigarette to her lips.

"I forgot how much you love dance," Man says. "I should have thought to take you." He untangles his body from hers and gets out of bed, throwing on the shirt and pants he has draped across a chair. "I've been so distracted—this painting is taking everything out of me."

"It's all right," Lee says. "We've both been busy."

Later that day, Man stands barefoot on top of their mattress, facing his painting of her mouth. The bedsheets are covered with drop cloths. Lee is sitting in a chair in the corner of the room, contemplating the inverted V of the painting she can see between his legs. A swatch of cirrus, a blob of her lower lip. From this angle his body bisects the giant canvas.

Her mind is still on the ballet. "Let's go see it tonight," Lee says to him. "Come with me." Lee thinks the match the dance lit inside her will light him up too.

"Tonight? We can't," Man says. "It's the salon."

Lee has forgotten. Breton's big hoopla. Posters hang all over the neighborhood, the names of the featured artists printed in one big curve running the length of the page: DALÍ~ERNST~RAY~ARP.

"Do I have to go?" Lee has not been able to parse the difference between this salon and the other weeknight gatherings Man's been going to lately. Gatherings where, if she goes with him, she is never sure what role he wants her to play: coy ingenue, faithful mistress, bawdy tomboy. She tries out all of them and none feel like a fit or seem to fully please him.

"Of course! Everyone is going. Éluard wants that new girl of his to be included—what's her name? Nusch?—and got Breton to agree. And this is a public event, not just one of Breton's regular things."

"So Nusch and Paul—who else?"

Man ticks off names on his fingers. "Tristan, Soupault, Aragon. Most likely Tatiana, and Ilse Bing—have you met Ilse yet?"

Lee can't remember. She knows the core group of Man's friends, but the more peripheral members, the ones who come and go depending on the group's shifting alliances, leave her befuddled. Especially the women, whose entrée into these evenings is entirely dependent on whatever man they are attached to at the time. But Lee has gotten to know Tatiana, the blonde from Moscow whose accent is so thick it sounds as though she has sponges stuffed in her mouth. And she likes Nusch, a birdlike woman with whom Paul Éluard has recently fallen in love.

The rest of the women connected to Man's circle Lee can

do without. Recently, Lee bumped into a group of them at Le Dôme; they were gathered close around a café table like buzzards around carrion. Lee pulled up a chair but none of them moved to give her room, so she sat for a while on the outskirts of their group, her martini balanced on her knee because she could not reach a surface on which to set it. Lee realized then—and tells Man now—that the other women don't like her because she is too pretty; they are intimidated by her, all of them except Tatiana, who has a certain regal beauty of her own.

Man shakes his head. "They acted cold to you that day because you were supposed to buy them a round of drinks," he says.

"I don't have the money for that!" Lee says, shocked.

"They think you do, and that's all that matters. Besides—one round. You *do* have the money for that."

As always, Man's loose hold on finances annoys her. "Well, whatever the reason, they don't like me and I don't know how to fix it. And I don't see why I should have to fix it." Lee's mouth sets in a moue of disappointment.

"They like you fine. Everyone likes you. Éluard loves you. And Breton is showing a film of mine tonight. I want you to see it."

"A film? You gave that up."

"It's an old one. It's really Dada, but everyone was so drunk when I showed it that I can show it to them now and call it Sur-realist, and what the hell will they know?" Man smiles.

Lee stands up, stretches, goes into the bathroom. In front of the mirror she executes a faulty little pirouette, wishing she were go-ing back to the Garnier.

The gallery is set up with folding wooden chairs and a projector aimed at the back wall. It is more than half full by the time Man and Lee arrive. People clap for Man when he walks in. He waves modestly and finds them chairs near the center of the room. Two

poets walk back and forth in front of the projector, their silhouettes moving in strange distorted patterns behind them as they
recite. The room is full of smoke and men and low, hushed chatter, and it is impossible to hear the reading over the audience;
no one seems remotely interested in listening to the poets. Lee
catches sight of Fraenkel—she can always recognize him from
his little caterpillar mustache—sitting in a corner reading a newspaper and intermittently ringing a large brass cowbell.

After a while the audience quiets. Onstage, Philippe Soupault,
a fierce, bony man whom Lee has met at several previous gatherings, gives an affected bow, closes his eyes, and begins reciting.

"No matter, no matter,
Animal cracker
The dish ran away with the quadroon.
When all was a clatter
Spitter spitter spatter
The bride
a groom
Room
Room
Room
I took the lettuce off the wall
and ate it."

Someone in a middle row launches a crumpled ball of paper
at him, and soon everyone is booing and whistling. Lee is surprised they don't like it; the poem sounds to her like much of
the other Surrealist writing she's heard, which to her ears is all a
bunch of gibberish. Soupault is unperturbed by the booing, keeps
going, but finally Tristan gets on the stage and drags him off. A
few moments of nothing, and then there is the hiss of film mov-

ing through the projector and the audience settles again. Tristan announces Man's film, *Le Retour à la Raison,* and images project on the wall. Silhouettes of screws and pliers. The front of a Bugatti with a woman's eyes where the headlights should be, blinking. More tools, scissors and hammers, dark black against a white background. Riotous and weird like all of Man's work. As the film continues, some people in the audience, which quieted down initially, cough and shuffle. Chair legs scrape the floor. The combined rustle of restlessness. Beside Lee, Man sits coiled tight.

He leans toward her and whispers, "They don't understand it." Lee takes his hand. Though she'd never tell him, the truth is that Lee doesn't understand it either. It feels to her as though she is sitting in the studio flipping through a stack of unrelated photographs. But maybe that is the point? Lee grows hot with embarrassment on Man's behalf. She wants everyone to love the film. To love him.

Suddenly, there is the snap of nitrocellulose breaking. Man jumps up and moves to assist Breton, who kneels beside the projector and runs his hand along the film reel to stop the strip from unfurling further. The audience's murmur becomes a din. People relax in their seats or turn around in their chairs to talk to the people behind them. Lee scans the room for people she knows. A few rows up and over, the Mdivanis sit together, impeccable in plus fours. Lee has not seen them since Patou's party, and once she notices them she keeps her eye on them, wondering if and when they will talk to Man. She wonders if Man knows they are here, if he has seen them since he told her about them all those months ago.

Tatiana is wearing a trim hat with a veil and, perched on top, a small stuffed bird. Lee catches her eye and they nod at each other. A row up is Claude Cahun, looking more normal than usual in a black suit and red bow tie, and next to her is a dark-haired woman with a small camera hanging from a strap around her neck. Her hair is short, cut like Lee's, and she has a perfectly centered mole at the nape of her neck, just above the collar of her white linen dress. She looks familiar, and Lee realizes she's seen a picture of her before, posing with a Leica in the latest issue of *Das Illustrierte Blatt*. It must be Ilse Bing, the woman Man mentioned earlier. In the photo—and now, as she turns and scans the room—she wears an expression of calculating intelligence, and Lee is almost as intrigued by her as she is by her expensive camera.

Lee is just about to get up and say hello to Tatiana when the film starts up again. Man stands at the front of the room with Breton. More of the same images appear, tools and shots of a stark landscape, and this time the audience doesn't settle. People continue to murmur as the film projects in front of them. Man's gaze roves around the room, but he doesn't look perturbed that they are talking; he's more curious than anything else. Lee wonders if anyone—Man included—could explain the point of the film.

When it is over, there is a light smattering of applause. Man clearly expects some sort of follow-up, some questions, but Tristan just shouts from where he stands in the corner that it's time to go into the gallery, and the audience stands and moves en masse into the next room. A few people start closing the folding chairs to make more space. Someone sets out bottles of wine and immediately a cluster of people forms around the table. Lee sees Man across the room but decides to get a drink, finding herself pushed up behind Ilse and Claude in line.

Lee hasn't seen Claude since she had her gallery show, and she has heard through Man's circle that Claude traveled south in the summer with some of the painters and set up a studio in Antibes. The coastal weather has agreed with her. Her cheeks aren't as sallow, and she's let her hair grow in so that she looks like a stylish little boy. Claude stands close to Ilse, and as they shuffle forward in the slow-moving line they link arms and whisper secretively. They don't notice Lee until they've been handed their wine, and then as they pass Claude leans toward her, her breath hot against Lee's ear. "Are you coming tonight?"

Lee is not sure what Claude means. Aren't they already here? "Yes," she says.

Ilse looks Lee up and down, considering her, and then says, "Good," before reaching out and pinching Lee's nose between her fingers. Before Lee can register surprise, Ilse and Claude have moved away, and Lee is at the front of the line, being handed a glass, filled gauchely all the way to the brim.

In the gallery Lee looks at the art. Of everything displayed she likes best Dalí's canvas, *The Accommodations of Desire,* which she has to wait in line to view. It is a small piece, white lumpen shapes on a beach, covered over with lions' heads, a toupee, ants, and shells. The shapes look to Lee like labia, the red paint at their centers like menstrual blood, and this both titillates and horrifies her. She knows from Man that Dalí made the painting for Gala, Éluard's now-estranged wife; knows, in fact, that Dalí's creation of it co-incided with the end of the marriage. Lee wonders how it feels to Éluard to have it hanging here, a visual representation of his wife's infidelity. If Lee were in his shoes she would be mortified, she thinks, but then she looks across the room and there is Éluard with his arm draped across his new lover, Nusch, his expression sanguine. Nusch looks carefree as well, though she must know the drama about this painting. Gala herself is absent, but then again Breton has always despised her. Dalí stands surrounded by a circle of men in the far corner, untouchable, his hair wild and his mustache waxed to angry points. Lee gulps down her wine and goes to get another.

All these people, each with his or her private drama. Over the past year Lee has worked to get to know them—at first because she was hungry for their fame, to be in their orbit. And then she wanted to know them because Man knew them. As she spent more time with them they morphed from intimidating ciphers into real people, with the same quirks and foibles as everyone else. And now Lee is part of it. This is her set, for better or worse. She feels they have accepted her begrudgingly, because she is Man's girl, and it is such a different feeling than how she feels with Jean's crew, with which she was immediately at ease. Perhaps it's because she showed up at the film set unencumbered. None of that group had any preconceived notions of how she would be. She wasn't Man's girl there—she was just another actor, working as hard as everyone else.

Lee wishes she was at Jean's studio right now instead of here. She closes her eyes and is backstage again, passing around the bottle of brandy. When she was there, she was thinking about Man. Now she is with Man and she's thinking about the film set. Lee can't believe it was just yesterday that she was at Jean's, just yesterday that she saw the ballet—and Antonio.

Lee needs to stop the thoughts that lead back to Antonio, so she begins to walk around the gallery again. Max Ernst is showing a few of his forest paintings, the paint textured with metal and sticks. Jean Arp has a sculpture and a strange painting that Lee likes, black-and-white blobs cut out of wood and arranged in a random pattern. Perhaps these people are sometimes ill behaved, but here in the gallery, their beautiful work hanging on the walls, Lee is reminded that they are serious about their art, and talented too. If only Lee's work were hanging here also. She's wanted this so many times, but what has she done to make it happen? Most of these people probably don't even remember that she's a photographer—that she's serious, just like them.

The thoughts make her melancholy, make her take another

swallow of her wine, which is cheap and terrible, as if it were made from raisins. On the other side of the room, Man stands with Soupault and Tristan, and when he sees Lee looking at him, he beckons her. As she approaches he holds out a hand to her and pulls her close, and when she is against his side she feels an easing, the familiar feeling of relief.

By ten o'clock glasses clutter every surface, overturned bottles have left viscous red stains on the wooden floors, and the air in the room feels humid. No one is looking at the art anymore. Instead, they are knotted into tight groups, arms slung around one another, their conversations slurred. Five drinks in, Lee leans heavily against Man, who absentmindedly rubs his hand up and down her arm. People start to disband, to say good night, and soon there are only two dozen or so of them left. As if responding to the change in the room, Breton claps his hands and announces that the show is at an end. Man kisses Lee's cheek and she asks, "What's next?"

"More drinks, I imagine," he says, pulling her in closer.

A few final stragglers leave and Breton locks the gallery door. The remaining group moves upstairs to a private space above the gallery. At the top of the stairs stands Soupault, blindfolded and holding a large wooden box. Lee realizes *this* must be what Claude and Ilse were talking about, the real festivities of the evening.

"Forfeits!" Soupault shouts. Lee almost laughs. She hasn't played forfeits since boarding school, when she and the other girls would gather after lights-out, toss their few pieces of jewelry into a box, and dare one another to do ridiculous things, like throw eggs at the headmaster's house or eat rotten food.

The line slows as people decide what to give up. Valuable items—a tiepin, a pocket watch—get cheers; smaller items—a cheap tortoiseshell comb, a pair of dice—get booed. Standing a few people in front of Lee, Tatiana takes off her beautiful hat and places it carefully in the box. A writer whose name Lee can't remember pulls an ivory fountain pen out of his pocket and tosses it in. Claude pulls a heavy signet ring off her finger and adds it to the collection. Lee rarely wears jewelry and has only a paste clip in her hair, which she drops into the box as she passes Soupault. She waits for people to jeer, but as the line moves forward a few more steps, she hears instead laughter and whoops of approval. They aren't for her. Lee turns to see Ilse pulling her Leica strap over her head and fumbling at her dress. For a moment Lee thinks she is going to put the camera in the box, but then Ilse unhooks her brassiere, snakes her arms out of its straps, and drops it on top of the pile.

In the upstairs room, everyone sits on the floor in a big circle, Soupault and the box in the middle. A whiskey bottle makes its way around. When it gets to Lee she circles the neck with her lips and tips her head back, loving the earthy burn of the whiskey as it goes down, loving, in a sudden liquor-fueled burst of magnanimity, these people and the lightheartedness of this activity, that she is here drinking with them just as she was doing the other night on the film set. She feels more relaxed, sits with her legs folded casually, her shoes cast off to the side. Man is to her left, Breton is to her right, and when the whiskey moves a few people away from them, Breton reaches into his jacket and pulls out a flask, which he hands to her with a collusive raise of his eyebrows. Lee takes a nip and whatever's inside the flask is even better than the whiskey.

Soupault looks around the room and then picks up the box and sets it on his lap. He peers inside for a few moments before pulling out a bow tie. "I have here a silk bow tie, two decades out-of-date," he says to ripples of laughter. "Blue with white stripes, and smelling of a certain someone's gardenia perfume." More laughter, and Nusch laughs along with them but then covers her face with her hands.

Paul Éluard, his shirt collar unbuttoned, says, "Mine, of course. What is my forfeit?"

Soupault rubs his chin. "Go to town with Nusch."

This, too, Lee remembers from when she was younger, when she played this game at a birthday party and had to go to town with the boy from a few farms over, Johnny Whiting. Every time he asked her a question she had to take a step toward him, and he chose the easiest questions he could think of so that he could kiss her sooner, his breath smelling of the cucumber sandwiches they'd just eaten.

Éluard laughs. "That's too easy."

"I'm starting us off easy," Soupault says.

Éluard nods and he and Nusch rise and stand in the middle of the circle about eight feet apart. For a few moments they just look at each other. "Do you like rainy weather?" Éluard asks her.

"Yes," she says. Nusch is tiny, delicate, dressed all in black with a lace scarf tied in her hair. She stands with her eyes cast down and there is something raw and honest in her voice that sucks the drunken hilarity out of the room. They take a step toward each other.

"Do you like T. S. Eliot?" she asks in a whisper.

"Yes." They take another step toward each other.

Soupault stands up and claps his hands. "I take it back. This is too easy. I will ask the questions. Paul, do you like Salvador?"

"Not particularly," Éluard says, and a wave of knowing laughter goes around the room. Neither Éluard nor Nusch moves forward.

"Nusch, do you think Paul is handsome?"

"Yes," she whispers, and they step toward each other.

"Paul, do you like being in bed with Nusch?"

A pause. "Yes." Another step. The gap between them is only a foot wide now.

"Nusch, has Paul asked you to marry him?"

Nusch does not answer, but they move the final foot toward each other and then they are kissing, and Paul lifts her off the ground and holds her in the air, and there is an uncomfortable feeling in the room that this isn't something they should be watching, but then someone whoops and sets everyone to clapping. Éluard puts Nusch down and raises his arms above his head like a boxing champion and then they both sit down in the circle. Lee moves her hand along the floor until it's touching Man's, and watches the other couple, who sit with their arms around each other, their obvious mutual attraction setting them apart from the rest of the group. Lee glances at Man and he smiles at her and squeezes her hand.

Soupault slingshots Éluard his bow tie and then digs around in the box again. This time he pulls out Tatiana's hat and says, "I have here a fine example of Russian millinery. This elegant confection formerly graced the head of none other than . . . ?"

Tatiana raises her hand.

"Tata, put lipstick on André, blindfolded!" someone shouts, and everyone laughs as she gets up and puts on the blindfold and then fumbles at Breton's face with a lipstick someone hands her, drawing a second pink mouth a few inches larger than his real mouth.

A few other people are chosen and the forfeits grow stranger. Max Ernst fashions an outfit out of newspaper for Fraenkel and makes him strip to his underclothes, then ties the outfit to him with shipping twine. The writer whose name Lee doesn't recall walks across the room with a potato held between his thighs. One man has to sit on another man's lap for thirty minutes.

During it all the bottle has made its way around to Lee several times, and she has gone from feeling warm and limber to dazed and floaty. She closes her eyes and thinks how desperately nice it would be to have a glass of water. It has to be getting close to her turn, and she wonders what they will make her do when they pull her clip out of the box.

As the forfeits have continued the organization of the circle has changed, and now when Lee opens her eyes she finds herself sitting next to Ilse.

"What do you make of all this?" Ilse asks her, gesturing to the circle.

Lee blinks her eyes a few times to focus. "It's all in good fun, I suppose?"

"Fun. Yes. Do you know I wanted to have my work in this show and André told me no?"

"Oh, I didn't know that." The whiskey makes the words roll like marbles in Lee's mouth.

"Of course you didn't know. Why would you?" Her tone is strident. "*You*. Claude has told me all about you."

What could Claude have to say about her? Lee looks over at where Claude lies on her back with a cigar between her lips, blowing smoke circles above her head in little puffs.

When Lee doesn't answer, Ilse continues. "My photographs are *good*. They're as good as anyone's in here, and André won't even *look* at them. What do you have to do—suck a man's cock to get him to look at your work?"

Ilse glares at her. Lee has no idea what to say. "I'm not sure . . . I'm sorry he wouldn't let you in," she finally says.

"You're sorry. Everyone is sorry. André will be sorry too. Claude and I are going to have our own show."

"Good for you." Even as Lee says it she doesn't mean it. Jealousy already coils its tentacles through her.

Ilse says, "You know, I gave up everything when I moved here. My studies, my family. I'm alone except for this"—she points to her camera—"and when I got to Paris, I thought: I should meet other women. We can help one another. And then I heard about you, and I thought perhaps we could join together. That you would be interested in doing something with me, in saying

263

piss off to all these men. But I can see just from looking at you that you wouldn't want to do it."

Lee straightens up, fights off the fug of drink. "How can you know that?"

Ilse shrugs. "You—you're like a piece of pretty glass, with your pretty eyes and your pretty face, but that's all you are. Just clear, through and through."

The woman's harshness shocks Lee. "You don't know the first thing about me."

"I know that Kiki hit you in the face the other night. Everyone knows that story by now. I don't blame her. She must hate you, how you stole Man Ray from her."

From the floor, Claude, who Lee didn't even know was listening, says, "She does hate you."

Lee is trembling. "That's not at all how it went," she says, but Ilse has turned away dismissively and is bent down and whispering something to Claude. Lee strains to make out what they're saying but can't.

Kiki, now Ilse—these women are crueler than the men. At least Lee knows how to manage men, how to flirt with them and get them to do what she wants. But these women are entirely different. Judging her before they even know her.

In the center of the circle, Soupault stands up again. He pulls something sparkly from the box. "I have here a triangular clip. Diamonds, maybe, but"—he puts the clip between his teeth and clamps down—"probably not."

Lee gets to her feet, still buzzing from her conversation with Ilse, and says loudly, "Me. What's my forfeit?"

"Oh ho!" Soupault says. "Madame Man Ray."

As always, Lee wishes they wouldn't call her that. Éluard stands up too, his bow tie drooping crookedly around his neck, and the two men confer and then laugh. Man is now all the way on the other side of the circle, and Lee can tell how drunk he is by how he's slumping, practically lying on the floor.

Finally, after a dramatic pause, Éluard says, "We want you to tell us if Man Ray is a homosexual."

Drunken shouts and whistles. Man sits up quickly from his slumped position. People look at him and Lee, waiting for one of them to do something. Lee has no idea what to do, so to ease the tension she says, "Can't I just walk across the room with a potato?"

This gets a laugh, but Éluard shakes his head and reiterates the question.

This is not the first time homosexuality has come up; in fact, Lee heard them discussing it the one time she joined the men at Tristan's. Together they are preening, frightened roosters. Lee thinks they should all just fuck one another and get it over with; their childish ridiculing of what they desire disgusts her. Even Man, still sitting on the ground, suddenly disgusts her. Why not ask *him* this question? Lee is not his mouthpiece. And what does Man expect her to do? She knows his secret—what he has done with the Mdivanis, who luckily aren't here anymore. Lucky for Man. But what Man has told her in their bedroom is for the two of them to know; she would not break that trust for all the world. So she'll say no, and then she'll walk across the room and kiss him, and the night will go on as it was meant to. Because it is none of these men's business who Man has loved, or how, or why. It is none of their business how he loves her, how different he is when they are alone together. But before she can speak, Man stands up and goes right up to Éluard, his spittle catching the light as he shouts boastfully.

"All these rumors swirl around because I don't discriminate at my studio. Are you a whore who wants her picture taken? Are you an addict? I will take your picture. I will do it."

"That doesn't answer the question," Éluard says, his voice hoarse. "*Are you* a homosexual?"

Man has a crazed look on his face and a bottle in his hand, which he swigs from before wiping his mouth on his sleeve. "I answer your question with a question. If I were bent, how would you explain Exhibit A?" He points to Lee and all eyes turn back to her. Ilse snorts with laughter.

Anger fills her. Man's arms are outstretched as if he's a preacher in a two-penny tent, the wine bottle still clenched in his fist. His clothes are rumpled and there is a big streak of dust on his pants from where he was lying on the floor. Lee glares at him and his gaze slides away from her. She can tell he's embarrassed, but something seems to have taken him over, caught him in this strange male posturing. She is even more angry than when she left him with Kiki the other night.

Suddenly, Claude stands up and stomps her foot on the wood floor. The sound brings everyone to attention. "You people," she says, her words a slow drawl. "You people are all so fucking boring." She stubs out her cigar in an empty wineglass and then saunters over to the doorway, where she turns back to face them and slaps down her hand on her biceps, raising her other hand in an obscene gesture. Then she disappears down the stairs.

The room is quiet for a moment. Then Aragon says, "I always liked her," and everyone erupts in drunken laughter.

No one seems very interested in forfeits after that, and soon someone puts on a record, the needle shrieking across the shellacked surface before the song begins. Nusch and Paul start dancing, and others join in, but Lee and Man stand still, sizing each other up. Finally Lee pulls the bottle out of his hand and takes a big slug from it, wincing as the brandy sears her throat.

"'Exhibit A'?" she says, crossing her arms over her chest and glaring at him.

"Not here, Lee."

"Not *here*?"

Man reaches out for her, then stops himself. "I'm sorry," he says, his voice so low she can barely hear him over the music.

"For which part?" Lee gestures around the room. "For all of it?" The anger is dissipating and she does not like the new feeling that has sprung up in its place: a gulf between them.

Lee turns from him. As she walks away, someone turns out the lights, and in the darkness the music sounds louder. The thin wooden floor booms with all the stomping feet. Lee could go—this could be the second time in as many weeks that she leaves somewhere without him—or she could stay. She contemplates the shadows of the dancing figures around her. Right in front of her is Ilse, dancing by herself, all limbs and elbows. Lee kicks an empty bottle out of the way, sending it jangling across the floor, and puts one hand on Ilse's side, damp with sweat, and pulls her close. Together they move around the floor with ease. As they dance Lee moves her hand up from Ilse's back to her neck, to the place where her hairline is razored neatly against her soft skin, not with longing, but with curiosity. Since the ballet yesterday it seems all Lee has thought about is the feel of strangers' bodies against her own, and right now holding Ilse makes Lee feel as though she's taking charge in some small way, showing this woman—showing her and Man and everyone—that she's someone they should pay attention to.

The song ends and they step away from each other, and as another begins, a man—Aragon, or the writer, maybe; Lee can't make him out—steps up to Ilse. She looks back at Lee but moves away from her and starts dancing with him.

Lee dances by herself for a while, a lazy shimmy. Somewhere in the room Man is watching her. She twirls around, slowly, and then she sees him, standing off in the corner. Lee goes over to him. "Puttin' On the Ritz" starts playing, a song Lee finds ridiculous, but she doesn't care: she dances with Man watching her and she can tell he wants to join her but isn't sure if she wants him to. Lee isn't sure herself, but it is so natural to be with him, so when the next song starts, a slower number, she pulls him to her and they start moving together.

They dance for minutes or hours—later she will not remember. Everything is fogged with whiskey, reduced to snapshots of emotions, snippets of disjointed sound. At the end of the night, or practically morning, Lee and Man stumble out of the room. At the doorway leading to the stairs, Ilse blocks their way, smoking a cigarette in a long silver holder. As they push past her, Lee leans woozily into the other woman's face. She clamps her fingers around Ilse's arm. "You're wrong," Lee says. "I would have worked with you."

Ilse lifts one slim shoulder. "Perhaps," she says.

As they descend the stairs, Lee looks back: Ilse above them, her nipples, freed from the brassiere she never put back on, casting pointed shadows through the light linen fabric of her dress. On her face a hard proud smile.

CHAPTER TWENTY-FIVE

The next morning, after the salon, Lee's mouth is as dry as cotton batting and her head is pounding. She gets up before Man and sits in the kitchen, gingerly sipping a glass of water. The night comes back in flashes—the paintings in the gallery, Claude's smoke rings, Man embarrassing her, Nusch and Paul, the feel of Ilse's hair—and connecting all the fragmented memories is a sick feeling of failure, as if there was a test and Lee didn't pass it. Of all that happened, it is her exchange with Ilse and Claude that bothers her the most, their view of her as empty, nothing more than Man's companion.

Lee wants to go back to bed, to crawl under the blankets and pull them up over her head. She wants Man to get up and see what state she's in and take care of her. Or better yet, she wants to be back in her childhood bed, her father bringing her cambric tea.

But today is the last day of filming, and after another glass of water and a piece of unbuttered toast, Lee musters the energy to get dressed and go to the set. Man still lies in bed; he far outdrank her last night, so it is the kind thing to leave him be, and the truth is she doesn't even want to talk to him. There is no way they can talk without addressing what happened during forfeits and the fight they almost had afterward. She leaves a note in their usual spot on the table, telling him where she'll be. Signs it *Love, L* after a moment's hesitation.

Filming goes smoothly. They reshoot a final scene in which a guardian angel removes an ace of hearts from a cardsharp's pocket, and Lee transforms into the statue and walks through fake snow without leaving any footprints. Afterward, as she takes off the complicated costume for the final time, she thinks she might miss it, even though it's so uncomfortable.

At the end of the day, Lee, Enrique, and a few other cast members stay with Jean until everything is done and it is time to lock up the set. One by one they leave, until finally it is only Lee and Jean who remain. They walk outside and Jean turns the key in the lock, but neither of them is ready to go.

Jean has booked a ticket to Rome, where he says he can focus and get his edits done. Enrique is not going with him. Perhaps the men's relationship cannot be sustained outside the insular world of the film studio. When Jean says goodbye to Lee, his face looks sad and drawn.

"Take care of yourself, Mouse," he says.

"Find me when you get back to Paris."

"Of course. And you will be one of the first to see the film."

Lee hugs him and is surprised to find tears stinging her eyes. She can't believe filming took only a few weeks. It feels as though months have passed since she first got there.

"Ah—I almost forgot." Jean digs around in his jacket pocket until he finds a small white calling card, which he hands to her. *Madame Anna-Letizia Pecci-Blunt,* it says in an embossed heavy serif font, with an address in the Trocadéro beneath it. "Do you know her?" he asks.

Does Lee know Madame Pecci-Blunt? Everyone knows her, or at least her name. She is one of the richest women in Paris, almost royalty, somehow related to the Pope. "I don't know her person-ally, if that's what you mean."

"I never know who you are going to know. She has a big party every year. Everyone goes. I saw her out one night recently and she told me this year she is going to do a white ball. The Bal Blanc. All the decorations in white. The guests in white. Every-thing like a ghost, like purity. She asked me if I would help her make it incredible. I can't do it, so I gave her your information."

"Mine?"

Jean makes an impatient noise. "I gave her the address of Man Ray's studio. But it was you I told her about. When she calls, you should be the one to talk to her. It can be your shoot, if you want it to be. With that in your portfolio you could get more business, start your own studio. I spoke very highly of you."

"You did? I didn't even know you liked my work." When she showed him her photos at the studio a few weeks ago, she felt as embarrassed as she used to feel when showing her work to Man. She didn't even want Jean to see many of them, and rushed through her portfolio, as if letting him linger on any one image would reveal her as the imposter she always worries she is.

"Mouse, of course I do. You should already know this, but you are good. Are you as good as you'll be in years to come? Surely not. But you have that something. I had it too, and look at me now. This business—it favors the bold. It doesn't favor the assis-tant. You need to find a wealthy patron. It is the only way to do it. The vicomte—he gave me my million francs. Without him, no film."

This is the first time Lee has heard this figure and she is im-pressed. But more than that she is happy to know that Jean thinks she's talented. She says, "What would Madame Pecci-Blunt want me to do? Take photographs?"

"Here is what you do. You meet with her. After proper introductions you ask if you can call her Mimi—it will put you on the same level. You hear what she has to say. She tells her vision. Ghosts, white, purity. You say, 'What you are saying is so exciting. I have so many ideas—too many to choose from.' You get her to keep talking until you understand what she wants. These people—they think they want to hire a talented artist, but what they really want is to think they've come up with the idea themselves. And then whatever trifling concept she comes up with you take it and make it something worthwhile. Maybe you...I don't know...put everyone in white and they all have to carry white parasols or wear the same white mask. Or give them white paint and let them paint all over things. I'm sure you'll think of something."

Jean loops his scarf around his neck and kisses her on both cheeks. Lee holds the card in her hand and looks at the ornate font of Madame Pecci-Blunt's name and tries to picture herself in the meeting Jean described. It is easy to turn it into the fantasy she wants it to be, in which she confidently charms the rich woman over a lavish afternoon tea. Lee likes the fantasy very much. She thanks Jean, gives him a hug, and rests her cheek against the soft fabric of his coat. They stand that way for a while and then Lee watches as Jean walks off toward his home. She heads in the other direction, down Boulevard Raspail, and as she walks she rubs Mimi's card between her fingers.

The fall air is mild, the sun just beginning to set and turning the light thick and yellow. Lee decides to take a long way home, past the Sorbonne and the Panthéon, its columned facade deep in shadow. When she gets back to Montparnasse she ducks down a side street she's never been on before, and at the corner of Rue Victor Schoelcher and Rue Victor Considérant there is a small sign in the ground floor window of a narrow building: STUDIO SPACE TO LET: INQUIRE WITHIN. Lee pauses in front of the building and tries to look inside, but it is all in shadow and she can't really see anything. The windows are large, running almost from the floor to the ceiling, and she imagines what the room might be like, what she could make it look like if it was hers. Like the party she might create, she would paint the studio white: floor, ceiling, walls. She would have a white couch, a white stool. And when the afternoon light came filtering through, the room would glow like a candle and the clients who came for their portraits would be their most beautiful selves, illuminated, the light washing their eyes clear and their skin smooth and creamy. On the door she'd hang a little sign. Simple, small, discreet. Three words: LEE MILLER STUDIO.

She keeps walking, and by the time she gets home the sky is purple with sunset. In the apartment, she finds Man in the bedroom, painting. His hair is wild and disheveled, and before he notices her he bows his head and rakes his paint-stained hands through it. Lee clears her throat and he turns to her, his expression a mix of relief and anxiety.

"I didn't hear you come in. Is the filming wrapped up?"

"Yes, all done. Jean is leaving for Rome."

"Needs to get closer to the muse, no doubt."

Lee smiles despite herself, goes over to the bed and flops across the mattress. Man almost loses his balance and scowls at her. Lee stares up at his painting. The canvas is filled edge to edge now. He watches her as she takes it in.

Before she can say anything, he says, "I've gone back to Lautréamont. When I was younger it was the part of the poem about leaving home and abandoning the past that spoke to me, but now I see something different in it. I didn't make the connection until this morning: these aren't only your lips. They're the sapphire lips of Maldoror. The temptress. The devil. But they're your lips too. I want the viewer to hold both images in his mind at the same time."

Man has shown Lee the Lautréamont poem before—she despised it, though she didn't tell him so. To her it is pure onanism, scene after scene of violence and bloody sex and destruction. His love of it—they all love it, all his friends; Soupault carries a battered copy of it around in his coat pocket—mystifies her.

"It's a fascinating idea," Lee says. "But to me the painting's so sensual. I don't see the violence in it."

Man steps down from the mattress and goes over to the dresser, where he picks up a dog-eared book and starts rifling through the pages.

"This part," he says. "This is what I was reading today while you were gone. Let me read it to you."

A pair of nervous thighs gripped tightly against the monster's viscous flesh, and arms and fins wrapped around the objects of their desire, surrounding their bodies with love, while their breasts and bellies soon fused into one bluish-green mass reeking of sea-wrack, in the midst of the tempest still raging by the light of lightning; rolling and rolling down into the bottomless ocean depths, they came together in a long, chaste, and hideous mating! At last I had found somebody who was like me . . . From now on I was no longer alone in life . . . Her ideas were the same as mine . . . I was face to face with my first love!

Man's reading quickens as he goes along and when he is done he looks at Lee expectantly. The whole poem repels her. It is like all that is evil and dark in the world, and when she hears it she can feel herself teetering on the edge of her own darkness, where she does not want to go.

In the painting above her head, her red mouth floats calmly in the cloudy sky. No matter how hard Lee tries she can't connect the painting to the murky shipwreck of the poem. Finally she says, "Is that how you see me? Like some sort of . . . monster?"

Man goes over near the wall and gestures at the painting. "No, of course not. In the painting your mouth is your mouth. But there's the devil from the poem there too. Good and evil. Pain and pleasure."

Man has a delirious look in his eyes that reminds her of how he looked last night during forfeits. Lee gets up and goes over to the vanity and starts running her hairbrush through her hair, pressing the bristles so hard against her scalp it's almost painful.

"I don't like it. You using me like this." In the growing gloom, her reflected face in the mirror is a pale orb, like one of the white shapes on the beach in Dalí's painting.

"I would think you'd be flattered. This painting—honestly, I think it's my greatest work."

"Do you think that's what Salvador said to Gala when he made that painting of her?"

Man looks confused at the change in subject. "The one at the gallery last night?"

"Yes. Did you look at it? I loved it, actually. It was so evocative." Lee says this just to provoke him—he hates when she compliments other artists' work.

"There's no comparison."

"No comparison between the merit of your painting and his, or between Salvador using Gala and you using me? You told me yourself about Salvador's painting, that he made it when he was persuading Gala to leave Paul. And there are elements of her in it—it's obvious. So I don't see what the difference is. And what I'm saying is that I don't want you using me and then telling me I'm a monster."

"I'm not *using* you, Lee. You inspire me. You know that."

Lee holds her hairbrush to her mouth like a microphone. "And here we have Exhibit A," she intones, "the woman who inspired Man Ray to produce his greatest work."

Man gets a knowing, almost condescending look on his face. "Ah. So that's what this is about. I was drunk. I needed to shut Paul down. And it worked. I'm sorry if I offended you."

"You *did* offend me."

As often happens, when Man realizes Lee is really upset, his demeanor changes. He comes over to her, pulls the hairbrush out of her hand, and wraps his arms around her.

"Lee, my darling. I'm sorry," he whispers. "They were just words. You know how I feel about you."

She lets herself be held by him. For a moment she pictures his arms as the tentacles from the Lautréamont poem, gripping her body as they sink to the bottom of a stormy sea. She feels her pulse quicken, but shakes her head to focus on what is actually in front of her. Man. Her Man, who loves her. He kisses her neck, right behind her ear as she likes him to do, and the image dissipates. Lee relaxes into his arms. He smells comforting and familiar, of turpentine and pipe tobacco, vetiver from yesterday's cologne. In his embrace the poem and the events of last night seem less important: they are all just words.

After a little while he pulls away from her and goes over to his palette. He picks up a paintbrush and daubs it in some red paint. "Come here," he says.

He hands her the paintbrush and they both step up on the mattress. He points to a section where he has painted her bottom lip, and Lee reaches out and swipes the brush across the canvas, at first with hesitation, then with growing confidence, the red he's given her adding a touch of brightness to a darker section of her mouth. She hasn't painted since she got to Paris.

"The Lautréamont," he says. "I'm the monster, you're the temptress. That's what I meant. That part I read to you about not feeling alone—finding someone the same as me. That's what I want the painting to convey."

Lee keeps painting. "I see."

"I get a little crazed when you aren't here," he says with a laugh. "My imagination gets the best of me. And you've been gone a lot lately."

Lightly, she says, "Well, as I said, filming's done. I'm all yours again."

"Thank God for that."

"Yes." Lee hops off the bed and loads her paintbrush with more paint. "What's the painting going to be called?"

"It's called *The Lovers*."

"No devil in that," Lee says, and steps back up on the bed. They paint together for a while. She gets her face so close to the canvas her lips are all she sees.

CHAPTER TWENTY-SIX

With filming over, Lee and Man return to their old schedule and habits. As the weeks pass there is comfort in the familiarity of the work. When occasional clients come, Lee falls back into assistant mode, setting up lights, fetching diffusers, swapping out the drop cloths before Man takes the shots. Now and then she suggests a tweak to the framing, and almost always he agrees; she can tell his heart's not really in the work, which always happens when he spends a lot of time painting.

At the end of one shoot, Man says, "Lee, can you collect payment from Miss DuBourg?"

"Now?" Lee is surprised. Usually they bill later, long after the pictures have been delivered.

"Yes. Just bill for the session time and we'll follow up for the rest of the fees when everything is done."

So, with embarrassment, Lee explains to the client that they do require payment that day. Miss DuBourg doesn't hide her shock, but she pulls a checkbook from her purse and dashes off a check, handing it to Lee pinched between two fingers.

After Miss DuBourg is gone Lee goes into the office and gives Man the check. "Was that really necessary?" she says.

He rubs his hands through his hair and coughs. "I'm in a bit of a bind," he says. "Nothing too bad, but we need to drum up some more business, get a commission. Something."

Lee thinks back to her recent accounting. "We have a lot outstanding, but most should come in by the end of the month, and with the Patou catalog work—"

"Patou just dropped me."

"Really? Why?"

"They're hiring someone in-house. Blumenfeld. So expected."

Lee grimaces. "I hate his work."

"I know. Me too. There's no energy there, nothing provocative. The models may as well be taking pictures of themselves while they look in the mirror."

"That would be more interesting, actually."

Man laughs, but then his face falls again. "I need a big commission—a Rothschild or a Rockefeller who wants their portrait done. But I'm worried I'm falling out of favor with that crowd. If I were to win the Philadelphia prize, I think I'd get some attention."

"Can I see the pictures you've chosen . . . or help you with the artist statement? I was helpful last time, with your essay . . ."

Man stares at the check. "I don't know. I still haven't decided what to submit. In the meantime, the most helpful thing you could do would be to see if there's anyone we haven't billed or who hasn't paid."

Lee thinks of Madame Pecci-Blunt's card. She had been intending to listen to Jean and keep it a secret, figure out if there is some way she can do the party herself, but the moment is too perfect. She can't help herself.

"Well," Lee says, smiling slyly and walking over to where she's hung her handbag, "it's not a Rothschild, but look at this." She hands Man the card.

He reads it and shakes his head, confused. "Where did you get this?"

"Jean gave it to me."

"Does she want her portrait done?"

"No. Apparently she has a party every year, and she's looking for an artist to help make it really memorable. Jean can't do it so he passed it on."

"Never thought Cocteau would do me any favors," Man says.

Lee takes the card back from him and returns it to her bag. "I think he's doing *me* a favor."

"Hmm."

Lee waits for him to say more and when he doesn't she continues. "Jean gave her my name"—she puts a slight emphasis on the word *my*—"so hopefully she'll call soon."

A smile spreads across Man's face. "Oh, this is good. This is very, very good. If there's one thing we can do it's make this party interesting. I did something like this for the Wheelers once—did I tell you about it? They were having a dinner party and I made sculptures for the table and took film footage when everyone was dancing after dinner." He stands and wanders around the room as he talks, picking up some of the clutter and organizing it, as he often does when he is agitated. It is the only time he tidies anything.

"We can charge a lot," Lee says. "Jean says we can name our price."

"We'll charge aristocracy prices—that's what we'll do."

Lee laughs. "Ah, aristocracy prices! What's the going rate for those these days?"

"Enough that I don't have to sell the Voisin."

Lee is surprised to hear him say it, even though selling the car makes perfect sense. They barely use it, and just keeping it garaged is an expense they really don't need. Yet she doesn't want to lose it. She thinks of the drive to Biarritz, the way the wind whipped off her scarf and left her skin tingling, the countryside unspooling past her, framed in the open car window. She wishes, powerfully, that they could be back there right now, lying in the sun and looking out at the sea. Or sitting in the cabaret, her knees pressed tight against his, their forearms touching on the small table as they share a bottle of wine. But then she realizes she could re-create that feeling right here in Paris, that their happiness is not some irretrievable thing; she can create more of it if she wants to.

She wants to bring it up, to remember Biarritz with him. Just thinking about it eases the tension of the past few weeks, of being away from him on the film set and the fight they should have had after forfeits, the bitterness still simmering inside her. But it's obvious Man's head is not in the same place as hers. He squares a stack of magazines on the corner of the desk.

"Also . . . Arthur Wheeler called this morning," he says.

Lee waits for him to continue. She has met the Wheelers just once, when Tanja was in town. Arthur does something in business—Man is always vague about exactly where his money comes from—but what Lee does know is that the Wheelers have funded many of Man's more experimental projects and taken Man on several trips, to Italy and the Côte d'Azur, among other places, where he's done some of his best work.

"They were hit hard—Arthur's pulling out of his oil venture. And he's still on me about making another *Emak Bakia*."

"But you told him you don't want to, right?"

"The conversation was more tangled than that. He was rather distraught, actually. But it's clear I can't depend on them anymore, film or no film. It wasn't even clear if there is funding for more work if I was willing to do it. Which I'm not."

Man goes over to the far wall and straightens one of the picture frames that gets crooked every time they open or close the door. Lee thinks for the hundredth time that she really should get a little piece of putty and put it behind the frame to keep it steady. There are so many chores like this, and she doesn't want to do any of them. Sometimes the studio and the apartment exhaust her with their daily requirements, the grind of the mundane. There was none of that in Biarritz, none of it, in fact, on Jean's film set either, where everything was meant to be transitory. Here, watching Man as he rounds the room and sets things in order, she feels a sudden crushing need to escape. She doesn't want to talk about the Wheelers or the crash or selling the Voisin.

"Let's do something fun. Let's go to the ballet," she says. "You know I've been wanting you to go since I first saw it, and we don't have anything to do tonight."

Man shakes his head. "You're like a child sometimes," he says, but his voice is kind. "I'm telling you we have no money and you're saying we should go to a show."

"Well, why shouldn't we? We can sit in the back. The tickets aren't expensive."

"I don't sit in the *back*," Man says, but after a little grumbling he agrees and they head home to dress.

But after they've gotten back to their apartment, Man changes his mind. He's tired. He doesn't like dance—she knows that. All he wants is a quiet night with her. He misses her, wants to sit across a table from her and just enjoy a simple meal.

This is not at all what Lee wants—eating together is all they ever seem to do. They have become an old married couple in every sense but the legal one. Well, with the added exception that Man is the only one of them who is old. But she agrees to dinner, because it is not worth fighting him over something so trivial. If she were to force him to go to the ballet, Lee imagines him squirming in his seat, checking his watch as he always does when he is bored. And as it always does, her acquiescence makes Man happy; his mood lifts instantly, lifting Lee's too.

He takes her hand. "Let's go to that bistro in the Fourth that I mentioned to you. They have the most delicious roast chicken."

They debate a taxi but decide to walk, pleased with themselves about this small act of thrift. They walk in silence in the direction of the bistro, a good twenty minutes from their apartment. The wind cuts through Lee's thin dress under her coat and she can feel the metal in her garter belt go cold against her thighs. Already the lift in her mood is deflating. She can think of nothing to say, and compares how she is feeling now to how she feels when she talks with Jean, how his infectious energy always cheers her. Thinking of Jean makes her think of the ballet, and before she knows it she is thinking of Antonio, of how much she was looking forward to seeing his sets again, to knowing he was up in the rafters behind the stage.

As they walk, Lee feels her face go warm against the cold. She keeps her eyes trained on the sidewalk and does not look over at Man. Nothing has changed. All she is doing is thinking. She used to think about other men all the time, before she was with Man. But the *things* she is now thinking: Antonio's cock inside her. Bruises on her legs from his hands. Her makeup smeared, his fingers hooked into her mouth. She feels the imaginings in her bones. If Man were to look at her, there is no doubt he would be able to see it in her face. She keeps her head completely still and stares straight ahead.

"We'll see the ballet another time," Man says, even though she hasn't mentioned it.

Lee sucks in her breath. Has he read her mind? "It's all right," she manages to say. "But I think you'd like it."

"Oh, maybe." Man's tone is dismissive. "You don't know the intricacies of it because you haven't lived in Paris long enough. Rouché wants the opéra ballet to matter again, so he hires Lifar. Lifar can probably do it. But why start with *Prométhée*? The music is so lilting, so flippant. I would have thought he would have wanted to make a bigger start. *Giselle,* maybe. Or something grittier. *Le Sacre du Printemps*."

"I don't know," Lee says, willing her mind to engage with this change of topic. "All I have to compare it to is what I've seen in New York."

"You don't need anything to compare it to to be able to gauge its success. It should stand alone. Lifar's a dancer, and a good one. But that doesn't necessarily translate into artistry. It's as if . . . oh, I don't know . . . as if Amélie were to suddenly start taking pictures."

They have just turned down another street, and his words make Lee stop in the middle of the sidewalk.

"Are you being intentionally rude to me?" she asks, pulling her arm from his.

Man looks at her with surprise. "What? No! I'm not talking about you at all."

"So you're just talking in general terms about a model not being able to be a good photographer."

Man lets out a little laugh. "Not everything is about you, Lee."

"Not even the things that are *exactly* about me?"

Man groans and reaches out to hold her shoulders. "The ballet is probably good. We should see it together. You are a good photographer. I love you. I'm hungry, and tired, and I just want to find this place and sit down with you and relax over a glass of wine."

They keep walking and walking, and finally Man admits the bistro might have closed down. Ravenous now, they choose another place, fancier probably than Man intended, and once they are seated several waiters fuss around them with wine lists, napkins, and small adjustments to their place settings. They both get chicken—Man has made her crave it—but when it comes it is disappointing: lukewarm and undersalted.

They are quiet while they eat. Lee's mind swirls. Antonio. Man's comment about Amélie. She wants to probe him, as if Man is an infected tooth she can't stop touching with her tongue. Or maybe she wants to shock him—wants, suddenly, for him to know where her mind has been, that he is not everything to her. She takes a bite of chicken and wonders what he would do if he knew what she was thinking on the walk here.

Instead, she says, "It's been so long since Tristan's printed *221*."

Man chews and swallows, his Adam's apple bouncing in his neck. "I know. Money troubles. Just like the rest of us."

"Is he ever going to put it out again?"

"I have no idea. It's a bit of a tense subject. And I'm certainly not in a place to help fund it." Man puts down his fork and rubs his hands together as if he is washing them.

"So . . . my pictures?"

He looks at her blankly.

"My pictures. In the magazine."

Man drops his head. "Lee," he says. "Now's not really the time to ask Tristan for a favor."

Lee waits for him to continue, to apologize. When he doesn't, when he just keeps sitting there, she says, "I thought you'd already asked him. And I didn't realize it was a favor."

Man makes a sound that is half growl, half laugh, and covers his face with his hands. "It's not a *favor*. That's not what I meant. I just—I have a lot on my mind right now. You would have known that if you'd been around lately."

He is done with his chicken. Even though it wasn't very good, he has decimated it. The bones are so bare they seem almost boiled, stacked neatly at the edge of his plate. Lee takes slices out of the center of hers and doesn't care how much she wastes.

"I had an idea," Man says. "You know how you asked me this afternoon how you could be helpful? I saw George Hoyningen-

Huene at Le Boeuf sur le Toit the other evening. He's working for *Vogue* and he said he's bored with all the models he's been using. He wants someone new, modern. Of course I thought of you."

Lee sits back in her chair. "I've told you I don't want to model anymore—"

"Oh, I know. But they pay so well. And you did ask how you could help."

"I meant ... What about the Bal Blanc? Should we phone Madame Pecci-Blunt? You said we could charge a fortune."

Lee wonders if he can hear the frustration in her voice, or if his own worries are drowning out hers. She does not want to model again; he knows that. He must.

"The party's in six weeks," Man says. "We won't get paid until the new year, if we're lucky. Hoyningen-Huene is looking for someone *now*. How about this: I'll call Madame Pecci-Blunt and you'll drop by *Vogue*. Just see how it is. He's supposed to be really good, actually. It might be fun."

"How about this: *I* call Madame Pecci-Blunt."

"Don't you think the call would be better coming from me?"

Lee puts down her fork and crosses her arms. "Jean recommended *me*. He also said she wanted to work with a woman on this, so I think I should call her. I'll explain that you and I work together."

The "woman" part isn't true, but Lee figures Man can't refute it. He drums his fingers on the table. "I think I should call her," he finally says. "But I'll use both our names. I'll present us as a team."

Lee considers this. "Fine. But I want to *be* a team. I want to come to all the meetings, and I want to help come up with the concept. And I want my name in the papers next to yours."

"I can't control what they put in the papers."

"Well, you can try. We can call it a Man Ray–Lee Miller production, or something like that."

Man nods and uses a piece of baguette to sop up the last of his drippings. "All right," he says.

On the way home Lee insists they stop for a drink in the hope that there is something they can salvage from the evening. They choose a place where they've never been before, with a crowd that is mostly men, as if they are all there in the bar to do business deals. Lee downs her first martini and flags the waiter for another before Man has finished his. She lets the gin warm her and looks around the room at all the other patrons, trying to find a way for each of them to remind her of Antonio: the way one man has a silk scarf looped around his neck, the way another's hair brushes his collar, the way another's legs spread wide in front of him. She finds herself imagining that they really *are* Antonio, all of them, that she could simply sit down at another table and be with him instead of Man. Her thoughts embarrass her but she doesn't stop herself. After a few moments, Lee forces her attention back to Man, to his wide forehead and the two little lines between his eyebrows, to the small patch on his chin where stubble doesn't grow, to the bright whites of his eyes and the memory of how they made her feel just a few short weeks ago, when she couldn't think of another man in the world she wanted to look at but him.

MUNICH,
PRINZREGENTENPLATZ 16

MAY 1, 1945

It is Lee's idea to stage the picture. She sits on the wicker chair next to the tub and unlaces her boots, leaving them where they land, then unbuckles her uniform and slips out of it, Dave watching from the door with that smirk on his face. He's seen it all before and she's seen him too. It doesn't matter. What is shocking right then is how white her skin is under her clothes, pale and tender in the hard overhead light. It will be her first bath in three weeks and in the little vanity mirror her neck and face are army issue brown, the dirt almost topographic where it has dried on various layers of sweat.

"Dirty auslander," Dave says in a fake German accent, and they both laugh.

She runs the tap as hot as she can get it, even pours in some Epsom salts from a little container on the nearby counter, and the bathroom fills with steam and a sharp saline smell that reminds her of the ocean and makes her realize how long it has been since she's seen anything beautiful.

Dave putters with his camera and tests the shot. He leaves the room and comes back with a small portrait of Hitler, which he places on the rim of the tub.

"Too much?" he asks.

"There's so many goddamn pictures of him in this house I'm shocked he doesn't have one in here. Leave it."

She steps in and the water is so hot it gives her goose bumps.

"You're going to leave a ring around that tub, rub-a-dub," Dave says, referencing an ad for a cleaning product they made fun of a few years earlier. Dave is drunk. So is she. They've been nipping slowly at their stash since leaving upper Bavaria, their stomachs sour from what the Krauts call wine. Here at 16 Prinzregenten-platz they rejoiced when they opened a bar cabinet and found it full of Braastad, a luxury they haven't seen since before the war. They pour it into snifters etched AH and emblazoned with swastikas and get properly ossified.

Lee sits down in the tub and Dave hands her a washcloth and a bar of soap. There, under the accusing eye of the Führer, his hands on his hips in a pose that Lee is sure is supposed to look commanding but instead looks priggish as a schoolmarm, she scrubs at the dirt of Dachau until her skin stings.

"Wait till *Life* gets their eyes on these," Dave says.

"You wouldn't."

He laughs. "No. These are just for us. To commemorate—"

"Not commemorate. To bury that fucking monster."

Dave takes enough shots to fill a roll and Lee sits in the bath until the water gets cold. Then she steps out and puts her uniform back on, the buckles and buttons as familiar to her now as her own body, and she picks up the framed picture and lets it drop facedown on the bathroom tile. In one quick motion, she pivots her foot on top of the frame, the glass screeching on the ceramic, and leaves the room.

They spend three more hours in Hitler's house before the rest of the regiment arrives. Lee feels as though she knows the Führer a little bit by this point. She's sat at his desk, read his letters from Eva, looked through his sketchbooks, seen his bedroom and his sock garters and his headache tonics. The more normal he seems, the more she despises him. She is filled to the brim with hatred, choking on it.

CHAPTER TWENTY-SEVEN

Frogue, as everyone calls it, is more than *Vogue.* To say it is more French is to miss the point. It is more everything. Epicenter, nexus. Here in the ornate cluttered offices, the editors are choosing the fashions that American *Vogue* copies; they are setting the trends instead of emulating them.

When Man asks her how it is going, Lee talks dismissively of it, but to her surprise she loves being there. Does she wish she were behind the camera? Of course. Does she have to stop herself from shouting directives in the middle of a shoot, bite her tongue when the photographer makes a choice she doesn't agree with? *Mais oui.* But at *Frogue* she and all the other models are treated with a respect never shown to her in New York. From the moment Lee arrives at the main office, foul-tempered, feeling forced into being there by Man, she has been treated as if she is important. In the waiting room, the assistants' obsequiousness saps the grumpiness right out of her. They usher her directly to a studio to meet the photographer; they do not keep her waiting. They seem, in fact, to be honored to have her, to be reacting to a reputation Lee did not fully recognize she had. And the reputation is not from her connection to Man Ray: it comes from her, from her past work for Condé Nast, from Steichen's pictures of her, and because everyone at the magazine knows she will make the clothes more beautiful. Here the clothing matters above all. Fashion made totemic. Lee has not forgotten that she is beautiful, of course, but it is nice to have an outside reminder, and from such a place as this.

Her life suddenly has a balance to it. Madame Pecci-Blunt has hired them, but she's been impossible to pin down on details, so Lee and Man spend a few hours a week making preliminary plans on their own. Then Lee spends a few days at *Frogue,* and the rest of the week in the studio. She likes the rush of a day spent modeling: fitting in lunch, the way the *Frogue* employees have their favorite bistros only steps away. And she likes George Hoyningen-Huene, the photographer she works with most closely when she is there.

George takes photos of her dressed in Paquin, dressed in Chanel. She is zipped into bias-cut dresses that cling at her waist and puddle elegantly on the floor around her feet. When Lee expresses admiration for a particularly lovely Vionnet, white linen with eye-shaped geometric embellishments, it arrives at her apartment door at the shoot's end, the box tied with a bow and a card that says *Compliments—G.*

George is a consummate professional, fastidious, laboring over a shot long after Man or Lee herself would have called it a success. He is fussy but not to a detrimental degree. His shots are clean-lined, modern; his style perfectly matches the current mood in fashion. It is why Lee is a successful model for him. She feels—as she felt in New York when she began her career—lucky to be living at a time when her beauty is the *right* beauty. Framed illustrations from years past hang on the *Frogue* office walls—wasp-waisted girls dripping with frippery—and Lee thanks the Lord she wasn't born three decades earlier.

Some of the pictures they take of Lee are reproduced in American *Vogue* as well, and before long she gets a letter from her father about them. Lee has barely been in contact with him since his visit—she has been trying Man's approach of not reaching out and finds she barely misses him. His letter is full of praise for her modeling spreads. He says he's glad she's working again and that he always thought she was so beautiful and talented. Before it would have bothered her—she's been working at her real work: making photographs—but she feels very little when she reads his words. Something shifted when he visited; he has lost his power over her. She puts his letter in her handbag and doesn't respond.

There is a model with whom George often pairs her. His name is Horst P. Horst and he looks so much like Lee that he could be her brother. He's tall, lean, with clear blue eyes and blond hair that falls in a perfectly coiffed wave over his forehead. Like Lee, Horst is training to be a photographer and wants to be taking the photos instead of modeling. As Man is for Lee, George is for Horst, and often during a shoot the two of them will work together on an image, the air crackling with sexual tension. Lee just watches—amused, on the periphery and glad of it.

Though Lee doesn't yearn to be taking the fashion stills, she does bring her Rollei, capturing images she finds behind the scenes. A row of shoes, their laces undone and tongues lolling, looking for all the world like a line of smiling mouths. A crying woman on the telephone in the hallway, her mascara running in black rivulets down her cheeks. When Lee develops the pictures later, she feels almost as though she is getting away with something, stealing ideas and beauty from her place of employment.

One evening after a shoot, when they are lingering in the lobby, Horst invites Lee to join him and George for dinner, and though she usually says no, this time she agrees and asks if she can invite Man.

Lee calls the studio and they arrange the meeting time and place. Before they leave the office George crooks his finger at Lee and Horst and leads them back to one of the closets, and they each pick out something to wear to dinner. Lee chooses an aquamarine chiffon she modeled earlier, backless with an embroidered halter neck. Horst hands her a silvery fox fur stole and jeweled heels and both men match their pocket squares and ties to her. Outside the building one man takes her right arm and the other her left. The fur is soft against Lee's bare arms and she has never felt more lovely.

For once, she thinks, Parisians are looking at her—it just takes two escorts and a Schiaparelli original to break through their snootiness. Man is waiting outside the restaurant when they arrive. They spot each other from a distance, and she likes seeing him watch her as she promenades down the sidewalk. When their trio is just a few feet from Man he steps forward and puts his arm around Lee's waist, kissing her possessively and running his hand up her bare back.

"Doesn't she look ravishing?" asks George, and Man nods in agreement, staying close by her side as he shakes George's hand and goes through introductions with Horst.

"An honor," Horst says, "an absolute honor to meet you. Your work inspires me."

"Is that so?" Man's tone is falsely modest.

"God yes. Your fashion shots—especially your earlier work, the *Vogue* work from twenty-five, twenty-six. I've actually tried to re-create some of them on my own just to see if I can get the lighting right."

Lee knows that Horst's words are the wrong ones—referencing Man's older work rather than his current projects always feels to him like an insult, and he's never pleased when people use his ideas—but of course there is no way for Horst to know this.

"And I can't tell you how lucky I feel to be working with this beauty," Horst continues, cocking his head at Lee. "You must spend half your time fighting off other desperate suitors."

Man gives Horst a strained smile, and Lee can tell he's already made up his mind not to like him. She pulls Man closer and bends and kisses his cheek. "I can fight them off myself just fine, thank you," she says, and she can feel Man relax against her as the other men laugh with more amusement than the statement deserves.

They go inside and when the waiter comes to their table they order escargot, deviled quail eggs, and hearts of palm, which they wash down with pastis and, when they have drunk the pastis, a bottle of Riesling, which Horst insists is the best wine to drink before dinner.

Now that they are seated, Man is charming. He likes Hoyningen-Huene, likes trading stories with him and discussing technique. The two men are soon trying to outdo each other with stories of strange clients and botched photo shoots. Man tells the story of taking Hemingway's portrait—even fashion photographers like a story about a celebrity—and Horst leans across the table to hear him better.

"Tell me," Horst says. "What is he like? I liked his latest book very much."

Man gives a knowing, dismissive shrug. "It was six or seven years ago, I think, and he was really a nobody still. Gertrude Stein asked me to do his picture. Said he was the real thing. She was always asking me to take pictures of her artist friends back then. He shows up half an hour late for a one-hour shoot, and rings the bell about a dozen times. I go down to greet him and he's leaning against the doorframe like a drunkard with this huge white bandage wrapped around his head." Man circles his own head with his hand to show what he means. "I ask him what the bandage is for. He says a skylight broke and fell on him. It seemed like a bizarre excuse to me, but what do I care if he's a lying drunkard? Some of the best portraits I've taken are of drunks." Everyone at the table laughs. "So we go upstairs to the studio. He's not weaving, doesn't smell like whiskey, but when I get him situated for the portrait I ask him to take off the bandage and he refuses. I tell him I'll turn him to the side so no one will see the cut. He says no again. Instead, he takes this little triangular felt hat out of his jacket pocket and unfolds it and sets it on his massive head, looking pleased with himself. It doesn't cover the bandage at all. But I think, no matter. No one but Gertrude Stein knows who he is, so if he wants a picture of himself looking like a leprechaun with a head injury, so be it." Man pauses and takes another sip of his wine. "In the end I rather liked that portrait of him, actually."

"And then he published *The Sun Also Rises,*" Lee prompts.

"Yes, and they used my photo of him in the *Atlantic Monthly* review. Portrait of the writer! He doesn't even have his shirt buttoned."

"It's a good picture, though," Lee says. "Hard to take a bad picture of Ernest Hemingway."

Man gives her a look.

"Agreed," Horst says.

"Oh, I almost forgot the best part," Man continues. "When it comes time to pay me, he insists he wants to give me a painting. Says he doesn't have any money, but he has this little Picasso that Stein told him to buy. Brings it over personally. He doesn't seem to understand that I know Picasso. Like he's letting me in on this secret—a real investment opportunity."

"Did you take the painting?"

"Of course I did. Wouldn't you?"

Lee looks at Man as he holds forth and she feels a rush of affection for him, looks around the table at George and Horst, dressed in their borrowed evening wear, and thinks to herself that this is how she always imagined life in Paris. Delicious food, wine in elegant glasses, men around her treating her like delicate glassware herself, slim and radiant and special. Man has his arm resting on the back of her chair, and every once in a while he runs his hand up and down her arm, and it is warm and comforting against her skin. And she thinks, with a feeling of wonder, that her life is like a giant turning crystal, each surface catching the light at a different time. Who would have thought that going back to modeling would be a good idea? But it is making her happy. It is her own thing, not Man's, and it is a facet of her life she never realized was missing until it was there again. And somehow, sitting at this table with her lover, her photographer, and her fellow model, she feels as if all the facets are coming together. She moves her chair a few inches closer to Man's and he holds her a little tighter.

It is the sort of meal that lasts for hours. The Riesling is replaced by a Burgundy, big and dark. Plate after plate of food arrives. More escargot, stuffed with garlic and parsley and butter they have to wipe away when it runs down their chins. Baked Camembert, so rich and stinky it makes Lee's tongue ache. *Moules marinières*. A veal stew she's never tried before. Green beans and summer squash with garlic. Through it all, more wine, and the wine loosens a screw in Lee's spine, leaving her pliable and content.

George is talking about their swimwear shoot that afternoon. He took Horst and Lee up to the roof, where he posed them against the sky and told them to pretend it was the sea.

"It's hard to get *Vogue* to pay for location shots anymore," he says, turning companionably to Man, who is pushed back from the table, his ankle crossed over his knee, the picture of relaxation. "So I've been doing more of this sort of thing, shooting close and letting the background *suggest* a mood rather than dominate the image." George picks up his glass and swirls around the inch of wine in it. "But they want a big shoot for the summer issue, and Horst had this idea of Biarritz or Saint-Tropez, on the beach. Wouldn't they be stunning? Those two blond heads in that light?" He tips his glass at Lee and Horst in turn. "You know the magazine better than I do. How can I convince them to let me do it?"

George is looking at Man, eager. Man says, "You have to have a better reason than the light to get them to let you go on location. In fact, I'm sure whatever you're thinking of shooting there you could easily do here. You're right when you say the setting doesn't matter as much in fashion right now."

Horst leans in toward the center of the table, makes his voice low. "But *we* want to go to the beach. Let them pay us for lying in real sand, with real sun on us." He laughs and gives Lee a wink.

He and Lee had this conversation this afternoon, as they sat back-to-back, shivering in the strong rooftop wind, on the wooden plank George fashioned to look like a diving board. "If my balls were any colder they'd crack right off my body," Horst whispered to her, and to forget the frigid air they spent the rest of the shoot describing to each other the sun-splashed paradise they'd be in if they were shooting in the Côte d'Azur. It felt funny then, a lark, but now, with Man staring at them as if they are naughty children, Lee just wants to change the subject.

"I can never tell if it's a good thing or a bad thing to fantasize about warm weather in the winter," Lee says. "I grew up in the coldest wasteland in America, so I have a lot of practice."

But Horst won't let it go. He reaches out across the table and touches Lee's cheek. "A face like this *deserves* the perfect setting. As does this one." He puts his hands to his own face and frames it, giving them a joking smile. "I want to get out of this city. Have an adventure."

"Well, try to get *Vogue* to pay for it if you can. They never did much for me," Man says, his voice clipped. He raises the end of the napkin he has tucked into his shirt collar and wipes his lips with it before looking over at Lee. "Obviously, if it works out, you wouldn't be going. You're needed here, in my studio."

Lee sees Horst and George exchange a glance, and she lifts her wine goblet and takes a deep swallow so that she can look into the bottom of the glass instead of at their expressions. The moment is a small one—right afterward the conversation shifts to Dalí's latest film, set to premiere in just a few days—but it is the end of the good feeling of the evening for Lee, and she cannot help but feel as she did so many times when she was young, as if she has been chastised for doing something she didn't even know was wrong.

CHAPTER TWENTY-EIGHT

Over the next few weeks, as Lee continues to switch off between modeling and Man's studio, she keeps thinking back to the dinner with Horst and George, keeps seeing Horst frame his face in his hands and insist he wants an adventure. And then she pictures herself on the beach, her skin warmed by the sun. And every time she thinks of it, she thinks of Man's reaction, and the dinner becomes the moment when distance opens up between them. Nothing huge, just a crack in the sidewalk, with her on one side and him on the other. Just the sense that he is suddenly unfamiliar to her. And that she herself might be unknowable to him.

She works more, stays out later, goes out for drinks with Horst and some of the other people she's met at *Frogue*. In addition to her modeling, Lee starts to take on small writing assignments, fluff pieces, mostly, but she finds she enjoys pounding out the stories on her typewriter, likes even more seeing her name as the byline. Lee becomes friendly with one of the women in the finance department, a British expat named Audrey Withers who is desperate to get back to London, the first woman Lee has become true friends with since Tanja. And she starts staying out so late each night that Man is asleep when she arrives home, and then it's Thursday and she realizes she needs to be at the studio and she hasn't had a real conversation with him since Sunday, and she hasn't even noticed, not really, hasn't even missed him all that much.

One day when she shows up at the studio, at first she doesn't pay much attention to his mood. He is hunched over his desk, scribbling furiously in a large notebook, with an extra pen stuck behind one ear and lots of crumpled sheets of paper dotting the floor around him.

"Tea?" she asks.

He looks up briefly. He is unshaven, with pouches under his eyes. "Yes, thanks."

She puts the kettle on. From the other room she hears him rip another sheet of paper out of the notebook, then silence, then the loud scratching of his pen. When the water boils she gets out their two teacups, fills the teapot, drops sugar cubes in the empty cups, and places everything on a tray, which she carries into the office with the grace of someone performing an action perfected over time. She sets the tray at the edge of his desk and slides the cup near him, stands for a few minutes waiting for the tea to steep, and pours it in the cup, twirls a spoon around. Through all this Man doesn't speak, just scratches at the notebook without stopping.

"Is that your artist statement, for the Philadelphia prize?" she asks when he pauses.

"Yes—it's finally coming. I figured out what I wanted to say late last night."

"That's wonderful," Lee says, and means it. After fixing her own cup of tea and standing over him for a few more moments, she continues. "I'm going to start printing the Artaud shoot. We said we'd deliver it Friday."

Man looks up at her with an unreadable expression. "Actually, do we have anything this afternoon? I'd love to shoot you. I have an idea for a project."

Lee is surprised. Flattered. It has been a while since he's taken any pictures of her, and it hits her that this is what must be missing between the two of them right now, the collaboration that used to fuel everything.

Lee works all morning and when she comes into the studio in the afternoon he has two of his Graflex cameras looped around his neck. She feels almost shy. He stands at the window and stares down at the street below. He says, "The light is good right now." Lee starts unbuttoning her shirt, but he shakes his head no. She poses by the window where he places her, resting her palms on the windowsill. Man gets very close to her, the camera lens only inches from her face, its eye peering at her eye. He focuses and releases the shutter quickly, a few times in a row.

"What are the pictures for?"

"I can't quite explain it yet," he says. He switches to the other camera, again getting as close to her as he can. He takes pictures of her ear, her eye, her mouth, her nose. Lee holds perfectly still, hardly breathing. The camera obscures Man's face, and she can actually feel the chill emanating from the metal of the camera case. In the curved surface of the lens, she sees her features, shrunken and distorted, and feels a rising sense of panic at the idea of his camera touching her. It doesn't help that Man is completely silent, engrossed in the work.

"Your eye," Man says, pausing to reload one of the cameras with a new roll of film. "When I get this close to you, I can reduce it to pure geometry, to the golden rule. I *see* it that way when I'm shooting it."

Lee's heart is beating fast; she can feel it in her throat. "It's just my eye."

"Your eye is what I make it into." He moves her shoulder gently so the light will hit her face. "Now there is a beautiful shadow across your iris that's going to run the length of the frame. I might crop it even more when I print it. Total abstraction. Geometry. That's it."

Lee wishes he would move away, give her space. She closes her eyes but he keeps shooting. Her eyelids flutter wildly. After a few moments, she can't take it anymore and steps away from him.

"I don't . . . Just stop." Lee steps back again, into the shadow of the curtains, and he finally puts down the camera. They stare at each other for a moment.

"I'm done with this," she says.

"But I'm not."

Lee walks out of the studio. She is shaking. Man follows her. He is angry; she can feel it rolling off him.

"Your eye is *my eye*," he says. There is a tremor in his voice, and he has his mouth clenched so that two curved grooves are cut into his cheeks. "You're mine in every way. You know that, don't you? You're *my* model. *My* assistant. My lover."

She backs away from him.

"Tell me you're mine. Say it."

Lee's throat has closed to the size of a straw and her words when she says them sound strangled and reedy. "I'm yours."

Even though she has said what he asked her to say, he doesn't seem satisfied. Lee wonders what it is he *does* want, if there are any words she could say that would placate him. They don't break eye contact.

"You're no one else's model. Not Hoyningen-Huene's, not Cocteau's, not anyone's. And if you want to go somewhere, back to Biarritz or anywhere else, *I* will take you."

Lee has never seen him like this. He holds the camera like a shield in his hands, but she can see he's trembling. She's trembling too. He has confused her, filled her with a need to leave but a conflicting need to soothe him.

"I'm yours," she whispers, the words like stones in her mouth. Her repeating the words seems to satisfy him. His shoulders relax. He lets go of the camera and lets it hang from its strap. The other times she has seen him angry have been like this: brief flares, quickly extinguished. So different from how she is, the embers burning for days. But right now Lee feels a deep sense of relief that she has calmed him.

"Good. Let's finish the shoot—I have a few more ideas I want to try out." With that, Man seems to think it's over. He reaches out and touches her cheek.

Lee nods. As she follows him back into the studio, she has trouble moving her body; she feels as if she is made of wax. Man has to move her into position, and she lets him. But as he picks up his camera she feels her old wild mind. She stares right at him but doesn't see him, imagines instead that she is a pilot in the cockpit of a plane, flying above the city and looking down at the ribbon of the Seine. The goggles press into the bones of her face; the air is filled with the smell of acrid smoke and burning fuel. Her heart pounds; she grips the yoke and points the plane straight up, to where the atmosphere is thin above the cloud cover. When Man puts the camera near her eye again she squints, closing him out of her view and filling her eyes with sky.

Afterward, when Man is finally done, Lee gathers up her things and leaves without saying goodbye. As she goes down the stairs she keeps seeing his camera looming toward her and feels the heat of his breath on her face. She makes sure Man doesn't hear her leave, and as soon as she is on the sidewalk, she inhales and lets it out slowly. She loops her Rollei around her neck and walks north with no destination in mind, her only thought to get far away from where she's been. She walks up Boulevard Saint-Michel, letting the city move past her in an uninterrupted rush. Across the street a young boy clings to his mother's hand while sucking on a gigantic lollipop that has smeared his whole face pink. A white-haired man tucks his hands into his pockets and hunches against the wind. A woman in front of a bakery trails her gloved hand along all the baguettes before selecting one. Again and again Lee wants to pick up her camera and snap a picture, but she doesn't. She lets life stream by without inserting herself into it, uninterrupted, uncaptured. Who is she to make herself a part of it?

Lee continues on across the Seine, through the Île de la Cité and across the Pont au Change. She walks and watches. At Les Halles she takes a quick right, wanting to get onto a quieter street, then turns again onto Rue Saint-Denis, where the bordellos are. Lee has walked here before but without her camera. The street has a furtive, debauched atmosphere that suits her mood. The buildings, painted bright colors years earlier but now fading, have paint peeling off in some places and all their shutters closed at all hours of the day. A few women, their stockings sagging down from their garters and their dresses outdated by several years, lean against the buildings or sit on the steps with their legs spread wide. One of them looks familiar. She has a sharp nose, a small mouth, black hair marcelled in tight waves against her scalp. Her flesh stretches against the seams of her thin black dress.

Lee approaches her. "Kiki?" she asks. With a feeling of elation, Lee starts dialing the settings into her camera. But as the woman looks up, her face dissolute, her makeup blurry, Lee realizes it's not Kiki. Of course not. Up close this woman looks nothing like her. As the woman puts her hand out to stop Lee from taking her picture, Lee puts the camera to her eye and releases the shutter. When she sees what Lee is doing, the woman starts yelling, a stream of French invectives. After she gets the shot, Lee leaves quickly, looking back only once to make sure the woman isn't following her. As she turns the corner, Lee feels a rush of clarity and power. The photo—Lee does not need to develop the film to know what she has gotten—will show the woman with her mouth twisted into an angry circle, her hand outstretched like a beggar, the fabric of her dress straining as she leans forward. There will be in it a feeling of surprise, of unexpected juxtaposition, as if in taking the picture at the exact moment when the woman's anger flared, Lee has shown her honestly, both supplicant and whore.

On Rue Pierre Lescot, Lee stops and works to calm her breathing. She holds her camera in both hands and it feels as though it is bonded to her skin and completely connected to her. Getting the shot has erased Man from her mind and hinged her to the present. The people, passing by her, appear in flashes, a film reel unspooling as she walks. She heads back toward Les Halles. The street is crowded. Lee watches the lives around her and begins to come back to herself—or to come to herself for the first time. Her eyelids are like a camera's shutter snapping; she blinks the motion around her into pictures. Every once in a while, one of the pictures she creates in her mind is worth saving, so she picks up her camera and freezes it on film. Every picture she takes feels alive and unexpected. And Lee herself feels more alive than she ever has, just taking them.

CHAPTER TWENTY-NINE

By now it is six o'clock and the last rays of the November light angle across the city, everything gray in the growing shadows. Lee doesn't want to go back to the apartment, but she must. Her feet hurt; she has walked for hours; she is hungry. She thinks of telling Man about her picture: the woman's mouth rounded into a perfect O, her emotions as visible as her flesh. But it is not Man she wants to tell. She wants to tell *herself,* so she plays it back in her mind, reliving again and again the feeling of power she got when she released the shutter at the exact right moment.

Lee dillydallies outside their door, hoping Man is out, but when she finally goes inside, she can hear bathwater down the hall and sees the trail of Man's clothing left on the floor along his path. Lee even hears him singing. It's that new song "A Bundle of Old Love Letters," weepy and sentimental. Hearing him, she realizes she can't stay. Quickly, Lee pulls open the armoire and looks at her dresses. Which one will make her look her best? She chooses her green crepe georgette and puts it on hurriedly, along with a more comfortable pair of shoes, jams her paste diamond clip in her hair, and leaves without letting Man know she was ever there.

Though she's been walking for hours already, as soon as Lee is back outside she realizes she's not remotely tired. She wants to move, wants to be outside, and most of all she wants to be doing something that will turn off her brain, calm the thoughts that fill it.

It is an hour's walk to the Palais Garnier. A nice walk, as good a destination as any. She knows how long it takes because she's walked there before, a few weeks earlier. The night is clear and mild, and soon Lee unbuttons her coat and lets it swing out behind her. She picks up speed, moving so fast her heart beats hard inside her chest. She walks the hour in forty-five minutes and finds herself at the Garnier at seven o'clock, right when they open the doors to let the crowds in.

She buys herself an orchestra seat, even closer to the stage than she sat with Jean. Pays with a flourish. An extravagance, yes, but it is nice to pay for herself for once. As Lee waits for the dancers to take the stage, she reads the playbill, looking for names she recognizes—the patrons and the dancers and the crew. The set designers and musicians. Sees it printed there. ANTONIO CARUSO, in the same black font as the rest of the names but, to her eyes, burning.

As the first chords sound, the dancers take the stage. Again Lee is transported. It is the purest expression of emotion: feelings made physical and mapped onto the body. Oh, the bodies! Lee would love to photograph them. The hard fact of their bones, the connective tissue visible under their skin, as if she is meant to see how the bodies are made. Lee wants to take pictures of them against Antonio's sets, the dancers' sinews and the silk panels in contrast with one another. It fascinates her, the toughness of their bodies, and when they move Lee thinks about the pain of dancing, the ballerinas' feet crushed and aching as they go up on pointe, the tape and bandages wrapped around the men's strong calves. Lee's own body—soft in comparison. The only part of her that is toughened is her hands, the skin dry and flaking from the darkroom. She wishes all of her was thickened up, that her body was a callus, that she got that way through hours of work and training. Lee wants to be someone who exerts effort, tries at things. She does not want to be soft.

At the end of the show the audience members are as ecstatic as they were the other night, leaping out of their seats and pounding their hands together. Lee stands with all of them, claps and claps, waits until she can be the last one to leave.

She does not know what she is doing. Does not know what she wants. No. That is not true. She knows what she is doing and what she wants but does not want to admit it, thinks that maybe if she doesn't admit it, it won't be true.

She waits so long at the south door she almost thinks he's not going to be there. But then she sees him, recognizes him in silhouette, lean, lithe, a scarf thrown over his unbuttoned coat. He sees her too. Stops and stares. Lee stares back with no expression. Her gesture has been made. She wants him to come to her. And he does: he walks over. Stands so close his jacket brushes against her. He is so tall she has to tip back her head to look up at him. The streetlamp casts odd shadows on his face and she can see a starburst of fine wrinkles radiating out from his eyes, the skin tissue thin and delicate.

"Well," Antonio says.

"Well," Lee answers.

"Want to go somewhere?"

Lee nods. Without another word he hails them a cab. As she gets in, Antonio says something to the driver that she cannot hear. They sit in the back and watch the city go by, the passing streetlamps casting rippling ribbons of light across their bodies.

Fifteen minutes later, they stop on a familiar side street. When Lee gets out she realizes where she is: he has taken her to Drosso's. She should feel something, some guilt, she knows she should—

at the very least she should be worried that some of Man's friends will see her there—but she feels nothing. This time when Drosso opens the door and kisses her cheek she pushes her face against him to feel the pressure of his lips more strongly. She and Antonio go into separate rooms to change, and even the act of removing her clothing, of taking off the dress she now realizes she chose for him, feels somehow erotic, as if she is stripping for him even though he's not there, and she rubs her hands along her body and between her legs before she puts on the robe, the silk cool against her skin. When they emerge into the hallway, both dressed in robes, Lee fills with a powerful giddiness, bubbling up in her throat so that she cannot help but laugh.

The sweet smell of smoke seeps out from under the bookshelves, and Lee hangs back while Antonio moves the lever on the bookcase to let them inside. Tonight, the secret room is crowded, a dozen people sharing the hookah on the bronze table in the middle of the room, all of them curled up on floor cushions and drowsing against one another. On a couch in the far corner, a group of mustachioed men are deep in conversation, their voices hushed but urgent. Someone somewhere is playing the piano, the same phrase over and over again. It takes Lee a moment to realize it's actually the phonograph skipping. As soon as she notices, she can think of nothing else, but no one in the room seems to care. Lee goes over to it and sets the needle back in place at the start of the record. A pause, and then the room fills with a beautiful series of cascading classical notes. She takes a deep breath. Antonio watches her from across the room, and she gives him a little smile just to see the returned smile spread across his face.

He comes over to her and inclines his head toward the bar cart. "None of that for you tonight," he says.

"I suppose not," she says, but part of her wants the cold glass in her hand again, like last time, the oblivion that came after.

A man approaches them, dressed in a Chinese robe with a small fez on his head. He bows and points toward the hookah.

"Do you smoke?" Antonio asks Lee.

"No."

"That's a shame. Could be fun."

The words hang in the air. Lee thinks of her mother. For many years Ellen tucked her Pravaz on a ledge on the underside of her bathroom sink, where she must have been certain no one would see it. Lee found it one afternoon when she was ill; she had gone into the bathroom to be sick and then lain down on the cold tile, liking the way the porcelain felt pressed against her cheek. And there it was, a small black leather case with her mother's initials stamped on the outside in gold foil, and secured inside with loops of elastic were several slim blue vials and a surgical-looking needle. After she found it Lee would feel under the sink every time she was in the bathroom, just to see if it was still there. For many years it always was, the vials at varying levels of fullness. But after a while, her mother stopped being so sneaky, and the case instead stayed in the pocket of her dressing gown, pulling down the fine fabric with its weight. One day while her mother was napping, Lee went in to see her, and the noise of the bedroom door opening and closing disturbed her so that she turned and stretched a naked arm above her head, the delicate white skin dotted with scabbed marks. Lee stared and stared at that arm, until finally her mother stirred again and Lee snuck out so she wouldn't be caught.

Now, at Drosso's, Lee takes a breath. "How does it feel?"

Antonio shrugs. "Like you're awake but not. Like happiness."

The man in the fez tugs at her robe and gestures to an unused hookah tube.

"I'm happy enough," Lee says. It costs her effort to say it, and part of her wonders if by saying no to this she is ruining everything with Antonio.

But Antonio just nods, waves off the man, and puts his hand at the small of her back, where she can feel the warmth of it like a brand through the thin silk. He moves her gently toward another door at the back of the room. They go down a short hallway. A pulsating beat of syncopated jazz vibrates the floorboards under her feet. Antonio opens a door at the end of the hall and they enter a large room, much bigger than the hookah room. Everything in it is a soft washed pink, pink flocked wallpaper and pink velvet banquettes, pink carpet and small pink tables at which people, dressed in blush-colored robes that seem, impossibly, to be coordinated with the surroundings, sit in small groups, talking loudly over the music. Who *are* these people? They lean in toward one another across the tables, put hands covered in diamonds up to their throats as they throw back their heads in open-mouthed laughter. The women's robes expose high arched collarbones and deep-colored pendants that nestle in the hollows of their necks. The men have smooth chests, olive skin, hard, sharp shoulders that make their robes somehow masculine. They are impossibly chic. At the far end of the room, a bar is set up, with a female bartender behind it, wearing a silk dress no thicker than a slip. The wall behind the bar is covered with rose gold foil, and the bottles are displayed against it on glass shelves so that the entire bar seems lit from inside and glowing.

"Oh," Lee says, "I will definitely have a drink in here."

No one pays Antonio and Lee any attention. They move toward a table and before they sit down he says, "I helped Drosso paint this room. We finished it a couple of months ago."

"It's gorgeous," she says, and means it. "Was it your idea?"

"Yes. I wanted it to feel like you were inside a mouth. I thought it should just be plain pink, but Drosso had the idea for the serpent, so I added it."

Lee looks around again and sees that the wallpaper is actually a mural, painted in gold, of a giant snake that coils around the room, each of its scales the size of a dinner plate and embellished with smaller drawings of snakes and what she thinks must be the Garden of Eden.

She tells him, "I'm not very good at that—making things up. I could take a good picture of it, though."

Antonio pulls out her chair for her and her knees buckle into it. He says, "It's not what I want to be doing—none of it is, really, the sets and everything—but I'm good at it. I can take a box and make it look like a palace."

Lee thinks of his set pieces for the ballet, the forest and ballroom, how real they seem. Imagines what it would be like to have an entire room as a canvas, to place viewers *inside* what they are viewing. "What do you want to be doing?"

"My own work. Not things I'm getting commissioned to create. But no one seems very interested in what I'm interested in."

"Which is what?"

"Oh, lately it's little paintings made out of oil and candle wax. 'Depressingly murky,' according to the one critic who's ever written about my work."

"I'd like to see them. I bet I'd like them."

Antonio raises his eyebrows at her and gives her a half smile. "You know? You just might."

The pink room reminds Lee of a costume party she went to in New York a few years ago, a night that got written up in the *Times* and talked about for months afterward. Guests were instructed to dress as either devils or angels and to make sure no one could tell who they were underneath. Once there, depending on what identity they had chosen, they were sent to a particular floor of the house. Lee was a devil, of course, with a red silk mask that covered most of her face and tendrils like flames that ran through her hair and curved around her neck.

The room she was directed to was illuminated by red lights, had a huge fire roaring in the hearth. She begins to tell Antonio about it and then says, "Oh!"

"What?" He leans toward her, staring right into her eyes, and tension crackles between them like wood popping in a fire.

"It's just...I took on this big job recently, and being here in this room and thinking about that party, it made me realize what I could do."

Antonio waits for her to continue.

"It's a white party. The Bal Blanc. Madame Pecci-Blunt does it every year. But what if we make it the black-and-white party? Everyone dressed in white, with words and images projected on their bodies as they go through the rooms. Like photographs. The guests themselves can be the paper and we can develop the pictures right onto them. Weird pictures, words and phrases—"

"That's fantastic," Antonio says emphatically. "Wish I had thought of it." He doesn't laugh, doesn't take his eyes off her, and she knows the idea really is a good one.

A waitress comes over to them. Antonio orders quickly, and she returns with a tray laden with cut crystal. With great ceremony, she lays out a sugar bowl, two Pontarlier glasses, two slotted spoons, a small carafe of ice water, and a green bottle.

"Absinthe!" Lee says.

"Drosso," Antonio says in explanation.

He fills the bottom bulbs of their glasses, the liquid gleaming like jade against the pink background. They each put their spoons, holding sugar cubes, across the lips of their glasses, and then he pours the water over her spoon in a slow trickle. Coming from him, the gesture is sensual, teasingly slow. In the bottom of the glass the green liquid grows cloudy. Lee takes the carafe from Antonio and does the same to his glass, conscious of his eyes on her. They use their spoons to stir, clink their glasses together, and tip them back at the same time. Lee's mouth fills with peppermint and licorice; her nose tingles as she swallows.

Antonio sips, coughs, reaches into his pocket, and pulls out his tobacco. In one fluid motion he rolls a cigarette and lights it, taking a deep drag off it so that the ember hisses and crackles. He hands it to Lee, who almost refuses but then thinks, *Why not?* As she inhales, the smoke sharpens the absinthe in a way that makes her feel as though she's burning from the inside. As though she is flaying herself and starting over. She takes another long sip of the drink, another drag off the cigarette, and soon they are refilling their glasses and starting the process over. The force of their attraction to each other hangs in the air like a suit of clothes they could step into.

"So," Antonio finally says, his expression curious.

Lee takes another sip and puts her hand on the table, and he rests his hand on top of it. Her world narrows to a point and he is at its center.

The crowd ebbs and flows. The music gets louder, the beat more insistent. Several couples stand and push aside tables so they can dance in the middle of the room. The dancing women hold up the bottoms of their robes and expose lean unstockinged legs. Lee and Antonio sit close together. Around them swirls the world. It feels like that to Lee, as if this strange room contains everything anyone would ever need. The dancing couples—as she watches them, time slows, and she sits back and just lets details wash over her: a bruise on someone's knee, the way an earring casts a sliver of prismatic light on a woman's neck, the expressions the dancers make as they move, both self-conscious and uninhibited, their eyes closed while smiles and grimaces of concentration flash across their faces. Lee catches snippets of conversation from other tables: "I was growing *gardenias,* of all things." "We made it down the mountain before it started to really snow, but I had lost a ski." "Patrice is a real hussy when she's around him."

Lee leans close to Antonio so her lips almost touch his ear. "You know what I want? I want to take pictures of this place."

He pours more absinthe in her glass. "You're good, aren't you? Your work. You really care about it."

Lee doesn't know how he's gotten this impression, but it's true. His knowing it makes it truer, somehow, than when Man or even Jean has said the same thing to her.

"I *do* care about it. I feel . . . " She looks around at the dancers as they jump and hop, at the other couples at the tables nearby. "I feel like I finally understand what I'm trying to do."

Each time they talk they have to lean in so they can speak at a normal volume, which feels incredibly intimate in the loud room.

"I think the world . . . ," she continues, "the world just goes on doing what it does whether I take a picture or not. My art—it's about choosing when I release the shutter. It's not about setting up a scene and making a picture of it. It's about being somewhere at the exact right moment and deciding it's a moment when no one else might think it's anything."

He nods. "I like that."

She feels flushed. She is not sure if he has understood her—Lee has never voiced this thought to anyone. She is still just figuring it out herself. With a trembling hand she picks up her absinthe and takes a long searing swallow, then refills the glass herself. The water hits the absinthe and swirls like smoke in the glass.

What she longs for more than anything is that moment of decisiveness, of clarity. She wants to create moments and capture them on film. Capture lived experience, the feeling of being alive.

From across the room she sees the bartender extend a wineglass to a man as if she is holding out a rose. She sees a man lower his head and rub his neck. The room smells of liquor and perfume and it is humid with all the bodies—exactly, she thinks, as Antonio must have imagined when he wanted it to be a mouth. Lee picks up the bottle and fills his glass again, and then she leans across the table and kisses him.

Hours later, drunk, their bodies thrumming, they stumble down a darkened hallway in a part of Drosso's apartment that Lee doesn't think she's seen yet. Antonio's hand is clenched around hers; her thumb rubs the round knob of bone in his wrist.

Someone walks toward them in the semidarkness.

"We need a room," Antonio mumbles.

The person doesn't answer, staggers away.

They try doorknob after doorknob. Giggling now, simultaneously drowsy and alert. So many doors! They open one on a bathroom, catch each other's eye. Almost consider it. Antonio puts his arm around her, his big hand wrapped tight around her rib cage. He is so warm she feels as if he is melting her.

Finally, at the end of the hall, double doors with large matching pull handles.

"Are those . . . ?"

They are: two giant erect penises, cast in bronze, curving up from their bases to make the handles.

"Do you think"—Lee begins speaking, then hiccups—"those are *Drosso's*?" She starts to laugh again and worries she's not going to be able to stop.

"Probably."

"Well, they're very . . . impressive."

But Antonio just gives them a yank and leads her into a large bedroom that must be Drosso's. Antonio, who all the time Lee has known him has been a man of few words, is whispering things to her, his voice a low rasp in her ear. The things he wants to do to her. All the ways he'll fuck her.

"Yes," she says. "Yes." Lee wants to say more but her mouth isn't moving right and she doesn't want to miss what he is saying. They find the bed; he lifts her onto it. Their robes are off, crumpled on the ground, there is just skin on skin on skin. Lee is on her back; Antonio kneels between her legs and grabs her around the waist, lifting her up and onto him so that their positions are reversed. With no effort he slides into her. She presses her thighs against him and feels the sharp blades of his hip bones as she moves above him, setting the tempo. Each time she lifts herself up he raises his hips to meet her. As he pushes into her she feels the same as she felt with the absinthe, as if she is scraping herself out from the inside and starting over. She leans forward and runs her hands all over him, feels every inch of his body, puts a hand between her legs and circles the base of his cock so she can feel how hard he is. Soon enough she stops thinking of anything. It is all just smoke and heat and licorice, the feel of their bodies as they move against each other. Her orgasm, when it comes, is a wild and terrible wave. She holds it off for as long as she can but it rolls in anyway, an obliteration, and she is lost to it, senseless, the wave is the blackness crashing over her and she lets it come.

Afterward Lee lies next to him, her head resting on his shoulder. The room is dim, and she stares at the wallpaper, letting her vision blur so that the pattern of vines and flowers seems to undulate on the wall. Or perhaps the flowers *are* undulating; in the gloom she watches, fascinated. Then she shifts her gaze and stares at Antonio's profile. He is looking up at the ceiling, unblinking. Lee rubs her hand along his arm until he looks over at her.

"What are you thinking?" she asks.

He props himself up on an elbow so he can look right at her. "You know? I'm thinking I don't really even know who you are."

In her drunken, sated state, Lee considers this. She could tell him that *she* doesn't know who she is, that she never has, that sometimes she just feels like an empty vessel to be filled by who-ever she is with or whatever she is doing. She has the sense he might understand.

But instead she says, "Does it really matter?"

He rolls toward her. "I think it does. Because I want to see you again. Can I see you again?"

Lee feels herself sobering up. In an unwelcome rush, she pictures the list of excuses and alibis she will have to create to keep this from Man. It is exhausting just to think about. And yet she cannot imag-ine herself *not* doing this again now that she has done it.

She looks at the way the shadows play over Antonio's chest, the dark line of hair that runs down his stomach. "Of course you can," she says.

"You're not with Man Ray? I thought I'd heard...?"

"What if I were?"

Antonio raises his hands above his head in a conciliatory ges-ture. "You don't have to explain to me. I remembered you from that other time we met, and then once I thought I saw you with him at the Dôme. You looked...I thought you looked happy."

Lee pictures what Antonio might have seen. The camera lens zooms back and she is in the middle of the shot, smiling, Man's arm around her protectively, possessively. Man sees someone he knows, smiles and waves, goes over to say hello. If Lee were to snap a picture of that scene, in it she would be watching Man without wanting anyone to know she was watching him, sidelong and hungry. But what might Antonio have seen? Under the sur-face, love? There is no way for her to know. The moment is gone; the moment never existed in the first place.

"We *were* happy," Lee says, and swings her legs over the side of the bed and searches for her robe until she finds it tangled with Antonio's by the door. She picks them both up and tosses his to him. He roots around in its pocket and finds his tobacco, then scoots up to the headboard and starts rolling a cigarette on his thigh.

Lee walks over to him and gives him a long kiss, neither of them wanting to break it off first. He tastes like smoke and sugar cubes. The nerve endings in her tongue pull taut a knot in her stomach, and it is all she can do not to lie down beside him again. But instead she moves away.

The truth is that Antonio is a stranger. It is Man she knows; Man the one she has built a life with, who made her into the person she is today. Lee thinks about what it would be like to leave him. She would take all her things from their apartment—and go where? To stay with Antonio? This man here is just another Man, but one she doesn't know and who doesn't yet love her. But Man loves her. His anger this afternoon, the camera pressed into her face, is a reaction to her pulling away when what she should be doing is getting closer. She cannot imagine her life without him.

"I said the wrong thing. I can't see you again."

Antonio laughs an incredulous laugh. "You are a mysterious woman."

"I guess I am."

"If you change your mind..." His voice trails off. She walks over and kisses him again, and rubs her hand down the length of his body. Then she gets up and pushes through the doors toward home.

The sun is spreading pink across the sky by the time Lee gets back to the apartment. In the changing room at Drosso's, after she left Antonio, she saw herself in the mirror. The only word she could think of was *ravaged*: lips puffy, eyes ringed with smudged liner, hair greasy and disheveled. In the small lav she turned on the cold tap full blast and pushed her face into it, the water spurting up her nose and in her eyes. She rubbed at her face with her fingers until the remains of her makeup came off, ran her wet hands through her hair to tame it. Then she wadded up her robe and ran it under the water, and scrubbed and scrubbed between her legs and at her armpits as hard as she could. But the rest she could do nothing about: the smell of tobacco on her fingers, the bruised appearance of her face, the scrim of guilt covering her like a thicker, blunted version of herself.

There is nothing right she can say to Man—no good excuse she can devise for where she's been. As she walks into their apartment she is not so much trembling as vibrating, every inch of her alive with worry. Perhaps Man is still asleep or has already left for the studio; perhaps she can delay their meeting for a little while longer.

But he is sitting at the table drinking espresso when she walks into the kitchen. He looks up at her curiously, as if he hasn't seen her for several months. Calmly, he brings the espresso cup to his lips and takes a sip.

"Where have you been?" he asks.

Lee takes off her coat and folds it over the back of a chair, wondering if this is what she would usually do. She clears her throat. "Jean is back in town. From Rome. I bumped into him on the street as I was headed to the studio and he wanted to show me some of the film. It's so good. I can't wait for you to see it. I'm sorry if you were worried."

It is a plausible lie. Jean *is* back. He wrote to her from Rome to tell her he was coming home, but she hasn't found time to visit him; she could easily have run into him in the neighborhood. Lee was practicing before she arrived, but now her words sound stilted even to her own ears.

"Ah," Man says, and places the espresso cup back on its saucer so gently it doesn't make a sound. "I look forward to seeing it."

"Yes, I can't wait to show it to you. It won't be long now— Jean says he has just a few more edits to do, and then it will be ready. The parts I saw, they were good. Really good. I want you to see it."

Lee is talking too quickly. Man gets up and puts his espresso cup in the sink and walks into the foyer. He grabs his coat, his keys. He opens the door, looks back at her.

"I'll see you later, when you get back from *Vogue*?" he asks. The look he gives her is mild; his lips curve up in what might be a smile.

Before she can even say yes, the door clicks closed behind him.

VIENNA

SEPTEMBER 1945

Lee names the kitten Warum, the German word for *why*, when she finds him in the gutter in Vienna. He fits snugly in her coat's breast pocket, purrs against her chest like a motorbike engine while she waits in line to get her clearance to move on to Moscow. Everywhere she goes she needs triplicated permits, and every bureaucrat she talks to is disorganized and incompetent. Of all the former Nazi strongholds, it is Vienna Lee hates most of all.

The liberated city is a study in contrasts. At night, the Austrians gorge on music. Frothy harpsichords and lilting violins tinkle through the streets. Concert halls are packed with people, but the operas Lee used to love no longer move her. One night she goes to a marionette show and the loose bodies of the dancing puppets remind her so much of Dachau she has to run from the theater to keep from screaming.

She's been trapped here for weeks, long enough for her mail to catch up to her, a stack of letters from Roland as thick as her thigh. She reads them in bed and laughs when Warum bats at the pages. Roland's tone is worried and insistent. He wants her home. The war is over, Hitler is dead, he can think of no reason for Lee to still be gone.

In the light of day, all Lee sees are signs of privation. Austrian girls in dead men's coats, begging for food in the rubble of their city. Malnourished babies dying in Viennese hospitals, their rib cages delicate as pick-up sticks, chests rising and falling as they struggle to keep their breath. If she were to write to Roland, she would say, *This is why I'm still here, to shine a light on the suffering that didn't end with the war*. But instead she doesn't write to him at all.

One afternoon, Lee is startled to find Warum missing from her pocket. She retraces her steps, stops at checkpoints she went through hours earlier to show the same permits the guards have already seen, each passing minute making her more convinced she'll never find him. She looks until the sun is setting before she gives up and heads back to her room. Something in the road by the hotel's door catches her eye. There he is, in another gutter: hind legs crushed, back arched like a fighter, his body already cold and stiffened. *Why?* Lee thinks. She picks him up, rocks back and forth. It is hours before she is ready to leave him. She uses her scarf as a shroud and buries the bundle in some nearby rubble. It is pointless to love things when in the end they'll all be taken.

CHAPTER THIRTY

After Man leaves the apartment, Lee is alone with her betrayal. She goes through the motions of getting ready for work, walks to *Vogue* with her head down, focusing her full attention on her feet. The air is bitterly cold, but she doesn't feel it. All her mind will do is replay scenes from the night before.

The deadline for the magazine's next issue is the following week, and there is always a ramping up of activity and energy as the date approaches. The offices are in their usual chaos when Lee arrives, models and assistants and illustrators running around as if by moving quickly they'll be able to get their work done on time. A few people say hello to Lee as she passes them in the hall, but she goes straight into one of the dressing rooms and sits in a chair. She can't believe she has a shoot today—Lee hasn't slept a minute, and she doubts even George is talented enough to obscure the bags she sees under her eyes when she looks in the mirror.

Man must know exactly where she was last night. He must know that for weeks when she was with him, it was Antonio's hands she imagined touching her, Antonio's body she pictured in the dark. Or maybe he doesn't; maybe he has no idea. Lee seizes on this thought and then finds herself getting indignant—how can he *not* know? How foolish can he be?

The door creaks open and Horst strides into the room. He takes one look at Lee and says, "You look run over."

Lee groans and drops her head, rubbing at her temples. Horst sits down in a chair across from her and stretches his legs in front of him, crosses them at the ankle. "Jesus. George isn't going to be pleased. We're shooting the hat spread today, I think." He sits forward and peers at her more closely. "Have you been crying?"

"No." Lee spits out the word. "And you don't look so hot yourself."

Horst looks at himself in the mirror and gives his reflection a toothy smile. "I look marvelous, and you know it."

Lee is supposed to laugh, but she doesn't, and Horst turns his attention back to her, a vague look of concern flashing across his pretty features.

"Let's get this done," she says.

The shoot goes fine—the makeup artist works what Lee feels is a minor miracle—but after it is over, and Lee realizes she has to go home again, she gets the same feeling she had earlier with Man, as if her tongue is swelling up and choking her.

Horst and George stand chatting in the hallway, flirting as always. Lee waits. Horst usually walks her home, and she wants his company even more than usual, so that she can stop her mind from its endless circling.

When they get outside, the afternoon air is milder than before. The wind has died down, and they walk along Boulevard Raspail, the cafés and bars thronged with people who, like her, Lee thinks, don't want to go home. The laughter and street sounds set her on edge, and after a few blocks she turns onto a quieter side street, Horst following along behind her. They pass a men's shop with a window display of wide silk neckties, and Horst pauses in front of it.

"Can you wait a minute? I love that blue one," he says, and darts into the store. Lee stands on the sidewalk and uses the opportunity to try to slow her thumping heart. Horst is gone for five minutes, then ten. Lee peers through the shop's murky glass door and sees him gesticulating in front of a mirror, four ties draped around his neck. She sits down on the shop's stoop. In front of the store is a lamppost covered with a palimpsest of signs and posters. Lost cats, new bistros, advertisements for upcoming films. And there, glued among them, is a familiar face. Lee stands up and goes over to the lamppost. ILSE BING AND CLAUDE CAHUN: OBJECTS AND OBJECTIFICATIONS, it says, with photographs of both women printed beneath the title, and below that, one of Ilse's photographs of a dancer and one of Claude's self-portraits. PIERRE GALLERY, DECEMBER 1930–JANUARY 1931.

"Fuck," Lee whispers. She rips the sign free and shakes it. They've actually done it—Ilse and Claude. At the Pierre, where not even Man has had a show. If she had handled things differently, befriended them months ago, perhaps Lee could be there with them. "Fuck," she says again, louder, and repeating the oath makes her feel better, a valve released.

A few moments later, Horst comes out of the store, two tie boxes under one arm. Lee quickly balls up the paper and tosses it in a nearby bin, and then she puts a smile on her face and walks back to Horst, who shows her his ties and seems content to walk in silence next to her.

They take a shortcut through the Cimetière du Montparnasse, where stately elm trees make an archway over the wide paths. Lee can't think of a day when she's felt worse. She crosses her arms and rubs her hands up and down them, trying to warm up.

"You sure you're all right?" Horst finally asks her.

Lee lifts her chin. "I'm fine."

He nods. She glances over at him, at his guileless face, at the tie boxes held casually in the crook of his arm, at the little comb marks in his perfectly slicked-back hair, his whole figure radiating self-content and vigor, and she feels a sudden, powerful dislike for him.

"You and George," Lee says abruptly. "Everybody knows what's going on between the two of you."

Horst stops on the path, knits his eyebrows together, and shoves his balled fists into his pockets. "None of their business," he says. "Besides, nothing's happening."

"Don't be ridiculous. Everyone has known for months you want to fuck him."

Horst takes a step back as if Lee has slapped him. She can tell by his face that she has crossed a line. But saying it releases more pressure within her. "It's embarrassing. All the gossip. Just do it and get it over with."

"What the hell? What is wrong with you?"

What *is* wrong with her? Horst blinks his long eyelashes at her. Horst is *nice,* one of the nicest people she's met in Paris, uncomplicated and fun to work with. Finally she says, "I'm sorry. I don't know what's gotten into me."

"Well, figure it out. You're no peach to be around lately." Horst starts walking, kicking at some of the larger pebbles in the path, and when she follows him, he holds up a hand to stop her. "You know?" he says, turning to face her. "You'd have a lot easier time in life if you treated people how you want them to treat you."

"What's that supposed to mean?"

Horst hesitates, then says, "Look. You're fun, when you want to be. But we've worked together for how long now? And what do you know about me? You never seem very interested in anyone but yourself. And if you *were* interested in me, you'd know that I made a pass at George, and he turned me down. So if there's gossip, none of it's true." He glares at the path in front of him.

"I'm sorry—"

"Are you, Lee?" Horst shakes his head, and then turns around and heads down the path to the south side of the cemetery. She watches him until he disappears around a corner, and then she stands there a little longer, wondering what to do. In her current mood, she is afraid to do anything, afraid of what else she might destroy.

She can't go home. Can't be there, in her and Man's space, even if he's not there. She also can't be alone with herself, so she turns around and heads for Les Deux Magots, where she'll have a cup of tea and try to get herself into a better state. But then as she walks up Rue des Plantes, she remembers that Jean is back. She changes course and heads for his apartment, suddenly desperate to see his friendly face. When he opens his door, Lee practically falls into his arms.

"Mouse!" he cries, picking her up off the step and holding her in the air. "I was thinking I was going to have to come find you if you didn't answer my letter soon, and here you are."

They go into Jean's sitting room. He pours Lee a glass of wine, the sight of which turns her stomach. He sits across from her and keeps up a stream of chatter, telling her about Rome and the brand-new train he traveled on when he came home and all the edits he's made to the film. "It is so, so good," he says. "If it were not my own work, I would use the word *brilliant*. Forgive me: I will use the word anyway. The film is brilliant, and you, my dear, are brilliant in it."

Lee smiles for what feels like the first time all day. "Really?"

"Would I exaggerate? Everyone is so pleased. The vicomte loves it. Well"—here a shadow crosses Jean's face—"all but the ending. We have to redo the ending, but that has nothing to do with you. I have to get Anush back to film those sections again— ah! Did you hear? Anush is having a baby."

Lee hasn't heard. She hasn't kept up with any of the people from the film except for Jean, and as he tells her about Anush and the others, she feels herself grow a little calmer. Anush liked her, accepted her just as she was. Everyone on the film set liked her. Lee doesn't need Horst's friendship, and if Man is angry with her, then maybe she doesn't need Man.

"When you make another film, can I be in it?"

"You can be in any of my films for all time," Jean says dramatically, placing his hand over his heart.

She imagines stepping onto Jean's next film set and just leaving the rest of her life behind. "What are you working on next?"

Jean picks up her untouched glass and takes a swallow. "Who can tell? I might not do another film for years. I have to get hit with an idea. Right now I'm writing poetry. Painting. Talking to Diaghilev. He wants me to do another project for his new ballet."

Just hearing the word *ballet* makes Lee shudder. She sits back against the couch and feels almost sick with thoughts of last night. Jean, always observant, notices instantly.

"What is wrong?"

He stares at her, his deep-set brown eyes intent. Lee knows she shouldn't talk about what she's done, but she feels an uncontrollable urge to tell him, to lay her guilt at someone else's feet, someone who cares for her. "I've done a bad thing," she whispers, looking down at her lap.

Jean moves over to the couch and takes her hands in his. "What could you do that is so terrible?"

Lee clears her throat, tries to swallow. "You know Antonio Caruso?"

A wistful smile crosses Jean's face. "Of course."

"I—I was with him. Last night. Man doesn't know, or I'm not sure: he might know. I didn't go home last night. I haven't slept in two days." The words rush out, tumble over themselves.

Jean has closed his eyes and still has the smile on his face.

"Jean?" Lee asks.

"Sorry." He opens his eyes. "I was making a picture of you and Caruso in my mind. He is such an attractive man. I'm always inventing reasons to need him on my set, just so I can look at him."

Lee wants to laugh, but she's too anxious. "I don't know what to do," she whispers.

Jean drums his fingers on his leg. "When Man Ray was with Kiki," he says, "they used to scream at each other in the street. Everybody heard them. Talked about them. I don't hear these stories about you two."

"We shout in private," Lee says with a choked laugh.

"Ah. Well, a cat never changes its stripes, as they say. Man was always telling Kiki what to do, so I can imagine that he does the same with you."

"Yes."

"Kiki—" Jean dismisses her with a snap of his fingers. "I don't have many feelings for her. But you: no one should tell *you* what to do."

Lee covers her face with her hands. How can she explain to Jean what Man means to her? Even if Jean didn't dislike him, she doesn't know if she can make him understand. She says, "Remember that night when I first met you, and you took me to the fountain and asked me if I was in love with Man?"

"Yes."

"I've thought about that night so many times. I didn't want to tell you how I felt about Man. You were a stranger. And so I told you that I didn't know how to be in love. And I do feel that way sometimes . . . but there's so much of Man's and my relationship— so much of any relationship—that no one ever sees. You can't explain it to an outsider. At least I can't. But there was something I regretted not telling you about that night. Months ago, I was working in the darkroom alone one night, and this mouse ran over my foot—"

"A mouse for Mouse," Jean says, nodding.

"Ha, yes. Anyway, I turned on the darkroom light and exposed my negatives to the light and it didn't ruin them, and afterward Man and I worked together to re-create the technique—we perfected it, and the prints we made together, they're my favorite work I've ever done. I think that was when I knew I could really be an artist."

Lee takes a breath. Jean says, "Everyone has that moment when they go from *trying* to *doing*. I had it too, a similar thing with a teacher. But you've always been an artist. Anyone can see that."

Lee nods, but she doesn't really believe him. "Maybe," she finally says. "But that was the happiest I've ever been."

"Ah. That's a different thing."

"Yes."

Jean holds out his hands. "You want my thoughts? You slept with Caruso because Caruso is a beautiful man and you're a beautiful woman. You're young and figuring things out. Tell Man Ray or don't tell him. It's up to you. But don't make yourself feel bad for what you did. Nothing good comes from that. You're an artist. Artists crave experiences because that's how they make art."

It would be so easy to agree with Jean: Lee has told herself the same thing several times already. But using a desire for experience as an excuse for an affair—it is just that, an excuse, a way to absolve herself of her transgression. And the reasons she slept with Antonio are so tangled in her head there is no way to explain them to Jean. Much of it has nothing to do with Man, but that doesn't change the fact that she has done something to hurt him. Lee says, "If I don't tell him, there will always be a lie in our relationship."

"So tell him."

"But then there won't *be* a relationship. Man would never—he would never betray me the way I just did him." Lee feels her eyes prick with tears and swipes at them with the back of her hand.

"Hmm. Then you, Mouse, are a lucky woman." Jean pats her leg. "Perhaps the best thing is not to think about this anymore, at least not right now. Do you want me to show you the film?"

They go into a room at the back of Jean's apartment, where the blinds are drawn and a projector is already set up. Together they watch the film from start to finish, and when they get to the part where Lee appears, her eyes closed, gliding across the stage like marble come to life, she sucks in her breath and holds it in as she watches. Jean glances at her and then takes her hand, threading his fingers through hers and squeezing.

"See?" he says when it is over, getting up and shutting off the projector. "Brilliant."

It is past suppertime, and Lee knows she needs to leave. She feels calmer now, even though she is still unsure what she will do or say when she sees Man. At the door, Jean embraces her and whispers into her hair, "Be well, Mouse," and she clings to him a little longer than necessary before she leaves.

Man has not left the note in the usual place on the dining room table. He has not left it in the kitchen, or on the little stand by the door. It is in their bedroom, propped on a pillow on the bed beneath his half-finished painting. It's folded in half, written on the business stationery he got years ago when he was feeling flush, his monogram letterpressed at the top of the page.

Lee stands beneath his picture of her mouth and reads it.

My love,

Do you know your power? How much power you hold over me? I think if you knew you would not hurt me the way you do. You would not promise to commit to me and then leave me constantly wondering, constantly confused. You would not make me a man who needs a promise.

I need to leave town for a few days, maybe longer. I can't write or paint or photograph when all I think of is you. The only way for me to get anything done is to leave for a while. If you want to write me you can reach me care of Arthur and Rose. I am sorry I am leaving when the Bal is just around the corner, but I'm sure you'll find a way to do it on your own.

Yours ever and always,
M

Lee reads the note again, and then a third time. Does he know? Does it matter? The room feels recently vacated; she has a sudden vision of catching him at the station. In her mind's eye she imagines it: the race down crowded sidewalks, her hand waving like a frenzied bird as she hails a cab, finding him just as he is about to board the train and shouting his name until he sees her. The scene feels false, ridiculous. In it Lee isn't covered in the lingering stink of her betrayal.

Lee puts down the letter, goes to the wardrobe, and gets out her dressing gown. Puts it on. Goes into the kitchen and makes a cup of tea. No part of her pays attention to what she's doing. The apartment is so quiet. On the street beneath their window people chatter, and in the distance is the rising wail of a police siren. Beneath the worry that has gnawed at her all day, Lee feels something different. She will have to do the Bal Blanc on her own. She knows just what she'll do—the idea she had last night at Drosso's. The new feeling inside her is so fresh and clean it is inchoate; she cannot yet pin it down with a name.

CHAPTER THIRTY-ONE

Days pass in ways that Lee does not remember. She stays in bed; she oversleeps. There is no one there to see her. She drinks espresso on an empty stomach; she eats the last remaining food. Without Man there the apartment is a cavern. The lights are off and still she pulls the covers over her head.

Lying on the mattress Lee can look up behind her and see Man's painting. She runs her fingers over the thick texture of the dried paint. From this angle her lips look even more like bodies, and Lee wishes powerfully that Man were next to her, that he hadn't gone away.

The same groove cuts into Lee's mind until she is sick of thinking. Antonio: he felt like a simple test of her bad behavior, of how far she was willing to go. But now: the sadness she is left with. Lee stretches her arms and legs to the edges of the bed and cannot find the end of her regret.

After a few days, Lee finally has to rouse herself. Get some food, get to work. On the street the sunshine is blinding; she wears dark glasses and pulls her hat down tight. As she runs errands she feels like an actress, better than she ever was on Jean's set. She wills the muscles in her face to move when she wants to smile, ties a rope

334

around her thoughts and drags them back to the moment at hand. It works, mainly. But at the bakery, in the middle of a transaction, she forgets what she is doing. Other times she has to leave a shop and take deep breaths to calm herself down.

At the studio, when she finally goes back, there is ringing and ringing. At first Lee can't figure out what it is. Some sort of alarm, a drill? When she realizes it's the telephone she runs to get it, her voice breathless when she says hello. On the other end of the line is Madame Pecci-Blunt, her voice imperious. Will Man Ray still be coming the next day so she can show him the solarium where the party will be held? Lee fumbles, blurts out that actually, it is she who will be coming, as Man has been called away unexpectedly.

"Ah, you are the assistant?" Madame Pecci-Blunt says.

"Partner."

"Yes, all right. The one Jean told me about. He said you were talented. But I need you both. I need Man Ray. Everyone knows him. This party has to be *exquisite*. It has to be the party of the year, the absolute *pinnacle* of the season. I don't want just white cake! White plates!" Her voice oozes money, sophistication, her French a waterfall of tinkling vowels.

There is a pause. Lee remembers Jean's advice, to just let the client talk until it's clear what she wants. "It's not about the food, or the plates," Lee finally says, encouragingly.

"Ah, you are right! These ideas—they are the ideas a child would have. That is why I'm hiring you both. All I know is that the Bal is about magic, transporting the guests to another place entirely. Like a dream."

"A dream in white. I had some ideas, actually," Lee says. She begins to describe them and then interrupts herself. "Mimi—do you mind if I call you Mimi?"

"Not at all."

The woman's agreement emboldens Lee further, so she continues, her words coming out in a rush as she explains the idea she had when she was talking to Antonio: projected images, words on the floor, on people's bodies.

"That is good," Mimi says. "Quite, quite good." Before long, they have figured out a plan so grand Lee is just as convinced as the woman that it will be the party of the century. The only problem is that Lee doesn't really know how to do any of it. For that she needs Man, and his equipment. She tells Mimi that he will be back in a few days.

When Madame Pecci-Blunt asks her to clarify the fee, Lee quotes the number she and Man agreed on, a number that feels so high, so outrageous, she half expects the woman to hang up the phone right then. The number is more than the Wheelers offered Man for his next film, more than three months' rent on the little whitewashed studio on Rue Victor Considérant. But the woman accepts the number without a question, and they agree to meet the next day to go over the details. Lee finds herself wondering if she should have asked for more.

The next afternoon Lee goes to the Pecci-Blunt mansion in the Trocadéro, where the Bal will be held. She brings her notebook, a measuring tape, and a small portfolio of her work, which Mimi doesn't ask to see. Instead, they walk around the property as if they are old friends. The grounds are astounding; Lee has never seen such wealth up close. In the gardens, everything is laid out tidily and squared off at right angles as if it's part of a prep school geometry lesson. Each topiary snipped with precision, the winter cabbages and hardy mums arranged in neat formations. Not a petal out of place. Along the paths, pebble mosaics of angular fish leap at forty-five-degree angles out of symmetrical ponds.

It's all so perfect that as she walks Lee feels the urge to kick out at something, to gash a hole in a box hedge and cover the ground with shredded leaves. Instead, she smiles, accepts Mimi's offer of tea, which is served in a sitting room whose ceiling is painted sky blue. Delicate porcelain cups, translucently thin at the edges, are filled with cambric liquid made weaker with too much cream. Espresso, the mud and stink of it, is what Lee wants now, but it would be too much for this refined woman's palate. Lee perches on the edge of a satin-covered settee and lifts her teacup with shaking hands.

After tea, Mimi takes her out a side door to a giant solarium, in which a tiled swimming pool is surrounded by blooming flowers. The air is heavy with the scent of lilies. Lee is enchanted: a winter idyll, here in the center of Paris.

"This is perfect," says Lee. "We can set up gauze curtains along the perimeter, and project the film on the curtains, and into the water."

As she says it, Lee can see it, more clearly than she has ever seen anything: couples in white tuxedos and ivory dresses, dancing at the edge of the pool, white-clad waiters weaving their way through the crowd. She sees the way the curtains will billow from the breeze let in through an open window, the images—her images—trembling as if they are alive. And as she and Mimi work out the logistics, Lee fills with such impatience it blots out all her other feelings— her guilt, her anger at Man, her loneliness—and leaves her with one imperative: to get to work. When Mimi smiles with pleasure at Lee's suggestions, neither of them mentions Man at all.

Over the next few days Lee exists in a sort of fever dream, her only focus to create the films she'll show at the party. She teaches herself to use Man's cine camera, which thank God he has not sold, and fills an entire notebook with sketches and ideas. Each afternoon, like a diver emerging from a pool for air, she comes to the surface of the world again, and goes out into the streets for supplies, which she charges to an account Madame Pecci-Blunt has given her. She comes back to the studio with rolls of

16mm film, canvas, materials she can use to experiment as her ideas change and grow.

First she makes a list of a hundred or so words and phrases, both in English and in French, words that will surprise and titillate when they are projected on guests' bodies. RACONTEUR, COQUILLAGE, FALSEHOOD, DREAMER, CHUCHOTER, PERMISSIVE, LACK-ADAISICAL—the words come in a flood and she scribbles them all down, paints them on the canvas she has purchased, and then films them. She pictures the words crawling across the wealthy guests' skin and clothing—GAUCHE, SEREIN, AWESTRUCK, FLÂNEUR, JOUR-NEYING—and as more words come to her mind she paints and films those too.

One evening Lee starts painting a story on a drop cloth, or maybe it's a poem, words and phrases that start to have a narrative. As she paints she realizes the words are a love story, they are Man and Antonio, they are a coded apology that only she and Man will understand. The words give her an idea, and she rifles through some pictures Man took of her months ago, and places them next to the phrases. As she works she suddenly wants Man to be there, for him to come to the party and see what she has done, the words she's written for him, the story she is making, the best way she can think of to tell him she regrets what she has done.

The more Lee works, the more she finds she is sorry. The more she misses Man. The way their eyes met in the darkroom, the looks they gave each other when something turned out well. The dance they executed around each other in their shared small space. Working alone is not the same. On a rainy afternoon she almost phones the Wheelers, but can't think what she would say.

One evening, after working for countless hours, Lee stops and looks around with bleary eyes. The studio is a disaster. Spent tubes of black paint litter the floor. The air smells of linseed and spilled wine and what might be Lee's feet. The ends of her fingernails are permanently blackened, the cuticles dry with turpentine. But the films are done. There are four of them: one of disconnected words, one of strangely juxtaposed images that she knows owe much to Man's Surrealist films, one of the words and images she thinks of as her love poem, and one of her hands in hundreds of poses—she hopes that when these are displayed on people's bodies it will look as if someone is touching them. Lee opens another bottle of wine and watches all four films, projected on the back wall of the studio, as she drinks straight from the bottle, the wine going down her throat in what feels like one uninterrupted swallow. When the last film slips loose of the reel at the end, Lee sits in the sudden hot bright light of the projector, listening to the *tock tock tock tock* as the film goes around the reel, and she feels overwhelmingly, drunkenly proud.

The next day, Lee goes back to the apartment for the first time in eight days. She needs clean clothes; she needs a bath. The mail slot is full of correspondence. Bills to be paid, friends to respond to. And as Lee goes through the stack she sees how many letters are addressed to her, all of them in Man's crabbed hand. There are fifteen of them: he has written her almost two letters a day. She gathers them up and once she has stripped off her dress and lain down on their bed she opens them and reads them as they must have been written, almost in one stream of consciousness.

Away from you I realize even more how much I need you—we are like twins of each other or mirror images—without you I'm less than half of myself—I've hardly eaten since I left you, food has no taste, my mouth is dry and water doesn't help it—and this trip becomes what I should have known it to be: a penance, an exile, a drying out, the only way I can get over the liquor that is you.

In some of the letters he seems angry; in others he is plaintive. He must have spent hours on them. Lee envisions him at some desk at the Wheelers', looking out at the sea but not seeing it.

I feel old. I probably shouldn't admit this to you, as one of the things I worry about most is that you will tire of being with me. But I do. My bones ache. My knees creak when I stand up from the floor. My head aches. I feel your beautiful fingers at my temples, rubbing the pain away. But then I think: no wonder she does not love me as I love her, if what I imagine is myself sick and needing to be taken care of. And you—you are so free. You only half realize it, I think, how much potential you have inside you, all the things you have left to do.

It is not until she reaches the tenth letter that he mentions the night she left and what she's done, and the letter trembles as she reads it.

I know you were with another man the night before I left Paris. I'm not sure how I know, but I do. I could feel it, while you were gone. Could feel what you were doing. I saw the man's hands touching you, I saw him making love to you as only I am supposed to do. It made me sadder than I have ever felt in my life.

And then in the last letter, he gets angry, the slant of his penmanship more pronounced, his pen gouging into the paper.

You have never let me in. You know this, don't you? For all our time together I have been knocking against the door of your skull and you have only opened it one crack. I have had to view you through a peephole. I know why—I understand how hard it is for you, that what happened to you when you were young is still with you—but

340

I thought I could break through that old, old pain, clean it up like a spill. But you! You don't even know that I am knocking. Don't even know that we could have been more than we were if only you had opened up to me. You didn't let me be all the things I wanted to be for you.

By the time she gets through all the letters, Lee is hollowed out. Exhausted. In the margins of the last letter Man has written *Elizabeth Lee Elizabeth Elizabeth Elizabeth Elizabeth Lee Elizabeth Elizabeth Elizabeth*. Her name a hundred times over. While she thinks, she traces her finger along the letters.

It is true, what Man has written. That she hasn't known how to let him in. Or perhaps she didn't want to. All along she has thought maybe he hasn't noticed. Lee doesn't have other love affairs to compare to this one, not real ones, so there was always the chance that what they had together was enough. But it wasn't. She has tried to move past the memories, to erase them, but instead they have become indelible, a scribbled darkness over what used to be light. She is so ashamed at her weakness, at how events from two decades ago have left such a permanent mark on her. If only she could have done as the analyst requested, as her father requested, and forgotten. And now, here, another erasure, another thing lost—or maybe it's something she never had in the first place.

Lee fills with such powerful self-loathing she has to lie back on the bed and close her eyes. Everything suddenly seems absurd— her own aspirations as an artist, her relationship with Man. Her love poem film: the thought of it is embarrassing. As if a few words projected on a screen could be a true representation of love. All of it is nothing. She puts an arm over her eyes and feels hot tears slip out from under it.

Lee gets under the covers and huddles in a little ball, Man's letters spread around her, until finally sleep comes and saves her for a while.

When the sun comes up it wakes Lee from a fitful night. She is still surrounded by Man's letters and all the other mail. She lies there, staring up at the ceiling, watching the shadows the curtains cast on the wall. She picks up one of Man's pages and reads a few lines. She already knows what it says; the words are burned on her brain like a photograph. As she sets down the letter, she notices a big envelope at the bottom of the pile, with the Art Deco monogram on it that the Philadelphia Camera Society uses on all its correspondence. It's addressed to Man, of course, and is thick and heavy. Good news is always thick and heavy. She knows she shouldn't open it, but then it occurs to her that if he has been accepted for the exhibition—or even better, if he has won one of the big prizes, the grand prix, even—it would be a good reason for her to call him at the Wheelers.

So she opens it, slipping her finger under the thick glued flap and peeling it open as carefully as she can. Inside, there is a letter and a big exhibit booklet. It has to be good news.

December 20, 1930

Dear Mr. Ray,

We are pleased to inform you that the Jury of Selection has awarded your triptych, "The Bell Jar Series," the Patterson-Shrein Award for Portraiture. The triptych will appear in the exhibition on March 1, 1931. The jury members were deeply impressed by the compositions, and especially by the new technique one of the photos employs, described in your accompanying artist statement as solarization. Furthermore, your photos have been chosen by Mr. Joseph Merrill Patterson

*and Mrs. Richard T. L. Shrein to receive a five-hundred-dollar ($500)
prize and a place in the Philadelphia Camera Society's distinguished
permanent collection.*

*Though we imagine it will not be possible for you to attend
the exhibit in person, if by happenstance you find yourself in the
Philadelphia area in March, we would be delighted to host you at
a small reception for the prize recipients. Otherwise, we enclose the
exhibit guide, and thank you again for submitting your outstanding
work.*

Our kind regards & etc.,
Dr. George C. Poundstone, Vice President
On Behalf of the Officers of the Philadelphia Camera Society

Lee picks up the exhibit guide and flips through the pages. A
few pages in she finds her bell jar series, with Man's name beneath
it. In his short artist statement, Man has defined solarization and
written, "I discovered this process by chance last year, and refined
it over a series of months." Nowhere is there a mention of Lee's
name.

It must have been weeks ago when Man mailed off these photographs, which means that for weeks he's known that he has
betrayed her, and yet said nothing. What could he have been
thinking? The photos are good—she and Man both know that—
but of course he has photos that are just as good as or better than
these. Photos that are his alone. Could it be that he has *forgotten*
that these are Lee's?

As she lies there, things he's said over the past few months come
back to her. "You're not *not* me," he said, and at the time she
didn't know what he meant. The sentence was nonsensical. But
now she sees. If that is how Man views her, then perhaps he views
her work the same way. His property.

Her father, then Condé Nast and Edward Steichen, and now Man. All of them using her for their own purposes, taking what they need with no regard for what's left for her when they are done.

In the winters in Poughkeepsie the windows in her childhood home got so cold they frosted over, and in the mornings Lee would get out of bed and scrape her fingernails through the frost flowers, screeching them up and down over the frozen glass until she could see through to the snow beyond. Her eyes feel like that now, scraped and freezing, as if she is seeing clearly for the very first time.

By the time she swings her legs over the side of the bed a few minutes later, she has a plan. Gets a piece of notepaper and dashes off a telegram she will send to Man that afternoon. *Bal Blanc on Jan 6. Want you to be there. Need your help. Your Lee.*

CHAPTER THIRTY-TWO

As they are setting up the projectors, Man tells her about the Wheelers' new seaside cottage outside Cannes.

"What makes it so lovely," he says, "is that it's genuinely simple. There's no pretense. Arthur washed the floors in an ebony wax, and left all the windows bare, so you feel the countryside even when you're indoors. The first day I was there we picnicked under a beautiful spreading oak at the edge of the property, and Rose served cold roast duck and pickled quail's eggs and a nice Chablis. That was it. It was delicious."

"Sounds wonderful," Lee says. She pays little attention to what he is saying and moves determinedly around the solarium, tying white sheets around the bases of the projectors' stands, then taking a few steps back to survey her work. Guests are supposed to start arriving in two hours, and there is much to be done. Plus, Mimi tells her that everything needs to be ready early, because some of her guests will disregard the time printed on their invitation and show up when they feel like it. Lee has never been good at getting things done early—or really, even getting them done on time—but tonight she'll do it if it kills her.

Man doesn't share her urgency. He seems calm. Ever since he returned to Paris two nights ago, he has acted as if everything between them is back to normal. When he arrived, he found her in the studio, unable to stop editing the films and still surrounded by the mess she created while she was working. There was so much clutter everywhere that Man tripped as he made his way across the room to her, and without meaning to, Lee moved forward to catch him as he almost fell, and they ended up with their arms around each other. Man's relief at seeing her was palpable. He laughed at her mess and kissed her the same way he often kissed her, the way that used to send a hot bolt from her lips to her groin, and she parted her lips and pushed her tongue against his in the way she remembered doing when she wanted him. And he—foolish man—did not seem to notice any difference in her reaction to him, did not notice how vacant she was, how her mind stayed on her work while her lips kissed him. And that night in bed, Man was tender with her, held her in his arms and stroked her hair and cheeks and shoulders and seemed content just to be next to her.

"I'm so glad you wrote to me," Man whispered into her back. "I was so angry when I left. But it was terrible being away from you. I've never been so lonely in my life. Did you feel the same?"

"Yes," Lee said into the darkness, but even that one small word she had to force out of her mouth.

The next day, Lee took Man back to the studio and explained what she was thinking about the Bal. She showed him the film of her hands and stood in the beam of light from the projector so that he could see how the images looked as they moved across her body.

"Ah, it's so *good,* Lee," he said, his voice full of admiration. "How did you learn to do it all so quickly?"

She told him about all her plans for the party, about the Pecci-Blunt mansion, the swimming pool and the solarium, where the films would be shown, and he nodded and made notes in the small notebook he always carried in his back pocket.

There are a few things Lee does not tell him. She does not tell him about his package from the Philadelphia Camera Society, which she has taken outside and thrown in a rubbish bin a few blocks from the apartment, digging with her bare hands until it is buried under the wet stink of other trash. Lee does not tell him about her fourth film, the love poem she made for him, which she has unwound from its reel and pitched into the studio's metal sink and lit on fire, the nitrocellulose igniting so quickly she was almost scared for her safety, the hot blue flames rocketing up to the ceiling and reducing the film to a twisted lump. And she does not tell Man about what she did the afternoon before he arrived, the hours she spent plotting how to hurt him, what to do to make him feel the worst. How on impulse she hired a cab to take her to the Palais Garnier with a note she'd written clutched in her hand, *Antonio Caruso* written across the front in big dark letters. When the cab got there, she asked the driver to wait for her as she ran over to the building, through the side door, and down the narrow dark hallways behind the stage. It was hours before the night's performance, so there were few people there, but when Lee bumped into a skinny, surprised-looking dancer in the hallway, she pushed the note into the woman's hand and asked if she knew who Antonio was and if she could deliver the envelope to him. The ballerina nodded, agreed, and when Lee got back into the cab she rested her forehead against the cold leather seat, trembling and almost nauseated from what she had done. All these things she keeps to herself.

Now, Lee looks around the party space and thinks that truly, she has thought of everything. Even her outfit—at the sight of which Man raised his eyebrows, saying, "You're wearing *that*?"—is perfect: a trim white sailor top and white shorts. She didn't even need to look in the mirror to know it was right. Effortless and modern. Standing in the verdant, sweet-smelling solarium, Lee looks as though she is on a pleasure boat, and as she puts all the pieces of the party together, she tries to channel that feeling, to empty herself of the anxiety and anger that jangle around her like a suit of chains.

It's only half an hour until guests are scheduled to arrive. Heat lamps are lit. Waiters in crisp white tuxedos are lined up at the side of the room, chatting among themselves. The projectors are ready. The bar, a shining creation made entirely out of ice—a last-minute idea of Lee's—is stocked with gin and vodka and white wine, the only drinks that will be served all evening long. Collins glasses rest upturned on the ice counter like rows of crystal soldiers. And Mimi has emerged to survey the space, dressed in a floor-length white column dress covered in white paillettes that quiver and shimmer as she moves around the room.

"Miss Miller has done a tremendous job, don't you think?" Mimi asks Man, and he nods in agreement. "Are you taking over from here?"

Before Man can respond, Lee interjects, "No, he's helping me run the projectors. That's it."

Mimi looks a bit startled at Lee's tone. Man stays silent. When Mimi is pulled away by a caterer, Man looks at Lee with a mild expression. He is being so patient that Lee almost wishes she wasn't angry at him. But there's nothing to be done. Her anger is like the cellulose fire: it cannot be extinguished.

Man goes over to one of the projectors and fusses with it, testing things Lee has already tested, and then asks her what else he can do to set up.

"I think everything is ready," Lee says, and even she feels a little surprised.

"Then let me get you a drink, and we can toast." Man goes over to the bar and returns with two gin martinis, orbs of onion, skewered with white cocktail picks, balanced on the rims. "To Lee, my love, and to the assured success of this lovely evening," Man says, raising his glass to hers, and they clink them together. The gin tastes like the forest on an autumn day.

The sun dips below the roofline of the grand house next door, and the air gets thick and yellow with the final moments of the evening light. And then as the twilight gathers, the cypress trees beyond the glass of the solarium turn black as sentinels and cast thin lines of shadow across the ground. The swimming pool picks up the last of the sun and for a moment reflects it back, a gigantic oval of fire, brilliant and blinding, and then the sun dips a little lower and the pool goes dark, and that is when Lee turns on the projectors, so that the guests will see the films as they arrive. And arrive they do: a great crowd of them promptly at six, dressed even more elegantly than Lee imagined. The women wear elaborately pieced satin dresses with draped cowl necks and trains they have to gather in their fists as they walk down the stairs, white fox stoles wrapped around their shoulders. Their heads hold up tiaras, or little hats delicate as clouds, the tops of their faces beautifully blurred with gossamer half veils, their teeth bright white in their rich, laughing mouths. The men all wear white tuxedos with long coattails, and some of them have white silk scarves thrown over their jackets.

Lee leaves Man with one of the projectors and kneels at the pool's edge, lighting milk glass hurricane lamps and sending them out on white rafts; an air current from somewhere pushes them languidly along the surface of the water. Once there are a dozen rafts floating, Lee stands back and surveys her work, watching as the images from the projector make abstract shapes in the water and cast shadows on the white sides of the lamps as they rotate slowly in the pool's currents.

It is a crowd that is not simply wealthy, but so wealthy it is of a class that Lee never encounters. Very few of these people recognize Man, and none of them recognize Lee, though she sees the men's heads turn toward her as they walk by, eyes looking hungrily at her bare legs, and she smiles at them, enjoying both her power and her anonymity. She feels men watching her as they sip their drinks, but she feels wholly untouchable, unapproachable, the person they will later ask about: "Who was...?" "Did you see...?"

Lee helps herself to a second martini. The little sphere of onion bursts in her mouth with a savory pop. Man—so eager! so solicitous!—is working the projectors, moving between them to rewind the film and reset the reels, so there is actually not much for Lee to do. Every now and then she wanders over to him and asks him if everything is going all right. Together they stand back and watch the crowd.

"There are a lot of people here who must need their portraits taken," Man says, his voice conspiratorial, giving her the sidelong smile that used to charm her.

Lee nods.

"Do you think you could get the guest list?"

"Maybe," she says. She stands beside him for a few more moments, taking it all in—the guests exclaiming as the film of Lee's hands projects over them; the couples at the far edge of the pool dancing to the jazz; the smell of the cloistered air, scents of lily and gardenia and freesia from the oversize floral arrangements— and then she walks away from Man and over to the bar, where the bartender hands her another martini without her even having to ask.

A group of four guests approach her. "Mimi says that you're the one who did all this," one of them says to her, making a sweeping gesture with his arm.

Lee stands straighter and smiles. "Yes, all me."

"It's aces," he says. "We've never seen anything like it."

Lee glances back toward the steps that lead into the main rooms of the house and sees a man silhouetted against the light coming from inside. He shades his eyes and looks around, hesitating on the threshold as though he's not sure he belongs. Lee knows immediately that it's Antonio. She would recognize him even if he wasn't the only person dressed in black at the entire party. Thanking the man and excusing herself, she walks over to Antonio, enjoying the way his face lights up when he sees her.

"You got my note," Lee says.

"I did. Figured I couldn't possibly have gotten the address right when I showed up here. Look at all these rich pips. Wish you had told me to dress."

"I didn't want to scare you away."

They look around and Lee is overwhelmed again by all the wealth around them: the pampered skin, the ostentatious diamonds and furs and silks, the stinking excess of it all. Just then a waiter with a small silver tray approaches and offers escargot, and Lee and Antonio look at each other and start giggling. Antonio takes a snail and sticks out his pinky finger as he eats it. Lee looks behind him, and points out a snooty woman making almost the same gesture. Soon it's all hilarious. Antonio leans close to her and pushes his shoulder against hers as they are laughing.

Lee glances over at the projectors. She and Antonio are too far away for Man to notice them. She grabs Antonio's hand and leads him to the bar, where she orders him a drink to match her own. When she hands it to him he sniffs it and shakes his head no, so she takes it back and he orders vodka. Now she has a drink in each hand and alternates sips. With Antonio here the gin has turned to water; she barely notices she's drinking it. Occasionally, he puts his warm hand around hers and takes one of the glasses from her, stealing sips, and soon enough all three glasses are empty. Lee takes

Antonio's hand again, leading him over to the dance floor, where she knows full well that Man can see them.

At first Antonio stands at the edge, watching Lee's word film project across the guests' bodies. An older couple twirls by and the man's white tuxedo flashes DARKNESS IN THE WOODS before he turns again and the words disappear. A woman's silk dress says I SLEPT ALONE; another's says WITHOUT REGARD TO FASHION. Antonio folds his arms across his chest and takes it in.

"Pretty incredible," he says to Lee.

She puts her hand on his arm. "Dance with me."

"I don't dance."

"Just this once?" Lee says, and looks up at him under heavy-lidded eyes. She knows he can't refuse her. Antonio nods, takes her arm, and leads her toward the other couples, where he sets up for a waltz, moving so gracefully through the steps that Lee says, "You don't dance. Ha."

"Well, I didn't say I don't know *how* to dance." As if to prove it, he pulls Lee closer and drops her into a deep dip. She is dizzy when he pulls her upright.

His black outfit and her shorts make them the most noticeable couple on the dance floor, and Lee knows it is only a matter of time before Man sees them. Her head whirls around as Antonio leads her, and she keeps glancing over to where Man fusses with the projector. The film has reached its end; it snaps off the reel and leaves the dancers twirling plainly for a few minutes as he re-loads it, and after he gets the projector running again, Lee turns at just the right moment to see him notice her. Man shakes his head, a look of surprise on his face, and then she is turning again, lost within the clockwork of the other couples, held solidly in Antonio's strong arms.

They dance through three songs and still Man does not approach. Each time Antonio spins her Lee sees Man watching, still

near the projector, his hands at his sides. Lee pulls herself closer
to Antonio, until their pelvises touch, and she feels him grow
stiff against her through his tight pants. His erection makes her
ache, and so she pushes more insistently against him until they
must look indecent. Her head is hot, her eyes blurry, and through
her fuzzy vision she catches Man's stare each time she turns.
And then—because isn't this why she asked Antonio here?—Lee
stops dancing, and in the silent center of the dance floor, in the
stillness she's created, she goes up on tiptoe and wraps her arms
around him, raises her lips to meet his and kisses him for all the
world to see.

As Lee predicted, this gets Man's attention. He walks toward
them, his fists clenched, his body sparking with anger. He comes
right to her, grabs Antonio's arm, and yanks him away from her.

"Who—the hell—are you?" Man hisses.

Antonio opens his mouth to say something, but Man has already wound back his arm, which pops out like a spring, his fist
slamming into Antonio's face. It is an amazing punch, and Antonio staggers back from it and drops to one knee.

Antonio puts his hand to his cheek and looks at Lee accusingly.
Immediately, she feels terrible. What was she thinking, bringing
him into this?

The dancers have stopped and taken a few steps back to give
them room. The film Man just reloaded is still going, projecting
words and phrases from Lee's poems on their bodies: DELIBER-
ATELY, TEA FOR TWO, LUEUR D'ESPOIR, A GREAT EXPLOSION IN THE
SKY. When the words flash on Antonio they disappear in the black
of his clothing, but they crawl across from Man to Lee and she
can hardly bear to watch them. TAKE A POWDER, L'APPEL DU VIDE,
CARESS ME, EXIST FOR NOTHING. This is the exact scene Lee envisioned when she sent the note to Antonio, but now that it is
happening she almost can't believe what she has done.

"I said, who the hell are you?"

Antonio stands up and faces Man. "I'm—"

Man cuts him off. "Never mind. Fuck you. Get out of here."

Antonio looks to Lee. She nods once, and mouths that she is sorry, and he throws his arms out in confusion, then turns and goes out the way he came in. Man grabs Lee's upper arm. His grip is so strong and his hand so hot that she can feel his pulse pumping through his fingers.

"You are *working*," Man says to her. "You are supposed to be *working*."

Lee feels the crackle of her anger. "I'm not worried," she says. "I know you're just going to take all the credit for it anyway."

Man's hand is still wrapped around her biceps. "What?"

Before Lee can say the words she's practiced, Madame Pecci-Blunt sweeps up to them and puts her arms around them both, pushing them as elegantly as she can back into the house. "Darling," she says to Lee, "let's move this wholly inappropriate scene off the dance floor, shall we?"

Man and Lee let her steer them into the house and down a long hallway, until they're standing before some sort of game room, with a billiards table in the center and trophies mounted on the walls. With a delicate shove, Mimi pushes them into the room. "Make nice, and do it quickly before anything happens to my party. A little drama will be good for tomorrow's papers, but I don't want anything else to go awry."

Mimi pulls the doors shut behind her and leaves Lee and Man alone together in the giant room. From this far away they cannot hear the sound of the partygoers; in fact, all sound seems to be swallowed up by the plush carpet and the thick curtains lining the windows.

As soon as the doors are shut, Man whirls to face Lee. "What the hell was that?"

"What was what?" Lee says childishly.

"You. That man. Is he the one who . . . ?" Man makes a sound that is almost a choke and doesn't finish his sentence. He moves away from her and goes over to the window, lifting one of the curtains and looking out on the grounds below.

Lee moves forward and leans on the pool table, gripping its felted lip so tightly her fingers turn white. In a loud voice, she says, "You—stole—them. My pictures. My bell jar. You put your *name* on them."

Man turns to face her. "What are you talking about?"

"What am I talking about? You can't be serious. You know what I'm talking about. You took my picture—*my* pictures—and you submitted them to the Philadelphia Camera Society."

Man looks genuinely confused. He rubs his hand through his hair. "Ah. The bell jar photos. Yes, I did submit those, along with a few others. One of the stipulations of the prize was that the images had to be a triptych. I do so few series, and they're always coming up with some ridiculous restriction like that, God knows why."

"Have you—did it cross your mind that what you've done is *stealing*?"

"What? Of course not. We did those together. They're as much mine as yours."

Lee's voice shakes. "We did *not* do those together."

"We did all the solarization together—that's how I saw it. I assumed you felt the same."

Lee's hands are like claws clenched around the pool table's rim. "*I* discovered it. Not you. Don't you remember? Do you *not* remember?" It occurs to her that maybe he doesn't. Maybe the memory that looms larger in her mind than any other from their time together—those weeks when she felt more in tune with a person than ever before or since—maybe they have left Man's brain like fog burning off in the morning sun.

Man moves from the window and faces her across the pool table. Above his right shoulder a deer's mounted head looks down at them. "Lee, it is absurd to be this worked up. What we create in the studio is, ultimately, my work. It's my studio. You're"—he pauses, as if suddenly realizing how his words might sound to her, and then says softly—"you're my assistant."

"Ah." It is as she suspected. All the anger goes out of Lee and her legs grow weak beneath her. Man sees the change in her posture and hurries around to her side of the table, where he reaches out to touch her. She flinches.

"Of course I only mean that about the studio work. Just the studio. You know how much you mean to me—how much I love you."

Lee bows her head and doesn't say anything, just gazes into the dark shadow of the pool table's corner pocket.

He tries again. "I should have told you I was submitting those photos. I'm sorry. But it was a busy time, and you were gone a lot, and I suppose I just forgot."

Still she doesn't speak. Her eyes fill with tears, and one of them drops and makes a dark spot on the green felt of the table.

"Lee, say something. I've forgiven you for cheating on me—I forgave you when I was in Cannes; I can't stay mad at you—and I can forgive you for whatever this little scene was tonight. I love you, Lee. I love you."

She lifts her head and stares at him. "What do you see when you look at me?"

Man shakes his head, confused. "What do I see? A beautiful woman. The woman I love."

A beautiful woman. But what was she expecting him to say? It's what everyone has always seen. Lee wipes at her eyes with the back of her hand. "You don't see me. You never have."

"What do you mean? I can't see anything *but* you. I've told you that."

"You don't. You don't." Lee is crying harder now, her face crumpling, and instead of hiding behind her hands as she normally would, she stands with her arms at her sides and lets the tears fall. "I can never forgive you."

Man takes a step back. His face registers his realization that she is serious, that this is more important to her than he first understood. "Lee, be reasonable. It doesn't matter—I'll write to the society. Take the photos back. Whatever you need me to do."

"Will you write to them and tell them they're mine?"

Man's eyebrows scrunch together. "I'd rather just withdraw them. I don't want the society to get the wrong idea..."

It is the worst thing he could say. Lee wipes her eyes once more and then steps away from him. "I'm finished," she says.

"Finished?"

"Finished. With this. With us." She waves her hand around the room.

Man looks stunned. "Are you saying that your photos matter more to you than what we have together?"

"Yes, I guess I am."

At first Man blusters, defending himself, and then he switches to contrition. The words don't matter to her. When Lee said she was finished, she meant it: by the time he begs her to forgive him it is far too late.

Before she can leave the room, Man sinks to his knees and wraps his arms around her bare legs. She watches him do it and feels no connection to him, bends down and peels his arms away from her, steps awkwardly out of his grasp. Purposefully, she retraces her steps down the maze of hallways and back to the party, where everything is still spinning on just as it was before. Lee goes over to one of the stalled projectors and numbly switches out the reel, then watches as her own hands begin to move over the surface of people's bodies, her fingers running up a man's suit

357

jacket and across his cheek before disappearing into shadow. The party lasts for hours, and Lee stays until the end, finally gathering her coat and heading out into the frozen winter air. Who knows where Man is by then? Maybe he is still kneeling, waiting for her to join him on the floor.

Weeks later, when Lee has gathered all her things from Man's apartment and moved into a hotel, after she has answered the SPACE TO LET sign on the little studio's window, written to her father for a loan, bought her own studio camera and a gurney to put it on, after she has written up an advertisement—LEE MILLER STUDIO: PORTRAITS IN THE STYLE OF MAN RAY—after she has had her first client, an older woman who saw the ad in the Sunday paper, a package arrives at Lee's new studio's door. It is wrapped in brown paper, tied with twine, and it's clear that it hasn't come by post.

She knows immediately who it is from, even though they have not seen or spoken to each other since the Bal; Lee made sure to pick up her things from the apartment when she knew Man would not be there.

Lee takes the package inside and unwraps it slowly. Inside the brown paper is a wooden box. Inside the box is Man's metronome, with something taped to the pendulum. Lee picks up the metronome and sees that what's taped on is a piece of paper, and on it is a photo of an eye, her eye, staring vacantly out at her. At the bottom of the box is a hammer with a note tied to its handle. *Destroy me,* it says, in Man's familiar hand.

Lee sets the metronome on the table in front of her and considers it. The emotion that fueled its creation is tangible in the jagged scissor marks where the eye has been cut from her face. The image is underexposed, as if the print was pulled from the developing bath too quickly. Her eye is vacant, depthless, the iris thin as water. Lee stares at the image and it stares back. What picture did Man cut it from? Which version of her face jigsawed into the trash from the scissors's slicing? With a finger Lee sets the metronome in motion, sits down and watches as her eye rocks back and forth.

And then Lee looks around the space—her space, all her own, her sparse white room, as clean and bright as she imagined it would be when she first saw it—and at the photos she's been working on lately, some of them still hanging on the line to dry. She's begun a new series, semiabstract street scenes that are carefully composed but have the energy of snapshots. They are some of the best pictures she's ever taken. Lee gets up and goes into her darkroom to get back to work, leaving the metronome on the table to tick out the last of its spring-wound power.

SUSSEX, ENGLAND

1946

"Liberated": the word was bound to degenerate. Lee wrote those words and sent them off to Audrey with all the rest. She wrote them with Dave Scherman, right after they liberated a case of Gewürztraminer from another Nazi storeroom. The word became hilarious. "I'm going to liberate your pants," Davie said, and they laughed so hard they knocked over their wine bottle, but it didn't matter because they just liberated another.

Vogue has stopped sending Lee on assignment, but she is still working. She travels throughout Europe and photographs what freedom looks like. In Denmark it is an outpouring of repressed gaiety despite the lack of power, people creating elaborate cardboard facades to hide the damage done to their city. In France it is big hats, a flagrant use of fabric now that rationing is through. In Luxembourg—a country whose war strategy could be summed up as "Whistle and hope they don't notice us"—it is polite small-scale parades, harvest celebrations.

Lee is the only photographer still there. After Munich, after Dachau, after Hitler's suicide in his Berlin bunker, the press corps leaves, called away to other countries, other projects. Even Dave leaves, when *Life* sends him on assignment in the States. He urges Lee to come with him, but she cannot imagine languishing in a country the war barely touched. Instead, she continues on to Eastern Europe, hoarding petrol and brandy, driving alone across the cratered landscape in a jeep she's liberated from the 45th. She misses Dave's company so much that as she drives she starts talking to herself in an imitation of his deep voice, but she resents him too: for abandoning her and going home to take comfortable photographs of socialites and public works projects.

Somewhere in Romania the money runs out, and the telegram Lee sends to Audrey is answered tersely. Her accreditation has been revoked. There's nowhere to go but home.

When she gets back to London, Lee reunites with Roland Penrose. After all the years of letters, at first his corporeality disturbs her: the warmth of his body next to hers, how clean and well-dressed he always is. But lots of things disturb her, and she finds he is the only person she can bear to be around for more than a few hours. He doesn't ask anything of her—unlike Man, who asked for everything, and unlike the war, which took it all. Together she and Roland travel to Sussex, near where he was born, and rent a small farmhouse, walk along the gravel drive. They talk about moving there permanently someday. He takes her hand in his, and squeezes.

The farm is green and pastoral and so quiet Lee's ears won't stop ringing. Once they've unpacked, she collapses on their bed and sleeps for days, waking only to drink brandy from the bottles she keeps by her side. Roland brings her sandwiches, the crusts curling up and drying out when she doesn't eat them. One night she wakes up screaming, and Roland rubs her back until she pretends to fall asleep again. She waits until he starts to snore before she reaches for the bottle.

Lee can't shut off the pictures, the endless film loop of her brain, but brandy helps, and cognac. It also helps to sleep, to let nightmares replace her memories for a while.

"It'll get easier," Roland tells her, patting her hand, rubbing her arm. He spent the war in Norfolk, running the army's Eastern Command School of Camouflage. He touches her too often—sometimes she has to grind her teeth to stop herself from flinching—but it is easier to tolerate it than to tell him to stop.

A few years later, they get married. It is a mistake, but at the time Lee doesn't care; she just wants someone who accepts her as she is. Roland wants to be in the country, so soon they buy Farley Farm. She arranges to have her things sent down from London, and the crates arrive while Roland is away on business. Boxes and boxes of negatives and old discolored prints. Lee doesn't even bother opening most of them before she heaves them up to the attic.

She puts the boxes in a far corner behind an old bed frame, where no one will ever find them. Roland won't ask questions, and with him she can move on, become a different person, let the years erase the past until all that's left is clean and empty. Once she's locked the attic door behind her she feels a sense of release, a crack of light in the darkness. What is the name for what she's feeling?

She wishes it were liberation.

EPILOGUE

LONDON
1974

You wouldn't know from looking at her that Lee is dying. She looks beautiful as she walks unescorted through the front doors of London's Institute of Contemporary Arts, where Roland has recently been promoted to director. It is the first time she's been in the ICA's new building here on the mall, and if anyone were to ask her she'd say it is atrociously ugly, a squat structure covered with an excess of fat Grecian pillars, like a child's rendering of high culture. Lee vastly preferred the old space—drafty and cantankerous as it was—but no one has asked her. Certainly not Roland, who never asks her opinion on anything anymore.

Lee wears a dress, the first she has put on in months. Dying has, ironically, brought back her love of fashion, as well as her hips and cheekbones, and before she pushes through the museum's glass front doors she catches a glimpse of her reflection in their surface and for once likes what she sees. Face flushed from the unseasonably cold air and the coughing fit she had a few blocks earlier. Bouclé wool sheath with a smart matching jacket in a blue that brings out the color of her eyes. The suit may be démodé but it's Chanel, and it fits the way it fit when Lee bought it years ago—a victory of sorts.

Roland promised Lee a private viewing of the new exhibit before the opening party scheduled for that evening. Lee deserves it—deserves, in fact, far more than she's gotten from him, especially since she is part of the reason the exhibit is even happening. The *Vogue* article she wrote about her time with Man Ray—she counts back and can't believe it's been seven years since it was published—sparked the interest of the ICA's former director, and Roland weaseled his way into being part of the team that put it all together. This exhibit is probably why they promoted Roland when the other director retired. He has Lee to thank for his new role, though of course he'd never say so.

She needs this time alone before she is forced to hobnob with all the museum people. And before she sees Man. At first Roland told her Man wasn't going to be able to come, that he was too frail to make the trip from Los Angeles, but then a few weeks ago he idly mentioned that he would be there after all. Forty years since they last saw each other. Try as Lee might to imagine what it will be like when he is standing in front of her, she can't make the image of him come together. Her memory has reduced him to impressions: the line of his jaw against his jacket, the slouching way he liked to stand. She's not even sure if those remembered fragments are real, or if they all come from a photo, that one she took of him on the bridge in Poitiers, the only one of him she saved.

Lee pushes through the groups of schoolchildren and tourists thronging the lobby, and takes the stairs to the second floor and past a temporary barrier. She almost laughs when she sees the exhibit's entrance. Hanging above the closed doors is a giant silk-screened sign, with Man's signature printed on top of a picture of Lee's naked torso. It's one of the many shots Man took of her against their old bedroom window, her body striated with evening light. Lee shakes her head and wonders if the museum's marketing people knows it is the director's wife they've printed on their banner.

She opens the doors and enters. No one is there. The room is completely quiet, dimmer than she would have expected. Small monolights illuminate framed prints, and some of Man's sculptures stand on pedestals in the center of the room.

The exhibit is set up chronologically, and the first few rooms are easy: artifacts from the life of the young Emmanuel Radnitzky, sketches and doodles, a mezuzah from his childhood home, early nude studies, even a copy of a term paper he wrote at school. And then a room of 1920s Paris: Kiki with the violin markings on her back, another of her sleeping. In an alcove *Emak Bakia* loops, already playing in preparation for the party later on.

It is not until Lee gets to the next room that she starts to have trouble. Painted on the wall by the door is 1929–1932, EROTIC PARIS. Photos are clustered in large groupings, and as Lee knew they would be, almost all the pictures are of her body. But knowing this in advance does not make it any easier. She walks slowly along one wall, taking it all in: her thighs and arms and breasts, boxed up in thick black frames, the harsh lights flaring off the glass as she moves past them.

Here they are, all those parts of herself she let Man photograph. All the parts he touched and painted and loved. She looks and looks, waiting for it to coalesce into a whole, but of course this does not happen. Why would she expect it to? In her attic there are dozens of self-portraits—Lee Miller *par* Lee Miller—and even those have never satisfied her. She knows why. It is because there is no whole to be found. No center. Or maybe that's not true. Maybe Lee has just never known how to find it.

Man's photos look old—they *are* old, Lee realizes, with a stab of sadness—and the girl in them has been lost to her for so many years. Here is her beautiful eye, her beautiful sternum. Lee wants them back, all the pieces of herself that have been taken. Her lips. Her wrists. Her rib cage. As she looks at the disembodied sections of herself she thinks of the X-rays the young pimply-faced doctor splashed up on the screen: the illuminated moth's wings of her lungs inside her chest, shot through with cancer. In the negative, there was a reverse effect, and the tumors appeared as bright white spots, but Lee knows what color they really are. In the examination room she had a small feeling of vindication: finally, proof of the blackness she always knew she carried inside.

Lee pauses in front of a print she remembers well, her solarized face in profile, a thin black line separating her skin from the white background. A small placard hangs next to the print, and Lee leans in close and squints to read it. SOLARIZATION, A JOINT DISCOVERY BETWEEN ARTISTS MAN RAY AND LEE MILLER, IS A PHENOMENON IN PHOTOGRAPHY IN WHICH THE IMAGE RECORDED ON A NEGATIVE OR ON A PHOTOGRAPHIC PRINT IS WHOLLY OR PARTIALLY REVERSED IN TONE. Lee reaches out and rubs her thumb over the words, leaves a smear on the plastic cover, and then smears it more when she tries to polish it away. *A joint discovery. Artists Man Ray and Lee Miller.* How much those words would once have mattered. All she gave up because she didn't hear them. How little meaning they hold for her now.

Lee gathers herself and moves to the next room. In it there is only one painting. Gigantic, eight feet in length, it hangs at eye level, vibrant and sumptuous. OBSERVATORY TIME—THE LOVERS she knows the placard says. It is like viewing a memory forgotten and then half remembered. The lips lying like bodies one on top of the other, spent and sated. Where did that girl go, the one who surrendered herself fully to sensation, to her lover, so close it wasn't clear where her body ended and his began? Lee wants that back too, that feeling.

The rest of the exhibit is a blur. Lee wanders through room after room of paintings and sculptures from later in Man's career. A room devoted to his time in California, another to the portraits he took in Europe in the 1950s. Lee has seen most of them in journals over the years; she has followed his career and so has Roland.

Before too long Lee reaches the end of the exhibit. She stands at the exit for a while, not yet capable of venturing out into the noisy mess of the rest of the museum. There is a bench against the wall, and Lee sinks onto it with relief. She'll just rest her feet before she goes home.

Lee is sitting like this twenty or so minutes later, eyes closed, when she hears a noise behind her, the squeak of rubber on the hardwood floor. Someone in a wheelchair is rolling into the room. And then as the person gets closer there it is: a voice, his voice, gravelly and thin now, but still familiar, a voice she wasn't able to recall until she hears it. She draws the deepest breath she can and turns to meet him.

"Lee?" Man says.

What passes between them will be just a memory. There are no pictures of it.

AUTHOR'S NOTE

Lee Miller first captured my attention when I went to an art exhibit at the Peabody Essex Museum in Salem, Massachusetts, called *Man Ray / Lee Miller: Partners in Surrealism*. Her work on display was incredible; her life, even more so. Yet in all my art history courses at school, it was Man Ray I'd heard of, not Lee Miller. After leaving the exhibit, I dove into two years of research before writing what became *The Age of Light*.

My fascination with Lee sprang from images—images of her, and images taken by her. Her confident gaze in her very first cover image for *Vogue* in 1927, her defiant stare in photos taken by her father, the love in her eyes as she looked up at Man, her utter transformation into a hardened war reporter. The images were access points into novel scenes, and remained touchstones for me as I was writing and revising the book. The novel, then, is the story behind the images. It is a work of fiction, and even though I absorbed facts from many excellent biographies and historical texts while I was writing, these characters are products of my imagination.

Historical fiction is a unique genre, and when a writer is writing about real people, the process comes with its own set of expectations and rules. Though I worked to render history authentically—especially geography, chronology, and other historical details—I chose to experiment and to invent scenes and actions, as long as they felt genuine to who the characters were, both as they lived and in my fictional representation. Above all, my goal in writing this book was to present Lee as the complicated woman she was: beautiful and talented, of course, but also flawed and fragile, and it was more important to me to get this right than to stay entirely inside the lines of written history.

For further reading about the real lives of Man Ray and Lee Miller, I highly recommend Carolyn Burke's biography *Lee Miller: A Life.* It is a book that I turned to again and again for research, and it does a wonderful job of exploring Lee's complex history. *Man Ray: American Artist,* by Neil Baldwin, and Man Ray's autobiography, *Self Portrait,* are good starting points for information on his incredible life and work. I include here a short list of other sources I consulted over the years. Any of these books would be a great place to learn more about the characters and the period. And, of course, there is Man's and Lee's art, which I hope inspires you as much as it does me.

FURTHER READING

Baldwin, Neil. *Man Ray: American Artist.* Cambridge: Da Capo Press, 2000.

Burke, Carolyn. *Lee Miller: A Life.* New York: Knopf, 2005.

Cahun, Claude. *Disavowals, or Cancelled Confessions.* Boston: MIT Press, 2008.

Conekin, Becky E. *Lee Miller in Fashion.* New York: Monacelli Press, 2013.

Flanner, Janet. *Paris Was Yesterday, 1925–1939.* New York: Viking Press, 1972.

Klein, Mason. *Alias Man Ray: The Art of Reinvention*. New Haven: Yale University Press, 2009.

Penrose, Antony. *The Lives of Lee Miller*. London: Thames and Hudson, 1988.

Penrose, Antony, ed. *Lee Miller's War*. Boston: Bulfinch Press, 1992.

Prodger, Phillip, with Lynda Roscoe Hartigan and Antony Penrose. *Man Ray / Lee Miller: Partners in Surrealism*. London: Merrell Publishers, 2011.

Ray, Man. *Self Portrait*. Boston: Little, Brown, 1963.

Roberts, Hilary. *Lee Miller: A Woman's War*. London: Thames and Hudson, 2015.

ACKNOWLEDGMENTS

It's said that writing is a solitary act, but this book would not exist were it not for the guidance, encouragement, and belief of the following people. It is such a pleasure to be able to express my gratitude for their support.

It was my dream to work with my agent, Julie Barer, long before she emailed me from the sky on her way to Japan, and she has turned out to be even more brilliant and wonderful than I imagined she would be. I owe her and everyone at The Book Group a thousand thanks. Special thanks as well to the unflappable Nicole Cunningham.

Huge thanks to my amazing team at Little, Brown, including Karen Landry, Sabrina Callahan, copyeditor Nell Beram, Alexandra Hoopes, and my superb editor, Judy Clain, who is a joy to work with and whose insight and wisdom have made me a better writer and this a better book. Thanks also to the wonderful people at Picador UK, especially Kish Widyaratna and my lovely editor, Francesca Main, who offered invaluable suggestions at the macro and micro levels. Heartfelt thanks to Jenny Meyer, Caspian Dennis, and Gray Tan, foreign agents extraordinaire: I still get goose bumps when I think of my book being translated into other languages and read across the pond! To my foreign publishers: our relationship is just beginning, but I look forward to getting to know you and thank you so much for believing in my work.

In some ways, my writing life began when I joined my writing group, the Chunky Monkeys, and I couldn't feel luckier to know such an awe-inspiring group of people. Chip Cheek, Jennifer De Leon, Calvin Hennick, Sonya Larson, Alexandria Marzano-Lesnevich, Celeste Ng, Adam Stumacher, Grace Talusan, and Becky Tuch: thank you for reading countless drafts, providing world-class feedback, making me laugh, giving me pep talks, and proving to me that hard work pays off.

A special shout-out to dear friends and superstar writers Jenna Blum and Kate Woodworth, for holding me accountable and cheering me on with Bitmojis and Manhattans.

Boundless gratitude to the talented writers I'm lucky to call friends, who have helped me with this book in countless ways: Christopher Castellani, Ron MacLean, Lisa Borders, Michelle Seaton, Sari Boren, Sean Van Deuren, Jaime Clarke, Mary Cotton, Tom Champoux, Alison Murphy, Chuck Garabedian, Vineeta Vijayaraghavan, Michelle Hoover, Karen Day, Stuart Horwitz, Crystal King, Cathy Elcik, and probably more people whose names I will wish I had remembered. Thank you for inspiring me.

I'm convinced that Boston has the best writing community in the nation. I spent ten happy years working at Grub Street, an organization that managed to feel like a home. I also love being a part of the Charrettes, led by the wonderful Daphne Kalotay; the Spitballers, who make brainstorming sessions productive, collaborative, *and* fun; and the Arlington Author Salon, which has been a joy to help organize and has gotten me better acquainted with the lovely Anjali Mitter Duva, Amy Yelin, Marjan Kamali, and Andrea Nicolay. I'm grateful as well for the financial support of two Boston institutions: the Somerville Arts Council and the St. Botolph Club Foundation.

I will be forever grateful for the time and space to write I've

Ringland
22|10|20
Library

been granted at residencies and in the homes of generous friends. The two weeks I spent at the Virginia Center for the Creative Arts were the most productive weeks I've ever had, and I value the friendship and inspiration I found there with other artists, especially John Aylward, Sarah McColl, and Jennifer Lunden. Thank you to Mo Hanley for sharing her Cape Cod home; to Alex Reisman for transforming her Berkshires house in Rowe, Massachusetts, into a writing retreat where we worked and laughed in equal measure; and to Arthur Golden for trusting me to take care of Missy at Salt Meadows while I finished my (fifth?) draft. Closer to home, I thank God for Diesel Cafe, Kickstand Cafe, and Caffè Nero, which have fueled my revisions with endless Americanos and served as havens where I can always look forward to bumping into someone I know.

Finally, my heartfelt thanks to friends and family who have helped me in ways too numerous to list here. Jennifer Chang, Alexis Wooll, and Julie Greb: you have known me since childhood, been witness to my awkward teen years and cringeworthy rebellious phases, yet somehow still love me. Thank you for being my chosen family. Gale and Richard Scharer, best in-laws, thank you for providing literal sunshine (Florida) and figurative sunshine in my life. My globe-trotting sister, Colby, who has such great stories she should write her own book—may we have many more adventures together. My parents, Anita and Richard Bemis, who encouraged my early love of language with countless blank books and trips to the Tattered Cover. Thank you for your unwavering and outsize belief in me. My husband, Ryan, the smartest and funniest man I know, who moved back and forth across the country with me to support my writing and took on myriad responsibilities to make it possible for me to finish this book. I love you. And finally, my daughter, Lydia, who lights up the world with her spirit and wit, and will always be my best creation.

NEWPORT COMMUNITY
LEARNING & LIBRARIES

Y020822

CRITICAL ACCLAIM FOR JAMES SALLIS

'Wry... Powerful... A rich tapestry of social unrest and vividly evoked characters and settings...'
– *New York Times*

'Allusive and stylish, this stark metaphysical landscape will leave a resounding impression' – *Guardian*

'Poetic storytelling of the highest quality, entrancing and yet utterly unexpected' - *Daily Mail*

'Sallis creates vivid images in very few words and his taut, pared down prose is distinctive and powerful'
– *Sunday Telegraph*

'Sallis' voice is unique among mystery writers, and this novel, like previous ones in the series, is unforgettable'
- *Publishers Weekly*

'Fast-moving, elliptical, and like a jazz trumpet solo, has a plaintive note of melancholy woven through it'
- *Washington Post Book World*

'Sallis is an unsung genius of crime writing'
- *Independent*

'James Sallis is a superb writer' – *Times*

'Sallis is a fastidious man, intelligent and widely read. There's nothing slapdash or merely strategic about his work ... peculiar and visionary' - **Iain Sinclair**,
London Review of Books

Also by James Sallis

The Long-Legged Fly
Moth
Black Hornet
Eye of the Cricket
Bluebottle
Ghost of a Flea
Death Will Have Your Eyes
Renderings
Drive
Driven
Cypress Grove
Cripple Creek
Salt River
What You Have Left: The Turner Trilogy
The Killer Is Dying
Others of My Kind
Willnot

Stories

A Few Last Words
Limits of the Sensible World
Time's Hammers: Collected Stories
A City Equal to My Desire
Potato Tree and Other Stories